Santa Montefiore

The _Italian_ Matchmaker

**SIMON &
SCHUSTER**

London · New York · Sydney · Toronto · New Delhi

A CBS COMPANY

First published in Great Britain in 2009 by Hodder & Stoughton
An Hachette Livre UK company
This paperback edition published by Simon & Schuster UK Ltd, 2015
A CBS company

1 3 5 7 9 10 8 6 4 2

Simon & Schuster UK Ltd
1st Floor
222 Gray's Inn Road
London WC1X 8HB

www.simonandschuster.co.uk

Simon & Schuster Australia, Sydney
Simon & Schuster India, New Delhi

A CIP catalogue record for this book is available from the British Library

Paperback ISBN: 978-1-47113-368-8
eBook ISBN: 978-1-47113-369-5

Typeset by Hewer Text UK Ltd, Edinburgh
Printed and bound in Great Britain by CPI Group (UK) Ltd, Croydon CR0 4YY

For Louis Dundas

Love for ever

Chapter 1

England, Spring, 2001

Luca stood alone in the library, gazing out of the window at the glistening gardens of Dinton Manor. The clouds hung low and heavy in the Hampshire sky, releasing a light but persistent drizzle. A couple of blackbirds pecked the grass in search of worms before returning to the towering lime trees that had just begun to sprout new green leaves. The peaceful silence was punctuated every now and then by whoops of laughter that erupted from the drawing-room on the other side of the hall where the rest of the house party were commenting loudly on the Sunday papers or playing Scrabble. Luca found their *joie de vivre* grating. He had only come for Freya, having lost touch with her over the years. He admired her home, her family, her obvious contentment, and realised that in the last two decades he had somehow drifted off course.

He blew smoke against the glass, lost in a fog of melancholy as he considered his life. He was forty-one. Single again. Father of two little girls entangled in the wreckage of an acrimonious divorce. Unemployed, having quit the City after twenty years as a fund manager, making money with such dedication that making money had become an end in itself – a greedy, empty existence that gave him no satisfaction.

He had left the City in a blaze of speculation. Telephones had buzzed as the news travelled across continents, leaving the banking world in a state of shock. Luca Chancellor, with a billion under management, had sold out to his two partners and just walked away. No one could explain it and Luca wasn't giving any answers. Instead, he had put his head down, turned off his mobile telephone and fled to the countryside. After a structured life in finance his newfound freedom made him uneasy; it had no limits.

Before he could dwell further on his unravelling life, he sensed he was no longer alone. The scent of ginger lily reminded him of that summer long ago when he and Freya had been lovers. She slid her arm around his waist and leaned against him.

'Here you are, Luca. What are you doing?'

'Thinking.'

'Thinking's dangerous. What are you thinking about?'

The smile in her voice encouraged him. 'You and me. Summer of seventy-nine.'

'You mean the summer I fell in love with you, only to be rejected when autumn came?' She laughed, able now to make light of a situation that had hurt her deeply at the time. 'Cast aside with all the other women who thought they'd be the one to tame you.'

'You've always been different. Letting you go was the stupidest thing I ever did.'

'Don't be so hard on yourself. It wasn't meant to be.'

'You would have been good for me.'

'I'm not sure *you'd* have been good for *me*. You were far too handsome and arrogant to stay faithful to one woman.'

'I'm a different man from the one I was back then.'

'Leopards don't change their spots. Once a bounder, always a bounder. Still, you lasted with Claire for what? Ten years? That's nine more than I expected.'

'Look at you,' he said, turning to face her, his cornflower-blue eyes intense with regret. 'Happily married to Miles. Big, beautiful country house. Four blond, rosy children.' He ran his gaze over her features. 'More beautiful with every passing year.'

She blushed. 'Oh, Luca, really, don't. You only want what you can't have.'

'Are you happy with Miles?'

'Very.' She curled a tendril of blonde hair behind her ear.

'Pity. I'd like to make love to you again.'

Freya withdrew her arm. 'Just because you're half Italian doesn't mean you can say things like that to a married woman.'

'You're my oldest friend. There's nothing I can't say to you.' He dragged on his cigarette, now barely a stub.

She lifted a china ashtray from the sofa table and handed it to him. 'That's a horrid habit. You should quit.'

'Now's not a good time.'

'It never is.'

'It's as if I'm dying and seeing my life pass before my eyes. I was so consumed with making money I never had time for the important things. I've messed up my marriage. I never wanted to be one of those fathers who tears his children's lives apart. But look at me. I've made more money than even Claire can spend in a lifetime. I doubt she can remember the last time she travelled commercial. Bloody woman's fleecing me for as much as she can get. Yet, if she's a monster, I've only myself to blame for turning her into one. Money's no substitute for love. In spite of all my worldly goods, Freya, I'm an empty vessel.'

She touched his arm. 'The girls will survive. I did.'

'You were lucky. Your mother married again very quickly. Fitz picked you up before you had time to fall on your nose. Your mother's not vindictive like Claire. She's sensible. She didn't poison you against your father.'

'It's still bewildering when you discover your parents don't love each other any more and want to be with someone else. However amicable, you still feel you're in some way to blame – they don't love you enough to stay together. But children are resilient. They adapt quickly. Yours will too.'

'John Tresco is no Fitzroy Davenport. It makes my skin crawl to think of him being a father to my daughters.' He paled and took a final drag before stubbing out his cigarette.

'Why don't you disappear for the summer? You were just telling me about that amazing *palazzo* your parents have bought. The Amalfi coast sounds the perfect place to go and check out for a few months. Decide what you want to do. London is stifling in the summer and everyone goes away. You'll only be miserable if you stay. Perhaps your girls could join you there in the holidays. Children love palaces.'

'There's nothing peaceful about my mother! I've spent most of my adult life avoiding her.'

'At the expense of your father.'

'She's relentlessly social. Can't think how he puts up with all those people. That's not what I need right now.'

'A change of scenery will do you good – sun, sea, time to reflect.'

'On all my mistakes!'

'No one's perfect.'

'I'm carrying a heavy load, Freya.'

'Then drop it. Go and visit your parents. I know Romina can be a bit over the top but she's got a good heart. Blood is thicker than water and besides, I'm sure they're longing to show you their *palazzo*.'

He looked at her and grinned. For an instant her stomach lurched as she glimpsed the handsome rogue of her youth in his now jaded features. 'You see how good you are for me,' he said, the twinkle in his eyes restored. 'I should have married you while I had the chance. It's taken me years to discover that the woman I have always loved has been right beside me all along. Miles is a lucky man.'

'You'll laugh at this conversation one day. You don't really love me, you love what I represent. I'm like a sheltered harbour, but once you've taken time to recharge, you'll real- ise that you don't want a sheltered harbour. You've always been a man for the high seas. I'm far too placid for you, you'd get bored with me again like you did in seventy-nine.'

'You're wrong. I was never bored of you, I wasn't ready to settle down, that's all. Bad timing.'

'Come, let's go back to the drawing-room. Mum and Fitz will be arriving soon for lunch.'

'No, let's go for a walk.'

'In this drizzle?'

'You're meant to be a country girl!'

'It's a huge pretence. I have to keep it up for Miles. He won't touch London with a bargepole. Are you sure you don't want to give Annabel a try?' she asked, changing the subject. 'I can tell she fancies you.'

'She's got that lean and hungry look that turns my blood cold,' he replied, watching Freya's nose crinkle with laughter.

'I've begun to notice it in the eyes of single women pushing forty – as well as the loud tick-tock of their biological clocks. Thank you, Freya, for thinking of me, but I'll pass.'

'A good hostess thinks of all her guests' needs.'

'My only need is one that you are unable to give me.'

'And one you shouldn't mention under my roof,' she retorted swiftly.

'You never used to be so proper.'

'I'm married,' she repeated, with emphasis.

He sighed. 'That's not how I like to remember you.'

'I don't want to know how you remember me.' She blushed again.

'Car bonnet, your parents' barn, midnight, summer . . .'

'Enough! I don't know what you're referring to! I'm ready for that walk now. Let's see if the others want a brisk route march before roast lamb.'

Luca wished she hadn't asked the entire house party – of adults, children and dogs – to join them on their walk. He didn't feel in the least bit sociable. Besides, there was no one except Freya he wished to talk to. Miles, every bit the land-owner in Barbour, boots and tweed cap, led them up the track towards the wood, his wife dutifully walking a few paces behind with her brother-in-law and his wife. Luca found himself accompanied on both sides by women. Annabel, whom Freya had picked as his date, was pretty but dry like a chicken roasted too long in the oven, while Emily, whose vertically challenged husband hung behind with their children, was red-faced and plump as a goose force-fed for *foie gras*. He disguised his scowl by lifting his chin, his height giving him a great advantage, and watched Freya's streaked blonde curls bounce against her back as she marched through the long grass to keep up with her husband. He couldn't imagine what she saw in Miles, nice as he was. Two of their children hurried past, chasing a black Labrador, and he observed their golden hair and skin, inherited, as fortune would have it, from their mother. Miles had that pale, Celtic skin dappled with freckles, his thinning hair a dull reddish blond. It irked Luca to see Freya with a man like that. Had she married a man like *him* he would have raised his glass and bowed out of the game, graciously accepting defeat from an equal player. Miles wasn't his equal; Miles was inferior on every level. Freya had clearly compromised.

'Come on, slow coaches!' Miles shouted at the entrance of the wood. 'You won't work up an appetite unless you put in a bit of effort.' His Labrador sat obediently at his feet, panting excitedly.

'It's like boot camp,' Emily complained. 'Miles always has to be the first, whether it's on the ski slope or tennis court, he always has to be the best.'

'And is he?' Luca asked, shoving his hands into his coat pockets.

'No,' said Emily dryly. 'At least not when he's playing tennis against Hugo. My husband might be short but he moves quickly around the court.' She lowered her voice. 'Miles is not a very good loser.'

'You've known them a long time?'

'Almost ten years. Since they moved down here. We live about twenty minutes away, just outside Alresford. We met through mutual friends. Freya's heavenly. Not a competitive bone in her body.'

'What makes them work as a couple?' he pressed. Emily's round face beamed at the chance to enlighten the handsome Continental.

'You could say they work because they're opposites.

Freya's so laid-back. Miles is sporty and competitive. Freya just rolls her eyes and smiles.' She glanced warily at Annabel and lowered her voice. 'I think Miles is rather pompous, actually. Perhaps Freya likes a man who takes control.'

'What do you think, Annabel?' Luca thought he might as well get something out of the walk. It was now drizzling heavily and he could feel a cold trickle down his back. Hunching his shoulders he wondered how long it would be until lunch.

'Miles is a very good lover,' Annabel stated authoritatively. Luca shuddered. The thought of Freya making love to Miles was as unappealing as the rain trickling down his spine.

'Did she tell you that?'

Emily honked with laughter. 'Did she really say Miles is a good lover?' she echoed, suddenly seeing him in a completely different light. 'Well I never.' She couldn't wait to tell Hugo.

'Yes, he's got an enormous cock,' Annabel explained as if she were discussing the size of his car. 'And he enjoys pleasuring her. He can stay down there for hours.' Luca looked more appreciatively at Annabel. He liked women who were unashamed of sex. It had been Freya's innocence that had frightened him back in '79.

'Secrets of the powder room?'

'I'm sure Freya would kill you if she knew you had told us,' said Emily, clearly titillated by the conversation.

'But she won't know, will she?' replied Annabel coolly. 'It's not the kind of thing one discusses over dinner, is it?'

'So how come she told you that piece of intimate gossip?' Luca asked, watching Freya walk on ahead of them, oblivious of her secrets being divulged.

'We got drunk one evening just after she'd met Miles. I'd

had a regrettable night with a man who looked like Sylvester Stallone but was a terrible disappointment, and she just came out with it. Looks can be deceptive. Miles is not only rich but a wonderful lover too. What more can a woman want?'

Up ahead, Freya joined her husband. He put an arm around her waist and drew her against him a moment while the others caught up. They shared a joke and she briefly rested her head on his shoulder. Luca felt jealousy rise in his throat. Miles wasn't handsome but he was a good lover. He couldn't help but wonder how *he* compared. It was so long ago now, Freya had probably forgotten. Yet, Luca hadn't forgotten her. His memories of making love to Freya were like scenes on a video. He could take it out and play them over and over again at will. She had been naïve, sweet as nectar, and shy. He had opened her up like a bud and deflowered her. He had kissed her embarrassment away and she had let herself go, abandoning herself to the pleasures of sex. Then he had casually tossed her aside, scared off by the intensity of her desire to marry and live happily ever after. He had dropped her, leaving her to be picked up by Miles with his big house, big ego and big cock. If he had been more mature where would they all be now?

While Emily whispered Freya's secrets to Hugo, Luca began to feel an unspoken connection with Annabel, like a pair of thieves recently returned from a robbery. They walked on, chatting like old friends, with the undertone of a growing sexual chemistry. Luca didn't notice the glances that Freya threw in his direction. She had invited Annabel for his amusement, but now that they seemed to be enjoying each other's company, she didn't like it.

The house party returned hot and flushed, their hair wet

but their spirits high. The smell of roast lamb wafted down the corridor from the kitchen. Heather Dervish had come from the village to cook and Peggy, the cleaner, who lived in the cottage at the end of the drive, had come to help serve. Peggy had replaced her usual dowdy clothes with a bright red smock dress with matching red tights and silver-buckled shoes into which she had only just managed to squeeze her marshmallow feet. Freya did a double take, gathered herself and said, 'Gosh, Peggy, you look splendid, but you needn't have gone to such trouble on our account.'

Peggy smoothed her hands down her dress. 'I haven't worn this in years,' she replied proudly. 'Do you think I'm mutton dressed as lamb?' Freya ran her eyes up and down the sixty-eight-year-old widow's fulsome body and decided not to tell the truth. After all, Peggy had dressed up for her stepfather's benefit and he'd be highly amused. She went over the top every time he came to visit.

'I think you look lovely,' she said. Peggy's plump cheeks managed a weak blush.

The house party assembled in the drawing-room and Miles opened a bottle of champagne. The fire was lit, filling the room with the sweet scent of apple wood. Outside, the drizzle had turned to rain that rattled against the window panes like small stones. Luca sat on the sofa with Annabel. He could smell her perfume, sweet and overpowering. She leaned against him so that their shoulders touched. 'If you had to fuck anyone in this room or die, who would it be?' she asked, her face as innocent as an angel's. 'Present company excluded,' she added hastily. 'That way you don't have to be polite.' He gazed down at her with sleepy eyes and, although he would have chosen Freya, beyond any shadow of doubt, the thought of Annabel after dessert was a tempting one.

'Present company *included*,' he emphasised. 'It would have to be you.'

At that moment the tall, handsome figure of Fitzroy Davenport filled the doorway. 'Any left for us?' he asked, nodding at the champagne bottle Miles had just emptied.

'Fitz!' Freya exclaimed, hurrying across the room to greet her stepfather. 'Where's Mum?'

'Here, darling, not far behind.' Her mother squeezed past her husband. Rosemary Davenport was slim and vivacious with highlighted blonde hair cut to her shoulders and pale grey eyes like her daughter's. She was proud of looking much younger than her sixty-six years and practised Pilates three times a week with a group of PLUs, the abbreviation Rosemary and her friends used for People Like Us. She was efficient and sociable and the first to admit that she was a little pushy: 'If I hadn't been pushy I would never have got Fitz up the aisle. A man like Fitz needs a pushy woman. Pushy women get things done.'

She glanced at her husband. He was blessed with enduring youth. His hair was still sandy with only the slightest hint of grey about the temples and he was more handsome now than when she had met him. For a man twice divorced he had been surprisingly acquiescent about giving marriage another go. She wasn't the type of woman to let a good man like Fitz slip through her fingers. She might not be the beauty that some of his ex-girlfriends and wives had been but, in spite of Freya and her three half siblings, Rosemary was in pretty good shape. If she let herself go, she'd look like his mother.

'For you, Fitz, I'll open another bottle,' Miles announced, working his thumbs under the cork.

'I've left Bendico and Digger in the car,' said Fitz, referring to his two yellow Labradors. 'Might take them out this afternoon. You can show me that coppicing you've been doing.'

'I'll need to work off Heather's lunch.'

'I should go and say hello. How is the eccentric Peggy Blight?'

'A fright. Don't let her put you off your lunch.' The two men laughed. Miles popped the cork and poured the bubbling Moët & Chandon into a tall flute.

'If I had to fuck anyone in the room?' Annabel mused, looking around. 'Present company definitely excluded, it would have to be Freya's delicious stepfather. I like tall men. He's a good example of a man who just gets better and better. He must be late sixties, but he has the appearance of a much younger man. Yes, I think there's a lot of life in that old dog!'

'And present company included?'

'Oh, I don't know,' she teased. 'Miles has already been road tested and proved very proficient indeed. Does a girl go for the dead cert or a man who looks like he has what it takes, but might be a terrible disappointment?'

'I can assure you, you won't be disappointed,' he said, grinning at her confidently.

'I'll think about it over lunch.'

'Of course, I have the advantage. Miles isn't available.'

'Nor is he handsome. That's an advantage too – but also a disadvantage.'

'Why?'

'Because handsome men prize themselves very highly, usually get what they want and therefore treat women badly. They have no respect for what doesn't challenge them.' She stood up as Peggy appeared in the doorway to announce that lunch was ready. Everyone stared in astonishment at the red ensemble, except for Fitz who approached her with a beaming smile.

'My dear Peggy!' he exclaimed. 'You're a vision in scarlet.' She blushed the colour of her tights.

'Thank you, Mr Davenport. Just something I threw on this morning. Nothing special.'

Lunch was in the dining-room at a large round walnut table. Freya had placed an elegant display of arum lilies in the centre and used the silver and crystal she'd been given as wedding presents. It was still raining, the clouds, heavy and bruised, moving slowly across the sky. Freya lit the candles because it was so dark, and the golden glow enhanced the cosiness of the room that was as stylish as its mistress.

Luca sat on Freya's left with Emily on his other side. Fitz was placed on Freya's right. As they tucked into the lamb Fitz caught up with Luca, whom he hadn't seen in a very long time.

'Freya married Miles, I married Claire, we drifted,' said Luca simply. 'Now I'm divorced I've returned to my old friends. Freya has welcomed me back without rebuke.'

'I'm sorry your marriage didn't work out.'

'So am I.' He shrugged. 'But it's life.'

'I've been through it twice. I sympathise.'

'Third time lucky, then,' said Luca. 'I don't think I'm going to be in any hurry to tie myself down again.'

'There's no need,' interjected Freya. 'You have two adorable little girls to give all your time to.'

'I like being married,' said Fitz. 'Rosemary picked me up when I was at a low ebb and has organised my life ever since. I don't know what I'd do without her.'

'Claire just spent my money and nagged,' Luca said wryly.

'All women nag,' said Fitz. 'I hear you quit the City.'

'Yes, I've done my bit.'

'It was all over the financial pages.'

'I didn't read them.'

'No one can understand it. You've put the fear of God into them. Do you know something they don't?'

Luca shook his head and grinned. 'I woke up one morning and realised I was working like a clockwork mouse programmed to make money. To make rich men richer. It's a soulless existence. Money, money, money. How much money do I need to be happy? How much do I need to be free? I want more, I just don't know what it is yet.'

'What are you going to do?' Fitz asked.

Luca shrugged. 'That's the million dollar question.'

Freya joined in. 'I told him to take the summer off. Go to Italy and stay with his parents in their new *palazzo* on the Amalfi coast.'

Fitz's eyes lit up. 'The Amalfi coast?'

'It's a small fishing town called Incantellaria. You've probably never heard of it.'

'Incantellaria,' Fitz repeated, turning pale. 'Bill and Romina have bought Palazzo Montelimone?'

'You know it?' Luca asked.

Fitz glanced nervously at his wife. 'I went there once, many years ago. The *palazzo* was a ruin.'

'My parents bought it about three years ago. It took two years to renovate.'

'But what a perfect team!' Freya exclaimed. 'Bill's an architect, Romina's an interiors painter. I bet it's stunning.'

'They wanted to recreate it as it was before a fire almost destroyed it in the sixties. Return it to its former splendour. I haven't gone out there yet. I've been too busy. I haven't seen them in months. Now I'm free I just might pay them a visit.'

They turned to Fitz expectantly. 'What took you to Incantellaria?' Luca enquired.

Fitz stared down at his plate. 'A very special woman.' He said the words with such tenderness Freya felt the hairs stand up on her arms. 'Before I met your mother, Freya,' he added tactfully.

'Apparently it's a very secret place,' said Luca.

'Secret and secretive,' Fitz confirmed. 'Once you start digging in Incantellaria, there's no telling what you'll uncover.'

Chapter 2

Fitz took the dogs out alone after lunch. Miles was required at the bridge table. This was a relief for Fitz who wanted time with his memories, as bright now as if they had just received an unexpected polishing. He strode up the track towards the woods. Digger and Bendico disappeared into the field in pursuit of hares. The dark clouds had moved on, taking the rain with them. Now, patches of blue were visible and occasionally the sun shone, catching the wet foliage and making it glitter.

Incantellaria. The very word pulled at his heart, creating a mixture of regret and longing. He couldn't help but think of what might have been. Now he was old he appreciated the miracle of love and the fact that, having let it go, he would never get it back.

He remembered Alba as she had been when he had fallen in love with her, now thirty years ago: her expression defiant, her strange pale eyes at odds with her Mediterranean skin and dark hair, her laugh wild, her careless disregard for other people, her irrepressible charm. He remembered her vulnerability too, her need to be admired, her unexpected love for little Cosima, the niece she had found with her mother's family when she had set out to Incantellaria in search of them.

The joy with which she had accepted his proposal and returned with him to England. The day she had wrapped her arms around him and told him she wanted to go back to Italy. That she couldn't live in England. She had implored him to go with her. She had insisted that she loved him – but not enough. Not enough. '*Don't say it's over. I couldn't bear it. Let's just see. If you change your mind, I'll be waiting for you. I'll be waiting and hoping and ready to welcome you with open arms. My love won't go cold, not in Italy.*' He had let her go and he hadn't followed her. Her love must have gone cold. Alba needed love like a butterfly needs the sun. He entered the woods and walked up the well trodden path. Ferns were beginning to unfurl with the first signs of bluebells, their shoots bright green and vibrant against the brown leaves and mud. The air was sweet and damp, the twittering of birds animated as they went about building their nests. He wondered where Alba was now. Had she stayed in Incantellaria or had she grown bored of that sleepy little town and moved to somewhere more exciting? Perhaps she had married, had children. At fifty-six she might even be a grand-mother. Did she think of him as often as he thought of her? The twist of regret in his heart would never go away. Oh, he was happy enough with Rosemary. But, after Alba, there was no falling in love again. He had closed his heart and married with his head. However, he often wondered what his life might have been like had he followed her to Italy. Dreams that came and went like clouds across the sky, some dark, others light and fluffy, but always the sense of having missed a golden opportunity.

'Is Fitz all right?' Freya asked her mother as they sat on the sofa in the drawing-room, sipping coffee out of pretty pink cups. 'He went very quiet over lunch.'

'Things are a bit tense at work. One of his favourite authors is moving to A.P. Watt.'

'Poor Fitz. He should retire.'

'So I keep telling him. He works so hard. But he loves what he does. He won't quit until he's dead. But losing Ken Durden is a real blow.'

'I should have gone out with him.'

'Don't be silly, darling. He likes going out on his own.' She patted Freya's knee. 'What a lovely house party you've got this weekend. I'm pleased you've found your old friend Luca again. My goodness, isn't he handsome?'

'He's been through a ghastly divorce.'

'Well, he does look a little frayed around the edges. More rugged than he used to be. You did well marrying Miles. Men like Luca are good for fun, but not for ever.'

'Oh, Mum!' Freya protested. 'That was a long time ago.'

'I'll never forgive him for hurting you. But that's all water under the bridge, isn't it? I bet he regrets it, though. They always do.'

'Have you heard of Incantellaria?' Freya asked her mother.

'Yes. Only because your stepfather nearly went out in pursuit of an ex-girlfriend just after we met. I talked sense into him, though. No point trying to put something together that's irreparably broken. Besides, it's a sad little place. No life. It's between Sorrento and Capri. Overlooked on the map. Italy wasn't the place for Fitz. He's too English. Can you imagine Fitz marrying a foreigner?' She gave a shrill laugh.

'So, she wasn't his "big love"?'

'Gracious no!' Rosemary retorted a little too quickly. 'She broke his heart, but I put it back together again. Why do you ask? Did he mention her?' The sudden flash of anxiety surprised her. Thirty years was a long time to hold on to fear.

'No, Luca brought up Incantellaria,' Freya replied hastily. She couldn't tell her mother of the wistful look on Fitz's face when he had mentioned the woman who had taken him there. 'I'm just curious about his past. Everyone has a past and I bet Fitzroy's is rather colourful.'

'He was quite a catch.' Rosemary smiled proudly. 'Not only devilishly handsome, but also a budding literary agent. You know he used to represent Vivien Armitage?'

'Vivien Armitage. She's huge.' Freya was suitably impressed. 'You never told me that.'

'She's dead now. But she'll continue to be read for decades. People never tire of stories of unrequited love and broken hearts. Don't forget, I had had my heart broken too, by your father. Fitz and I healed together and I saved him from dying of boredom in Incantellaria.'

'Luca's parents have bought a *palazzo* there, overlooking the sea.'

'How lovely,' said Rosemary, her tone patronising. 'A pleasant escape.'

'He might be spending the summer there, while he works out what he wants to do. He's quit the City and everyone's talking about it, so Miles says. He's really put the cat among the pigeons.'

'A sleepy little place like that is probably just what he needs right now, though I bet he'll come scuttling back to England in the autumn. I can't imagine there's a great deal to do in Incantellaria.'

Fitz returned from his walk and put the dogs in the back of his Volvo Estate after giving them their lunch and a bowl of water. They lay on tartan blankets panting against the glass and he lingered a while, stroking their silky heads, his thoughts lost among the olive groves, his senses recalling the smell of figs that had always pervaded that place. Finally, he shut the boot and pushed his memories back into the far corners of his mind to gather dust. There was no point dwelling on regret.

The drawing-room was tranquil. The children raced around outside while the grown-ups played board games, sat chatting or reading the Sunday papers. Peggy cleared away the coffee cups, bumping into Fitz in the hall as she returned to the kitchen. 'My dear Peggy, you can't carry all that on your own,' he said, taking the tray from her.

'Oh, I'm used to it now.'

'Perhaps, but none the less, it's heavy.' She followed him down the corridor into the kitchen where Heather Dervish was packing up her things to return home.

'What a splendid feast you cooked for us today,' he exclaimed.

'I'm glad you enjoyed it,' she replied, placing her apron in her bag and zipping it up. 'I'm coming back to cook dinner.'

'Shame I won't be here to taste it.'

'I'm cooking a cheese soufflé and there's treacle tart for dessert. I know you like treacle tart.' She picked up her bag and made for the back door and her little white van.

Fitz pulled a face to show his disappointment. 'My favourite.'

'Next time,' she said, giving a little wave. 'See you!'

'I'd better go home and put my feet up, too,' said Peggy, loading the cups into the dishwasher. 'Otherwise I won't make it around the table tonight.'

'The prospect of treacle tart will get you through dinner, Peggy,' he replied.

'Oh, I don't imagine there'll be anything left for me.'

'Then we're in the same boat.'

'It's my favourite, as well. Though, at my age I have to be a bit careful.'

He looked her over appreciatively. Peggy sucked her stomach in, barely daring to breathe. 'You're a fine figure of a woman. I'd say a little treacle tart would do you nothing but good.'

She giggled. 'I admit I don't deny myself much.'

'I'm glad to hear it. Life's too short to make those sort of sacrifices.' He gave her a genial smile. 'Have a restful afternoon, Peggy. If anyone deserves a rest, it's you.'

Peggy watched him leave the room and then slumped into a chair with a sigh. She felt a little light-headed and picked up a magazine with which to fan herself. A cup of sweet tea would revive her. Mr Davenport always made her feel special in a way that no one else ever had. She'd happily cook him a treacle tart that he could eat all on his own.

Fitz and Rosemary left shortly after tea. Freya and Miles went out to see them off. Their black Labrador attempted to jump up against the boot of the Volvo to see Digger and Bendico before cocking his leg on a back wheel instead. Luca wandered out from the croquet lawn having been given a guided tour of the estate by Annabel. He leaned in at Fitz's window.

'Good to see you, Fitz,' he said, patting his shoulder. 'Tell me, what am I to expect in Incantellaria?'

'Magic, miracles and wonder.'

'I don't understand.'

'The statue of Jesus in the little church of San Pasquale weeps tears of blood. There is an account of the tide mysteriously covering the beach with bright red carnations . . .'

'The Mediterranean has no tide.'

'Exactly,' said Fitz darkly. 'Incantellaria abides by her own rules.'

'The south of Italy is full of such superstitions,' Luca
argued.

'Incantellaria is special. You will see. As for Palazzo Montelimone, that is possessed by an altogether different kind of
magic.'

'I don't believe in ghosts, if that's what you're referring
to.'

'It's not the dead you need worry about, but the living!'
Fitz looked across at Rosemary. 'Ready, darling?'

Luca watched, perplexed, as they drove away. He wasn't
sure whether Fitz had been joking.

That night the guests came down to the drawing-room in
dinner jackets, the girls in pretty dresses and discreet jewellery. When Luca saw Freya, her beauty gave his gut a sudden
wrench. She had pinned her hair up, displaying her fine bone
structure and long neck. Her skin was smooth and pale, her
grey eyes light against the dark mascara on her eyelashes, her
figure slim and willowy in a floral wrap-around dress. She
smelt of ginger lily, reminding him once again of his foolish
youth.

'You're still beautiful,' he said under his breath so that only
she could hear him.

'Thank you, Luca.'

'You're by far the most beautiful girl in the room.'

'I thought you and Annabel were finally hitting it off.'

'She's a sexy girl,' Luca conceded. 'But she doesn't have
your beauty or your poise.'

'But she's available and willing. I can tell.'

He grinned mischievously. 'So can I.'

'Well then?'

He gazed into her silvery eyes, suddenly serious. 'I'm
through with soulless encounters that leave me empty, Freya.'

'Maybe you'll find a voluptuous *signorina* in Incantellaria. I'm sure your mother will fill the *palazzo* with smouldering Latin beauties.'

'I don't want a Latin beauty.'

'You want what you can't have.'

'Yes.' He pulled his cigarette packet out of his breast pocket and tapped it against his hand. 'Do you mind if I smoke?'

'Does it make a difference?'

'Not really. I'm just being polite.' He placed a cigarette in his mouth and flicked the lighter. He smiled at her with intense blue eyes, causing the crows' feet to deepen into his skin, and she felt that familiar effervescence in the pit of her belly.

'Whatever you think you feel, Luca, I just want to say how happy I am that we are friends again. I'm sorry we drifted. I should have made more of an effort. But I didn't like Claire and I know how you feel about Miles . . .'

'Miles is a good man,' Luca interrupted. She raised an eyebrow. 'Okay, so I'm jealous, but that's not his fault. You came good when I needed you.'

'You'll be there when I need you too. That's what friends are for.'

At supper, Freya had put Annabel next to Luca in an attempt to throw them together. It gave her a mean-spirited sense of victory to see him so tormented with regret. How she had loved him. How he had let her down. But now she felt vindicated by the naked longing in his eyes.

Peggy had changed into a simple black dress over which she had tied a crisp white apron. Freya felt sorry for her. Her face looked grim in the flickering candlelight, now that Fitz was no longer there to flatter her. They dined on cheese soufflé and fish pie and Heather's famous treacle tart. The wine bottles were drained and replaced. Luca found he was constantly filling Annabel's glass. The conversation turned once again to sex, which appeared to be her favourite subject.

Freya addressed her husband across the table. 'Darling, did you know Hugo's psychic?'

'Really, Hugo?'

'A little,' Hugo replied bashfully.

'He's very psychic,' interrupted Emily. 'He sees spirits all the time and often knows what's going to happen in the future. Just the other day he told me he sensed that an old friend from New York was going to come over and see us. Five minutes later the telephone rang and it was Bobby, calling from Manhattan asking whether he could come and stay. That sort of thing happens all the time.'

'We're all psychic to a degree,' Hugo explained. 'Most people dismiss intuition as coincidence. Once you start to tune in, you'll find you're really very psychic.'

'Do you see dead people?' Annabel asked, squirming excitedly.

'I have done,' said Hugo.

'Do you ever mistake them for real people?' asked Sarah.

'I don't see them all the time,' said Hugo. 'I have to link in. I have learned to shut it off. I used to mistake them for real people.'

'Well, link in – go on!' Miles encouraged.

'Oh, do, Hugo. It'll be fun,' Freya added.

'One must never do it just for fun,' said Hugo seriously. 'It's not a game. We're talking about spirit energies. If you go about it with the intention of causing amusement or fear you will attract the same energy. Like attracts like. I don't want to encourage mischievous spirits to bang on the table and blow the candles out. But I can take a piece of jewellery off one of the girls and tell you things about her that may surprise you.'

'Oh, goodie,' said Freya. 'Take my wedding ring.' She pulled it off and handed it to him. She glanced at Luca and noticed that beads of sweat had formed on his brow.

Hugo took the ring and held it in his hands. 'This contains your energy, Freya. I'm simply going to tune into it and tell you what I see and sense.' He closed his eyes and took a few deep breaths. The room fell silent. No one moved. They only slid their eyes from one to another in nervous anticipation. Luca bit the inside of his cheek. The whole thing made him feel hot and uncomfortable.

'So, Freya, you have a very strong feminine energy. Like a sugared almond, sweet and pretty on the outside, tough as a nut on the inside. You're secretly obsessive about tidiness and vacuum the sitting-room when no one's looking. In fact, I can see you hurriedly putting the hoover away before Miles comes back from his walk.'

Freya laughed.

'There's no secret about Freya's need to tidy up all the time. She's positively anal!' said Miles.

'I see you spending a lot of time folding children's clothes and putting all the tins in lines with their labels at the front. I see you as a child in a red dress crying because your shoes don't match.'

Freya gasped. 'How could you possibly know about that?'

'But your mother tied red ribbons on your black patent shoes and now I see you smiling and dancing around the room.' Emily glowed with pride. Her husband became so attractive when he used his 'gift'. 'You had a little white dog called Pongo and I see an old lady in a pleated tweed skirt, beige sweater and sleeveless green jacket, you know, those quilted ones.'

'Husky,' said Emily helpfully.

'That's the one,' said Hugo.

'My grandmother,' Freya observed quietly.

'She's in spirit,' continued Hugo. 'But she's with you all the time, watching over you.'

'What was her nickname for Freya?' Miles asked, hoping to catch Hugo out.

'Pumpkin,' Hugo replied.

'No it wasn't!' Miles was quick to correct him. 'It was Frisby.' Hugo frowned.

'No, darling, Hugo's right,' said Freya. 'She did call me Pumpkin.'

Hugo nodded, eyes still closed. 'But you asked her to stop calling you by that name when you grew up.' Miles fell silent.

'Can you tell us what lies in her future?' Sarah asked.

'You're going to go to Italy,' said Hugo.

'To visit you, Luca,' Freya said happily.

'I hope I'm included!' Miles interjected.

Hugo's face clouded a moment and he frowned. 'Of course,' he said.

Miles's smile remained, but his eyes betrayed a certain discomfort. He had never liked Luca. He had been safe enough while married to Claire, but now he was single again he had that predatory glint in his eye that made him dangerous. Miles was very self-confident but he wasn't a fool. Freya and Luca were unfinished business.

'That place makes me feel uneasy.' Hugo opened his eyes and handed the ring back to Freya.

'You're joking,' said Freya, feeling a prickle of anxiety.

'Of course he's joking,' interjected Emily, but she knew from her husband's face that he had seen something too horrible to share.

'It's all a load of nonsense!' Luca had loosened his bow tie and was undoing the top button of his shirt.

'But how could Hugo know all those things about Freya?' Annabel asked.

'He could have heard them from Rosemary at lunch.'

'Give him something of yours, then,' Emily suggested. 'Give him your watch, let's see what he has to say about you.'

'Yes, the big City player,' said Miles heartily. 'What's the real reason you quit and where will you go from here?'

'No,' said Luca quickly. 'I've had enough of this game.'

'You can't accuse my husband of being a liar and then refuse to let him defend himself,' Emily continued, her voice rising a note.

'It's okay,' said Hugo with a smile. 'I'm not here to convince anyone. I come across cynics all the time.'

Luca stood up. 'Let's go into the drawing-room.'

'Good idea,' said Freya, following him out.

'That's the behaviour of a man with something to hide,' said Miles.

Once in the hall Freya grabbed his arm. 'What was that all about, Luca?'

'I just don't want him inventing things about me.'

'He wasn't inventing. He was telling the truth. He couldn't have known any of those things. What about my grand-mother's nickname for me? How do you explain that?'

'I can't.'

'I understand you not wanting to let him read your watch. It's not a game. You never know what he might reveal. But you needn't have put him down.'

'He has a wife to defend him.'

Freya frowned. 'You've gone all funny, Luca. What's the matter?'

He stared down at her for a moment, as if about to divulge a terrible secret. His eyes were glassy, his mouth twisted at one corner. He looked afraid. But Annabel and Miles stepped out into the hall, interrupting them with their cheerful banter.

Luca went to the bathroom and stared at himself in the mirror. He splashed water on to his face and rubbed his eyes but still he looked terrible. He felt that familiar sensation of falling very fast without anything to hold on to. He dared not close his eyes for fear that the voices would return. That the shadows would once more walk about the room. That he would invite back in all those beings he had struggled to evict. He could hear his mother's voice telling him to grow up, not to invent imaginary friends. That if he really was hearing voices they were the spirits of Hell trying to persuade him to follow them into the fiery furnace. He recalled the doctor telling him to pull himself together and stop frightening his mother with lies, the teachers telling her he was making it up to get attention. Eventually, he had learned to keep quiet. Little by little he had shut them out and they had been silenced.

That night he did not want to be alone. He lay staring up at the ceiling, the light on the bedside table throwing shadows into the corners of the room. At last he crept down the corridor to where Annabel slept. Her door was ajar as if she were expecting him. She sat up when he entered, her white breasts exposed above the sheet. 'What took you so long?' she asked, throwing back the covers invitingly. He untied his pyjama bottoms and let them fall to the ground. Making love to Annabel was the best way to forget his boyhood and make him feel like a man again.

Miles took Sinbad for a walk around the garden before bed. It was drizzling again on to the phosphorescent green buds and daffodils. The dog trotted into the darkness, sniffing the grass and wagging his tail. When he was far enough from the house not to be overheard, Miles pulled out his mobile telephone and pressed redial. 'Hi,' he said in a low voice. 'It's me.'

Chapter 3

The following morning Luca returned to London. He had promised Annabel he would call her, but knew he wouldn't. As for Freya – happily married, beautiful Freya – there was no point chasing angels. He'd had his chance and missed it long ago. He drove up the M3 in his silver Aston Martin ruminating on what might have been. Would he be in the middle of a divorce had he married Freya instead of Claire? Or was he simply not made for the institution of marriage? He considered his daughters, Coco and Juno, then shuddered as he thought of them climbing into bed with John Tresco every morning. He hoped Claire would have the sensitivity not to bring him home until they were married, then the wisdom to resist forced intimacy with a man who was not their father.

John Tresco's shallow features were more suited to a shop dummy than a man of flesh and blood. Luca didn't trust men who looked like pretty boys, preening themselves in the mirror and taking too long to dress in the morning. John Tresco was too in love with himself to muster up emotion for anyone else. Arrogant and pompous, he was a know-all and a show-off. Having inherited a fortune, he had never done a day's work in his life, floating from party to party, shooting weekends in Scotland to weddings in Saint Tropez, mingling with the famous and fatuous. He invested the family money and employed armies of staff whom he spent hours training and seconds firing when they didn't come up to scratch. At least Luca had made all his money himself.

He had suspected Claire was having an affair long before she was caught out at a hotel in Beaulieu supposedly on a two-day break with her mother. Being so busy he had given it little thought. The spark between the two of them had died a few years after they had had the girls. Once the fire of passion had diminished to a mere glow they were left with the two very different people that they were. The girls united them briefly: early mornings and interrupted nights and shared moments watching the little miracles over the side of the cot. Then even the glow died and they existed as acquaintances or house-mates who didn't laugh with each other any more. He didn't blame her for finding someone else to love her but she felt guilty and chose to accuse him of driving her into John's arms. Years of resentment gushed out in a venomous torrent: he hadn't been there for her; she'd had to raise the girls single-handed; he didn't listen to her any more; he only talked about himself; he was a shocking father; he didn't deserve to have children. As deftly as he defended himself, he suspected she was probably right. He was guilty of all those things. They divorced on the grounds of irreconcilable differences. They were yet to work out a financial settlement but she was ensconced in their family house in Kensington, taking the girls to their home in Gloucestershire on alternate weekends and during the holidays. Her monthly maintenance was more than most people required in a year. If she was spoiled, he only had himself to blame.

Reluctantly, she let him see the children. He had bought a mews house in Chelsea, hiring an interior decorator to do it up for him so that the girls had bedrooms of their own and a playroom full of toys. It didn't feel like home to him; he was pretty sure it didn't feel like home to them either. The weekends he had them he relied on his friends who had children the same age. Coco, although only seven, was a precocious little girl one would almost expect to see smoking Marlboro Lights over a *cappuccino* in Starbucks. Dressed in clothes from Bonpoint and Marie Chantal, she was pretty and slim with dark hair and blue eyes like her father, but her face was joyless, as if she had seen and done everything already, so nothing excited her anymore. Juno, four and a half, was less blessed in the looks department, but she was effervescent and smiley, caring more about her toy caterpillars than her own wardrobe of beautiful clothes. Since Luca had stopped working he had begun to get to know his daughters. He realised there was not an awful lot to like in Coco. Juno was more malleable: with her there was still potential.

He considered Freya's advice. The thought of leaving London was a very tempting one. His parents' *palazzo* would offer just the sort of tranquillity he needed to search for the point in his now pointless existence. He'd find a corner away from his mother and her friends, take a suitcase full of books he had always wanted to read, and spend time on his own. He'd swim in the sea, go for long walks, unwind the years of tension that had slowly begun to choke him like a noose around his neck. There was something unsatisfying about his life but he wasn't sure what it was. He had money, children, women whenever he wanted them, but there was an emptiness that, since leaving the frenetic world of banking, he had begun to feel more acutely; a silence in his heart as loud as clashing cymbals.

He arrived in Chelsea just before lunch time. His house looked like a hotel, beautiful but impersonal. The housekeeper had cleaned it, tidying away any signs of life. Only the neat pile of post on the kitchen table indicated that somebody lived there. The light on his telephone winked at him, displaying messages. He pressed the delete button without even listening to the complaints of friends accusing him of not having confided his plans.

He opened the fridge. It was empty but for a couple of bottles of Chablis and some *pâté* from Lidgates. He left his suitcase in the hall and walked round the corner to Vingt Quatre where he read the papers over smoked salmon and scrambled eggs. Opposite, there was a table of children supervised by two mothers who sat gossiping while the children flicked food at each other and got up and down from the table to play hide-and-seek. The mothers were both pretty, late thirties, blonde, with expensive highlights, designer handbags and manicured nails. One of them noticed him watching and began to flick her hair self-consciously. She said something to her friend, who turned around to look. She smiled flirtatiously before telling her children off for making a din. *So this is the road ahead?* he thought bleakly. *Catching the eyes of good-looking mothers with small children?* He felt his stomach plummet.

That evening he was in the bath when the telephone rang. He listened to it ring and ring without any intention of getting out to answer it. He soaked in fragrant bubbles, thinking about nothing, heavy with apathy. When he finally got out, he wrapped a towel around his hips and listened to the message. His heart sank when he heard Annabel's chirpy voice. Surely Freya wouldn't have given her this number? 'Darling Luca,' she said. 'Last night was lovely. How about another round? I'll come over and make you dinner if you like. Call me.' She left her number. He had no intention of calling her. The thought of Italy became even more enticing. There was an awful lot in London he wanted to run away from. Shame he couldn't run from himself. The one telephone call he couldn't avoid was to his ex-wife. If he was going to disappear to Italy she needed to know. 'Oh, it's you,' she said. 'Everyone's talking about you. Your ears must be on fire!'

'I'm going to Italy to visit my parents,' he said.

'You sound like you've murdered someone.'

'Not yet.'

'How long are you away for? I can't imagine you're calling me if it's a mere weekend abroad.'

He chuckled. Claire had always been as sharp as a dart. 'I don't know. I'm heading out for the summer.'

'We're only in April.'

'It's going to be a long summer.'

'Are you telling me that you're going to leave me with the children for four months?'

'Of course not.' The truth was he hadn't given them more than a passing thought.

'I should hope not. I think it's only fair that you have them for at least a few weeks over the holidays. John and I want to get away. We've been asked to Saint Tropez again by the von Meisters. They've invited Elizabeth and Arun, which will be lovely for the girls, Damien is a darling, so after that I'd like to leave them with you so we can have some quiet time together.'

'Sounds great,' he said, trying to muster some enthusiasm. As long as their nanny came too it would be fine. His mother adored her granddaughters.

'I'll call you on your mobile, shall I?'

'I'm not answering. I'll call you with the number of the *palazzo*.'

'You really are running away.'

'Just need a break.'

'If you had taken a break a few years ago we might have avoided this mess.' Her voice quivered with bitterness.

'I doubt it. Ours was a crash waiting to happen.'

'Easy for you to say. You've been married to bloody Turtle Management for so long you can't imagine life without it.'

'I'm about to find out.'

'Three years too late.'

'How are things with John?' he asked, changing the subject.

'Heaven,' she replied a little too quickly. 'He's everything that you are not. Shall I list all his good qualities or can you work them out for yourself?'

'I'll have a good think about it then discuss it with my therapist. With a little professional help I'll try to become a better person.' He loathed himself for rising to her bait.

'Oh, shut up. I hate it when you get sarcastic.'

'I'll call you from Italy.'

'Whatever,' she snapped.

'Kiss the girls for me.'

'Is it fair to raise their hopes when they're not going to see you for months?'

'I'll have them as soon as you're willing to share them. The ball's in your court, Claire. As it always is.'

That night he listened to the whirring of his own thoughts, like a constant fan inside his head. Living in a mews was quiet. There was no rumble of traffic, no sirens screaming, dogs barking, people shouting, horns tooting; just the dead sound of sleep. When he had worked in the City he had stayed up so late he had fallen asleep the moment his head touched the pillow. Now he lay awake, ill at ease with his new existence. It didn't feel right having no plans. No goals. He had that nervous feeling in the pit of his stomach as if he had forgotten something important.

A thought popped into his head from nowhere. *Darkness is only the absence of light.* He wondered what it meant and why he had thought of it. He stared at the dark ceiling, at the streaks of light that entered above the curtain pole from the street lamp outside, slashing through the darkness. With his mind focused on that thought, he drifted into a deep sleep.

By morning a calmness had come over him. He lay dozing in bed until the telephone rang, jolting him out of his trance and thrusting him back to the present. His stomach tightened with nerves and the lightness he had felt was replaced by the familiar heaviness of heart. There was no one he wanted to talk to: not Annabel, the City, the press, his disgruntled friends. Freya was right, he needed to get away. He'd sort out his affairs, then leave everything and everyone. He'd be totally free.

Chapter 4

Luca sat in the motor boat on his way to Incantellaria. His gaze swept over the rugged red rocks that rose sharply out of the sea and paused on a couple of birds dancing flirtatiously on the breeze. Spring breathed new life into the vegetation that sparkled green against a bright cerulean sky, and little yellow buds were beginning to flower. He inhaled the scent of pine and felt his spirits rise, as if the negativity in his heart was expelled with each outward breath. His mother had told him to come by boat.

'Incantellaria is best seen from the sea,' she had explained, her accent more noticeable since they had moved to Italy. 'You won't believe the magnificence of it. I'll pick you up in the car. Darling, I'm so pleased you are coming, finally! It has been so long I was beginning to wonder whether you'd ever come.' Her voice was buoyant. She hadn't asked about Claire or the children, not out of tact – no one was less tactful than Romina – but because the acrimony of their divorce hurt her too and she didn't want to spoil her day.

The boat motored around the rocks, opening suddenly into a horseshoe bay of such beauty that Luca stood to get a better look. The medieval town basked in the midday sun, the red-tiled roofs shimmering above white and sandy-pink houses. Delicate, wrought iron balconies were decorated with pots of red and white flowers and, rising above them all, was the yellow and turquoise dome of the church. As they approached he could see the pale grey pebbles of the beach and the sky-blue and white fishing boats dragged up out of the water. He recalled Fitz's account of the red carnations and smiled at the absurdity of it. The south of Italy was full of such 'miracles'. His mother was Italian but even she dismissed them with a disdainful snort. They reached the quay. A few cars were parked beyond the beach where busy restaurants spilled out on to the road among a couple of chic boutiques and a kiosk selling sweets and postcards. An elderly couple in black sat on a bench, chewing on rotten teeth and fading memories, while a trio of scruffy children took turns to jump off a concrete bollard. Luca noticed his mother immediately. She was wearing over-sized sunglasses, her black hair swept off her face with a bright Pucci scarf, and waving frenziedly. He waved back, hoping to subdue her enthusiasm, but she only waved with more vigour, shrieking 'Darling, darling, you're here! You're here!' As he prepared to disembark, his eyes were drawn to a dark-haired woman with a little boy, ambling slowly up the beach. He shielded his eyes from the sun so that he could see her better. She was attractive, with long brown curls, skin the colour of toffee and a curvy, femi-nine body wrapped in a simple black dress. As she walked closer he noticed the serious expression on her face and her downcast eyes. The little boy chattered beside her, but she seemed distracted, her arms folded defensively, her gait slow and melancholy. The child chattered on, undeterred.

'Darling, Luca,' his mother enthused, throwing her arms around him although she only reached his chest. 'You've grown. I swear it. You're taller!'

'Mother, if I'm still growing in my forties, by the time I'm old I'll be a giant!'

'But I swear it!' She smiled, her teeth white against her olive skin. Luca spotted the pretty girl going into one of the restaurants.

'Are you hungry?' he asked his mother, without taking his eyes off the door. 'How about these restaurants?'

'They're good,' she replied. 'But I have lunch already prepared up at the *palazzo*. I can't wait for you to see it. You won't believe what your father and I have done to it. You should have seen it when it was a ruin.' Luca was disappointed, but he could not refuse her. He picked up his bag and followed her to her small yellow Fiat, parked badly on the curb.

'These streets are too narrow for cars really. They've improved the road up to the *palazzo*, which is a blessing,' said Romina, turning the ignition key. 'At least it stops the town becoming over-crowded with tourists. There's a divine hotel in the square and the little church of San Pasquale, which is enchanting.'

'Ah, the church where the statue of Jesus weeps blood.'

'So you already know about Incantellaria?'

'Only because Fitzroy Davenport told me about it.'

'How is darling Fitzroy? Still henpecked? I didn't know he'd been here?'

'Yes. A long time ago.'

'It hasn't changed that much, you know. It's hidden away, like a jewel, and I like it that way. The locals keep themselves to themselves. Tourists are few. You see, there's no sandy beach, no glamorous hotels with swimming pools. There isn't the room. It attracts bird watchers and old people who come for the beauty. The fashionable people go to Portofino and Capri. *La dolce vita*. To tell you the truth, life is more *dolce* without that crowd of models and film stars.'

'Do you know any of the locals?'

'A few. We are quite detached up there on the hill. As you know I don't go to Mass and I don't involve myself in community life, but the locals are perfectly friendly, if a little in awe of us. No one wanted to buy the *palazzo*, it was just a pile of rubble. The man who owned it no longer lived there. He hadn't wanted to sell at first, but we made him an offer he couldn't refuse. I think the townspeople consider us rather eccentric, what with all the coming and going of friends calling in on us from all over the world. We are like a hotel, except we don't charge. What is the point in having earned all this money if we don't permit ourselves to enjoy it! Your grandmother would want me to spend my inheritance like this, restoring a beautiful house in her native country, not wasting it on gluttony and booze like that idiotic brother of mine! By the way, your father insisted on building a swimming pool, so you can bring the children next time. I haven't seen them for months and I miss them terribly. They are my only grandchildren and now I have no communication with their mother it is even harder.' She gave him a sidelong glance. 'Don't let Claire monopolise them. They need their father too.'

They drove up the narrow streets, past sandy coloured houses with tall, ornate windows and large wooden doors that opened on to pretty courtyards and gardens. A couple of bony dogs trotted against the walls in search of scraps while the local people watched the car with curiosity as they motored past. Luca rolled down the window and rested his elbow on the window frame, taking in the old buildings, the women hanging washing on shady balconies, the ugly white satellite dishes nailed into the medieval walls, savouring the warm smell of spring that rose into the air with the heat. His thoughts were drawn again to the woman he had seen on the beach, though she was clearly a wife and mother. There was no way he wanted to further complicate his life by chatting up a married woman, certainly not in an Italian town where the men were sure to be protective of their women and suspicious of foreigners. He put her out of his mind.

'So, you've quit the City,' said Romina as they left the town behind and started climbing the hill. 'About time too! Now we will see more of you.'

'I've come to a crossroads in my life. I need to take time to work out which way I want to go.'

'The world is your oyster, Luca. You have enough money to do anything you want. You don't even have to work if you don't want to.'

He sighed. 'That's the trouble, there are too many options. It's better when you have limits, easier to make a choice. The truth is, nothing inspires me.'

'That's because the divorce has knocked you for six. Claire is a great disappointment. But you're young. There is still time to marry again and begin a new life. You have come to the right place. Palazzo Montelimone will fill you with inspiration. We are nearly there.' The road turned sharply round a bend and began to get steeper, appearing narrower in the shadow of the encroaching trees and shrubs. Finally, they forked off to the right. 'Now we are approaching the gates. We have kept the original ones. They were too beautiful to throw away,' Romina explained. 'There! Aren't they splendid?'

The gates were black and imposing as gates to a magnificent palace should be. His parents had gone to so much trouble he wondered why they hadn't put in electric gates that opened with the press of a button. He got out to open them and looked up the drive that swept in a graceful curve through an avenue of cypress trees, opening at the end into a pool of bright sunshine. There, in that magical pool of light, stood the *palazzo*. His mother tooted the horn to hurry him. 'Do get on, darling. I'm hungry.'

'I think that's the loveliest entrance I've ever seen,' he said when he returned to the car.

'You know, when we saw it for the first time it was nothing but stones and ivy. The garden had taken over, climbing in through the holes and seeding itself in the rooms. Only one of the two towers was left standing. It was so sad. So neglected. It was as if it had given up, abandoning itself to its fate like a beautiful woman crippled by age. I fell in love, Luca.'

'How did you find it if the owner didn't want to sell?'

'By chance. I was painting a *palazzo* just outside Sorrento and the lady who owned it mentioned this place. She said that if she had had the money she would have bought it and resurrected it herself. She had beautiful taste, so I was intrigued. I drove here on my own and took a look around. No one was at home. I called your father and told him he had to come and take a look. We were thinking of retiring to Italy anyway. I knew this would be an incredible project for both of us. Having worked for other people all our lives, what fun to work for ourselves!'

Romina parked the car on the gravel in front of the *palazzo*. The building was of the same sand-coloured stone as the town. The windows were capped with ornate baroque pediments and opened on to ornamental iron balconies. Heavy brickwork gave way to plaster on the first and second floors and the roof was covered with pink tiles, rising into two magnificent towers. It stood nestled among lofty pine trees and inky green cypresses. 'Come, darling. Let me show you inside.'

The door was vast and arched and made of old oak. Within it was a smaller door that opened into a hall of large square flagstones. 'These stones are the original ones,' said Romina, leading him through into a pretty courtyard. 'I scraped my foot over moss and grass to find them underneath. What a find!' In the centre of the courtyard was a stone fountain where the trickling sound of water was gentle and constant. Against the walls between the windows, were lemon trees in large terracotta pots. The floor was a mosaic of smooth round pebbles and flat square stones. The effect was stunning. Luca wasn't surprised. His mother might be eccentric but she had a sharp intelligence and enormous talent when it came to aesthetics.

In the main body of the house, the rooms had tall ceilings, bold mouldings and walls painted in the original colours of pale blue, duck-egg grey and dusty pink. 'I wanted to return it to its former glory,' Romina explained, gesticulating at the antique tapestries and marble fireplaces. 'We kept everything we could from the original building. It represents two years' work. Your father and I have poured our souls into it, not to mention a great deal of money. Now, where is he?'

Luca followed his mother into a drawing-room where French doors opened out onto a terrace overlooking the gardens. He was surprised to find an old man in a three-piece tweed suit reading *The Times*. He looked up over his spectacles and nodded formally. 'This is my son, Caradoc,' said Romina, her wide trousers billowing as she glided over to him. 'And this, Luca, is our dear friend Professor Caradoc

Macausland.' The professor extended a bony hand, so twisted with arthritis that it resembled a claw.

'Please don't consider me rude for not getting up to greet you, young man,' he explained in his clipped 1950s English accent. 'I walk with a stick and it seems to have walked off without me! Must be that charming girl.'

'Ventura,' said Romina with a melodramatic sigh. 'She thinks she's being helpful leaning it against a wall way out of reach.'

'So, you are the famous Luca,' said the professor. 'Your parents speak very highly of you.'

'They are biased,' Luca replied, wishing he didn't have to bother with the old codger.

'It would be unusual if they weren't. Isn't it splendid here?'

'It certainly is.' Luca noticed how at home the professor looked in that leather armchair. 'How long have you been here?' he asked.

'Oh, a couple of weeks now. One loses track of time. Your mother is such a perfect hostess, I don't see much point in going home.'

'What are you a professor of?'

'History,' Caradoc replied. 'I specialise in Ancient History. This *palazzo* must have a rich heritage and I have told Romina that once I have found an interpreter I will endeavour to uncover its past. You see, I don't speak Italian, only Latin which is helpful up to a point. Beyond that point it is utterly useless. The locals here don't seem to speak any English at all.'

'Ah, an obstacle then,' said Luca.

'Obstacles can be surmounted, if one uses a little lateral thinking. You are in my lateral vision, young man. Surely you speak Italian?'

'Of course.'

'Good. I will enlist your help, Luca. The two of us will make a formidable team.' He smacked his lips. 'Holmes and Watson! What fun we shall have. I so enjoy unravelling mysteries.' Luca was already planning to make himself scarce.

'Darling, don't dither. The professor likes his quiet time before lunch,' she said now, waving at her son to join her on the terrace. Caradoc returned to his newspaper and Luca returned to his tour, following his mother out into the sunshine.

There, at a long table nibbling on *bruschette*, sat a group of strangers. Luca's heart sank. He had come away to avoid people. He had planned to spend time taking stock of his life, not sit around gassing with old people.

He looked around. The view of the sea and town was spectacular, down into the heart of Incantellaria. Romina sailed up to her guests. 'My friends, allow me to introduce my son, Luca.' He wondered, looking at the group so comfortable there in the shade with their glasses of wine, if they had all been in residence as long as the professor.

Romina proceeded to introduce them one by one, starting with a petite woman with curly blonde hair and big blue eyes. She wore a pale pink chiffon shirt tied in a bow at the neck. 'This is Dizzy and her husband Maxwell, who live in Vienna, and that darling little creature on her lap is Smidge.' Dizzy was stroking a fluffy white dog with long manicured nails.

'Hello, Luca. We've heard so much about you.'

'Hi,' said Maxwell, running a hand over his balding head. 'Good to meet you, finally! A man who bats on the same team!'

'Maxwell works in finance too,' explained Romina. Luca tried to stifle his irritation. Everything about Maxwell and Dizzy was repugnant.

'And this is Ma Hemple.' Romina placed her hands on an elderly lady's soft shoulders. Ma was totally grey except for dramatic black streaks that swept from her forehead to the bun that was tied on top of her head, like a racoon. When she took off her large red-rimmed sunglasses her eyes were a surprisingly pale shade of green. Her lips were crimson, matching the poppies on her dress which she wore over wide black trousers. She was a large woman with a dry sense of humour some could mistake for rudeness.

'About time!' she said without smiling. 'We were beginning to think your mother was making you up.' Her accent was as upper class as the professor's, her tone deep and fruity.

'That is why I came, to save her face,' Luca replied solemnly.

'Well, just in time! Come and join us. There is a *bruschetta* left and it has your name on it.' Luca had no option but to remain among this extraordinary gathering. He wondered where his mother had found them all. Her appetite for new people was voracious.

'Isn't this fun!' said Romina, casting her eyes to the French doors in the hope that Ventura would appear with refreshment. 'Silly woman! I'd better go and get her. We need more wine. Wine for my son!'

As Romina disappeared inside, the professor emerged on Luca's father's arm. 'Ah, here's my boy,' said Bill, grinning at Luca. He was tall and lean with thinning grey hair partially hidden under a stiff panama hat, a good-looking man with a wide, infectious smile. He was even tempered and consistently jovial, which was just as well, being married to the mercurial Romina.

'Hi Dad,' said Luca. They embraced, clearly pleased to see each other.

'So, what do you think of our new home?'

'It's spectacular.'

'Not bad for an architect and a painter, eh?'

'Not bad at all.'

'How long are you staying?'

'I don't know. I'll take every day as it comes.'

'Like us. That's the joy of being retired,' interjected the professor.

'Or unemployed,' Luca added wryly.

'So I gather,' said his father. 'Time to try something different.'

'What exactly, I don't know.'

'You'll figure it out. Here, have a chair and a glass of wine, that'll do you the power of good.'

Romina returned followed by Ventura, an attractive young girl with long brown hair and dark eyes, carrying the professor's walking stick in one hand and a bottle of *rosé* in the other. 'Don't forget to put some food out for Porci,' said Romina, pulling out a chair. 'Porci was a house-warming present from your uncle Nanni, Luca.' Luca raised an eyebrow. His mother didn't usually like dogs, even little white fluffy ones like Smidge. 'He's a pig,' added Romina, flapping her napkin and placing it on her lap. 'A darling little pig!'

'Who wears a nappy inside,' said Ma. 'A most uncommon sight. Though, I would say he has a certain hoggish charm.'

'He's a cutie,' chirped in Dizzy. 'But he's naughty because he doesn't like Smidge.'

'Who's to blame him?' said Ma under her breath.

'The only reason he's not on the menu is because your mother wants the children to see him,' said Bill to Luca.

'They'll adore him,' Romina gushed.

'And if they don't, we'll eat him,' said Ma.

Two butlers in uniform appeared on the terrace with trays of food. The professor's eyes brightened at the sight of the feast, but Ma gave a heavy sigh. 'What are we to do with all of that? Am I not fat enough already? The little pig is going to be a *lucky* little pig, troughing on the remains of our banquet.'

'Remember, I don't eat carbohydrates,' said Dizzy with an apologetic laugh. 'They make me bloat.'

'More for the pig,' Ma said, obviously irritated by Dizzy. 'Is there anything else you don't eat?'

'Oh yes . . .' Dizzy began but Ma's snort silenced her.

'You must be fun to live with.'

'Right, darlings, tuck in!' Romina instructed excitedly.

'Except for you, Dizzy. You can watch us eat,' said Ma. Dizzy looked sternly at her husband, who chose to ignore her, helping himself to a healthy bowl of spaghetti.

They dined on tomato and garlic pasta, steak and vegetables followed by cheese and a raspberry soufflé. By the time coffee was served they were light-headed with wine and sleepy from so much food. Luca lit a cigarette and sat back in his chair. Romina smoked too, inhaling contentedly while her guests settled their stomachs with mint tea and black coffee.

'I'm going into town after a little nap,' said the professor. 'Do you want to come with me, Luca? I could do with your help.'

'I think I'll hang around here this afternoon,' he replied. He rather fancied lying in the sun by the pool.

'There's a lot of local talent,' said Maxwell.

'Italian girls are so pretty,' gushed Dizzy.

'But they all end up as fat as me,' said Ma.

'It's those carbohydrates,' said Dizzy with a smile.

'I want to show you the folly,' said Romina.

'The one thing we kept exactly as it was,' Bill added.

'Oh, it's a fabulous little Hansel and Gretel house,' enthused Dizzy. 'Though Smidge got a bit restless in there, didn't you, darling?' She kissed the dog on her mouth, provoking a grimace from Ma as the dog's little pink tongue flitted across her mistress's lips.

'Consider your husband!' said Ma. 'Dogs lick their bottoms.'

'Because they can,' Max said with a smirk. Ma's fleshy lips twitched in suppressed amusement.

Romina stood up. 'Come, Luca,' she said.

'Who are all these people?' he asked as they walked down a narrow path that wound its way through the garden to the cliffs.

Romina shrugged. 'People we have picked up along the way.'

'Do you always have the place full of . . . freaks?'

'Darling!' she chided. 'We have all sorts, old friends and new friends alike. I love to fill the *palazzo* with interesting people from all over the world.'

'When are they leaving?'

'I don't know. People come and go, but most of them want to stay. Incantellaria has a particular magic. Once you come here, you don't want to leave.'

'I think that has as much to do with your free and bountiful hospitality as it has to do with the magic of the place.'

'Darling, that's very unfair. My friends are not unwelcome parasites, but people I choose to entertain in my house. I have a gift for friendship.'

'So I have to spend my holiday with a bunch of nutters?'

'If you came more often I wouldn't have to fill the house

with other people. You know I would put you and the children above all my friends. Anyway, don't write them off so
quickly. Caradoc is fascinating. His knowledge of history is
vast and wonderful. You should ask him about it. I think that
is what keeps him young – history and poetry.'

'What about Maxwell and Dizzy? They're beyond
dreadful!'

'Yes, they are rather dull, aren't they? Friends of your
cousin Costanza. It is not often that I come across bad apples
in the apple cart! They must leave. We might have to pretend
the *palazzo* is haunted!'

Chapter 5

They wandered down the hill, through a second avenue of cypress trees to the folly, a small grey stone building overlooking the sea. 'This is it,' said Romina. 'Isn't it enchanting?' It was perfectly symmetrical with a tall window either side of a large double door.

'What is it?'

'I don't know,' she said, turning the key in the rusty old lock. 'A lovers' hideaway perhaps.' The door creaked open, revealing a harmonious square room with terracotta walls and a domed ceiling painted with a fresco of fat little cherubs in a pale blue sky. In the centre was a four-poster bed with heavy silk drapes that were once green. In front of one window stood a pretty walnut desk; before the other, a dressing-table. The walls were covered with paintings of nude boys, the bookshelves full of erotica. In an alcove stood a replica statue of Donatello's David.

'The previous owner clearly loved sex,' said Luca in amusement. 'Who was he?'

'We don't know. The sale was done through solicitors. I think the man must be very old. He didn't take anything with him. The *palazzo* was built by the Montelimone family about four hundred years ago. A famously grand family. I

gather the late *Marchese* was quite a character because whenever I mention him people raise their eyebrows. After he
died I don't know who bought it. No one wants to elaborate.
Perhaps they don't even know. Anyway, when we found it
it was a ruin and completely empty but for an old leather
chair and a bed, which we burned. But *this* was beautifully
preserved. It didn't feel right to change it. It's rather beautiful, don't you think?'

'Have you been sleeping in here?' Luca asked, pointing at
the unmade bed.

'No,' said Romina, pursing her lips irritably. 'I think your
father must have been coming in here for a nap. The only
place to get a little peace. I don't allow our guests to come in
here. I keep it locked.'

'I don't blame him, the bed looks very comfortable.'

'Yes, it does, doesn't it?' she agreed, placing her hands on
her hips. 'Still, I don't like anyone to use it, not even your
father. There's something rather sad about its state of neglect.
Now you're here to translate, I'll send the professor off to
find out about the previous owner. Give the old man something to do, he's such a character. And I'm rather intrigued,
aren't you?'

'Yes,' Luca replied, his curiosity mounting. 'Why would
someone leave without taking their belongings with them?'

That afternoon he lay beside the pool reading a Wilbur
Smith novel. The sun was warm on his skin, a silky breeze
keeping him pleasantly cool. He forgot about the professor.
Later, he borrowed his mother's car and drove into town,
parking the car in the square that was dominated by the
church of San Pasquale with its white walls and mosaic
dome. In the centre there was a little park with palm trees

and benches where women sat gossiping in the shade while children played around a fountain, giggling with excitement. Luca recognised one little boy as the child on the beach. He was the only one not wearing a school smock. He looked around for the boy's mother, but she was nowhere to be seen.

It was pleasant not having to talk to anyone or explain himself. He wandered over to a *caffè* and ordered an *espresso*, then sat back and smoked languidly. It wasn't long before he had company. '*Buona sera.*' The woman was slim and olive-skinned with curly brown hair and the confident gaze of a sophisticated manipulator. 'Do you have a light?' Her full lips curled into a smile, her eyes promised more.

'Sure.'

She leaned forward and puffed on the flame. 'You're not from here.'

'No, just visiting.'

'You're a tourist?'

'Yes.'

'You sound Italian, but with a hint of something else. Where are you from?'

'London.'

'An Italian living in London. Why ever would you want to do that when you could remain here in God's own country?'

He laughed. 'I'm beginning to wonder myself.'

She let the smoke float out between her lips. 'May I join you?'

'Sure,' he replied, finding it hard to resist when she was offering herself on a plate.

'I'll have an *espresso*. My name is Maria Fiscobaldi.'

'Luca,' he said.

'The coffee here is good. But if you want a tip, the best

coffee is at Fiorelli's. Down on the quay. You should give it a try.'

'I will.'

'How long are you staying?'

'I have no idea.'

She grinned. 'Long enough to see the best view in Incantellaria?'

'Sure. Where's that?'

'I'll show you after coffee. I assure you, you won't see better.' She had mischief in her eyes.

Luca summoned the waiter and ordered two coffees. He was going to be buzzing on so much caffeine. Maria sat back on her chair and appraised him. He knew that look well: the sleepy eyes, the knowing expression, the flush of admiration on her cheeks, the naked lust vibrating in the invisible space between them. He knew sex could follow, but he wasn't in the mood. He hadn't come for that, even though she was beautiful. Their coffees arrived and they chatted. She told him about her life and he was content to listen, weary of talking about himself. After an hour, he paid the bill and got up to leave.

'You're not coming to see the view?' she asked, disappointed.

'Another time, perhaps.'

'You don't know what you're missing.'

'Then it's my loss.'

'Thank you for the coffee.'

'It's a pleasure.'

She smiled suggestively. 'On the contrary, the pleasure is all mine.'

Luca returned to the *palazzo*. His mother was talking to Ventura and another maid in the hall. 'My darling, where have you been?'

'Into town,' he replied.

'Isn't it pretty?'

'Prettier than I expected,' he said with a grin.

'Come out and have a drink. Dinner is at nine.'

'I think I'll go and take a shower.'

'Don't be long. The professor was asking after you.'

Luca rolled his eyes. 'I don't want to have to talk to that old codger. I'm here on holiday.'

'Well, you're going to have to and that's that.'

Luca retreated upstairs. When he finally stepped on to the terrace, Dizzy was sitting talking to his mother. Bristling with irritation, he joined them. 'So, how was your afternoon?' he asked Dizzy.

She smiled sweetly, tossing her blonde hair. 'I had a very relaxing time lying in the sun and reading my book. Then Max and I slunk off for a little nuggy bunny.'

'Nuggy bunny?' Luca repeated.

'Yes, when you cuddle up in bed together like two little bunnies.' She pulled a face of mock guilt. 'So indulgent, but the bed is so comfortable one doesn't want to get out.'

'I'm so pleased. I bought the very best Frette sheets,' said Romina.

'We're going to Capri tomorrow. Why don't you come with us?' Dizzy asked Luca.

'Thanks, but I think I'll hang around here and play nuggy bunny all by myself.'

His mother shot him a look. 'Luca's very tired. He needs to rest.'

Luca conversed in monosyllables during dinner and didn't stick around for coffee. Romina made excuses for him. 'He's going through a very difficult time. He's quit the City, divorced his wife and doesn't know what he wants to do. I need to find him a nice girl.'

'There are plenty of girls in town,' Caradoc suggested. 'Italian girls are very easy on the eye.'

'Not a local girl,' Romina scoffed. 'Gracious no! I'd hope for a girl with a bit more class.'

'I don't think marriage is high on Luca's agenda,' cautioned his father.

'It's very high on mine. Men are better when they're married. Look at Nanni,' she said, referring to her brother. 'He's a disaster!'

'I wouldn't wish Nanni on anyone,' said Bill.

'On second thoughts, neither would I!' Romina agreed.

For the next few days, Luca managed to make himself scarce. He was polite but aloof. He spent most of his time reading by the pool or walking along the stony beach, lost in thought. In spite of the beauty of Incantellaria he was unable to lift the heaviness in his soul. He considered Maria and felt his heart sink. Maria, like so many other women he had encountered, was like a delicious honey pot. After eating all the honey there was nothing left but the empty pot. His spirit yearned for something more. A pot that remained always full. A honey that lasted. Maybe he wasn't cut out for long relationships, but destined to flit like a bee from flower to flower, never settling for long.

He had managed to decline the professor's invitations to accompany him into town for almost a week, but he couldn't decline them for ever. At lunch, when Dizzy suggested a trip to Positano he decided that the professor was the lesser of two evils. He didn't think much of the idea of spending the day with a pair of nuggy bunnies.

The professor enjoyed a long siesta, waking at four to go into town. Romina lent Luca her car and waved them off. The air was thick with the scent of pine and eucalyptus, the light twittering of birds ringing out from the branches. 'I believe the *palazzo* has a tragic history,' said Caradoc. 'I can feel it in the rooms. They are beautiful but the atmosphere is melancholy with something I can't quite put my finger on. I've felt it before in ancient Greek temples and palaces. The energy of the events that took place there imprints itself into the stone. If those events are tragic, it is as if the very walls are draped with sadness. I want to get to the bottom of it. Two minds are better than one. Are you in, boy?'

Luca couldn't help smiling at the old man's enthusiasm. 'I'm in, Professor. Where do you want to start?'

'In the centre of town. In the church.'

'What do you hope to find there?' *Apart from a weeping statue of Christ*, he thought cynically.

'Old people,' said the professor. 'Old people spend a lot of time in churches. Old people know things. And old people love to talk about the past.'

Luca helped the professor out of the car, handing him his stick. 'Give me a minute to find my legs,' said Caradoc, giving each one a little shake. 'I'm lucky to have them. Jolly nearly got them blown off in the war.' He chuckled as they walked slowly along the road towards the church. There were boutiques, a pharmacy, a butcher's, a barber shop, a bakery, all open for business after the siesta. Luca noticed the little boy he had seen a few days before, roaming aimlessly among the trees like a lost dog.

The church was cool and dim inside the enclosure of its thick stone walls. There was no sound but the echo of silent prayer. At the end, where the altar stood in a large alcove, were tables of candles flickering eerily through the gloom, illuminating the marble statue of Christ on the cross. Luca didn't think for a minute that that statue had ever wept blood. Some clever person with red paint and a penchant for theatricals was no doubt responsible. He followed Caradoc down the aisle, not quite sure what they were looking for. The place smelt of warm wax and incense. He swept his eyes over the frescoes of the Nativity and Crucifixion, and the iconography decorated with gold leaf that glittered in the candlelight. It was a charming chapel and no doubt well attended, which wasn't a surprise in a place such as this, where Catholicism was at the core of the community.

There were people either side of the aisle: an old lady with her rosary beads, an elderly man in a black hat kneeling in prayer, a young woman in a black veil lighting a candle, closing her eyes and making an impossible wish. Caradoc leaned on his walking stick. 'What now?' Luca hissed, putting his hands in his pockets. How on earth had he got himself involved in the professor's mad quest?

'I'm looking for the oldest person here.' He chortled. 'Someone as old as me. Ah, there he is.' The man kneeling in prayer was so still he might already have been dead had it not been for the sudden twitch of his foot, like the tail of a dozing cat.

'You can't interrupt his prayers.'

'Of course not. I'll wait until he's finished.'

'He might take all evening.'

'I'm in no hurry. I have one or two things I can tell the good Lord while I'm waiting,' said Caradoc, shuffling over to take a seat near him.

As he sat down to wait, Luca noticed the woman by the candles turn and walk up the aisle towards him. It was the woman he had seen on the beach, the mother of the child playing outside. He recognised her immediately by the way her hips gently swayed with each step. 'I'll be back in a moment,' he whispered to Caradoc, then followed her out into the *piazza*. She was dressed in black, her veil reaching down to her waist. He noticed her bouncing hair and the fine curve of her hips and bottom, her slender ankles and calves. Before he had thought about what to say, he found himself greeting her in Italian. She turned, startled.

'I'm sorry if I surprised you,' he said, trying to make out her features behind the embroidered lace. 'I didn't mean to sneak up on you. I've just arrived in Incantellaria from England. My parents live up at the Palazzo Montelimone.' The mention of that place grabbed her attention. She looked less timid than curious. *Good*, he thought, *I'll have this all wrapped up before the old man is even half way through his prayers*. 'We're trying to find out a little of the history of the place. Who lived there, what he was like, you know, it's natural that one would want to know about the past. It's such a beautiful *palazzo*.'

'I know nothing,' she said. Her voice was soft and low like a reedy flute. She turned away and walked on through the square.

'Perhaps you have a grandmother who might know something?' he continued, hurrying after her.

'No,' she replied, quickening her pace. 'No one has lived there for decades. It was a ruin.'

'It's not a ruin now. It's glorious. Is there someone you can recommend? A local historian perhaps? Is there a library?'

'No one,' she said briskly.

Luca felt foolish chasing after her. 'Well, thank you for your time,' he shouted.

She smiled politely and hurried on, her pretty little feet moving swiftly over the paving stones. The boy left the shady trees and skipped up to join her. Luca grinned at him and gave a little wave. The boy's big brown eyes looked stunned. He hesitated a moment, his mouth agape, then turned to run after his mother who was leaving the square by a narrow street, almost lost in shadow.

Luca returned to the church. It wasn't going to be as easy as he thought. No wonder his mother hadn't had much success in finding out the history, if no one wanted to talk. He took his seat next to Caradoc. 'I bet you found out nothing,' whispered the professor.

'You're right. She didn't want to talk.'

'Of course not. She must have thought you were just chatting her up.'

'Which I wasn't!' Luca joked.

'Beware of the men in her family. You don't want to cross an Italian man.'

'You're telling me?'

'You're only *half* Italian. These southerners are very passionate. Men are killed for less.'

At last the elderly man picked up his prayer book and prepared to leave. Caradoc tapped him on the shoulder.

'Good day,' said the professor in Latin. The old man looked confused.

'*Buona sera*,' whispered Luca. 'Forgive us for disturbing you. We're new in town. We live at Palazzo Montelimone on the hill. Would you mind if we asked you a little about the history of the place? We thought you looked like the sort of person who would know.'

The old man sniffed noisily. 'Come outside,' he hissed, standing up stiffly. Both men followed him to the *piazza* and took a seat on one of the benches. The gossiping mothers had gone home, the *piazza* was quiet.

'Professor Caradoc Macausland.' The professor shook the man's hand.

'Tancredi Lattarullo. So you live up at Montelimone.' He smiled at the professor, revealing large black gaps between a few long brown teeth. His skin was tanned and bristly, life's joys and sorrows imprinted in deep lines like arid rivers in a desert. He sniffed again.

'My parents live there,' interjected Luca in Italian. 'My name is Luca.'

'Yes, I know who lives in the *palazzo*. You'd never get a local living up there. They must be very brave, Luca,' said Tancredi, his laugh rattling in his chest like an old engine.

'Have you always lived here?' he asked.

Tancredi was only too pleased to tell them a little about himself. Luca offered him a cigarette and lit one for himself. 'I have lived in Incantellaria all my life,' said Tancredi, exhaling a puff of smoke. 'I survived the war. I fought for my country. The things I've witnessed are enough to turn your blood cold. But I was a hero. They should have given me medals for the things I did at Monte Cassino. Now look at me. No one cares. Life was better then. People looked out for one another. Not like now. Everyone is out for themselves. The young have no appreciation of what their countrymen fought and died for.'

'Who lived in the *palazzo* during the war? Was it occupied by the Germans?'

Tancredi shook his head. 'It belonged to the Marchese Ovidio di Montelimone. He was a little prince. Too good to mingle with the common folk down here. He had his own private Mass daily up at the *palazzo*. Father Dino would have to bicycle up that hill and back down again in the heat even though the *Marchese* had a chauffeur and a shiny white Lagonda. Like a panther it was, purring as it went, a real beauty. I remember it even now. It could have been yesterday. The only other person to have a car was the *sindacco*. Now it's not just the mayor who has a car, but everyone and the smell gets up my nose.' He sniffed again to make his point. 'People become animals behind the wheel. They think they are invincible. In those days we travelled by horse and life was better.'

'What happened to the *Marchese*?'

'He was murdered up there in your *palazzo*.' Tancredi drew a line across his chicken neck. Luca quickly translated for Caradoc.

'Ask him whether it was an honour killing?' said Caradoc, looking years younger with excitement.

Tancredi shrugged, pulling a face like a fish. '*Bo!* Nobody knows the truth. But my uncle was the town *carabiniere* and I have heard it whispered that the *Marchese* killed Valentina, his mistress, so Valentina's brother killed *him*.'

'An honour killing,' repeated Luca. 'No wonder no one wants to talk about it.'

'Valentina's death was all over the newspapers at the time because she was in the car with the infamous *mafioso*, Lupo Bianco, when they were both murdered. A small-town beauty in diamonds and furs on her way to Naples in the middle of the night.' He raised his eyebrows, clearly taking delight in divulging the dirt. 'You can imagine, it was a sensational story. Her daughter, Alba, lives here in Incantellaria. English, like you. But she came here thirty years ago and has never gone back to England. That's what happens to people who come here. They don't go back. But you won't get her talking about it. It was a long time ago. No one likes to drag up the past. The *Marchese* got what he deserved. Valentina was the light of Incantellaria and he extinguished her.'

'So that's it?' said Luca. 'That's the reason no one wanted to buy the *palazzo*?'

Tancredi looked shifty. 'It is haunted.'

'Haunted? By the *Marchese*?'

'Of course.'

'How do you know?'

'Everyone knows. For years the *palazzo* was uninhabited. The *Marchese* left it to a man called Nero who let it rot like an unwanted cake. Then Nero left. I think he ran out of money. No one would buy it. I don't know what became of him. But during the years that passed, on dark nights, you could see candlelight flickering through the rooms. The police went to investigate on numerous occasions but found nothing.' He took a deep drag, pausing for effect. 'Of course, there were stories, accounts of sightings, screams, noises. No one is in any doubt that the *Marchese* is still up there on that hill.'

'Well, now Mother has her history,' said Luca as he walked back to the car with the professor.

'A murder indeed,' exclaimed the professor. 'And a ghost thrown in. I would expect nothing less from the south of Italy. A truly satisfying piece of detective work. Well done, my boy.'

'That Valentina sounds quite a player.'

'Quite a girl,' agreed Caradoc with a chuckle. 'The war took people to extremes. There were no limits. One had nothing to lose. I fought for king and country. It was brutal and romantic. Death in every corner, a girl in every port. Then I came back and married my childhood sweetheart, Myrtle.'

'What happened to Myrtle?'

'She died. Cancer.'

'I'm sorry.'

'The best die young.'

'Children?'

'Four. All grown up. But since I retired I've travelled. Nothing gives me greater pleasure than to see the world. I think I'll hang my cap up here for a while. Like Tancredi said, people come to Incantellaria and they never leave.'

'Say, Caradoc, what do you think about having a drink on the sea front?'

'I'd say jolly good idea, young man. There's a nice little *trattoria* called Fiorelli's. They serve *espresso* on the terrace and the girls are easy on the eye.'

'Sounds just my thing,' said Luca, taking the professor by the arm.

Chapter 6

Alba stood in the shadows with her daughter as the two men took a table on the terrace. 'That's the man,' said Rosa, her pale eyes appraising him appreciatively. 'Cosima said he was tall, dark and handsome.'

'I'm glad she noticed,' said Alba. 'It's time she moved on. It's been three years.'

'He's gorgeous! If I wasn't married . . .'

'The way you and Eugenio behave it's a miracle you still are. You two fight like cats and dogs.'

'But the making up is so delicious,' Rosa countered, with a smile.

'Who's he with, I wonder? His father?'

'The old man? He's English. He's been here before – from the *palazzo*.'

'You'd better serve them, Rosa. Don't leave them to Fiero. I want details.'

Alba withdrew to the kitchen where Alfonso sweated over a cauldron of soup while his son, Romano, in a clean white apron and hat, chopped vegetables at the butcher's block in the centre. She sat at a small wooden table in the corner and rubbed her forehead wearily. At fifty-six she was still beautiful. Her hair was lustrous, tumbling down her back in thick waves, her skin the colour of rich honey, though the bloom of youth had been replaced by a more worldly hue. Her pale grey eyes still had the power to captivate, being so unexpected on such a Latin face, and her body was as voluptuous as a ripe peach. She was once formidably plain spoken, yet the years had mellowed her and children softened her, buffing her sharp corners and bestowing the gift of generosity so that she was well loved and respected in her small corner of Italy. She sighed. The goings on up at the *palazzo* were giving her nothing but worry. She liked Incantellaria as it was; quiet, secretive, undeveloped. There was little doubt that those newcomers were nothing but bad news. Since they had moved in there'd been a steady stream of people into the town. Old and young, all looking for amusement. A few were good for business. More than that was a threat to her way of life. Were they turning the *Marchese*'s palace into a hotel? She envisaged nightclubs and beach parties, and dreaded developers. Why didn't they buy a place in a more fashionable town that already had the infrastructure to accommodate them? 'Over my dead body,' she muttered to herself. 'Where's the ghost when I need him?'

Rosa sashayed out on to the terrace, swinging her hips, her bottom protruding to accentuate the pretty curve of her back. Her red dress was tight and low cut, her glossy brown hair fell over her shoulders in dark waves. She had her mother's pale eyes and black lashes, the same petulant bow to her lips but her father's strong chin and wide, angular face. She knew she was beautiful. Most of the fights she provoked with her husband, Eugenio, were due to her flirtatiousness: Eugenio was so handsome when angry and life would be dull without the fire of their battles and the sweetness of their making up.

Luca raised his eyes and Rosa's heart skipped a beat. He was devilishly handsome. 'Good afternoon,' she said brightly. Her flawless English threw them both.

'My goodness,' exclaimed Caradoc. 'A Latin beauty who speaks English like the Queen.'

'I'm so pleased you think so. My mother's English, my father Italian.'

'Well, that accounts for it,' said the professor. 'What did I tell you, Luca? The girls are easy on the eye, are they not?'

'My friend here tells me you serve a good coffee.'

'He isn't your father?' said Rosa.

'We're brothers,' quipped Caradoc. 'Can you not see the resemblance?'

Rosa giggled. 'Of course. Silly me! Two coffees then, brothers?'

'Make it strong, with hot milk on the side,' said Luca. 'Piping hot milk.'

'You didn't bring your wife?' she asked innocently.

'I don't have one.' He was used to women like her, but she didn't look a day older than twenty-five.

'What a shame,' she replied with a sympathetic smile. 'Tell me, you're from the *palazzo*, aren't you?'

The professor nodded. 'The ghosts haven't scared us off yet.'

'Oh, that rubbish!' She rolled her eyes. 'Let me get your coffees. Then I'll tell you all you want to know about that place. My grandmother was Valentina, you know.' She watched the younger man's eyes light up with interest.

Alba emerged from the kitchen. 'So, who are they?'

'The younger man is called Luca. They're not father and son. Luca called him "my friend".' She grinned mischievously. 'He's not married.'

'Divorced,' observed Alba.

'How do you know?'

'Just a hunch. He's got the look of a man who's been dragged through the law courts by an avaricious woman.'

'He's gorgeous!' breathed Rosa as she placed two cups beneath the *espresso* machine. 'I could make him happy.'

'You watch out,' cautioned Alba. 'You'll only upset Eugenio and I don't think I can take much more of your bickering.'

'We'll move out if you wish,' Rosa said sulkily.

'Don't be silly. And leave me with Cosima?'

'She looks like a witch dressed in black all the time.'

'She's in mourning. It's her choice and her right.'

'Well, it's very dull for those who have to live with her. You know, my children call her *la strega* behind her back.'

'If they call her witch, darling, it's only because they've been listening to you. Have some compassion.'

'It's wearing thin. As you said yourself, it's been three years.'

'That kind of loss stays with you for ever,' Alba said fiercely. 'By God's grace it won't happen to you. Now take them their coffee – you're here to serve, not to flirt.'

'I wonder who I take after?'

'Don't be cheeky.'

'*Papa* said you took some taming.'

'Rubbish, I was his from the moment I saw him on the quay.' Alba watched her daughter walk provocatively across the terrace. She saw the young man's eyes linger a moment on her cleavage before returning to her face. Alba shook her head resignedly. He *was* very good-looking. She was reminded of Fitzroy Davenport, the man she had nearly married – might have married had he had the courage to follow her. She recalled their adventure at the *palazzo*, sneaking into the ruins in search of the mysteries surrounding her mother's death. What fun they had had searching for clues in the damp rooms overrun with ivy and mildew. Then they had met the emaciated Nero, smelling of alcohol and decay, rotting in the *palazzo* the *Marchese* had left him. Why had Nero finally chosen to sell the place? She was angry that he had. It should have been left a ruin. Nature would have devoured it in the end, swallowing the past and the darkness that shrouded her mother's secret visits there, when she had let the *Marchese* make love to her in the folly. The thought of strangers building over the past without a care and erasing the history with paint and wallpaper was an insult to her mother's memory. Nero should have allowed it to crumble, leaving it to the spirit of the *Marchese* who most certainly walked those corridors in a hellish limbo of his own wickedness.

And what of Fitz? She had loved him; but she had loved Cosima and Italy more. She often thought about him. Wondered what he was doing, whether he still remembered her. She had broken his heart. She had left England and started a new life. She had never regretted it. Two of her children had moved north to Milan, but Rosa remained with her own three small children. They were a constant joy. If it wasn't for Cosima and her tragic past, Alba would have said that she was totally content. She remembered her grandmother, Immacolata, and the shrines she had built to Valentina and the son she had lost in the war. She could still smell the candle wax in the house, infused into the fabrics of the home she had inherited. Immacolata had nearly died of grief, as Cosima was in danger of doing. Alba kept her niece busy with accounts for the *trattoria*, tried to keep her mind occupied so it didn't dwell on her loss. But Francesco had meant the world to her: the sun, the moon, the stars. Without him Cosima's days were heavy with sorrow and guilt. If she hadn't taken her eyes off him he might not have drowned.

Rosa took the seat the professor pulled out for her. 'Professor Caradoc Macausland,' he said, extending a gnarled hand. She took it with the tips of her fingers as if his arthritis were contagious.

'Rosa Amato,' she replied. Luca didn't offer his hand. He didn't want to encourage her, lovely as she was. Judging by the rings on her finger she was married, and her rounded stomach indicated that she was also a mother.

'Luca,' he said simply and added hot milk to his coffee.

'So, gentlemen, what's it like up there?' Her eyes were wide with curiosity.

'It is a wonder,' said Caradoc. 'Luca's mother has beautiful taste.'

'My great-uncle Falco knew the *Marchese*,' volunteered Rosa. 'He took lovers, both male and female, the old pervert.'

They were distracted by a gust of wind as a flash of black swept furiously past their table and into the *trattoria*. 'Oh dear, that's my cousin, Cosima. She doesn't look very happy.'

Luca recognised his mystery woman from the church. 'She's related to you?'

'Yes, my grandmother and her grandfather were brother and sister. Don't we look alike? Though black really isn't my colour.' She stood up. 'I'd better go and find out what the trouble is. I'm sure it's my fault again!' She left the two men straining to hear what was being said inside.

'I wonder if she's married,' said Luca.

'Rosa's definitely married,' replied the professor with a smile. '*Go, lovely Rose! Tell her, that wastes her time and me,*

That now she knows, When I resemble her to thee, How sweet and fair she seems to be.'

'Not her. The cousin, the one in black.'

'Ah, Edmund Waller. Do you know his poetry? What a genius! The mysterious woman in black, eh? A widow, I would assume. That's why she's in mourning.'

Luca raised his eyebrows hopefully. 'You think so?'

'Ah, my boy, you're looking for an opening.'

'She's fascinating.'

'Only because she won't talk to you.'

'She will.'

The professor shook his head. 'It's that kind of arrogance that will ensure you never get the woman you really want.'

Cosima spoke so fast her words were like a round of machine-gun fire. 'They've taken his things again. They're all over the house!' Her arms flew about, agitating the air around her. 'Do I have to lock my door against my own cousins? How many times do I have to tell them not to come into my room? Not to disturb his things. They are all I have left of him. If they are all over the house they will get lost and then I will be lost. Don't you see? Doesn't anyone see?' She began to cry.

'Sit down, Cosima,' said Alba gently, helping her into a chair. Rosa appeared, her shoulders already tense with irritation.

'What's the matter?' she asked, trying to sound concerned.

'The children, they've taken Francesco's things again.'

Rosa's face darkened defensively. 'That's not true. They know not to go in there.'

'Then if *they* haven't, who *has*?'

'I don't know,' said Rosa, crossing her arms. 'But it wasn't my children. I swear it.'

'We'll ask them when we get home,' said Alba diplomatically.

'Fine. Ask away. But I know I'm right. You can't go on blaming my children every time one of Francesco's trinkets appears in the sitting-room.'

'Well, darling, we can hardly blame your father, or Eugenio or Toto.'

'I don't like the way you're always accusing me.' Rosa's eyes glittered. 'I skulk around the house, terrified of doing something wrong or saying something wrong. Terrified my children might offend you or cause you pain or worse, blow out the candle you have burning all the time. It's three years, Cosima.'

Cosima stared at her cousin. 'Three years?' she said slowly. 'You think three years is long enough? You think I shouldn't feel pain after so long? Well, let me tell you that every day is an effort to live through. Every second is torture. Every moment of my pitiful life I feel his loss as if I am without my limbs. I wish I could end it and join him wherever he is. But I'm afraid. Because I don't know if anything comes after.'

'Oh, Cosima,' Alba sighed, pulling her head against her stomach. 'Francesco is with God.'

'I've had enough!' Rosa snapped. 'I'm fed up of being accused. We'll move out and find a house of our own. It's too ridiculous all living together. We're like a tin of sardines.'

'Rosa, don't be silly,' Alba began, but Rosa stomped off into the kitchen.

'I'm sorry, Alba,' Cosima sniffed. 'But she doesn't understand.'

'She's young, my love. She hasn't experienced death like you and I have. We all go in the end and I promise you we go to a better place. Your Francesco lives on in another dimension.'

Cosima wrapped her arms around Alba's waist and sobbed. 'I wish I had the courage to end it all.'

'It takes far more courage to live.'

Luca and the professor remained on the terrace until late afternoon. The restaurant began to get busy. Rosa appeared, looking strained. She seemed not to want to discuss the *palazzo* any more. Luca smiled sympathetically as she brought them the bill and he made sure he gave a generous tip. She nodded at him gratefully before returning to her other customers. After a while Cosima emerged. Her face was red and blotchy from crying, her skin pale against the hard black of her dress. If she saw Luca she ignored him. 'There goes your beautiful widow,' said Caradoc. '*Grief for a while is blind, and so was mine. I wish no living thing to suffer pain.* That, my boy, is Percy Bysshe Shelly.'

As they got up to leave Luca noticed the little boy standing in the doorway of the trattoria, staring with eyes as round as saucers. Luca helped Caradoc with his stick and waited a moment while he shook out his legs. When he looked up, the little boy pulled his hand slowly out of his pocket and opened his fingers to reveal, sitting in his palm, a beautiful blue butterfly. It extended its wings and quivered with pleasure as the sun shone directly on to them. Luca smiled at the sight. This startled the little boy who seemed to want a reaction but was surprised when he got one. Luca wanted to talk to him, but the child slunk around the corner into shadow, making way for Rosa who emerged with a tray of steaming dishes.

There was something strange about the boy. He seemed very much alone; or lonely. Luca found that he occupied his thoughts all the way back to the *palazzo*.

'So what have you discovered, professor?' asked Ma, putting down her needlepoint and looking at him over her sunglasses. 'Or should we call you Holmes?'

The professor took a chair at the table that was already laid for dinner. The terrace was deserted, except for Porci the pig who trotted over the stones in search of a cool spot to lie on. 'Nothing that surprised me.'

'How dull,' said Ma. 'I much prefer surprises.'

Caradoc grinned like a schoolboy. 'Only a couple of murders, an illicit love affair and a ghost.'

'Not so dull. Go on.' The professor told her what they had found out. Ma listened, enraptured. When he finished she gave a little sniff. 'I don't think you should tell Romina. She's already over-excited at having discovered someone's been sleeping in her folly. She accused Bill, but he's protesting his innocence. If she thinks there's a ghost up here she'll expire.'

Caradoc chuckled. 'Well, that would be most inconvenient considering I'm just beginning to feel at home here.'

'Me too,' Ma agreed, shuffling on her sun-lounger, her sparkly blue kaftan spilling on to the stones like water. 'But remember, she's Italian and, although she claims to think nothing of the primitive superstitions of the natives, it'll be in her blood. By the way, she tells me there's the famous Festa di Santa Benedetta next week. Some sort of religious festival in the church. The marble statue of Christ apparently used to weep blood to ensure a profitable harvest. It hasn't done so for fifty-seven years, not that it seems to have affected the olives or lemons. They are flourishing as far as I can tell. I'm going to go just to see what it's all about. You might like to be my date, Caradoc, if only out of curiosity.'

'I would be honoured,' he said. 'I'll bring young Luca as our translator.'

'Don't mention it to anyone else. I can't bear the sight of Dizzy's ridiculous dog. It looks like a powder puff and what sort of a name is Smidge? Soppy or Rat-in-Rabbits'-Clothing would be more appropriate. Dizzy is aptly named, though. I'll tell her where she can put all those carbohydrates she goes on about. If she gets any thinner, she'll disappear altogether.' She ruminated a moment. 'Not a bad idea, actually. I can't see what Romina sees in them. Anyone whose conversation revolves around first-class airport lounges and short cuts deserves a medal for banality. No, we'll go just the three of us. Don't breathe a word.'

'So, which one of you took Francesco's things out of Cosima's room?' Alba looked sternly at the three little faces. There was seven-year-old Alessandro with his chocolate-brown hair and silky brown skin; five-year-old Olivia who had inherited her mother's beauty and her pale grey eyes, and three-year-old Domenica who was as brown as her brother and as mischievous as a squirrel. They stared up at their grandmother, their eyes wide and innocent.

'You see,' said Rosa. 'None of them is guilty.'

'Then who took them?'

'How do I know? Cosima probably did it herself and doesn't remember.'

'You know you are not allowed into Cosima's room, don't you?' Alba reiterated. The children nodded, then skipped off outside.

'You're going to have to decide between me and Cosima,' Rosa said gravely.

'What do you mean?'

'I can't continue to live in the same house as her. She's like a living ghost. It's depressing watching her wander about half dead.'

'Don't say such things!'

'Come on, *Mamma*! Do you want your grandchildren growing up in this soup of misery?'

Alba walked over to the window and gazed out on to the garden. The scent of eucalyptus and jasmine wafted in on the breeze as the sun sank into the sea. 'When I first arrived here I was only a little older than you,' she said wistfully. 'Your great-grandmother, Immacolata, was like Cosima, dressed in black like a little squat crow, her face pinched with grief. She had lost her daughter, my mother, and one of her sons in the war. She dwelt in a limbo between life and death, just like your cousin. She had two shrines, illuminated by candles, and she prayed there every day. The house felt heavy and unhappy. But she wasn't alone. She had her son Falco, Beata his wife and their son Toto, and her great-grandchild, Cosima.' She turned to her daughter and took her hands. 'The point is, darling, Cosima needs us. We're her family. We are the strength she lacks. If every day is a struggle, we must make that struggle easier to bear. One day she will move on. She might even fall in love again. She's not too old to bear more children. Things won't be like this for ever. But you have to be patient. Imagine if you were in her shoes.' Rosa lowered her eyes. 'Imagine if you had suffered the same loss.'

'It's too terrible to imagine.'

Chapter 7

In the farmhouse on the hill that had belonged to her great-grandmother, Cosima painstakingly replaced every one of Francesco's knick-knacks. She brought each object to her nose and sniffed it like a pining dog. Sometimes she felt that she'd find him asleep in her bed as if the last three years hadn't happened. She could almost hear his breathing and feel his presence in the room. But she'd turn to look and he wouldn't be there, just the memories that lingered like ghosts. She felt so alone. So abandoned. Closing her eyes, she willed herself to die.

Alba sat on the terrace with her aunt Beata and watched the sun set slowly into the sea. The place hadn't changed much since Immacolata's day. Back then there hadn't been a road to the house: they had had to park beneath the eucalyptus tree on the hill above and walk down a narrow path. Alba and her husband, Panfilo, had built a proper drive and added to the house to accommodate their growing family. Toto, Cosima's father, had married again and taken his wife to live with his parents, a few hundred yards through the olive grove in the house where he had grown up, leaving Cosima with Alba, where she felt most at home. Cosima's half brother and sisters had married and had children, buying houses nearby so the once quiet hillside rang with the happy laughter of young people. The place still smelt the same, of jasmine and vibur-num, eucalyptus and gardenia. The wind swept in off the sea, bringing with it the scent of pine and wild thyme, and, in the evenings as the air grew cooler and the light more forgiving, crickets rang out with the flirtatious twittering of roosting birds. 'I worry about Cosima,' Alba said, watching the chil-dren rag about on the grass. 'She's thirty-seven. She should be enjoying marriage and motherhood. She should focus her thoughts on those who are living and who love her.'

'I know,' Beata agreed. 'The children play around her and she barely notices them. Little Alessandro follows her like a lost dog, as if he senses the reason for her unhappiness and is trying to compensate, but she ignores him. It's the guilt, you see. She blames herself for Francesco's death.'

'They say those who drown don't suffer.'

'How can they know?'

'I hope it's true.'

'I wish she had faith.' Beata put down the shirt she was mending and a frown drew lines across her smooth forehead. 'Then she would know that Francesco is with God and that God is looking after him as He is looking after Immacolata and my dear Falco.'

'And Valentina,' Alba added gently. Her family still had trouble saying her mother's name, as if to mention it was somehow sacrilege. 'But she has lost her faith. Death often brings a person closer to God, but Francesco's has taken her away from Him.'

'One has to accept what comes. How can we presume to know God's plan?'

'Do you know what Rosa said to me today?'

'That she wants to move out? Don't listen to her, Alba. She's headstrong and passionate, just like you were at her age.

Rosa's quite a handful. It's no surprise that she doesn't like her cousin getting all the attention. After all, it always used to be Rosa everyone talked about. She was the noisy, excitable, vivacious one in the family, and so much younger than Cosima. We all spoiled her terribly. Now she's having to watch while Cosima steals the limelight, wandering about dressed in black, weeping and wailing.'

'Do you think Cosima's self-indulgent?'

'I would never say such a thing about my granddaughter. How can I pass judgement on a young woman who has lost her world? My heart goes out to her.' Beata crossed herself.

'It's the Festa di Santa Benedetta next week. I'm going to encourage her to come with us.'

Beata resumed her sewing. 'That statue hasn't bled for over fifty years. The last time was the year your parents met. Your father was so dashing in his naval uniform. They made a handsome couple.'

'Then it failed to weep blood the following year, the day before they were due to marry. The day she was found on the road to Naples in furs and diamonds, murdered with Lupo Bianco.'

'But still we keep celebrating the miracle even though the statue has dried up.'

'You never know, it might happen again.'

'God works in mysterious ways. Anyway, you must take your place in the festival as your grandmother did. You are a descendant of Saint Benedetta.'

'It's hard to keep a straight face, Beata. They all take it so seriously. The disappointment when Christ's eyes remain dry is terrible. It was probably a hoax in the first place. Father Dino and a bit of tomato ketchup.'

'May you be forgiven, Alba!' But Beata's mouth curled up at the corners as she suppressed a smile.

'Ah, Cosima,' said Alba as her niece came out to join them. 'Is everything in its proper place now?'

'Yes, thank you,' she replied, taking a seat in the wicker armchair that used to be Immacolata's. 'Everything is where it should be.'

Alessandro stopped playing and stood watching his aunt, his face serious. Then, inspired by a feeling he couldn't understand, he plucked a rose and walked tentatively up to her. 'For you.'

Cosima frowned. 'For me?'

'Yes, from Francesco.'

Cosima's eyes welled with tears and for a moment she was unable to speak. Alba exchanged glances with Beata. They held their breath, waiting for Cosima's reaction – anticipating the worst. But she took the rose with a little smile. It was yellow; Francesco's favourite colour. She looked at Alessandro with such tenderness his heart swelled. She touched his face with her fingertips.

'Thank you, *carino*,' she said. Alessandro blushed a deep crimson and looked to his grandmother for approval.

'That was very sweet of you,' said Alba encouragingly.

'He's a darling,' agreed Beata, relieved that Cosima hadn't taken it the wrong way. Alessandro returned to his siblings and cousins, making off through the olive grove.

'I'm so touched,' said Cosima, twirling the flower between her thumb and forefinger. 'He's very good to apologise.'

Alba was pleased Rosa wasn't around to hear her. As far as she was concerned, her children had nothing to apologise for.

'Yellow is a good colour on you,' said Alba, tired of seeing her niece look so pale and ill in black. 'Do you remember that pretty dress with little yellow flowers?'

'It's in my cupboard,' said Cosima.

'Don't you think you've worn black for long enough?'

Cosima's face hardened. 'I will never wear colour again. It's an insult to Francesco's memory. I will never stop mourning him.'

Cosima scattered the ground around her with eggshells so no one knew where to tread any more. Everything caused offence. Beata was right: she had been allowed to grow self-indulgent and it had to stop or she'd drive the family apart.

It was fortunate that just then Panfilo's truck drew up under the eucalyptus tree to stop Alba from speaking her mind. They heard the motor behind the house and the barking of his dog, Garibaldi. 'How nice,' said Alba, getting up. 'I wasn't expecting him until later.' She left Cosima and Beata on the terrace and walked around the house to greet her husband.

Garibaldi jumped out of the back and galloped down the path as fast as his short legs could carry him. His stumpy tail wagged furiously. Alba bent down and patted her knees, calling his name. The dog flew into her with a yelp and she laughed as he ran rings around her. 'Hello, wife!' exclaimed Panfilo, striding down the path towards her with Toto. 'Look who I picked up on the road!'

'Hi, Toto,' she called, waving. Then she rested her eyes on her husband and felt the warm glow of love spread across her body as if seeing him for the first time. At sixty-seven he was still ruggedly handsome with shoulder-length silver hair, a broad forehead creased with lines and a long Roman nose above a large, sensual mouth. His eyes were turquoise, deep set, with crow's feet that fanned out onto his temples, reflecting the laughter within them. He was tall and broad, his skin brown and weathered, his hands large and tender. She grinned as he approached, his camera bag slung over his shoulder. He wound his free arm around her waist and kissed her, lingering on her skin for as long as he was able to.

'I've missed you,' he murmured, running his eyes over her face.

'Work is work,' she replied, casually. 'I've missed you too.'

'How's everything?' He meant Cosima.

'Same.' She pulled a face which said more than words ever could.

'What's happened to your car, Toto?' Alba asked as her cousin joined them.

'It's with Gianni. The brake's gone again.'

'It's important to get that mended,' she said with a laugh. 'We don't want you driving it off the cliffs.'

'I gather those people from the *palazzo* came for coffee?' said Toto. 'Rosa was full of it.'

'She's a great deal more excited about it than I am,' replied Alba. 'If you ask me they are nothing but trouble.'

'Aren't you even a little curious to see what they've done?' Panfilo teased, squeezing her waist playfully.

'Why would I be? My own uncle committed a murder in there. It should have been destroyed, not rebuilt and redecorated by people with too much money and no tact.'

'They probably don't know the history,' said Toto.

'Then someone should have told them.'

'I'm very curious,' said Panfilo.

'That's because interiors is your job,' said Alba. 'I suppose you're going to photograph it now.' Panfilo remained silent. Alba turned and stared at him. 'Panfilo?'

He shrugged guiltily. 'Work is work.'

'You're not. Over my dead body!'

'You don't have to come with me. I thought you'd be pleased that I was taking a job close to home instead of travelling all over the world.'

'But it's the *palazzo!*' she gasped.

'It's not the place you knew thirty years ago, my love. You don't even know whether Nero had anything to do with the sale. He might have died a long time ago, or moved away. It's all buried in the past.'

'But you're going to dig it all up again.'

'I'm taking photographs, that's all.'

'Then who's writing the article to go with the photographs?'

'What difference does it make? It'll be a story of design.'

'So, it's *House and Gardens.*'

Panfilo looked bashful. 'No,' he replied.

'You *know* it's not just an article on decoration, don't you?'

'It's none of my business. I just take the photographs.'

'What's the magazine?'

Panfilo glanced at Toto who grinned mischievously and shook his head, then thrust his hands into his pockets and walked tactfully on ahead, leaving them alone.

'The *Sunday Times.*'

'The *Sunday Times!*' She pulled away. 'You know that means some pretty in-depth reporting.'

'What does it matter? If I don't do it, someone else will.'

She brought her hand to her throat. 'Oh God! They'll dig up everything. They might even find out that Falco didn't act alone in killing the *Marchese.*'

'There's no proof that Falco even killed him, let alone whether or not he had an accomplice. Don't worry, your father's quite safe. I promise.'

★   ★   ★

Rosa hoped that the handsome Luca would return to the *trattoria* but, in spite of her pretty red dress and the Yves Saint Laurent perfume Eugenio had given her the previous Christmas, he did not come back. She was surprised her face hadn't managed to lure him. After all, she was a local beauty and constantly compared to her grandmother, the legendary Valentina. She even worked extra hours in the hope of seeing him. A little flirting was a healthy thing, she told herself. Having got away with one affair, however, she wasn't going to risk her marriage a second time just for the thrill of taking a bite of the forbidden fruit.

Since her children had been blamed for a crime they did not commit, Rosa had barely spoken to Cosima. The two women breakfasted under the vine on the terrace with Alba, Panfilo, Eugenio and the children, and each managed to behave as if the other didn't exist. Rosa was fed up of tiptoeing around her cousin, aware that the very existence of her children must cause Cosima pain. Wasn't it time she put on a pretty dress, tied her hair up, applied a little blusher and lipstick, and threw herself out into the world again? If she left it much longer no man would want her. Francesco was dead; mourning him wasn't going to bring him back.

Alba seemed not to notice the growing rift between the two young women. She was wound up like a clockwork mouse over Panfilo's commission up at the *palazzo*, but Panfilo just teased her, knowing he would get his way in the end. Why her mother cared so much about that place Rosa couldn't imagine. Thirty years was a lifetime ago. She was amazed Alba's memory stretched back that far.

Rosa had told Eugenio she wanted to move out, knowing that it was impossible. They hadn't the money to buy a big house of their own – and only a big house would satisfy

Rosa. Eugenio had told her how insensitive she was and she had accused him of being disloyal and of not loving her any more. It had developed into a full-blown row. If she had feared her marriage was becoming dull she certainly revived it with their making up, pleased that the passion was still there to be reawakened when necessary. She didn't consider what it cost her husband to have to reassure her of his devotion time and again. She didn't realise that she wore him down with each tantrum and each reunion. His policeman's salary was small. He was aware of her love of fine things, like a magpie always attracted to shiny baubles and glitter, and he was only too aware of his inability to satisfy her.

Chapter 8

Luca sat alone on the beach, gazing out to sea. He enjoyed the solitude and the new sense of freedom Incantellaria offered him. Everything about the place pleased him, from the clamour of birds to the sweet scents of fertility that rose up from the earth with the medicinal smells of the wild herbs that grew among the long grasses. He took pleasure from the coming and going of the little blue boats as the fishermen went about their business. His skin soaked up the sun's rays by the pool and he lost his city pallor. He slept more than he had in twenty years and his dreams grew less troubled until he no longer dreamed at all. He took twilight walks on the stony beach reached by a path that meandered down the hill from the *palazzo*. Crickets chirped in the undergrowth and the rustle of grass gave away the odd rabbit or snake. It felt good to be alone, blanketed by the night.

He thought of Freya with a yearning for the comfortable and familiar, regret for what he had been too young and foolish to hold on to. He thought of Annabel and their soulless coupling, and the dull stream of similar meaningless encounters that blurred into a grey fog of pointlessness. He thought of Claire and the girls and how he had let them down.

When he hadn't been working, his life had been a merry-go-round of glamorous parties, dinners in expensive restaurants, knocking back cocktails in fashionable clubs, weekends in Saint Tropez, waterskiing off fully-staffed yachts, skiing in the Swiss Alps, forging relationships on the fragile foundations of wealth and status. The merry-go-round had got faster and faster, louder and louder, until his divorce had brought it to a sudden, mortifying halt. In the quiet that followed he was at last able to stand back and examine his life. The extravagance and waste disgusted him. His friends had separated into two camps, those supporting Claire and those supporting him, but most just blew away to the next party like pretty petals on the wind. Picking up the children from school once a week was like running the gauntlet through a crowd of disapproving mothers and, to his shame, he recognised himself reflected in their eyes. Here in the silence of Incantellaria, he realised he didn't want to be that man any more.

It was early morning when he returned to his senses. He blinked and stood up stiffly. He looked at his watch. It was five o'clock. He stretched and felt the blood rush to his muscles. He stood, watching the sunrise. Its beauty filled his spirit with longing. He felt a tremendous desire to dig the soil with his hands, plant a seed and watch it grow – to create something tangible. Yet, he didn't know how or where to start.

When he returned to the palazzo his mother was doing yoga on the terrace. 'What on earth are you doing up at this hour?' she asked, without moving from the lotus position. She was dressed in a long white shirt and white linen trousers, her feet bare, her scarlet toenails shocking against the serenity of her clothes.

'I could ask you the same thing.'

'I do yoga every morning before anyone gets up. It clears my head and settles my spirit. Ready for the day ahead.'

'I thought you didn't believe in that rubbish.'

'It's a form of exercise like any other.'

'Not if you start levitating.'

'I don't think I'm likely to defy the force of gravity. I'm too earthly minded.'

He laughed. 'I've been down on the beach.'

'Isn't it beautiful!' she gushed. 'Incantellaria is so magical. I never want to go back to dreary grey London.'

'I can see why. You live in paradise, Mother.'

'And it's being photographed by the *Sunday Times*.' She beamed with pride. 'Leyton Hughes came for the weekend and fell in love. And you know what?' Too distracted to continue her yoga she stood up, tossed the mat against the wall and took the chair next to her son. 'Guess who's going to photograph it?'

'I don't know, who?'

She took a breath, articulating each syllable with relish. 'Panfilo Pallavicini.' Luca looked blank. 'Darling, you don't know who he is?' She clicked her tongue disapprovingly. 'He's the most famous interiors photographer in the whole of Italy. There's no one who even comes close. He's devastatingly attractive too! Leyton has promised me.'

'I hope you won't be disappointed.'

'I trust Leyton absolutely. I gave him the best bedroom overlooking the sea. He adores me! And his wife adores Porci. She played with him all weekend and he followed her around like a lapdog.'

'When is all this happening?'

'It's scheduled for June to come out in the September issue. They plan so far ahead, they're working on Christmas in the summer. Must be very hard to muster up Christmas spirit in the heat! The journalist is coming in a few weeks. She's going to stay for the weekend so she really gets a feel for the place. Perhaps you and Caradoc can help with her research. Have you found anything out yet?'

Luca shrugged. 'Nothing that you don't already know.'

'You are useless. What did you do? Spend all afternoon drinking coffee?'

'Something like that. The professor's good company.'

'Didn't I tell you! You might be a grown-up but some-times your mother knows best! Well, the journalist can dig around for herself. After all, that's what she's being paid to do. Let her earn her salary.'

'Maybe she'll discover who's been sleeping in the folly.'

'Don't mention that place! It's your father, of course. He just won't admit it. He doesn't want to acknowledge he's getting old and in need of naps.' She laughed. 'I'll catch him at it and then he'll feel very ashamed of lying.'

'Maybe it's the ghost!' he teased.

'Not you too! Dizzy says she saw a man walk across the garden in the middle of the night and that silly girl Ventura complains the whole time that the *palazzo* is haunted.'

'And you don't believe in ghosts?'

'Of course I don't. I don't want to. Your grandmother . . .' She hesitated a moment. 'Oh, let's not talk about her. If anyone was going to come back as a ghost it would be my mother and I haven't heard a squeak since she died. Believe me, if she was squeaking on the other side the whole of Italy would hear her. It's for simple-minded people with nothing better to do.' Her face hardened and Luca felt his stomach clench as he remembered when she had dismissed his child-hood fears so brutally.

He got up. 'Where are you going?' she demanded. She had hoped to share an early coffee.

'To bed,' he replied with a yawn.

'You mean, you haven't gone to bed yet? What on earth were you doing on the beach?'

'Meditating.'

Romina laughed incredulously. 'Is that what bankers do in their spare time?'

'I'm not a banker any more.'

She shook her head and went to retrieve her yoga mat. 'You can take a man out of the bank, but not a banker out of the man!'

There was a snuffling noise as Porci trotted out on to the terrace. Romina was distracted and Luca slipped away, leaving her with her precious pig in her lap. He retreated to his bedroom and climbed into bed. No sooner had his head touched the pillow than he was asleep.

When he awoke it was midday. Ma's strident voice rose from the terrace with Dizzy's high-pitched giggling, punctuated by the professor's wise interruptions. He lay a while enjoying the warm breeze that slipped through the gap in the shutters. It was good not to have to get up at dawn to go to work. He didn't miss the carbon fumes, the rumbling engines and tooting horns, the frantic heartbeat of the City. He felt years younger. In the quiet of his new existence he was beginning to sense parts of himself he had forgotten existed.

He thought of Cosima, and pictured her storming into the *trattoria*, her face tear-stained and furious. He felt himself drawn into her drama by the compelling magnetism of her mourning and her obvious rage. She was too young to be wearing black all the time and much too attractive to ignore the men around her. Her rejection when he had tried to talk to her had left him with a strong feeling of desire. He wasn't used to being rebuffed.

He got up and showered, then went to find his mother.

'Can I borrow your car? I want to go into town for coffee.'

'You don't need to go into town, darling. I'll make you coffee myself.' Romina couldn't imagine why anyone would want to leave the *palazzo*.

'I like it there by the sea.'

She gave him a knowing look. 'Pretty girls,' she said, winking at Ventura. 'Men are all the same! Go on then. You can fill the car up with petrol while you're down there.'

She watched him go and her heart swelled with pride. He was so tall and handsome, with his wide shoulders and straight back. What he needed was a nice Italian girl to love and look after him. Claire had become an avaricious creature who expected everything to be done for her. She was selfish and ungrateful.

'Now, Ventura,' she said, brushing Claire out of her mind. 'You have to get over your fear of going upstairs. Ghosts don't exist. They are all in your imagination. Control it or find another job. I don't want you frightening the maids and I cannot carry excess baggage around this place. Pull your weight or leave.'

Ventura looked at her in astonishment. 'But I *know* there is someone up there.'

'The house is full of guests. It is hardly a surprise that you hear footsteps.'

'They say it is haunted.'

'Who says?'

'Everyone.'

'Gossip. This place hasn't been occupied for years. Really, Ventura, you can't believe the idle chit-chat of peasants who

have nothing more to do than spread rumours.' Ventura
made to speak, but Romina silenced her with the wave of
her hand. 'Enough. Now, you go and make up the rooms. I
don't want to hear another word about ghosts.' *It's all I ever
heard as a child, and I won't listen to any more!*

Luca parked the car in the *piazza*. The little square was
busy. The *caffè* where he had met Maria was full of customers
sitting at round tables beneath green parasols. Waiters in black
and white took orders and poured wine into large glasses. A
few elderly tourists emerged from the hotel, and children
played on the grass while their mothers and grandmothers
chatted on benches. The town had a festive air and Luca
wondered what was going on.

The narrow street down to the quay was blocked by cars
and scooters, tooting their horns in fury at the car in front
that had stalled on the incline. On the sea front, children ran
about looking at the boats and chatting to those tending
them. The restaurants were filling up, especially on the
terraces as everyone wanted to be outside. He saw a large
boat arrive, laden with tourists, and decided to grab a table at
the *trattoria* before they were all taken.

Rosa was taking an order when Luca appeared. She
shouted to Toto, her voice quivering with excitement.
'Show Luca to a nice table. He's a very special customer.'
She winked at him flirtatiously. Luca smiled; Rosa's ebul-
lience was contagious. Toto showed him to a table on the
edge of the terrace, beside a large stone container of red
geraniums.

'From here you can watch the world go by,' said Toto.

'What's going on today?' Luca asked. 'Is there some sort of
festival?'

Toto shrugged. 'Nothing unusual for a Saturday.'

'Of course, it's the weekend. I'm on another planet!' He sat down, amused that he had lost track of time. While he had nothing to do, all the days were the same.

'You're not from here?' Toto asked. The younger man's Italian accent was not familiar.

'From London,' Luca replied.

'But you speak Italian so well.'

'My mother's Italian. She lives up at the *palazzo*.'

'Palazzo Montelimone.' Toto gave a slow whistle. 'That's quite a place.' Toto was caught off guard. He rummaged around for something else to say but only managed, 'What will you have?'

Rosa appeared in a flash of crimson. 'I'll take the order,' she said, dismissing him with a gentle nudge of her hips. Toto withdrew to seat a group who had just disembarked from Sorrento. 'So, what will you have? I can recommend the red mullet, it's fresh today.'

'I wasn't planning on having lunch, just coffee,' he replied.

'You can't come here and not eat! A growing man like you. Besides, Fiorelli's is famous for its cooking. My great-grandmother passed her recipes to my mother and she has passed them to me. We guard them possessively. Why don't you let me choose something for you? Go on! Live a little.'

Luca was won over. Besides, he had nothing else to do. 'All right,' he said, handing back the menu. 'You choose. I'll have some wine, too. A glass of Greco di Tufo, chilled.'

'Right away,' she replied with a long, lingering look.

Luca sat back in his chair. He enjoyed people-watching. It was something he had never had time to do. Now he noticed everyone around him, from what they were wearing to the small gestures that passed between them. He tried to work out relationships, dynamics and moods. Rosa brought him wine. He took a sip.

'You like it?' she asked.

'Perfect,' he said, taking off his sunglasses. His blue eyes were the colour of the little fishing boats on the beach. 'Are you still in trouble?' he asked, angling for news of her mysterious cousin.

'I'm always in trouble with Cosima.'

'How long has she been in mourning?'

'Too long. Three years. It's time she put on a pretty dress and found a husband.' She gave a little sniff. 'You know, she can be quite pretty when she makes the effort.'

Luca was amused by her unguarded malice. 'What does she do?'

'Very little, because my mother feels sorry for her. She's meant to keep the books. Of course, she used to work here full-time, but she became a drag. This is a pretty place – we don't need a black widow spinning misery.'

'She didn't eat her husband, did she?'

Rosa laughed. 'Sometimes, I'd like to eat mine,' she murmured and Luca wondered how many times she had been unfaithful. This flirtatious dance seemed very well practised.

Rosa went away to serve other customers. She walked about the restaurant with her bottom out, her stomach in, her gait slow and sexy, conscious that Luca might be watching. In fact, Luca had turned his attention to the quay where Cosima's little boy was jumping off a bollard. He sat up: if the child was there, his mother would surely follow.

Sure enough, Cosima appeared on the terrace, carrying a bunch of pretty white and yellow flowers. She walked past him without a glance, the scent of lemons in her wake. He watched her weave deftly through the tables and felt his desire mount. She wasn't overtly sexy like Rosa, or as dramatically beautiful, but there was something about her that aroused him. He wasn't used to women being aloof. He knew there was fire beneath the ice because he had seen it here on this very terrace. He took a swig of wine and watched her disappear inside. She posed a tremendous challenge.

Rosa brought him a plate of red mullet with roasted vege-tables and potatoes. She insisted on waiting while he took a bite. 'Very good,' he said truthfully.

'It's all in the oil, infused with herbs and spices.'

'Well, it reaches the spot!'

'I'm so pleased. Can I get you anything else?'

'Your cousin seems in a better mood today.'

'She has her ups and downs. At least she has come in to help. She can do some washing up!'

'Doesn't she serve? You're very busy.'

'No, she'll frighten the customers away. It's important to smile and Cosima doesn't smile very much.'

'Doesn't anyone make her smile?'

'I smile enough for the two of us,' said Rosa, bringing the conversation around to herself again. He noticed that she had reapplied her lipstick. It was as red as her dress.

'You have a very pretty smile.'

'Thank you, *signore*,' she replied. 'If you need anything else, just shout.'

Luca observed Cosima's little boy and thought of his own daughters. He felt a wrench of guilt. He wasn't the most attentive father. Oh, they had the best education money could buy, beautiful homes, and holidays in the most exclu-sive resorts. He spoiled them with presents and treats when they came to stay every other weekend. Now he realised that he was just buying their forgiveness for all his failings. He resolved to make it up to them.

The little boy stood on the bollard and threw a white feather into the air. Then he jumped after it, catching it before it fell. It was a solitary game. Other children played nearby, but he didn't seem to want to join in. Eventually he stopped and wandered over to the *trattoria*. Luca looked to see if his mother was coming out of the restaurant, but she wasn't so he turned back to the child. He was standing a short distance away, watching a large blue butterfly that was sitting on his hand, basking in the sunlight with open wings. He looked up and saw Luca. He froze with surprise and caught his breath, staring at him with big brown eyes.

Luca gave a little wave. The child approached tentatively. 'Hello,' said Luca quietly so as not to alarm him. 'That's a very beautiful butterfly.' The child stopped a few feet away, a frown lining his young brow. Then he blew on the butterfly and it fluttered into the air, circling the geraniums a moment before settling on Luca's hand. Luca was astonished. 'You should give this to your mother,' he said, but the little boy had run off, back to the bollard. Luca was left watching the extraordinary butterfly, which settled on the table, its wings like oil, reflecting all the colours of the rainbow.

He ate his lunch and drank a second glass of Greco di Tufo, then remained at the table with an *espresso*. The butterfly fluttered into the geraniums and the child grew bored of his game and mingled with the other children, pottering around the boats like street urchins. Finally, Cosima appeared and stood talking to Toto. The older man looked at her with tenderness and Luca deduced that they were father and daughter. Then he said something that made her smile. The sight gave Luca a jolt. There was a gentle beauty in her smile.

As she turned and began to walk towards him, the butterfly fluttered off the geraniums and into her path. She stopped in her tracks and watched its erratic flight a moment. She was still smiling and Luca felt emboldened to speak to her again.

'That's a very friendly butterfly.' She turned her dark eyes to him as the butterfly settled on her shoulder, striking against the black of her dress. 'It likes you.'

'I think it does,' she replied. 'I shall wear it as a brooch.' She began to walk away.

'Your son has a real gift with insects.'

Her shoulders stiffened and she turned around to glare at him with stunned disbelief. 'What did you say?'

'Your son brought it to me. It belongs to him,' Luca explained.

She squeezed her eyes shut and shook her head, as if his words had caused her pain. Luca's heart lurched at her reaction and he frantically tried to work out what he had said to cause offence. He made to speak but she dismissed him with a sniff, muttering 'Foreigners!' under her breath. Then she turned and strode off without a backward glance. Her son broke away from the other children and hurried after her. The butterfly remained on her shoulder.

Luca finished his coffee, his good mood evaporating. He waved at Toto for the bill, but it was Rosa who brought it. 'I think I offended your cousin,' he said, handing her some notes. 'Keep the change.'

Rosa waved her hand dismissively. 'She is easily offended. Think nothing of it.'

'I didn't mean to upset her.'

'You'll get used to it. I upset her all the time. Join the club, it's very large.'

'Tell her . . .' he began, then stopped himself. There was no point. He was nothing to her, just a tactless foreigner. Maybe he shouldn't have mentioned her son. He hoped he hadn't got the child into trouble.

'Don't bother to apologise, *signore*,' said Rosa with a grin. 'If you have offended her, she'll *never* forgive you.'

Chapter 9

Luca returned to the *palazzo* and lay by the pool, so disgruntled that he could barely concentrate on his book. Dizzy and Maxwell came to join him, which irritated him all the more. Finally, in order to escape them and lift his mood, he called Freya.

Freya was at her desk writing letters when the telephone rang. Mildly irritated by the intrusion, she picked it up and hooked it under her chin. She had a village fete meeting at four and she had wanted to get all her admin done beforehand. 'Hello,' she said briskly.

'Is this a bad time?'

'Luca!' She put down her pen and sat up excitedly. 'You haven't returned any of my calls!'

'I'm deleting my messages without listening to them.'

'Is that wise?'

'I need a break.'

'So, how is it? Is it wonderful?'

'Well, I'm lying by the pool. It's hot and sunny. Life is good.'

'I'm so pleased. You really needed a rest. What's the *palazzo* like?'

'They have done the most splendid job. It's glorious. As you can imagine, Mother has paid attention to every detail.

It's going to be photographed by the *Sunday Times*. The journalist arrives in a few weeks. God knows what she's going to dig up. The place has a rather bloody history.'

'Tell me!' Freya had forgotten all about her admin. It wouldn't matter if she was late for the meeting. She'd make some excuse.

'An old marquis lived here during the war. His mistress was a local beauty called Valentina. She was also fucking a famous mafia boss and a Brit whom she was on the point of marrying. The marquis, in a fit of jealousy, murdered her.'

'Oh my God! That's terrible.'

'Then, Valentina's brother murdered him in the *palazzo*.'

'*Your palazzo*?'

'Exactly. Ventura, the maid, won't go upstairs because she says the place is haunted.'

'Well, is it?'

'Of course not!'

'Great story, though.'

'It gets better. Valentina had a daughter called Alba, by the Brit. She lives here in Incantellaria.'

'It all sounds thrilling.'

'Its beauty takes your breath away, Freya.' He suddenly sounded serious. 'I'd love to show it to you.'

She hesitated a moment. 'I wish you could show it to me, too.'

'Where's the lovely Miles?'

'Out and about. I don't know.'

'Are you getting bored of him?'

'No!' she laughed. 'Whatever gave you that idea?'

'Optimism.'

'Haven't you found a pretty Italian yet?'

'I don't want an Italian,' he replied, feeling once again the sting of Cosima's rebuff.

'What about Annabel? She's been asking after you. You haven't returned any of her calls either.' She heard him groan. 'You slept with her, didn't you?'

'Mistake,' he replied.

Freya was pleased. 'I'll fend her off. You were obviously too good . . .'

'You remember?'

'No! It was a long time ago.'

'I remember every inch of you.'

'Oh, Luca. You shouldn't.' But his words made her feel so desirable.

'We were good together. Why don't you come out?'

'I couldn't.'

'You have a nanny.'

'What would Miles think?'

'Bring him too. I'll find suitable distractions for him.'

'Don't be silly.'

'Come with the children in the holidays. I'm sure to have the girls while Claire goes social climbing. They can all play together and I can show you around Incantellaria.'

'Miles would never let me. He's suspicious of you.'

'How very unreasonable of him. Bring your mother.'

'She thinks Incantellaria is a dull little place.'

'Only because Fitz once had a girlfriend here. There's nothing dull about it; if anything, it's far too colourful for its own good. Think about it. It's perfect. *Almost* perfect,' he added with emphasis. 'You'd make it complete.'

She hesitated a moment. Luca was feeling much more cheerful. 'I don't think I can, Luca,' she said at last.

'Why? I'm not going to eat you.'

'You're a dangerous flirt and Miles knows that.'

'Then I'll just live off the memories.'

'Make some new ones, Luca, with someone else. We're just friends, remember.'

He sighed. 'I remember. Game, set and match to Miles.'

Energised by his conversation with Freya, he swam some lengths, his mind on Freya and the improbability of an affair. But, for every moment he thought of Freya, he twice rejected Cosima's face. It surfaced continuously to eclipse hers like an unexpected moon.

Dizzy moved her sun-lounger farther away from the water as Luca splashed her with his energetic swimming. Maxwell received business calls from Vienna and spoke very loudly in German, pretentiously adding the odd English word for emphasis. When Luca got out, Caradoc had appeared, sitting in the shade, reading a book.

'Ah, Professor,' he said, wrapping a towel around his waist.

'You *are* full of energy,' Caradoc observed, putting down his book.

'I went to the *trattoria*,' Luca explained.

'Was that delightful girl there? The one in red?'

'Rosa.'

'Ah, the lovely Rosa. Yes, was she there?'

'She works there, Professor. I think she's always there.'

'Then I should make a daily pilgrimage.'

Luca laughed. 'She'd love that.'

'I'm past my prime now but, between you and me, I was a bit of a rogue in my day.'

'I'm sure you still are.'

'I'm a bit long in the tooth now. I can only remember the good old days.'

'I saw the widow too,' Luca said ruefully.

'She rejected you again? That must have dented your pride.'

'I don't know what I said to upset her.'

'Well?'

'Long story, but her son was there and he gave me a butterfly. Then, when Cosima passed, the butterfly flew on to her dress. I told her it looked pretty and she almost smiled.'

'You thought you had her then. A pretty fish on the hook,' the professor said shrewdly.

'Let's just say she was warming to me.'

'Then what?'

'I mentioned her son and she looked at me with such venom.'

Caradoc frowned. 'Now, why would she do that?'

'I can't imagine. Then she muttered "foreigner" under her breath and stalked off.'

'You're not entirely foreign. You were speaking to her in Italian, were you not?'

'Of course. What she meant was that I'm not from here.'

'She doesn't trust you. That's the problem.'

'She doesn't know me,' Luca complained.

'Girls have noses for men like you. Don't deny it, Luca, my boy. I know you. Takes one to know one. Why do you think we get along so well, you and I? Because we're the same underneath. We like pretty girls and in my day they liked me. I got into a fair bit of trouble. Then I grew up.'

'What made you grow up?'

'Love. Love changed everything.'

'Myrtle.'

'My Myrtle. I won't love again.' He looked at Luca with affection. 'You'll know what I mean one day.'

Luca shrugged. 'I'm not sure I'm designed for love.'

'That's just when it hits you. When you don't think you need it. Then, you can't believe you lived so long without it. Now going back to that delightful girl . . .'

'Rosa.'

'*And she was fayr as is the rose in May.* Fancy taking tea with me at the *trattoria*?'

Luca shook his head. 'I've had enough of that place for one day.' When the professor looked disappointed, he relented. 'We'll have lunch there on Monday. They do cook a good red mullet, I recommend it very highly.'

That night they ate on the terrace. The candlelight drew moths and midges, and crickets rang out from the under-growth; the moon hung low and heavy in a sky full of stars. Luca couldn't stop thinking about Cosima. How dare she rebuff him when he was only being kind?

'I read in my guidebook that it's the festival of Santa Benedetta next week,' said Dizzy. 'Maxwell and I would love to stay for it.'

Ma caught the professor's eye and pulled a face of mock horror.

'It's very dull,' said Romina. 'The statue never weeps and everyone goes home disappointed.'

'Don't you think it'll be interesting from a cultural point of view, to see how the locals celebrate religious festivals?'

'Not at all,' said Romina. 'They are very primitive.'

'Actually, I think it is very interesting,' interrupted Bill. 'Ignore Romina! She doesn't know what she's talking about.'

'Darling, even you found it dull.'

'Disappointing, not dull. It's in celebration of a miracle that happened some hundred years ago. The descendants of Benedetta still live here in Incantellaria. They lead the procession . . .'

'Then they have a jolly good party afterwards, in spite of their disappointment,' said Romina scathingly.

'They continue to celebrate the original miracle,' corrected Bill patiently.

Romina rolled her eyes. 'Italians love a good party – and we love fireworks. It's all very noisy and over the top.'

'You sound like an old woman,' her husband teased.

'I *am* an old woman. I like a little peace and quiet.'

'Well, I think we should go,' said Maxwell.

'It's dangerous,' interjected Ma. 'Pickpockets.'

'Here?' said Dizzy.

'They look out for people like you. People who don't blend in. You're too blonde.'

Dizzy looked at her husband. 'I'm sure Maxwell will protect me,' she said with a little-girl smile. Maxwell took her hand.

'But why risk it?' said Ma darkly.

'Indeed,' added the professor.

'We'll think about it,' said Maxwell. 'Perhaps if we all go together?'

Ma scowled into her wine glass.

That night Luca slept fitfully, disturbed by conflicting thoughts of Cosima. On one hand she had bruised his ego. He found her attractive but she had rebuffed him. On the other hand, she was rude and he didn't care for women like that. He wished he could just forget about her, but somehow she had got beneath his skin.

He awoke with the residue of ill-feeling. At first he couldn't remember what caused it then, little by little, the memories of the day before came flooding back. He was contemplating what he was going to do with his day, when a butterfly fluttered in through the open window, the same species as the one from the day before: uncommonly large and vibrant blue. It fluttered about the room, then alighted on his hand. It was as if the butterfly knew him. He raised his hand to get a better look. The butterfly had closed its wings and was tasting his skin with its proboscis. Luca went to the window and threw open the shutters. He half expected to see the little boy on the terrace below, or in the garden, watching him with his big brown eyes. But it was empty except for the odd bird hopping about in search of worms.

Luca held out his hand, willing the butterfly to fly off, but the creature remained in the room while he brushed his teeth and turned on the shower. Finally, he copied the little boy and blew at it. The butterfly saw sense and fluttered into the air, disappearing into the garden.

After breakfast he lay by the pool reading his book. This time he was able to concentrate and was grateful for the distraction. He had promised Caradoc he'd accompany him to the *trattoria* for lunch the following day. After having written off the professor and Ma as two old eccentrics, not worth his time and effort, he was growing fond of them; they were life-enhancers. He resolved that if Cosima were there tomorrow he would not acknowledge her. He had twice made an effort. He wouldn't make another.

Caradoc sat in the shade reading poetry while Dizzy sunbathed, her walkman plugged into her ears, her right foot tapping to the beat, while Smidge lay sleeping in her Birkin handbag. Ma detested swimming pools. She was too fat to swim herself and resented those like Dizzy with beautiful bodies. She remained on the terrace with Porci, embroidering a pair of slippers for her nephew, trying to work out how to get to the *festa* without Dizzy and Maxwell muscling in to ruin their party.

After lunch, the professor retired for his siesta and Ma challenged Luca to a game of Racing Demon. Dizzy and Maxwell returned to the pool to lie in the sun and 'fry like a pair of slugs', as Ma put it meanly.

'I don't see the point of Dizzy,' she added, shuffling the pack.

'Does there have to be a point?' Luca asked, lighting a cigarette.

'A person without a point is like a pencil without a point. Useless. She's pretty enough, at least that's something.'

'She's not so bad.'

'I haven't heard her say a single interesting thing.'

'Some men like women like that.'

'What do you like, Luca?'

Luca took a long drag. 'I like a pretty girl, too.' Ma rolled her eyes disdainfully. 'Okay, I like intelligence, wit. I want to be amused and challenged. I like a woman to be independent and confident.'

Ma snorted. 'That's all very dull, Luca. What you need is a woman who fascinates you and who goes on fascinating you until the day she dies. As soon as you feel you know her, she shows you something you haven't seen before. That's what you need. Otherwise you'll get bored with her.' She dealt the cards. 'Yes, find someone fascinating and she'll always be a challenge.' They played Racing Demon all afternoon. Ma was a shrewd opponent who seemed to go at a slow, thoughtful pace, but somehow finished first.

'You're a dark horse, Ma! What's your secret?'

She tapped her temple with a finger. 'It's all in here and I'm not sharing it. If we were playing for money, I'd be a very rich woman by now!'

'If we were playing for money, I'd have quit long ago,' Luca retorted. 'I'm not one to toss away my fortune.'

'No, you had a wife who did that for you. What on earth inspired you to marry Claire?'

'She was a challenge,' Luca replied.

'Was she fascinating?'

'Not fascinating enough.'

'What happened?'

'I spoiled her.'

'They change once they get the ring on the finger. If I were a man, I'd never marry.'

'You're a woman and you've never married!'

'Marriage is like a pencil without a point, Luca.' She leaned over and hissed the word with relish. 'Pointless!'

When the professor reappeared at four he recruited Bill for a rubber of bridge with Ma and Luca. They played until dinner. Romina and Dizzy returned from a brief visit to town. Later, Dizzy could be heard through the upstairs window arguing with Maxwell. They came down to dinner, only to sit at opposite ends of the table, ignoring each other. Ma found this rather compelling and itched to know what the argument was about.

The following day the sky was grey and overcast. As promised, Luca accompanied the professor into town. The streets were quiet, the air cooler, a storm brewing on the horizon where purple clouds gathered like a congregating army. The professor's enthusiasm was in no way dampened by the inclement weather. 'We'll eat inside,' Luca suggested as he parked the car as near to the quay as possible. As soon as he spotted the little boy again, playing among the boats, he knew Cosima must be at the *trattoria*.

'That poor child is always on his own,' said Luca disapprovingly.

'What child?'

'Cosima's son. He follows her around and she barely acknowledges him. It's all very well mourning her husband but she mustn't forget the living!'

'I wouldn't mention it, if I were you,' said Caradoc, making his way slowly across the terrace to the restaurant.

'Don't worry. I'm through and out the other side. Where's the lovely Rosa?'

Inside, the *trattoria* was old-fashioned with small tables and simple chairs. The floor was tiled, the air sweet with the smell of dried lavender and herbs hanging from the walls above rows of framed photographs. There were bowls of lemons on the sideboard and bottles of wine in tall racks. A few tables were taken but the weather seemed to have kept people away. Rosa appeared in a green dress that clung to her body like seaweed. Her hair was up, exposing her long neck, and her lips were scarlet to match her nails. Luca noticed her toenails, painted like her fingers, peeping out of a pair of very high heels. He wondered how she managed to walk on them all day.

'We've come back for the red mullet,' said Luca with a smile.

Rosa smiled back. 'I thought you'd come for me,' she replied.

'*I* have come for you, pretty Rosa,' interjected the professor.

'Well, one out of two isn't bad. Would you like some wine?'

'Greco di Tufo, chilled,' said Luca. 'It looks like there's going to be a storm.'

'And a very dramatic one, too,' said Rosa. 'You might be trapped in here all afternoon.'

'I can't think of a nicer place to be trapped,' said the professor.

'Who are all those photographs of?' Luca asked.

'My family.' Then she pointed to a sketch of a reclining nude, placed high up on the wall. 'That is a portrait of my grandmother, Valentina, painted by my grandfather. Wasn't she beautiful?' Rosa's eyes glittered. 'I'm told I'm very like her. Sadly, my life is rather uneventful by comparison.'

'I hope you live longer, my dear,' said Caradoc. 'And come to a better end.'

In the middle of lunch the skies opened, thunder shook the hills and rain pounded the quay. Cosima, if she was in the kitchen, didn't appear. Luca resented her all the more for not giving him the opportunity of ignoring her. He looked out at the storm, at the dark, tempestuous sea, and hoped the little boy was safe at home.

Chapter 10

Luca didn't go down to the *trattoria* again. He took to visiting a *caffè* in the square instead, where they made a good, strong coffee and served *brioches*, and tried not to dwell on Cosima. The professor and Ma plotted against Dizzy and Maxwell and managed to convince Romina to encourage them to stay at the *palazzo* and avoid the famous Festa di Santa Benedetta altogether.

'I'll give them a nice dinner,' she said. 'I'm rather bored of Max and Dizzy myself. They contribute nothing. Surely, they have something they have to get back to. Can he really do all his business over the internet and on the telephone?'

As fortune would have it, the day of the *festa* Maxwell suffered a migraine and spent all afternoon in bed while Dizzy, bored and bad tempered on her own, lay in the shade reading a novel. Ma crowed with glee, while Luca antici-pated the *festa* with some foreboding. Surely Cosima would be there?

At dusk the three of them set off into town. Ma only just managed to squeeze her large bottom through the door of Romina's car and wound up sitting on the gear stick so that Luca had to ask her to move every time he changed gear.

'If I had known we'd be squashed into a baked bean tin I wouldn't have come,' she complained.

'Courage, dear lady,' said Caradoc from the back. '*Ring in the valiant man and free, The large heart, the kindlier hand.*'

'The large behind, the wandering hand,' said Ma as Luca reached under her trousers for the gear stick. 'Now is not the time for Tennyson, professor. They shouldn't make cars so small, it's insulting.'

'Why don't you hire a big car, Luca?'

'Laziness, I suppose, or just the need to be free of all belongings.'

'Being free is having a nice big car to spread out in,' said Ma. 'Hiring a car won't impede your spiritual quest, I assure you. And it'll certainly enhance mine!'

'Spirituality isn't giving up material things, it's not giving them undue importance. Don't let money be your god but your slave.'

'I hope you've taken all that in, Luca,' said Ma. 'Caradoc's a little cranky but he's a wise old bird. I'm just an old bird. Now what are we to expect tonight, I wonder?'

'Entertainment,' said Luca. 'At least, I'm hoping for something spectacular.'

'A weeping statue that hasn't wept for half a century,' said Ma. 'I'm not putting my money on that.'

'A town in the grip of religious madness,' said Caradoc fruitily. 'Mass hysteria, I suspect.'

'Thank God we haven't got any hangers-on,' said Ma. 'With you, Luca, speaking the language so fluently, we can blend in.'

Luca glanced at her to check whether she was serious. Ma wasn't the sort of woman who blended, ever.

They parked the car near the quay and walked up the

narrow streets to the square of San Pasquale where the people of Incantellaria gathered in front of the chapel holding small candles. The air was thick with the smell of wax and incense and charged with anticipation as they waited impatiently for the great doors to open. Luca saw Rosa immediately; her red dress and shawl stuck out of the crowd, shouting to be noticed. Children clustered around her and she was with a man who was presumably her husband. Then he saw Cosima, dressed in black, her face obscured once again by a lace veil. She was too far away for him to make out her expression. She stood beside a tall man with long grey hair and a kind face. Occasionally, he put his arm around her shoulder and drew her close, bending down to whisper something in her ear. Luca's fury melted to make way for pity that a woman so young and pretty should waste away for love.

Rosa couldn't stand still for the excitement. There was nothing she enjoyed more than a ceremony followed by a party. If Christ didn't weep they'd celebrate anyway, in remembrance of the original miracle. She looked around her; she knew most people. Then she spotted Luca staring at her cousin and Panfilo and felt her excitement ebb away. Cosima was a compelling sight in her mourning dress and veil. He must have felt her eyes for he shifted his gaze to look at her. She smiled jubilantly and gave a small wave. Luca waved back.

'Who are you waving at?' Ma demanded to know.

'The waitress from the *trattoria*.'

'Is she pretty?'

'She's married.'

'That never stopped anyone.'

'Luca's a man of honour!' said Caradoc. 'Though her beauty could launch a thousand ships.'

Ma squinted and identified Rosa. 'By the expression on her face I'd say she's already launched a fair few.'

The great doors opened with a loud clank and the people hurried inside, eager to find the best seats. Ma linked arms with the professor, who leaned on her gratefully. He liked full-bodied women. Luca noticed that they had begun to attract attention. He sensed the locals knew they came from the *palazzo* and were both fearful and intrigued. Children were less subtle, pointing and whispering behind their hands.

The little church was ablaze. On every ledge and surface there were clusters of ivory candles, their yellow flames flickering in the dusk. The smell of incense filled the air. The gold leaf glittered and the statue of Christ glowed eerily as if lit up from inside. Luca found three chairs together near the back, beside the aisle, and stood aside as Ma and Caradoc settled themselves. Cosima was at the very front with Rosa and the rest of her family. The children wriggled on their chairs and looked around to wave at friends, except Cosima's son, who was playing in front of the altar using a white feather as a sword, stabbing the air. No one seemed to mind that he wasn't sitting. The townspeople continued to file in, crossing themselves before the altar and ignoring the little boy.

A hush descended over the congregation, a buzz of anticipation straining the silence while they waited, barely daring to breathe. The little boy sat at the foot of the altar, running the smooth feather across his lips. Suddenly the doors reopened and three women dressed in black walked in like a coven of witches, their faces illuminated by the candles they held. One walked a little in front of the others, her chin raised, her eyes fixed upon the altar. Behind them walked the priest, reciting prayers in a deep monotone, and a little choirboy in red, waving a thurible of frankincense.

As they filed past, Luca noticed the eyes of the woman who walked in front. They were disarmingly light against the rich brown of her skin and hair. She shifted her gaze for a second and looked at him, her expression unchanging. Only the apples of her cheeks flushed to betray her surprise. Luca nodded, copying those around him who knew the ritual by heart. She continued to walk slowly, settling her gaze on the statue that held so much hope and expectation.

The three women took their places in the front pew. The priest and the little choirboy stood before the altar. There were no hymns, no music, only the inaudible prayers of the hopeful congregants who never tired of the ceremony, returning every year, their optimism refreshed.

Ma squinted but could only see a very blurred statue. 'Has he bled yet?' she hissed into Caradoc's ear.

The old man shook his head. '*My soul, sit thou a patient looker-on; Judge not the play before the play is done.*'

'Oh my, how the good Lord takes His time,' she grumbled.

'And tests our faith,' Caradoc replied.

They all waited for twenty minutes, after which the congregation gave a collective sigh. The miracle hadn't happened. Christ's eyes remained dry. The bell began to toll, shoulders were shrugged, a few old people wept, the children began to giggle and shuffle from one foot to the other.

Suddenly, there was a loud sob, the hurried tapping of shoes on stone, and the flurry of material as Cosima ran down the aisle and out of the church. Everyone stared, a murmur rising from the pews. Luca watched the little boy follow his mother, his face taut with anxiety, his hands gripping the feather. As he passed, he held Luca's eyes for a long moment, as if trying to communicate something. Luca could almost hear a cry for help.

'Oh dear,' said Ma in a voice of doom. 'She's taken it very badly.'

'The widow,' said Caradoc. 'Luca's got his eye on her.'

'That heart will be impossible to win.'

'Nothing a man likes more than a challenge.'

'Nothing a man hates more than losing,' Ma added pessimistically. 'Now what do we do?'

'Go home, I suppose,' said Caradoc.

'I wonder what's for supper.'

The procession of women walked slowly back up the aisle and out of the church, the priest and the choirboy close behind. The bell tolled dolefully but the musicians were ready to pick up their instruments and play in the square. Rosa wasn't going to let Cosima spoil the party, though she knew Alba would run after her as she always did. She wondered whether the handsome Englishman would stay to dance and whether she'd manage to speak to him with Eugenio present.

Luca felt flat with anticlimax. He was about to ask the professor whether he wanted to stay or return to the *palazzo* for dinner, when a cold gust of wind swept up the aisle, and there was the little boy with the feather standing in the doorway, red-faced and out of breath, searching the sea of faces. When he saw Luca, he began to scream at the top of his voice: 'Help! *Mamma* is in the water. Help! Please!'

Luca was right beside him, hurrying out of the church. 'Take me to her!' he commanded.

They ran through the square, ignoring the surprised look on the faces of the priest and the three *parenti di Santa Benedetta*. The little boy ran nimbly down the cobbles to the quay, from where Luca could just make out a figure wading out to sea in the moonlight. He threw off his shoes and jacket and ran after her, striding through the water as fast as he could. 'Cosima!' he shouted. At first she ignored him, as if in a trance. When he shouted louder, she accelerated her pace until her head disappeared beneath the waves. Luca began to swim, trying to locate where she had gone down. Then he saw an arm rise above the water as her instinct struggled to hold on to life. With a monumental effort he managed to grab it. There was a brief struggle and then she went limp.

Luca pulled her up and manoeuvred her on to her back so that he could hold her in the crook of his arm, her head resting on his shoulder. He swam back towards the shore until he could feel the stones beneath his feet. Then he took her in his arms and carried her out of the water. No one had followed him in spite of the child's pleas. Hastily, he placed Cosima on the stones and put his ear to her breast to check her heart. It was still beating, but she was not breathing. He tried to resuscitate her, pounding her chest and pumping oxygen into her lungs. Her lips were cold and salty, her body lifeless. He'd never forgive himself if the boy lost his mother because he was unable to save her.

At last, her body jerked as it expelled water from her lungs. She gasped and inhaled a gulp of air, opened her eyes and stared at him in bewilderment. Luca mumbled a few words of encouragement. He needed to get her somewhere warm. Hastily, he covered her with his jacket and lifted her into his arms. He struggled to hold on to her wet body, limp as she drifted in and out of consciousness. Gritting his teeth with determination, he set off towards the square. He looked around for the little boy, but he must have gone to the *piazza* to get help. Luca could hear the music from the party and the cheerful voices of the locals as they compensated for the disappointment of the ceremony.

He held Cosima against him, trying to keep her warm; her breath encouraged him to stagger on. Finally, he reached the square. 'Somebody help!' he cried. People turned, their faces registering horror as he walked towards them bearing one of their own, wet and lifeless. The music stopped, the dancing ceased, the crowd flocked around him like a herd of curious cattle. People crossed themselves as he passed, believing her dead.

Alba rushed forward. 'Cosima!' she cried as Luca laid her gently on the ground. 'Is she . . .?'

'She's alive,' Luca replied, catching his breath. 'But she was trying to drown herself.'

'Oh my God! Panfilo!' she shouted. Panfilo was right beside her, taking off his jacket to place across the girl. 'I should have known this would happen,' Alba moaned.

'We have to get her home, quickly,' said Panfilo, taking control. 'To the car!' He lifted her up in his strong arms and waded through the throng that parted reverently.

Alba turned to Luca. 'You saved her life. How did you know?'

'The little boy.'

'What little boy?'

'You didn't see the little boy in the church, screaming for help?'

'No.'

'I presumed he was her son.'

She stared at him for a long moment then touched his arm. 'Cosima has no son. Francesco died three years ago. Drowned. He was six years old.'

Chapter 11

Luca watched Alba disappear through the crowd. He was bewildered. The little boy followed Cosima everywhere. How come Alba hadn't heard him screaming for help? The whole church must have heard. He searched for Ma and Caradoc while the townspeople stared at him as if he were an alien.

'There you are!' Ma emerged from the sea of faces. 'What on earth is going on? You're soaking wet!'

'You're a hero, young man,' said Caradoc.

'You look like you need a strong drink,' added Ma. 'Are you all right?'

'Did you see the little boy?'

'Which one?'

'The child with Cosima, screaming for help.'

Ma stared at him blankly.

The professor chuckled. 'I think you need a hot bath and a hot toddy.'

'Wait!' Luca felt light-headed. 'Are you telling me that you didn't see the little boy come into the church and shout for help?' They shook their heads, looking at him askance. 'You didn't see him chase after the woman leaving the church in a hurry? Come on! You must have seen him?' He turned to the professor. 'Am I going mad? A little boy told me to save his mother. So I ran down to the sea and found her wading out, determined to drown herself. I swam after her and rescued her. I did not do that on my own. How could I have known if the little boy hadn't told me?'

'This is most baffling,' said Caradoc, leaning on his stick. 'But I'm afraid the only one who saw the little boy was you.'

'I thought he was Cosima's son,' he said in a thin voice. 'Maybe she's not a widow, after all.'

As they went back down to the quay to retrieve Luca's shoes and find the car, Rosa appeared, flustered and close to tears. 'Luca,' she cried, stopping him in his tracks.

'I'm sorry,' he said as she began to cry.

'She's alive. That's all that matters. I want to thank you. You saved her life.'

'Why does she want to commit suicide?'

'I feel so bad. I've been so unkind. I didn't realise how unhappy she is. I didn't believe her. I thought she was just wanting attention.' Rosa took a deep breath. 'Her son, Francesco, was drowned three years ago. She blames herself, because she was with him. One minute he was beside her and the next he was in the sea. Cosima can't swim. There was nothing she could do. She's never got over it.'

'Where's her husband?'

'She's never married.' She shuddered. 'We're all she has.'

'So who is the little boy who follows her around?'

'My son, Alessandro,' Rosa replied.

'The one with the feather who cried for help?' Luca asked, relieved that he wasn't losing his mind after all.

Rosa looked confused. 'No. My son was with me all the time tonight. I didn't see anyone cry for help.'

'For God's sake, he shouted so loudly they must have heard him in Naples.'

Rosa flinched at his raised voice. 'I don't know what you mean,' she said sheepishly.

'Don't worry, I'm obviously the only person who saw him. I'm going mad, that's all.'

'Well, thank you. On behalf of all my family, thank you for saving her life.'

Once again they all squeezed into the little car and set off for the *palazzo*. Ma and Caradoc were thrilled with Luca's heroism. The evening would have been an anticlimax had Cosima not chosen to throw herself into the sea. The drama had given them both a new lease of life and they couldn't wait to get back to tell the others. But while they chatted, Luca's mind was elsewhere. Was he losing his mind? Or was it something altogether darker?

Back at the *palazzo*, Luca helped Caradoc and Ma out of the car. 'Who'd have thought you'd turn out to be a knight in shining armour? There are precious few heroes these days, Luca, but you deserve a medal for what you did tonight. I'm going to tell your mother myself.' Ma patted his shoulder. 'You'd better go and change before you catch a cold.'

'*See the conquering hero comes! Sound the trumpets, beat the drums!*' sang the professor as Luca handed him his walking stick. Ma gave him her arm, waited a moment while he shook out his legs, then led him through the great doors of the *palazzo*. Luca fled upstairs to his room.

He stood under the shower enjoying the warm water as it pounded his skin and trying to block out his fears. Trying not to think about his childhood and the voices that had spoken to him in the night, the people he had seen, wandering about his room in the dark. His mother had told him ghosts didn't exist and that if he continued to talk about them she'd send him to a hospital for mentally ill children. After that, he hadn't mentioned them again. He had believed it was all in his head. He had shut them out until finally they had gone. If he was the only one to see the boy, did that mean they were coming back?

He dressed in a daze. How was it possible to feel the fear of a child when he was a man in his forties? He walked out on to his balcony and gazed across the ocean. Beneath the moon the water shone silver like mercury. He thought of Cosima and her little boy and his fear turned to compassion. Her pain was so great she had tried to end it all. She wouldn't thank him for saving her life. She had wanted to be with her son. But if the little boy was indeed her son, he too had wanted to save her. Luca knew he couldn't tell her what he had seen; she'd think him crazy. Everyone would think him crazy. He couldn't tell anyone.

He heard laughter down below where his mother presided over dinner on the terrace. Caradoc and Ma were obviously telling the story. The table listened, enraptured, their features illuminated by the flickering light of the hurricane lamps. He hoped they wouldn't mention the little boy. He'd shrug it off, make something up. He had shut them out once before, he was damned if they were going to come back.

His stomach rumbled with hunger and he was in dire need of a stiff drink. He would have preferred to eat on his own, but the *palazzo* didn't offer room service. Reluctantly he went downstairs. When he appeared on the terrace the table cheered and raised their glasses.

'Darling, I'm so proud of you!' his mother gushed, tears in her eyes.

'Have a glass of Taurasi,' his father said, reaching for the bottle.

'You look better now,' said Ma, turning to the rest of the table. 'He looked very pale. I thought he was going to faint. He was the only one in that entire church who rushed to her aid.'

'Who is she?' Bill asked.

'Is she pretty?' asked Dizzy.

Ma rolled her eyes. 'She's tragic and beautiful. If she'd been ugly he wouldn't have bothered.' Everyone laughed, except Luca.

'She's called Cosima,' he said, feeling a warm sensation as the wine reached his belly. 'Her son drowned in the sea three years ago. She was trying to commit suicide.'

Dizzy gasped. 'Oh, my God! I can't understand why anyone could do such a thing!'

'To be saved by a handsome stranger, of course,' said Ma sarcastically.

'I think you should pay the family a visit, Luca,' said Caradoc, thinking of the pretty cousin in the red dress.

'Of course!' agreed Romina. 'You must go and see them, darling. They will want to thank you.'

'They have already thanked me. But she'll hate me for having ruined her plans. It's only a matter of time before she does it again.'

'Then you have to tell her about the little boy,' said Ma. Everyone turned to Luca.

'What little boy?' Romina asked. 'You haven't told us about a little boy.'

'There was no little boy.' Luca drained his glass. 'I was confused. I was wet and cold.'

The professor was wise enough not to pursue it. 'Let them come to you if they want to thank you,' he said instead. 'I guarantee you, they will.'

When the others retired to bed, Luca went for a walk along the beach. On his return, as he approached the folly, he heard the sound of footsteps in the undergrowth. He knew it wasn't his father and it certainly wasn't Ma or Caradoc. He smiled at the thought of Maxwell and Dizzy making up after their quarrel, stealing into the folly for a bit of nuggy bunny in that large four-poster bed, surrounded by erotic pictures and literature. He dismissed the idea at once. They seemed as passionate as a couple of jellyfish.

Although the moon was high, the shadows were dark and impenetrable. There was a crackling noise, then silence. He stood still, his heart thumping in his chest. Perhaps it was an animal, maybe a deer. He strained his ears, but heard nothing except the breeze rustling the leaves and the chirping of crickets. He sensed he was being watched, that whoever it was was aware of him and waiting for him to make a move.

Eventually, he was left with no choice but to take a step. When no sound came, he realised he must have been imagining the whole thing, and walked the remainder of the path to the folly. After all, at six feet four with wide shoulders and a body that had been honed by daily work-outs, he needn't be afraid of anything.

Just as he reached the little portico of the folly a startled rabbit leaped out of the bushes into his path, before disappearing into the undergrowth. Luca took a deep breath, relieved. He tried the door, but it was locked. He shook his head and smiled wryly at his own stupidity. His mother had the only key. The episode at the *festa* must have shaken him up if he was imagining spirits in the shadows. He thrust his hands into his pockets and walked back to the *palazzo*.

That night he slept deeply with no intrusions. When he awoke to the dawn flooding the corners of the room, he wondered whether the events of the previous day had really happened. He got up and stretched, casting his eyes over the benign sea. The sky was clear and bright, the air infused with the smell of honeysuckle and lavender, the merry twittering of birds resonating across the gardens. He could see his mother practising her yoga on the terrace while a gardener watered the terracotta pots and borders with a hosepipe. He dismissed thoughts of the little boy and Cosima as if they had been part of a nightmare from which he had now awoken.

He breakfasted with his mother and Dizzy while Porci lay on the stones, his fat belly rising and falling as he slept. Smidge trotted around on her dainty little toes, avoiding Porci, whom she considered inferior on every level. Ventura came out with hot bread, fresh coffee and *brioches*. In the centre of the table was a bowl of pomegranates and peaches, from which Dizzy helped herself, avoiding the tasty *crescenti* which were damaging to her figure. Luca was starving, and sent Ventura off to make scrambled eggs, which he'd eat on toast with *prosciutto*.

The professor emerged in a cream linen jacket, Panama hat on his head, with Ma one step behind him in a long purple kaftan. 'Good morning, my friends,' he said jovially. 'Something smells good over here.'

'Darling Professor, come and sit down.' Romina patted the chair beside her. 'Did you sleep well?'

'Like the dead.'

'The dead don't sleep in this place,' grumbled Ma. 'I could have sworn I heard footsteps up and down the corridor all night. I haven't slept a wink.'

Romina tutted. 'That was probably Bill, he wanders about when he can't sleep.'

'Well, he has a very heavy tread,' said Ma grumpily.

Luca remembered the footsteps at the folly and wondered whether there had, indeed, been an intruder in the night.

'Strange things happen in Incantellaria,' he said as Ventura put a plate of scrambled eggs in front of him.

'Well, there was no sign of blood on Jesus' marble face,' said the professor.

'But they had a good knees-up anyway,' complained Ma. 'The fireworks kept me awake too.'

When Bill appeared, having been into town to get the English newspapers, the whole table turned and looked at him expectantly.

'Good morning, everyone.'

'Darling, did you corridor-creep in the middle of the night?'

'Not that I'm aware of.'

'And did you make a trip to the folly at about one in the morning?' asked Luca.

'There was someone at the folly?' interrupted Romina.

'I heard footsteps.'

'Not you too!' his mother wailed.

'Not guilty,' said Bill, dropping the papers on to the table, and pouring himself a cup of coffee. 'Looks like I'll be needing a strong one of these.'

'Then it can only be the ghost,' said the professor matter of factly.

'Surely you, Professor, with your good brain, don't believe in such things?'

'A good brain does not only accept the tangible. Think of radio waves, my dear, and ultraviolet light to name but a couple. There is far more to this planet than can be experienced with our five senses. The *Marchese* was murdered in this very house; who's to say his energy isn't still here?' Dizzy's mouth dropped open in horror.

Romina gasped. 'Murdered, here?' She turned on her son. 'You said you didn't find anything out!'

'I didn't want to frighten you.'

'You're not frightening me, darling. I was the one who sent you two out on a mission, the least I can expect is that you come back and tell me what you have discovered.'

'Well, as you're interested, the Marchese Ovidio di Montelimone was having an affair with a local girl called Valentina who fell in love with an Englishman called Thomas Arbuckle. In a fit of jealousy the *Marchese* murdered her. Her brother took revenge and killed Ovidio, here in this *palazzo*.'

'An honour killing,' said the professor. 'Very common in these hot-blooded countries.'

'Oh dear, that is gruesome,' said Romina. 'The *Sunday Times* will love it!'

'Ah yes, the *Sunday Times*,' said Bill with a sigh.

'Well, that accounts for the strange things going on up here,' said Ma. 'You should get the priest to come and exorcise the place.'

'Rubbish!' Romina scoffed. 'Anyhow, the priest won't come up here as I've barely set foot in his church. Religion is not my thing. I was given too much of it as a child and now I can't be doing with it. So I hardly think he's going to hurry to my aid.'

Ventura appeared with the telephone. 'A call for *signore* Luca,' she said, handing it to him. Luca got up to take it in private. Claire was the only person who had the number of the *palazzo*.

'Hello,' he said, positioning himself at the other end of the terrace.

'Are you having a nice time out there?' she asked.

'Sure. How are the children?' Her friendly tone made him suspicious.

'Fine. No one found you yet?'

'No.'

'People are getting desperate. They've even started calling me!'

'Who?'

'One or two journalists.'

'Tell them I'm abroad. They'll give up in the end.'

'I'm not your secretary. I've told your friends to leave messages on your mobile. You'll get back to them when you're ready.'

'You make it sound as though I'm ill.'

'Well, it is an illness of sorts, isn't it?'

'When can the girls come out?' he asked, changing the subject.

'Well, that's why I'm calling, actually. You see, we've been invited to Barbados over half-term and I was wondering whether you'd have the girls then. I'll send them out with Sammy. It's only for a week.'

'Of course,' he replied. 'I'd love to have them.'

'I'm so pleased. Friends of John's have a house in Sandy Lane.'

Luca didn't rise to the bait. 'When will you send them out?'

'Next Friday. You can send them back the following Friday.'

'That's fine.'

'I mean it's only fair that I take some time off, you know, I'm with them twenty-four seven. You were always travelling or working, so it's good for you to spend time with them other than alternate weekends. You'll really get to know them. They're adorable girls.'

'You don't need to tell me that, Claire. I've said I'm happy to take them. I'm not blaming you for going away. In fact, I'm delighted to have the opportunity to have them with me.'

'Oh, good.' She sounded relieved. 'I don't want you thinking I'm not a good mother.'

'Why would you care what I thought?'

'Don't be like that,' she snapped. 'I only want a little appreciation for all I've done over the years.'

'You have it, Claire.'

'So, I'll send them on Friday. I'll call you with the details. You will pick them up yourself, won't you?'

'Of course.'

'I don't want some chauffeur they've never met.'

'You have a great time in Sandy Lane.'

'Well, I'm sure I will,' she said brightly. 'John knows everyone.'

Chapter 12

'She won't eat,' said Alba in exasperation. 'She just lies in bed, staring at the ceiling, waiting to die.' She allowed Panfilo to wrap her in his arms. 'I don't know what to do any more.'

'You've done all you can, my love,' he replied, kissing her hair. 'She has to do the rest on her own.'

'But she'll die.'

'Then she'll be where she wants to be, with Francesco.'

'You can't say that! She's thirty-seven years old. She has her whole life ahead of her. I have a responsibility.'

'She's Toto's responsibility.'

'But I'm the mother she never had. I was there during her growing up. I love her like my own daughter.'

'Don't let Rosa hear you say that.'

'Rosa knows that. There are many ways to love.'

'Cosima needs more than love to rouse her out of the rut she's got herself into. She needs will and a change of mind. Perhaps Rosa's right, all this fussing over her is enabling her to wallow in self-pity. While she's doing that she doesn't have to face up to her life.'

'You mean, she's frightened to move on?'

'That's exactly what I mean.'

Rosa sat on the end of Cosima's bed. Her cousin was pale, her hair dark against her pillow. She looked frail. 'I'm sorry we haven't been getting along,' said Rosa, finding it difficult to apologise. 'I didn't understand.' When Cosima failed to reply, Rosa stood up and walked over to the little shrine with its burning candle. Francesco's face grinned out from his photograph. 'You know, the man who rescued you is called Luca. He's very handsome. I think you should thank him.'

'I don't want to thank him. He did me a disservice.' Cosima turned her face away.

'He risked his life for you.'

'He should have left me alone.'

'What decent man would watch a woman walk into the sea and not try to save her?'

'It was none of his business.'

Rosa decided to take a gamble. 'He said a little boy ran into the church and cried for help.'

'So?'

'He said he carried a feather.'

'A feather?' Cosima looked at her at last, eyes glittering.

'A feather.'

'Who was he?'

'No one else saw him.'

'You're lying!' Cosima's cheeks flushed. 'He's lying!'

'Ask him yourself.'

'I don't want to see him.'

'Then you'll never know.'

'It's impossible.'

But Rosa could see she was curious. Her heart began to race at the prospect of being the one to lure her cousin out of her mourning. 'Fine. Whatever you want, Cosima. But if I were you, I'd want to know.' She left the room, passing Toto on his way up.

'How is she?'

Rosa shrugged. 'I think she'll be getting up soon.'

Luca was in his usual spot by the pool when his mother appeared in a fluster. 'Good God!' she exclaimed dramatically. 'Someone's been in the folly again! Your father swears it isn't him. Didn't you say you heard footsteps there last night?'

'I was joking, Mother,' he replied, recalling the rabbit.

'Well, it's no joke. There really was someone there last night. The bed has been slept in again!'

'Why don't you change the lock?'

'Ghosts can walk through walls.'

'I didn't think you believed in ghosts.' He got up to help her to a chair.

'Maybe I'm wrong about that,' she hissed, in case anyone should overhear. She never liked to admit she was wrong. 'Your grandmother used to see them all the time. I'd find her deep in conversation with herself, but she'd insist she was talking to spirits. She'd lay extra places at the table for her dead relations. Nanni thought it was funny; I thought it was sad. My mother thought it the most natural thing in the world. I resented her for her madness. But was I wrong?'

'You're not wrong. You're a sane, intelligent woman. Ventura is a superstitious peasant. As for your guests, they're enjoying the idea of the ghost, but none of them really believes. There are no such things.'

Even as the words came out, he knew he was lying. He thought of the little boy in the church and the people who used to appear to him in the night as a child. Buried deep in the hidden recesses of his heart was the knowledge that there was more than this three-dimensional world. 'We'll get to the bottom of this, Mother. Trust me, the person lurking around the folly is made of denser stuff than Ventura's ghosts!'

That afternoon Caradoc invited him into town for a coffee. 'I'd like another look at that delightful girl,' he explained, meaning Rosa. 'Girls like her keep old men's dreams alive.'

'You're not going without me!' said Ma, catching them in the hall. 'Or have you forgotten our shared adventure?'

'Certainly not, dear lady. We are now linked for ever. Luca is coming too.'

'Dizzy is on the telephone to a long-suffering friend,' she grumbled. 'A good moment to escape. I can't tolerate listening to her gushing.' She looked at Luca. 'Ah, yes, the translator. I'm getting a sense of *déjà vu*.'

'I hope not,' he replied. 'I don't fancy wading out into the sea again.'

Ma arranged her red hat in the mirror. It was made of straw and decorated with brightly painted wooden fruit. She liked to keep the sun off her pale skin.

'I'd avoid the harbour then if I were you. If she's intent on drowning, nothing will stop her.' She grinned at him through the mirror, her face transformed by her elusive smile. 'Well, maybe you can. Men don't come more handsome. Italy is doing you good, Luca.'

'Ah, Luca,' said Caradoc. 'I was handsome once but age is a great leveller. *The flowers anew, returning seasons bring! But beauty faded has no second spring.* Enjoy it while you have it, young man.' They went out into the dazzling sunshine.

They borrowed Romina's car again, but this time Ma squeezed into the back where she could spread herself across the entire seat. Inside, it smelled of hot leather. Caradoc wound down the window to let in the breeze, lifting his nose like a dog. As the car hummed down the hill Luca felt his spirits rise in the company of these two most unlikely friends. How different this life was, and how different he was beginning to feel.

They arrived at the *trattoria* and chose a table on the terrace overlooking the harbour. Boats came and went, children played on the quay, a bony dog trotted along the pavement until he spotted a black cat lurking in the shadows and made chase. A pair of old men in caps sat arguing about the game of *scopa* they had played the night before.

Ma took a while to choose a chair in the shade and Caradoc nearly tripped over his own feet when Rosa emerged in her scarlet dress. She greeted them warmly and waited for them all to sit down. Luca hoped she wouldn't mention his 'heroism' again. It was an episode he would rather forget.

Rosa addressed the professor. 'So, coffee for you, *signore*?' Her voice was sweet as chocolate.

Caradoc beamed. 'You remember?'

'Of course. How could I forget?'

'Black coffee,' he said. 'And something sweet. You choose, I'm sure you will find me something special.'

'Shame on you, Professor,' said Ma disapprovingly. 'You're a silly old man.'

'The day I stop being a silly old man, I will simply be an old man, and a sad old man at that.'

Ma snorted. 'I'll have a nice cup of Earl Grey tea, with a little honey and milk on the side.' She expected the girl to shrug in that infuriating Italian way and declare that they didn't stock such a thing, but she nodded agreeably and turned to Luca.

'Coffee with milk on the side, piping hot?' she asked with a flirtatious smile.

'Thank you.'

Rosa's eyes lingered a little longer than was proper for a married woman. 'Can I get you anything sweet?'

'Yes,' interjected Ma stridently. 'We'll have whatever the professor has.' Rosa disappeared inside and Luca breathed a sigh of relief that she hadn't mentioned her cousin.

'Pretty girl!' said Caradoc with a sigh. 'If I were your age, Luca, I'd bed a succulent Italian girl like Rosa. They're like ripe fruit, ready to be picked and tasted.'

'Good God, Professor!' snapped Ma. 'What's got into you?'

'It must be the heat.'

'It's Incantellaria,' Caradoc corrected. 'I feel twenty years younger.'

'Well, it hasn't had that effect on me,' said Ma. 'I've never rated sex that much. I can't bear a man clambering all over me, heavy breathing and fumbling about. There are so many better things to do with one's time.'

The professor looked crestfallen. 'How about you, Luca?'

'I agree with you, Professor. The heat does turn one's thoughts to girls.'

'But divorce has the effect of a cold shower, I should imagine,' said Ma. She patted his hand. 'You'll have better luck next time. You're young and foolish enough to give marriage another go. I'd find a nice Italian girl to look after you.'

'Like Rosa,' said Caradoc.

'Not like Rosa,' said Ma sternly. 'If I were her husband I wouldn't trust her as far as I could throw her. She's got a mischievous glint in her eye that's nothing but trouble. Mark my words, she's a handful.'

Rosa returned with their drinks and three slices of lemon cake. 'My grandmother's recipe,' she said. 'It melts in your mouth.'

'Like a succulent fruit,' said Caradoc, gazing up in adoration. Luca saw from the intent look on her face that she was about to mention Cosima.

'My parents would like to thank you properly for saving Cosima.'

'There's no need.'

Her face fell with disappointment.

'You must all be going through a difficult time,' he added. 'I would hate to impose.'

'Impose? If you hadn't been so brave she would have drowned. It's the very least we can do. Besides, Cosima would like to thank you herself.'

'You'd better go,' said Ma. 'If only to ensure the poor girl doesn't try to drown herself again.'

'Now's no time for modesty,' cajoled Caradoc. 'If you play the hero you should accept gratitude with grace.'

'Please,' Rosa begged. 'You're the first ray of light she has had in such a long time. She just wants to say thank you. We all do.'

'Then I would be delighted,' Luca conceded, despite his apprehension.

'Good. Come tonight at seven and I will escort you myself. It is not easy to find the house and I'm no good at giving directions. You can drive me home. Everyone will be so happy!' she gushed, clapping her hands. No one would be happier than Rosa.

'Now that smile is worth a million gold pieces,' said Caradoc, watching her bottom as she went to another table to take orders. 'Do you want me to come with you?'

'No, I'll go alone,' said Luca. 'I'm a big boy.'

That evening Cosima waited with her family on the terrace beneath the vine. Curiosity had got the better of her as Rosa had predicted. Beata sat with Toto and Alba while Panfilo chased the children around the olive trees with his dog, provoking squeals of delight. The children were oblivious of the tension in the air as the adults waited for Rosa and Luca to appear.

Finally, the rumble of a car signalled their arrival. Alba went around the house to greet them, while Cosima remained very still, not knowing how to handle the situation. She resented him so for having thwarted her plans, and yet, there was a spark of hope in her heart on account of the boy with the feather.

Alba watched Rosa descend the hill with Luca. He was very tall and broad in his jeans and open-necked blue shirt. The sun had tanned his skin brown and his hair was thick and dark. His eyes were as bright as cornflowers. She greeted him warmly, disguising the trepidation she felt at his connection with the *palazzo*.

'Welcome.' She extended her hand. Luca recognised her as the woman holding the candle at the Festa di Santa Benedetta. 'You're so good to come. I'm Alba, Rosa's mother. Cosima is my niece.'

'I only did what anyone else would have done,' he replied humbly.

'Come. Everyone is waiting on the terrace. Rosa will bring you a *prosecco*.'

Rosa went into the house, her walk more of a dance, confident that Luca was watching her. She had put her hair up to show the pretty curve of her neck and applied more make-up, the red of her lips matching the red of her nails. If only she had some real diamonds to hang from her ear lobes.

The house was pretty – a sandy stone farmhouse with a grey tiled roof. The windows were framed by blue-grey shutters and protected with elaborate iron bars from which hung small pots of red geraniums. Surrounded by inky green cypress trees and large urns of lilies, it possessed a peaceful charm. Luca followed Alba around the corner, his heart accelerating as he, too, wondered how to deal with the situation. Make it brief and get out as fast as possible without causing offence, he thought.

Alba introduced him to the family one by one, leaving Cosima to the end. Her face was in plain view, no longer hidden by the black veil. He shook her hand but she refused to meet his eyes. Her lips were very pale, her cheekbones prominent, her skin almost translucent. She wasn't classically beautiful, but her features had a haunted quality that caused his heart to stall.

'Sit down,' said Panfilo, pulling out a chair. 'It's good of you to come.'

Rosa handed Luca a glass, enveloping him in a cloud of perfume. They all watched expectantly. He gulped his drink, paralysed by embarrassment. What does one say to a woman who's tried to commit suicide?

'So, how is it up at the *palazzo*?' Toto broke the ice.

Alba bristled but she repressed her feelings for Cosima's sake.

'It's splendid,' said Luca. 'It's got the most magnificent view.'

'Apparently the old *Marchese* used to spy on the village with a telescope,' said Rosa mischievously.

Luca grinned, grateful to her for lightening the atmosphere. 'I must get one then. He was obviously on to something!'

'You know, Panfilo is going to photograph it for the *Sunday Times*.'

Luca had quite forgotten the name of the famous photographer his mother had mentioned so gleefully. 'Of course. My mother has told me all about you. She says you are the best in Italy.'

'She flatters me,' said Panfilo with a shrug.

'No, she doesn't,' protested Alba. 'She's right. You *are* the best in Italy.'

'She's thrilled to be able to show it off. It was a ruin when they bought it.'

Alba was unable to contain her curiosity. 'Why *did* they buy it?'

'My father's an architect, my mother paints interiors. They are both retired. It's been a project for them both. My mother fell in love with the *palazzo* on sight. My father found it a great challenge. Now they hold court like a medieval king and queen, though I'm not sure where they pick up some of their guests. They are not all to my taste.'

Luca was aware that he was talking to Valentina's daughter, the same Valentina who was murdered on the road to Naples, whose brother took revenge on the *Marchese*. His curiosity was fired. He took another gulp of *prosecco* and felt the pleasurable loosening of limbs as it lightened his senses.

Conversation continued as the sun descended, casting long shadows across the grass. Cosima watched him warily, her eyes full of suspicion. The rest of her family compensated for her hostility with a slick routine they had been practising for three years. Perhaps they weren't even aware of covering up for her. Cosima's moodiness was as much part of their home as the shadows.

Luca saw the little boy from the church. He was standing quite still in the soft amber light while the others ran about him playing 'tag'. He held a large white feather. When he noticed Luca a smile spread across his face – a smile mature beyond his years, full of gratitude. The boy didn't look out of place with the other children but he remained detached, as if on an island of his own.

'Are those your children?' Luca asked Rosa, his voice little more than a whisper.

'Three of them are mine, the others are cousins.'

Cosima spoke at last. 'I had a son.' Everyone turned to stare. She looked steadily at Luca, her voice unwavering. He wanted to drown in her eyes. 'He was called Francesco,' she continued. 'He was six years old. He used to play here in the olive grove with his cousins. He loved toy cars and boats, but most of all he loved butterflies, insects and birds. He would search for them in the grass and try to catch crickets.' Her voice cracked and two spots of colour flowered on her pale cheeks. 'He collected white feathers.' The little boy had disappeared. The children had run off deep into the olive grove. Cosima continued. 'He carried them around in his pockets because he liked to feel their softness against his lips. He laid them in neat lines on the carpet and left them all over the house. But one blew away and . . .'

Luca was sucked into her compelling gaze.

'Do you want to see him?'

'Sure.'

'Come,' she said, getting up. 'Let me show you my son.'

Chapter 13

Luca followed Cosima through the terracotta-tiled hall and up the stairs. A cool breeze accompanied them and he shivered, sweat gathering in beads upon his nose and forehead. She opened the door to her bedroom. There was a shrine against the far wall. A candle burned in its glass lamp, illuminating the photograph of Francesco.

He entered slowly, half afraid of the face in the frame. But he had to see. He had to know. He crouched down and stared into the photograph. It was indeed the little boy on the beach, in the *trattoria*, the *piazza* and the church – the little boy who had been standing outside in the sunlight holding a white feather. But how was that possible? He looked as real as every other child in Incantellaria.

'Now you see why I want to die.' Cosima stood between Luca and the door. 'I cannot live with the guilt. Why did you save me?' Her voice was an icy wind.

'I had to.'

'How did you know I was in the sea?'

'I saw you run out.'

'But you didn't follow me, you stayed in the church.'

'Yes.'

'How, then, did you know? Who told you?' She stood behind him, silently demanding that he turn around and look her in the eye.

He rubbed his forehead in confusion. 'I think I'm going mad.'

'You saw a little boy, didn't you?' she persisted. 'A little boy with a feather?'

He turned and looked at her. He didn't want to give her false hope, but he couldn't lie. 'I saw Francesco.'

Cosima's eyes welled with tears and her lips trembled. 'Oh God,' she whispered, crossing herself. 'I want to believe you, but how can I be sure you're not lying?'

'How do *I* know I'm not seeing things?'

'No one else saw the child in the church. Only you.'

'I can't explain it. He looked real enough to me.'

'But my son is dead! You can't play with me like this! Look into his face. Are you sure it was him?'

'I know what I saw! I haven't lost my mind. Christ, I didn't ask for this.'

'Do you see them all the time? Dead people, I mean.'

'Spirits?'

'Yes.' He took a deep breath. He hadn't discussed this with anyone, not even Freya. But he could see that she needed some sort of explanation.

'As a child I saw spirits, but I didn't realise what they were. I'd hear voices. They frightened me. But my mother told me I was crazy and that she'd send me to a place for crazy children, so I blocked them out. Little by little they faded, became less frequent, until I stopped seeing them all together.'

'Why did you see Francesco?'

'I don't know, Cosima. I can't explain it. I saw him on the beach the day I arrived here. You were walking and he was beside you, chattering away, but you didn't seem to be listening. I imagined you were just ignoring him.' A fat tear dropped on to her thumb. She brushed it away. 'After that, I saw him at the *trattoria* with Rosa and in the church while you were lighting the candle. You remember I tried to talk to you?'

'Yes, I remember.'

'He was playing in the square. When you walked off he ran after you.'

'But I was alone.' She shook her head in disbelief. 'I'm always alone.'

Luca put his hand on hers, a spontaneous gesture that might have been presumptuous, but she didn't remove it. 'No, Cosima. You're not.'

Downstairs on the terrace, Alba and the rest of the family waited.

'What do you think they're doing up there?' Rosa asked, bristling with jealousy. 'How long does it take to show him a photograph?'

'Rosa,' chided her mother. 'If they're talking about Francesco, that's a very positive thing. I hope they take as long as they need.'

'What's this about the feather, Rosa?' asked Panfilo. It hadn't escaped his notice that Luca had blanched at the mention of it.

'Nothing really,' Rosa replied with a shrug. 'Luca says he saw a little boy with a feather in the church at the *festa*. That the same little boy alerted him to Cosima wading into the sea.'

Alba narrowed her eyes as her daughter jogged her memory. 'Yes, he did say something about a little boy.'

'What of it?' asked Panfilo.

'Well, no one else saw him,' Rosa continued.

'Are you suggesting that the child was Francesco?' Beata asked.

'I don't know. I mean, no, not really. But if Cosima thinks so, that's a good thing, right?'

'Good God!' Alba swore. 'You mean Luca's psychic?'

Panfilo grinned. 'It doesn't matter. If he manages to help Cosima he can be whatever he wants to be.'

'No, he's psychic,' Alba insisted.

At that moment Eugenio came around the corner, tired from bicycling up the hill. 'What's all this?' he asked, surprised. 'What's going on?' His children ran into him, wrapping their arms around his legs and waist. 'Hello, monkeys! Shouldn't you all be in bed?' He looked to Rosa for an explanation.

'We invited Luca up so we could thank him,' she said. He frowned, not recognising the name.

'The man who rescued Cosima,' explained Toto.

'They're upstairs. They've been up there for ages,' said Rosa huffily. She looked at her mother. 'Don't you think I should go and see if they're all right?'

'No,' said Alba. 'Leave them to it. It's good for Cosima to have someone to talk to who isn't family.'

Cosima hadn't intended to open up to a stranger. She had been aware of Luca from the first moment he had talked to her in the *piazza* and had dismissed him as an attractive foreigner not to be trusted. Despite that, she found herself telling him all about Francesco and Riccardo, Francesco's father.

Luca listened, intrigued, as she grew animated, telling stories against herself, laughing at her own foolishness in falling for a man who was clearly never going to leave his wife. She was transformed. The colour returned to her face and, although she was wearing black, it no longer sapped the life out of her. 'You see, Francesco was the part of Riccardo that was totally mine. He filled the hole in my heart Riccardo left when he declared that he wouldn't recognise my child and wanted nothing more to do with me. I was hurt but I had this baby growing inside that would belong to me exclusively. Francesco loved me. He would never leave me.'

'He hasn't left, Cosima. You just can't see that he's here.'

She slid her eyes around the room. 'Is he here now?'

'No.'

'Have you spoken to him?'

'Yes, but he didn't reply.'

She smiled tentatively. 'Next time he appears, will you please try again?'

'I'll do what I can.'

'Thank you.' They sat in silence for a moment. It didn't feel awkward. They were bound together by something beyond their control. 'Tell me something,' she said finally. 'When you said that butterfly was Francesco's, what did you mean?'

'Francesco was there at the *trattoria*. He was playing with a feather, jumping off a bollard. Then he had this beautiful blue butterfly. He came up to me and it flew from his hand to mine, where it remained until you came out and it settled on your dress.'

Cosima got up and walked over to her dresser. 'The Brazilian Blue Morpho,' she said, showing him a butterfly in an oval glass case. 'It was his favourite insect. The Brazilian Blue Morpho is native to Brazil,' she said. 'It doesn't exist in Italy.'

Luca returned to the *palazzo* with a spring in his step. His head buzzed with images of Francesco; he realised now he had never actually seen other people reacting to the child. He had always been isolated, as if separated by glass from his mother or the children he played amongst. No one else could see the boy but him. It was clear that Francesco wanted his mother to know that he was around her. Now she did, would he appear again?

Caradoc and Ma were on the terrace with his parents, drinking wine in the fading evening light. Small moths and flies hovered around the hurricane lights, flapping their dusty wings against the glass. Ventura had placed tea lights around the edge of the terrace and they twinkled through the twilight like fireflies.

'So,' said Ma expectantly. 'How did it go?'

Luca took a seat in one of the comfy armchairs and lit a cigarette. 'Well. Much to my surprise.' He was unable to restrain the smile that spread across his face.

'Have you saved the damsel?'

'Maybe,' said Luca cagily. His father handed him a glass of wine.

'Well, darling, don't keep us in suspense,' exclaimed Romina.

'What's the house like?' asked Bill.

Romina rolled her eyes. 'Like any other Italian farmhouse, darling. Don't interrupt Luca's story! I'm so proud of him!'

'The house is simple but pretty, with a view of the sea,' said Luca, humouring his father. He looked at his mother. 'And I met your fabulous Panfilo Pallavicini.'

'You didn't!'

'I did. He's Cosima's uncle, married to the famous Alba.'

'Ah,' breathed the professor. 'Valentina's English daughter. Well, you certainly fell into the right nest.'

'What is he like?' Romina was curious.

'Panfilo?' Luca shrugged. 'Handsome, I suppose. Longish grey hair, rugged – as you would expect.'

'When's he coming?'

'He didn't say.'

'But he *is* coming?'

'Yes, Mother, he is coming.'

'But what about Cosima, Luca?' said Ma. 'How did you fare with her?'

'Let's just say, she's talking to me now.'

'That's my boy. Persistence and diplomacy,' said the professor.

Ma's mouth twitched. 'So, she won't be rushing off into the water again?'

'I think not,' said Luca.

'Careful,' warned Caradoc. 'Her family has a violent history.'

'And an unlucky one,' added Ma.

'I'll make my own history, thank you very much,' said Luca, gratefully swallowing his drink.

Romina wasn't listening. 'Rewind, darling. Tell me, how is it possible that the most famous photographer in Italy lives in a simple farmhouse?'

Rosa was fuming. When she had put the children to bed she went to her own bedroom and reviewed the evening.

Cosima and Luca had finally come downstairs. For a woman who had spent the last three years in misery, she had sure recovered fast. Her face was flushed, her eyes sparkling, her lips full and pink. The black dress had faded into insignificance instead of dominating her like a shroud. Rosa saw Luca look at her, his gaze as tender as a lover's. Cosima's voice was so intimate she could have been thanking him for a night of passion. He seemed to have become a firm friend of the family, and no one remembered that it was Rosa who had found him in the first place.

'Rosa?' Eugenio closed the door behind him. 'Are you okay?'

'What does it look like?' she snapped.

'What's wrong?'

'Cosima.'

Eugenio sighed, anticipating another row. 'What's the poor girl done now?'

'She's not a poor girl. She's in love with Luca.'

'You should be happy for her.'

'Oh, so now I'm the bitch, am I?'

'Isn't she allowed to love again?'

'Of course she is. Only it was a little hasty, don't you think? She's been playing us all like fiddles for the last three years. Can't you see? Am I the only one in this house who's not blind? I work my backside off day and night in the *trattoria*, while she's allowed to keep the books. That's a holiday compared to what I do. It's been three years, *three*, but she still gets special nation status!'

'She does more than keep the books.'

'You're not around to see, Eugenio!' Rosa placed her hands on her curvaceous hips. 'She wanders in looking miserable, oh woe is me and all that theatre, and *Mamma* rushes to her like a mother hen. When she complains that our children have taken Francesco's toys out of her room, I get the blame. I swear on my life, our children are innocent! I feel like the outsider in this house. She's a big black cuckoo pushing me out! If anyone should move out it's her. Why doesn't she go and live with Beata, Toto and Paola? They're her family.'

Eugenio sat on the bed and patiently removed his shoes. 'You know very well that Alba's a mother to her.'

'She's *my* mother!'

'She's a mother to Cosima in everything but blood.'

'Why can't she bond with her stepmother?'

'Could you bond with Paola?'

'I don't have to.'

'Neither does she. Look, she grew up in this house. It's where she feels at home. It's where Francesco grew up. Face it, Rosa, nothing's going to change.'

She started to cry and Eugenio knew he was being pushed into a fight. 'You don't love me any more, do you?'

'*Madonna!* You know I do.'

'Then show me!' She sat astride him and pulled his head into her bosom. 'Tell me I'm more beautiful than Cosima. She's dry and old and I'm young and juicy.' She began to smother his face with kisses. He was aroused by the warm wetness of her mouth.

'You're more beautiful than Cosima,' he repeated obediently. 'You're more beautiful than any woman in Incantellaria.'

He felt her smile as she placed her lips on his. Her hands began to unbutton his shirt, slipping it over his shoulders. She threw her head back and let him kiss her breasts, flicking his tongue around nipples that were hard and expectant. She began to writhe on top of him, teasing him with her body, until he could stand it no longer. He threw her on to the bed, unzipped his trousers and entered her with a groan.

Her scarlet nails clawed his back. Then, in her imagination, it was Luca's skin she was ripping, his bristles scratching her neck, his lips kissing her throat, his hands running appreciatively over her body. She felt herself grow hot with arousal. How she would thrive on the wild, adventurous life of her grandmother, Valentina! To rise above the boredom of Incantellaria like she had done, to feel the hands of rich and dangerous men caressing her body, leaving trails of diamonds on her skin. Rosa kissed her husband and let her imagination take her to more exciting places.

Cosima stood beside the ancient stone fort that had once been a lookout point for the enemy approaching by sea and gazed over the water. Perhaps Francesco wasn't at the bottom of the sea, after all. Perhaps his spirit lived on, as Luca believed it did. What did he think of her mourning him in such despair? If he had indeed appealed to Luca for help, then he didn't want her to join him in death, but was willing her to live.

She smiled at the thought of Luca, his kind blue eyes, his raffish grin, the tender way he had placed his hand on hers to reassure her that she wasn't alone. She felt an unfamiliar mixture of fear and excitement, the tentative stirring of happiness long forgotten. Her tears weren't the habitual tears of despair, but water from her thawing heart. She gazed out at the black horizon and felt a quiver of anticipation. Perhaps there was something beyond the darkness, after all.

Below her, beneath the olive tree, lay Valentina's grave. Alba tended it regularly, pulling up weeds that seeded themselves in the soil, and occasionally laying flowers from her garden. She had faith. She knew that her mother wasn't actually there in the soil, but in a world beyond the senses of normal people. She had a certainty that Cosima envied. As much as Alba had tried to convince her, Cosima had refused to believe in what she couldn't see. Religion, so much part of her growing up, had seemed farcical in the face of her son's death, like pretty icing to hide a rotten cake. If Luca was right, the cake might not be so rotten after all.

When she returned home the lights in the house had been switched off but for the one in the hall. Everyone had gone to bed, or so she thought. She was making for the door when a voice came from the table beneath the vine. 'You're back.' It was Alba.

'Sorry, I didn't mean to alarm you.'

'I thought you'd gone to bed.'

'I've worried about you constantly for the last three years. Every time you walk down that path to the cliffs, I fear you won't come back. I have to be sure you're safe before I can lay my head on the pillow.'

'I'm sorry I've put you all through so much.'

'Sit down.' Alba leaned forward, her elbows on the table. 'What did Luca tell you?'

'That he saw Francesco. That's how he knew I was in the sea.'

'Do you believe him?'

'I want to.'

'I want you to as well. To try to explain faith to one who believes only in the physical world is like trying to explain a painting to a blind person. Faith is the only thing that will give you the will to live. Knowing that your son is with you in spirit is the only way you'll move on. Your life is an obstacle course. There are other obstacles you must jump and some will give you great happiness. Francesco had surmounted all the obstacles in his race and it was time to cross the finishing line. He's resting now and looking out for you, willing you to complete your course.'

'I'm feeling more positive,' she said with a smile.

'Then put on a nice dress. That black is so unbecoming.' Alba took her hand. 'I'll buy you something new. Yellow would suit you.'

'Francesco's favourite colour.'

'Exactly.'

Cosima smiled tentatively. 'Do you remember the fashion show we put on when I was a little girl?'

'Your father was so proud and you were so excited you twirled around like a ballerina.'

'You bought me so many dresses in the dwarfs' shop.'

'You couldn't choose, you liked them all. And you cried because no one had ever bought you so many before.'

'We didn't have much money.'

'But I did and it was the first time I'd ever thought of anyone besides myself. In fact, I think you were the first person to teach me the joy of giving.'

'Whatever happened to the dwarfs?'

'They grew.'

Cosima looked at her in amusement. 'You're not serious.'

'I'm totally serious. They grew. I don't think there's a dwarf left in the family. Incantellaria's not the same without them. But I'll find a pretty dress in Gaia Rabollini's boutique.'

'That's very expensive.'

'Consider it a coming-out present. It's about time Incantellaria saw how pretty you are.'

Chapter 14

At the end of the following week, Luca drove to Naples to pick up his daughters and their nanny, Sammy. He motored along the winding roads that hugged the red cliffs of the *costiera* and thought of Valentina, murdered somewhere on this very route – a small-town beauty playing a big and dangerous game. He wondered whether the *Marchese*, murdered in the *palazzo*, was somehow haunting the place just as Francesco was lingering close to his mother. Rather than suppressing those thoughts, he let them come. Whether he liked it or not, the spirit world was all around him. He didn't know why he had had the sensitivity to see it in child-hood, or why the spirits had come back now. Perhaps they had never really gone; he just hadn't allowed himself to see them.

Inevitably, these thoughts led to Cosima. She wasn't beau-tiful like her cousin, Rosa, but she had an allure that had nothing to do with lipstick and pretty dresses and everything to do with a vast capacity for love. He recalled the way her brown eyes had brightened as she talked about Francesco and what he had meant to her. The love she felt for him had no limit. His loss hadn't diminished her love but made it greater. She was a vulnerable flame; Luca wanted to put his hands around her to protect her. And he wanted some of her for himself.

He had no desire to go back to London. He didn't miss his colleagues and friends. He didn't miss the adrenalin rush of winning new clients and the triumph of making them richer. He had stepped off the treadmill into a quiet lay-by and at last he could hear himself think. He looked forward to showing Coco and Juno round Incantellaria but his happiness was mixed with apprehension; he didn't really know them, what they liked and didn't like. His work had meant he had seen very little of them, only snapshots of their growing up and frozen frames of them sleeping when he'd returned late at night. Their brief weekend visits to his mews house had been as artificial as a pretty shop window full of toys. It wasn't a real home and he didn't behave like a real father. He didn't even bother to help them with their homework. Sammy had always been there to fill the void and give them a sense of normality. Now he had all the time in the world, what was he going to do with them? He parked at the airport and strode into the arrivals hall. He waited, watching the people come out pushing their suitcases on trolleys, searching the crowd for their friends and family. He watched their faces light up with recognition and break into broad smiles, and he watched them embrace. He couldn't remember the last time he had been met with such excitement, or the last time he had kissed a lover with such passion. He thrust his hands into his pockets and looked away.

Finally, Sammy emerged with the two girls. She looked pretty, her blonde hair escaping from its clip, her cheeks flushed from the heat of the airport. Juno grinned broadly on seeing her father but Coco looked bored and tired and didn't smile. 'Hello there, girls,' he exclaimed, picking up Juno and kissing her soft cheek. She rubbed her furry toy caterpillar into his face. 'I've brought Greedy,' she said. 'Doesn't he smell nice!'

Luca pushed it away. 'Delicious, like cake. He likes you better.' He turned to the nanny. 'Hi Sammy. All well?'

'It doesn't matter how often they fly, they still get a kick out of it,' she said. Coco leaned against her and yawned.

'Ready for bed, darling?' he quipped, trying to perk her up.

'Is Mummy coming?' Coco asked. He looked at Sammy who rolled her eyes at the child's obvious attempt at manipulation.

'You've got Daddy all to yourself,' she said, her Australian accent giving her voice an inspiring bounce.

'Where are we going?' Juno asked, enjoying being carried.

'To a palace,' her father replied. He led the way through the airport with Sammy pushing the trolley behind.

'Is it a real palace?'

'A real palace, and you and Coco can be real princesses.'

'I didn't bring my princess costume,' lamented Coco. 'John brought me a new one. It's pink and sparkly and the prettiest I've ever seen.'

'I'm sure Granny will think of something.'

'Is Granny here?' said Coco, her voice brightening.

'Granny *Romina*,' Sammy corrected.

'Oh.' Coco barely remembered what Granny Romina looked like. Sammy strapped them into the back of the car and came to sit in the front. 'Lucky we didn't bring too much luggage,' she said, running her eyes over Luca's unlikely vehicle.

'It's my mother's,' he explained. 'Just what you need for the winding roads here.'

'I'll take your word for it.'

Juno began chattering to Greedy while Coco looked despondently out of the window. She'd already been to Italy, loads of times. She hadn't been to a palace, though, and her curiosity was roused, in spite of herself.

'So, how's Claire?' Luca asked.

'She's good, very excited about Barbados. She'll miss the kids, though. But we're going to have a good time, aren't we, girls?'

Romina was overjoyed to see her granddaughters. Juno allowed herself to be smothered in perfume and linen while Coco stiffened and grimaced until the ordeal was over. 'They are delightful girls,' she enthused. 'I'll get Ventura to show them to their rooms.'

Coco looked up at the *palazzo* with wide eyes. 'Is it haunted?'

'Absolutely not!' Romina replied. 'There are no such things as ghosts.'

'Yes, there are,' said Coco. 'All palaces have ghosts.'

'Run along, girls,' Sammy cajoled as Ventura disappeared inside. 'Go and unpack, then we can explore.'

Romina gave him a quizzical look. 'You should keep an eye on Coco,' she warned. 'I don't think Claire is on top of things.'

'She's just imaginative,' said Luca, feeling protective of his eldest daughter.

'I won't tolerate talk of ghosts. It's silly. Ventura is quite enough for me to have to deal with.'

Luca followed his mother on to the terrace where the professor was reading poetry to Ma while she worked on her needlepoint. Dizzy was by the pool, Maxwell absorbed in making business calls to Vienna and London.

'What are you going to do with the girls?' Romina asked.

'I don't know. I'll let them settle in, I think. They might like to swim.'

'Bill will be pleased. He put the pool in especially for them.'

'I might take them into town for tea.'

Romina raised her eyebrows, suspecting his motive. 'That's a good idea, darling. Perhaps I will come with you. I'd like to show them the harbour with all the pretty little boats. I'm sure they'll be enchanted.'

'I don't think Coco's enchanted by anything.'

'Give her time. Incantellaria will work its magic. There's still time to un-spoil her, even if it is too late for her mother.' Romina glanced anxiously at Porci who was lying asleep beneath the table. 'Most odd. Porci's been off his food for a few days now, yet doesn't seem to be getting any thinner. I wonder whether the staff are feeding him on the sly.'

'There's always enough food left over to feed an entire pig farm!' Luca replied.

'They've been told not to feed him between meals, but that belly looks full to me.'

Sammy appeared with the girls, a beach bag of swimsuits and towels hanging from her arm. She had changed out of her jeans into a pretty blue sundress and flip-flops. She was already tanned, her skin glowing and smooth. Even Maxwell did a double-take.

'Isn't this glorious, girls?' she exclaimed.

'Come and have a drink, you must be thirsty,' said Romina. 'Juno, my darling, come and show Granny your caterpillar. What's he called?' Juno approached her grandmother without inhibition. Coco remained glued to Sammy.

Romina made the introductions. 'This is Maxwell.'

Sammy extended her hand. 'Good to meet you.' Her smile was white and wholesome. Maxwell metamorphosed into a different species. He shed his dull, beige skin and emerged a new man, as if he had been hibernating and had suddenly woken up.

'Welcome. Can I pour you a drink?'

'Give the kids something first,' she said, sitting down. 'Poor lambs, they've had a long journey.'

Suddenly Coco spotted Porci under the table. She summoned her sister with a cry of delight and both girls disappeared, falling on the unsuspecting pig who awoke with a squeal.

Maxwell poured two glasses of lemonade. 'What will you have?'

'Same, please.'

'How long are you staying?'

'A week, isn't it great!'

'You will love it here. Romina and Bill are exceptional hosts.'

'How long have you been here?'

'Too long! We have accepted Romina's hospitality for weeks, using this as a base camp to explore the south of Italy.'

Ma watched with amusement as Maxwell flirted with Sammy though she seemed oblivious. 'She's jolly pretty. Maxwell's going to make a fool of himself. The blunderer!' Ma scoffed as Dizzy appeared in a diaphanous pink kaftan that barely covered her bikini bottoms.

'This should be fun,' said Caradoc, putting down his poetry.

'Dizzy!' said Maxwell, his voice rising a note. 'Come and meet Luca's children.'

Dizzy barely glanced at the girls before her eyes settled on Sammy. 'Hi,' she said tightly. She wasn't about to shake hands with the hired help.

'Nice to meet you. Right, girls. Time for a swim, eh?' Dizzy stood behind her husband, picked up his glass of lemonade, and took a sip. She rested her hand proprietorially on his shoulder.

'A good morning then?' she asked.

'Perfect,' he replied, his eyes never leaving Sammy.

Ma gave a satisfied snort. 'Dizzy should eat carbohydrates,' she said without bothering to lower her voice. 'Sammy's as sunny as a continental breakfast.'

'I predict trouble ahead,' said Caradoc.

'I think Maxwell's in enough trouble already,' said Luca, taking the chair beside Ma and picking up the thread of their conversation.

The drama continued to build over lunch. Dizzy found herself at the opposite end of the table to Sammy and Maxwell. Luca made eyes at Ma as Maxwell flirted over the heads of the children, who were between him and the object of his desire. He lowered his voice every now and then, sliding his eyes to the other end of the table to check his wife wasn't eavesdropping. His sudden interest in the children, making his napkin into a water lily for Coco and a caterpillar for Juno, was very out of character.

'I can't imagine why he doesn't have children of his own,' said Romina.

'Dizzy doesn't want to ruin her figure, I should imagine,' said Ma. 'Anyone who cares that much about what she eats is bound to be body obsessed. Sammy is a picture of health and sanity. I raise my glass to her.' The more Maxwell flirted the more enraged his wife became. The only person who seemed not to notice was Sammy. Finally, Dizzy raised her voice so her husband could hear and spoke to Romina across the table. 'It is such a shame we have to return to Vienna.'

Like a salmon he rose to the bait. 'Oh, darling, the lunch table is hardly the place to discuss our travel plans.'

'But we cannot impose on our good hosts a moment longer,' she said with a pout.

Romina made no attempt to encourage them to stay.

'The trouble with you, Romina, is that you make it so comfortable one wishes to stay for ever.' Maxwell gave a nervous laugh.

'We have commitments in Vienna, darling,' said Dizzy. There was an unmistakeable edge to her voice.

'Well, we've loved having you,' said Bill. 'I toast your good health and your safe journey home.'

Maxwell bowed, recognising he was outmanoeuvred. 'Thank you, Bill.'

After lunch, when Maxwell and Dizzy had retreated inside, Caradoc, Ma and Luca could hear the most monumental row through the open upstairs window. Ma raised her glass. 'To Dizzy,' she said with a wicked grin. 'Not so dull after all.'

Luca changed into a pair of pale blue Villebrequin shorts and dived into the pool to play with his daughters. Juno, who still wore arm bands, squealed with laughter when he chased her pretending to be a crocodile. He picked her up and threw her into the air so that she landed in the water with a splash, emerging, wiping her eyes and roaring with delight. Coco was harder to coax. She sat on the side in a pretty Melissa Odabash bathing suit, dangling her legs in the water, admiring her pedicure. Finally, Luca ignored her protests and put her upon his shoulders, then jumped up and down until her sullen face broke into a smile.

Dizzy emerged mid-afternoon, her eyes hidden behind large sunglasses, and lay listening to her music without a word to anyone. Sammy lay on her stomach watching the girls, her curvaceous body clad in a discreet yellow one-piece bathing suit. Luca drove his mother and daughters down the hill to the town. Sammy didn't fit in the car and remained by the pool, reading Sophie Kinsella. The children giggled in the back while Luca and Romina discussed the episode at lunch.

'I think it's high time they went home,' said Romina. 'For the sake of their marriage.'

'Don't you resent people staying so long, sponging off you like parasites?'

'Not if I like them. Caradoc and Ma are family now, I'll be broken hearted when they leave, which they won't, as long as I keep producing large bowls of pasta!'

Luca parked in the square and led the children down the hill to the quay. Juno held his hand while Coco walked beside her grandmother, her eyes peeled for pretty shops. There had been plenty of shops in St Tropez. When they reached the *trattoria*, Rosa was on the terrace to greet them. '*Buona sera, ragazze,*' she said to the girls.

'These are my daughters, Coco and Juno,' said Luca. 'And my mother.'

'Welcome,' she said cheerfully. 'When did they arrive?' she asked, showing them to a table by the geraniums.

'This morning.' He followed Rosa across the flagstones. She was wearing a pink dress the colour of Coco's toenails.

'What can I get you all?' She winked at Luca and added huskily, 'Well, I know what I can get *you*.' Romina shot her son a disapproving look.

'I think ice-cream and freshly squeezed orange juice for the girls,' interrupted Romina. 'Black coffee for me and . . .'

'Coffee for your son, with hot milk on the side,' said Rosa.

'She's nice,' said Juno.

'She's also unsuitable,' said Romina in Italian so the girls wouldn't understand.

'I'm not looking,' Luca replied. But he hoped Cosima would emerge with their order.

As they sat down, Luca's attention was drawn to the other end of the terrace where a sultry looking woman with scarlet lips was smoking over coffee with a silver-haired man. He recognised her at once as Maria Friscobaldi. Sensing she was being watched, she raised her eyes. When she saw Luca, she smiled seductively, pausing her conversation a moment. Juno tugged at his shirt. 'Daddy . . .' she began. Maria acknowledged his daughters with a little shrug, took a drag of her cigarette, then rested her gaze once more on her admirer. Luca turned back to his daughter.

Soon Rosa came out with a tray of ice-cream, juice and coffee. She chatted to the girls in English, telling them about her children, inviting them to play if they got bored of being with their father. Coco admired her pink nail varnish and jewellery. Juno liked the smell of her perfume. 'Yves Saint Laurent, Paris,' she said. 'One day when you're a big girl, your daddy might buy some for you.'

'How's your cousin?' Luca asked, tapping his teaspoon on the table absent-mindedly, trying not to look too interested.

'Better,' Rosa replied briskly. 'It was good of you to come.'

'How dreadful for you all,' interjected Romina sympathetically. 'I hope she is recovered.'

'She is, thank you,' Rosa replied politely. 'Your son is a hero.'

Romina's smile was genuine. 'I know. I am so proud. I would expect nothing less of him. He is very instinctive for a man.'

'Is she coming in today?' Luca sipped his coffee.

'No. She's feeling better, but not up to working. Now, isn't that a surprise!'

'Oh dear, I sense a little jealousy. *Stare attento, Luca,*' Romina warned. As Luca swallowed his disappointment he was distracted by a movement outside one of the small boutiques. It was Francesco.

'Excuse me a minute, Mother. There's someone I need to see.'

Luca strode to where Francesco stood playing with a yoyo. He was about to speak when Cosima stepped out of the shop. It took a moment for him to recognise her in a dress imprinted with little yellow flowers. She walked straight through Francesco.

'Luca,' she exclaimed in surprise.

'Hello, Cosima.' The boy had simply melted into thin air.

'Are you all right?' she asked.

'I'm fine. You look . . . beautiful.'

'Thank you.' She lowered her eyes and Luca noticed how long her eyelashes were. 'It feels a little strange, to be honest, not wearing black. I feel very conspicuous. It is better that we talk in private. Do you want to join me on the bench?' She pointed to one that was empty. They sat in the sunshine, looking out over the little blue boats that bobbed about on the water. 'Francesco would not want me to wear black all the time. He loved yellow.' She lifted the fabric of her dress. 'He'd approve of this.'

'I don't blame him.' He wanted to tell her that it was because of Francesco that he had hurried to the boutique, but he hesitated.

'Are you here with the professor?'

'I'm with my daughters,' Luca replied, pointing back at the *caffè* table.

'You have daughters?'

'Two.'

'How old are they?'

'Four and seven.'

'Are you married?'

'Divorced.'

'I should say that I am sorry, but I'm not.'

'I'm not sorry either,' he said. 'Not sorry at all.'

Chapter 15

Luca brought Cosima back to the *trattoria*. The children had almost finished their ice-creams and Romina was telling them a story that had them enraptured. 'Mother, this is Cosima.'

Romina's face crumpled with sympathy. 'My darling girl,' she said. 'I hope you are feeling better now. What a drama. You are so beautiful and young. It would have been a terrible waste!'

'I made a mistake,' said Cosima.

'Those who don't make mistakes make nothing at all,' said Romina. 'The professor told me that.' Sensing something going on, Rosa swept out of the restaurant.

'Cosima, what are you doing here?'

'I was passing and bumped into Luca.'

Rosa looked stony. 'You've barely touched your coffee,' she said to Luca. 'It'll be cold now.'

'Why don't you get him another one?' said Cosima.

'You should both come up to the *palazzo*,' said Romina, attempting to defuse the situation.

'Of course,' said Cosima. 'I'm curious to see what it is like.'

'Now, your father is Panfilo Pallavicini?' Romina asked Rosa.

'One and the same,' Rosa replied proudly. That was something Cosima couldn't lay claim to.

'Why don't you sit down and join us?'

'Some of us have to work,' said Rosa, making a face at her cousin.

'Then I'll get Luca another coffee,' said Cosima calmly. 'It'll be my pleasure. Would you like anything else, *signora*?'

'No, thank you,' said Romina.

Romina and Rosa sat chatting together for an hour, their heads almost touching. The girls ran around the quay with the other children who played there. Luca wondered what Claire would think of them mixing with the locals. Cosima brought his coffee but was unable to join them, as people needed to be served. Rosa deliberately left her cousin to take all the orders. It was about time she pulled her weight, she thought. Toto appeared for the evening shift, a spring in his stride because his daughter was restored to him. His eyes took in her new radiance as if he had never seen anything so beautiful.

The girls had found a couple of skinny mongrels and were chasing them up and down the waterfront. Cosima weaved gracefully through the tables, smiling at the locals, accepting their compliments with poise as they told her how pretty she looked now that she was no longer wearing black. Every now and then she turned and caught Luca watching her and her eyes softened. He was grateful that Rosa was distracting his mother, so he could savour those moments.

'Come to the *palazzo* with your father when he photographs it,' Romina urged Rosa. 'It would give me such pleasure to show you around. Bring your mother, too. I would love to meet her.'

'I don't think *Mamma* will ever step foot in that place again. She said it gave her the creeps.'

'Oh, all that was a long time ago, surely. Do ask her.'

Romina called the girls and they got up to go. Luca's eyes lingered on Cosima a moment then he was gone, taking her smile with him.

The following morning Cosima attended Mass. She took comfort from the embracing walls of the church and the invisible presence of God among the flickering candles and iconography. Was Francesco there, too, as he had apparently been during the Festa di Santa Benedetta? He'd be nearly ten now, not the little boy he had been when the sea had swept him away. She couldn't imagine him with big feet and long legs and a deep, gravelly voice. In her memory his skin would always be silky, more familiar to her than her own, his hair smelling of vanilla, his eyes gazing at her as if she were the most beautiful woman in the world. He used to stroke her face. '*Mamma*, you smell nice,' he would say, winding his arms around her neck and nuzzling her like a puppy. Her body ached with yearning to hold him again, to bury her nose in his neck and inhale the scent of his hair, to hear his laughter bubble up from his belly. She remembered the white feather he had been playing with on the beach and the wind that had whisked it away. She remembered him wading out to retrieve it. She'd never forget the moment he had lost his balance . . .

She opened her prayer book and focused on the words as best she could through her tears. The church was full, the priest chanting in Latin, incense rising from the thurible. She had made a pact with God the day of the *festa:* if Jesus wept blood she would accept that her son was with Him in Heaven. If He didn't, she would give herself to the sea because she couldn't bear to live knowing that she would never see him again. How strange, then, that Jesus's dry eyes had brought her Luca and a message from Francesco. God did indeed work in mysterious ways.

After Mass, she waited until the church was empty, then approached the table at the front where rows of little candles flickered eerily through the remains of incense that lingered in the warm air. As she reached for a candle she noticed a long white feather lying across the back of the table. She was quite alone. She picked it up and twirled it between her fingers. Was someone playing a cruel prank? Or was it evidence that her son was trying to communicate with her?

The priest walked down the aisle towards her, noticing the pretty cream dress beneath her black shawl. 'Hello, Cosima, are you all right?'

She held out the feather, her hand trembling. 'Did you find this here after the *festa*?'

Father Felippo knitted his bushy white eyebrows. 'No, I haven't seen it before. I don't believe we've had a bird in the church and besides, that's a rather large feather, isn't it?'

'Francesco loved feathers.'

'Then consider it a message from God,' said the priest. 'Miracles happen every day, my child. Much of the time we dismiss them as coincidence or luck.'

'Do you really believe that?'

'Of course. If Christ had the ability to turn water into wine and feed the five thousand with a few fish and loaves, leaving a feather for a mother in mourning is a very small thing.'

'Thank you, Father,' she said, bringing the feather to her lips as Francesco had done. 'I shall light my candle now.'

Father Felippo left her, confident that he had managed to return a lost sheep to the fold.

★   ★   ★

Rosa didn't know whether she preferred Cosima in or out of mourning. When she had draped herself in black, slipping through the house like a spectre, albeit a rather conspicuous one, at least she had been self-effacing. Now that she was wearing pretty dresses, smiling, *humming* even, her cheerfulness grated more than her self-pity had. Rosa wished she had never invited Luca to the house. Whatever had happened up there in Cosima's bedroom had had a dramatic effect. It would be intolerable if her cousin fell in love with Luca. He was out of bounds to *her*, of course, but if *she* couldn't have him she was damned if her cousin would. If Cosima hadn't been so foolish as to have given herself to a married man in the first place, Francesco would never have been born and all the drama that followed would never have happened. Cosima had only herself to blame. She did not deserve Luca.

It was night when Rosa crept out of the house. She loved the soft blanket of darkness, the silence of the cliffs, the gentle hiss of the sea below. Then she could imagine her life was different, the way it should be rather than the way it was. Valentina had shaped her life to her heart's desire. Outwardly a simple village girl, she had been the mistress of the *Marchese* and the lover of the infamous Lupo Bianco. *That* was glamour. *That* was living life on the edge. She had had it all. Rosa knew *she* could have it all, too; times were different now and she had the guile of a fox. It was in her blood. It had been in Alba's blood, too. But she had fallen in love with Panfilo who had his own unique blend of glamour and risk. Maybe if Rosa had found a man like her father, she wouldn't be dreaming of a secret life.

The trouble was, her life here in Incantellaria was so limited. She had met Eugenio and he had seemed to embody everything she desired. He was manly, strong, handsome – a responsible policeman with authority – but he was never going to be rich. She should have held out for a man with the means to keep her like a lady. Now she was a mother, she was forever tied to domesticity. A brief affair had been an invigorating interlude and she was lucky not to have got caught. Luca looked as if he knew how to please a woman and his family clearly had money. She should have held out for a man like him, not a local policeman with a peasant's salary. Then she could have travelled and seen the world, lived in London and Paris, shopped in New York and Milan, sat in the front row at fashion shows, worn the latest collections, been fawned over by Karl Lagerfeld and Dolce & Gabbana. Now she only glimpsed that world in the pages of *Vogue* and *Harper's Bazaar*.

When she returned home, Eugenio had not stirred. She climbed into bed and rolled over to face the window. She was twenty-six and this was her life. What was there for her to look forward to?

Eugenio opened his eyes and watched her breathing grow heavy as she slipped off to sleep. He wondered where she went at night, whether she was just going out for air or seeing another man. His jealousy mounted at the likelihood of an affair and his mind whirred with possibilities. He could confront her and cause yet another row, leaving himself open to be blamed for mistrusting her, or forget it and hope the affair petered out. He closed his eyes and prayed that she was innocent of his suspicions; the evidence was flimsy – nothing more than the result of a jealous mind. She wasn't an easy woman to be married to, but he had no choice; he was bound to her by love.

*   *   *

In spite of Maxwell's desire to remain at the *palazzo*, Dizzy was adamant that they leave. She had suffered him flirting with Sammy for long enough. Romina was pleased to see them go. Maxwell and Dizzy had outstayed their welcome.

'I'm rather sorry to see the back of them,' said Ma, as their car disappeared down the drive. 'They had become rather fascinating.'

'Any longer and I would have had to stand guard outside Sammy's door,' said Luca.

'Not before Dizzy had put a knife in the poor child's back,' said his mother. 'If looks could kill, Sammy would be dead as a doornail.'

Romina never tired of company. No sooner had she waved off Maxwell and Dizzy than her brother, Giovanni, arrived. Nanni was large and shaped like an egg, grown fat on pasta and cheese, with thin ankles that he showed off with short trousers and bright socks. Cancer of the throat had left his voice high and reedy. In spite of the disease, he smoked incessantly and refused to give up the foods he loved. His exuberance was irrepressible.

'My darling Romina!' he exclaimed, striding on to the terrace in a pair of scruffy beige trousers and a creased blue shirt. 'Every time I see the *palazzo* it is grander and more exquisite. What it is to have a good eye and a lot of money.' Nanni, of course, had neither.

Luca hadn't seen his uncle for many years but Nanni embraced him as if he were still a boy. '*Madonna!* How you've grown.'

'You sound like Mother.'

'That's hardly a surprise, we come from the same womb.' Nanni sat down and helped himself to a bread roll. 'Might I have a little butter?' he asked Ventura. 'And a large glass of wine.' He already knew Ma and Caradoc. The three of them were like a circus act.

The children appeared, chaperoned by Sammy, who wore a sarong over her bathing suit. Nanni adored children but was less at ease with young women. He ran his watery eyes over Sammy's lovely figure and felt the sweat gather on his forehead in large beads. To cover his embarrassment, he turned his attention to the children, and soon had them laughing at his funny imitations and silly voices. Porci, who had taken a shine to the girls, snuffled and grunted around them, competing with their great-uncle for attention. Sammy disappeared inside to change for lunch and emerged a little later in a sundress. Nanni recovered his composure and after he had tucked into all four courses he sat in the shade doing the *Times* crossword with a large glass of *limoncello* and a cigarette.

'The trouble is,' Romina confided to Ma as they sipped peppermint tea, 'my dear brother has a brilliant mind but a terrible weakness for alcohol and gluttony. He could have been a great man writing film scripts for the best Italian cinema, but he's indolent and self-indulgent. Now he is old, it is too late. Look at him, that crossword bores him, it's so easy, and English is not even his first language. He can speak ancient Greek and Latin as well as he speaks Italian, Spanish, French and English, and yet he hasn't two pennies to rub together.'

'I bet he used to be very handsome,' said Ma.

'He was divine, like a Greek god. But now he's grown fat and has lost most of his hair. He's nearly seventy; if he doesn't watch out he won't make seventy-one.'

'What does he do with his time?'

'Collects antique games. He has the largest collection of Tudor playing cards in the world. They're worth a fortune, but he won't sell them. He keeps them somewhere secret. He's paranoid someone's going to break in and rob him.' Romina finished her tea. 'Now, where's my darling Porci? He's as round as a football but isn't eating his food. I can't understand it.'

'Let's go to the folly,' said Nanni, putting down the paper.

'Have you finished that crossword, or shall I help you?' said Ma.

'I'm afraid I've finished. Perhaps you can check it for me to make sure I haven't made any mistakes?' There was a twinkle in his eye. Nanni didn't make mistakes.

'It would be a pleasure,' Ma retorted. 'But first I'll come with you to the folly. I can't sit on my behind all day or it will lose its shape.'

The three of them sauntered down the path to the little stone folly. Nanni breathed in the floral scents of the garden and sighed. 'You live in a paradise, Romina. I'd be happy to lie down one day and die amidst such peace and beauty.'

'Be my guest, Nanni, but do us all a favour and lie on something we can carry!' Romina unlocked the door.

Ma and Nanni followed her, their eyes adjusting to the darkness. 'Perhaps I will lie down in here,' he said. 'Though it looks like someone has already had the same idea.'

Romina ran her hand over the quilt, still imprinted with the shape of the intruder. 'Not again!'

'Just like Goldilocks,' said Ma.

Romina threw up her hands. 'This isn't funny any more. Someone has a key, or steals my key, to get in here. But who?'

Nanni picked up a silk scarf. 'What's this?' It smelled of perfume. Romina snatched it and held it up to the light.

'This isn't mine.'

'Nor mine,' Ma added. 'Pale pink and blue are not my colours.'

'It smells of a woman,' said Romina, narrowing her eyes. 'Dizzy?'

'Well, they left this morning. So, we'll soon find out if it doesn't happen again.'

'Could they have been so devious?' Romina turned the scarf over, looking for a label. 'Well, it's an Italian label. MOM.'

Ma shrugged. 'I've never been very good at brand names.'

'Means nothing to me,' said Romina. 'SOS would have been more appropriate!' Then her face darkened and she looked at her brother in alarm. 'Marchese Ovidio di Montelimone.'

Chapter 16

Romina sat in the shade with Porci in her lap, recovering from the discovery of the mysterious silk scarf. Ventura brought her a cup of coffee while Luca, Ma and Nanni discussed who the intruder might be. 'It's a woman's scarf. It smells of a woman's perfume, too.'

Luca brought it to his nose. 'A very sweet perfume. I'd recognise it if I'd smelt it before.'

'Who else has the key?' Nanni asked.

'Only me!' Romina wailed.

'Might she be climbing in through the window?' Ma suggested.

'No, there are bars on the windows and they are never opened.' Romina blinked back tears. 'Why on earth would someone want to sleep in there?'

'Change the lock.' Nanni was surprised that his sister hadn't done so already.

'No,' Luca intervened. 'Let's catch her. She's not doing any harm, so let's lie in wait. This old codger I met with Caradoc, in the church, said that rumours of ghosts have grown up over the years because lights were seen up here even though the place was uninhabited. Perhaps it's the same person.'

'Someone who doesn't want us here,' said Romina anxiously.

'A homeless person, perhaps,' said Ma. 'I do hate homeless people. They never bathe.'

'Whoever she is, I'm going to find her,' said Luca confidently. He thought of Cosima. 'You know, I know someone who might just shed some light on all of this.'

Luca was grateful for the excuse to go into town. He found Rosa in the *trattoria* with Toto. The place was very quiet; only one elderly couple sat drinking coffee on the terrace. His first instinct was to ask after Cosima, but the sight of Rosa's enthusiastic face warned him against provoking her jealousy. She rushed off to make him coffee, then sat down to join him. 'How are the children?'

'Having a blast.'

'And everything up at the *palazzo*?'

'When are you going to come and visit?'

'When my father gets around to taking the photographs. He's busy with a job in Positano at the moment.'

'Bring your children. They might like a swim.'

'I will.'

'Tell me something. What do you know about the old *Marchese*?'

'Only what my mother has told me, or let slip over the years. She doesn't like to talk about it. My father told me that during the war people did what they could to survive, even eating dogs! The *Marchese* was rich. He fell in love with Valentina. Times were hard, he was her ticket to a better life. She'd disappear to their love-nest up at the *palazzo* . . .'

'Love-nest?'

'Yes, there's a little house on the top of the cliff, overlooking the sea.'

'You've been in there?'

Rosa blushed. 'Yes.'

'How did you get in?'

She glanced around to make sure they weren't overheard. '*Mamma* has a key. Valentina's key. She'd let herself in and wait for the *Marchese*. Isn't that romantic!'

'Does your mother know you've been up there?'

'I haven't been in it for years,' she hissed. 'Don't ever tell her. She'd murder me.'

'Does your mother ever go up there now?'

'No. She won't go near the place. You see, when she came out here she was about my age. She came to find her family because her father had never told her about her mother. Of course, she never knew why. She thought it was because her step-mother was jealous of her. The truth was that her parents were never married and her mother was leading other lives. The *Marchese* was jealous that Valentina was going to take Alba to London with my grandfather – he wrongly believed the baby to be his – so, he murdered her. If he couldn't have her, he would make sure no one else could.'

'And Valentina's brother murdered him.'

'Yes. In your *palazzo*. My mother had an English ex-boyfriend who came out to win her back and they both went up to see the ruin.' Luca thought of Fitzroy and things began to shift into focus. If Rosemary had the slightest idea of Alba's beauty, she'd have a fit. 'They found Nero, this weird man who the *Marchese* had adopted as a child, I think. He told them that the *Marchese* was murdered because he'd killed Valentina. It was such a shock. *Mamma* found the place so desolate and evil she has never returned. Wild horses wouldn't drag her there.'

'So how does she feel about your father photographing the place for the *Sunday Times*?'

'She won't talk about it. My father teases her relentlessly. She shrugs it off, but I can tell she doesn't like it. The thing is, my father always gets his way. She can't deny him anything.' She paused. 'I wish my marriage was as solid as theirs.'

Luca finished his coffee and walked back to the car, heavy with diappointment at not seeing Cosima. Little by little she was seeping into his subconscious, carving a place for herself in his heart. Then it occurred to him that he might as well drive up to her house. There was no point skulking around hoping to bump into her. He didn't want to impose, but he was sure she liked him too. Perhaps because he was the only link she had to her son; he hoped it was more than that. He knew he had to take things slowly; she was fragile. It was that fragility that aroused in him a desire to protect her.

He reached the house and parked the car beneath the twisted eucalyptus tree. He felt awkward, like a teenager on his first date, and his stomach churned with nerves. The laughter of children was carried on the breeze with the barking of a dog and the occasional braying of a donkey. He shouted to alert them to his arrival. 'Hello! Is anyone at home?' To his surprise it was Cosima who herself came around the corner to meet him, drying her hands on a tea towel.

She was wearing a pale yellow dress with a short ivory cardigan and flip-flops. Her dark hair was clipped up on the back of her head, leaving long tendrils around her face and down her neck. She wore silver bracelets on her wrists and a little silver crucifix that shone against the creamy toffee of her skin. As she approached, he could smell the warm lemon of her scent. He longed to touch her and thrust his hands in his pockets, not trusting himself.

'This is a surprise,' she smiled. 'I was just baking a cake.'

'I hope I'm not disturbing you.'

'Of course not. You can help me ice it.'

'Somebody's birthday?'

'Panfilo's. He doesn't care much for birthdays, but the children like to have a party. They made such a mess baking it, I think I'll ice it myself. Are you any good at cake decoration?'

'The last time I baked a cake was a hundred years ago.'

'And the last time you ate one?'

'Very recently. I've never said no to a slice of cake.' He followed her around the house to the terrace. Beata was asleep in the shade, her sewing on her knee.

'My grandmother is in no position to help me,' she said with a laugh. 'It's lucky you showed up or I'd have had to do it all on my own.'

'Where's your aunt?'

'Alba's a law unto herself. When she's not at the *trattoria* she's out walking along the cliffs or on the beach. She's very solitary.'

Luca wondered whether Alba's refusal to discuss the *palazzo* was masking a deep fascination with it. She held the only other key to the folly. Could the mystery intruder be Valentina's own daughter?

The kitchen smelt of baking and Luca's mouth began to water. She poured him a glass of lemonade. 'You know, there's this beautiful old farm not far from here with a lemon grove that covers an entire hill. These lemons are from there.' She watched him take a sip. 'Good, isn't it?'

'Very good.' She took an apron off the back of the door and tied it around her waist.

'A wonderful old woman owns it called Manfreda. Of course she doesn't harvest the lemons herself, she's too ancient for that, but she always gets the boys to leave a basket for us. She knew Immacolata, you see, and is very fond of Alba. What she doesn't know about Incantellaria and the war isn't worth knowing. There's something magical about that farm because whatever the weather, her lemons are always big, yellow and juicy.'

'I'm beginning to think Incantellaria is magical.'

'So, you know about the carnations . . .?'

'Yes, the morning the beach was covered with them.'

'You should talk to Manfreda. Many strange things have happened here. Whether you choose to believe them or not is another matter. So, what do you do, Luca?' She began to pour icing sugar into a bowl.

'I worked in finance for twenty years, then I woke up one morning and realised I was spending my entire life on a tread-mill that gave me no satisfaction. Sure, it made me rich, but it didn't satisfy my creative side.' He grinned bashfully. 'I'm still looking for something that does.'

She listened as she stirred butter into the mixture with a wooden spoon. 'If you could do anything in the world, what would you do?'

'Good question. I'm not sure.'

'Do you paint?'

'No.'

'Write?'

'Sadly not. This would be the perfect place to write a novel.'

She paused for a rest and looked at him pensively. 'What was it that banking lacked?'

'It didn't leave me with anything concrete.'

'Just figures on computer screens. Nothing to take home with you at the end of the day, like these lemons.'

He took a lemon from the fruit bowl and squeezed it. 'Nothing concrete about these lemons. What are you grinning at?'

'You,' she replied, scraping her finger on the spoon and putting it in her mouth.

'Why?'

She added more icing sugar and continued to stir. 'Because it's very clear to me what you should do.'

'Do tell me. I've been trying to work it out for weeks.'

'Plant something and watch it grow.' It was as if she understood his deepest desire. She placed the spoon in front of his mouth. 'Try a little, it's good.'

The mixture melted on his tongue. 'Very good.'

'But it needs more lemon.' She cut one in half and squeezed it into the bowl. The juice ran through her fingers.

'You smell of lemon. Do you spray it on, or do you bathe in it?'

'Neither,' she replied, laughing. 'I drink it.'

She wiped her hands on her apron, went to the drawer and took out two spatulas. 'One for you and one for me. This goes all over the cake, not into your mouth.' She placed the sponge cake in the middle of the table then scooped a large dollop of icing on to the end of her spatula and began to spread it over the cake. Luca copied her.

'You're not bad,' she said. 'For a beginner.'

He pretended to be offended. 'Are you saying I don't know how to ice a cake?'

'You only know how to count. *This* is creative.'

'I have a dormant creativity, remember.'

'Well, let's wake it up then.' She brought over a tin of small colourful sweets. 'Let your imagination flow.'

'You want me to put these on the cake?'

'Yes. It's a children's cake. You can't go wrong.'

'I'm not afraid of a few sweets,' he scoffed. He longed to kiss her. How different she was from the woman he had chased outside the church. He placed the sweets around the edge of the cake.

'That shows a methodical mind,' she commented, leaning across and resting her chin on her hands.

'What does this show?' He dipped a red sweet in icing then very carefully stuck it on the end of her nose.

'Now I'm going to kiss it off,' he said softly. She didn't move. Luca leaned forward and kissed the end of her nose, licking off the icing and the sweet. He pulled back a little to gauge her reaction. 'I didn't come here to do this,' he said. 'But you're so beautiful, I can't restrain myself.' He placed his lips on hers and kissed her again.

There was the sound of footsteps. They sprang apart and continued to decorate the cake as if nothing had happened. Cosima wiped her nose with her hand.

'Hello Luca.' It was Beata, woken from her nap. 'I didn't see you come in.'

'You were asleep, *Nonnina*,' said Cosima calmly. 'Do you want to help us with Panfilo's cake?'

Beata leaned over to take a look. 'I think you're doing a good job of it by yourselves. How are you, Luca?'

'Well, thank you.'

'Good. I'll leave you to it then. The children will be thrilled.' Beata left the room.

Cosima began to giggle. 'We're behaving like school children.'

'I never kissed anyone at school.'

Cosima shook her head. 'I don't believe that for a minute!'

'Why don't we go somewhere where I can kiss you properly, without being caught by the headmistress!'

Cosima put the cake in the fridge, took off her apron and led Luca out through another door. 'I'll show you my favourite place in the whole of Incantellaria,' she said. As they walked through the olive grove, he took her hand. She didn't pull away. 'I used to play here as a child,' she said. 'I didn't have brothers and sisters to play with, so I played with my father or Alba. We'd always walk here and I'd skip around the trees. It's quiet but for the rhythm of the sea and the chirping of crickets. I like the smells too. Pine and wild thyme. Can you smell them?'

'Yes. And lemons.' He looked at her and the sweet way she looked back at him made his stomach flip.

They reached an old lookout tower, crumbling and redundant. 'This is where I feel most at peace. Where I come to remember Francesco. When I look out over such a vast horizon, to the mists that blur the line of the sea, it's hard not to believe in Heaven.'

Luca pulled her into his arms, longing to erase her frown with his lips. 'Don't be sad, Cosima,' he said. 'Francesco found me so that I could pass on a message to you. That he's in spirit. That he's always with you.' Luca curled stray wisps of hair behind her ear.

'I hope you're right.'

'I'm either right, or I'm mad.'

'You're not mad, are you?'

'Mad for you,' he replied softly, then kissed her lips that parted for him.

Luca had kissed many women, most of whom he couldn't recall. But he had never had such a deep feeling of tenderness. She pulled on his heart so hard that it almost hurt. He wanted to wrap her up and protect her from her fears, to kiss away her pain and watch her cry with joy instead of sorrow. Most of all he wanted her to love him back.

Chapter 17

When Rosa came home she found Cosima in the kitchen humming cheerfully as she bustled about washing up a bowl and two wooden spatulas. The room smelt of baking. A few sweets were scattered on the floor.

'Hi.' She opened the fridge. 'The children sure made a mess of that!' she laughed, on seeing the cake. Cosima didn't comment. 'So, how are they?'

'Very excited about Panfilo's party.'

'Excited about staying up, too,' said Rosa, sitting down with a glass of juice. 'It was quiet today. Very dull. Where's *Mamma*?'

'She hasn't come back yet. Beata's gone home and left the children with me. She's coming back for the party.'

'What have you got?'

'Balloons, of course.'

'He hates birthdays.'

'But the children love them.'

'He's very indulgent.' There was a buoyancy to Cosima's movements that made Rosa suspicious. She was far too happy for a woman who, only a week ago, had tried to drown herself. 'Why are you in such a good mood?'

'It's such a beautiful day.'

'It's beautiful every day.'

'But today is more beautiful than all the others.'

'Well, if you say so. It's the same as all the others if you ask me.' Rosa glanced down at her chipped nail polish. 'I'm going outside to find the children.'

Luca returned to the *palazzo* for a swim. It was hot and he needed to cool his ardour. As he propelled himself up and down the pool he recalled that kiss by the fort; sweet, tender, passionate, but much too short. He would have stayed there all the night had she been willing. It was all he could do not to unfasten the buttons on her dress and slip it off her shoulders. Instead, he had forced himself to take things slowly: this was Italy, not England where the girls were only too eager to jump into bed. As he came up for air he heard his daughters with Sammy.

'Daddy!' cried Juno, running over and crouching by the side of the water. 'Where have you been?'

'In town,' he lifted himself up to kiss her cheek.

'You're all wet.' She wiped her face with her caterpillar.

'Are you going to get in?'

'Can we play Naughty Crocodile?'

Luca pushed himself away into the middle of the pool. 'The Naughty Crocodile is feeling very hungry today,' he growled. Juno wriggled out of her dress and scrambled into her bathing suit, Coco watching warily from the side. 'Come on Coco,' cajoled her father. 'You're not going to ruin your manicure in the water. If you don't get in, the Naughty Crocodile will have to climb out and catch you.'

'You're not allowed out of the pool,' protested Coco. 'That's the rule.'

'Who makes up the rules?'

'I do,' said Coco, as Sammy unzipped the back of her dress. 'Granny is making me a tutu,' she added breezily. 'She's going to cover it in sequins.' Luca looked quizzically at Sammy.

'She's promised, hasn't she, Coco?' said Sammy.

'More work for poor Ventura!'

That night Luca lay with his hands behind his head, gazing up at the shadows cast by the silver light of the moon across the plaster, and indulged himself with thoughts of Cosima. He had left the shutters open so that the gentle sounds of the night could enter the room: the ringing of crickets, the scuffling of small animals, the breeze rustling through the trees. He longed to tell Caradoc, but he wasn't a teenager bragging about his latest conquest. He was a man in his forties, falling in love for the first time. Previous relationships he had enjoyed, from Freya to Claire, had only scratched at the surface of his heart. Cosima had entered the very core, like an arrow, where she remained, digging a little deeper with each uncertain smile. Everything about her fascinated him. He touched her but she still felt out of reach; he kissed her, yet she held herself back. And each time she smiled, he felt she gave him something special which she gave to no one else.

He must have drifted off to sleep for he was awoken at three o'clock by one of his daughters crying. At first he thought he was dreaming; the girls never cried for him. But the crying grew louder and more urgent. He stumbled out of bed and threw his dressing-gown over his pyjama bottoms. When he reached their room Juno was being comforted by Coco. He gathered her into his arms. 'What is it darling?' he asked gently, stroking her forehead.

'Daddy!' Juno sobbed. 'I'm frightened.'

'She's had a nightmare,' said Coco importantly.

'You're all right now. Daddy's here.'

'I think it's the bear again.'

Sammy appeared in the doorway, her hair dishevelled, her eyes half closed. 'Is everything okay?' she asked, folding her arms in front of the skimpy vest top that she wore over floral shorts.

'It's fine, Sammy, thank you. You can go back to bed.' Sammy sloped off. 'Now, sweetheart, tell me what you dreamed about?'

Juno hugged her caterpillar. 'A big bear chasing me.'

'There are no bears in Italy.'

'It's not a real bear, Daddy. It's a monster bear,' said Coco, climbing back into bed.

'Well, there are no monster bears. Do you think Granny Romina would put up with any monster bears in her palace?' Juno smiled timidly and shook her head. 'Now, I'm only down the corridor if you need me. But if you think of nice things you'll dream of nice things.'

'Like Greedy,' said Coco.

'And playing Naughty Crocodile,' Juno whispered, closing her eyes.

Luca tucked her back into bed and kissed her forehead. Then he went over to Coco. 'I'm sorry she woke you up, darling.'

'It's okay, Daddy. I'm used to it,'

'Would you rather sleep on your own?'

She shook her head. 'Juno needs me.'

'You're a good sister, Coco. Juno's lucky to have you.'

'Can I have a cuddle too?'

Luca was touched. Coco's devotion was harder to win. When he climbed back into his own bed he had experienced an unfamiliar emotion: what it was to be needed.

The following morning, after an early swim with the girls, Luca slipped away to the *trattoria* to meet Cosima. She was waiting for him in a green dress, her hair loose about her shoulders. 'Hello, beautiful,' he said, slipping his hand around her waist and kissing her cheek. The scent of lemons transported him back to the evening before up at the fort.

She looked around furtively. 'Careful, Luca. Things are not so good between Rosa and me. Let's not make them worse.' He looked puzzled. 'She likes you,' she explained, tilting her head. 'Are you surprised?'

'Not really,' he conceded. 'I can't say I haven't encouraged her a little.'

'You're a flirt.'

'You wouldn't talk to me,' he protested. 'But you grabbed my attention the first moment I saw you.'

'On the beach, with Francesco.'

'You looked so sad. You broke my heart.'

'Is he here now?'

Luca looked around the quay and beach. 'No, he's usually playing on that bollard. That's how I know you're near.'

'I'll take your word for it, because I so want it to be true.'

'I wish I could prove it to you.'

'I have to trust you.'

'You know you can.' He took her hand. 'You can trust me completely.'

They walked along the sea front to a secluded pebble beach where they sat, gazing out at the vast ocean.

'You're very special, Cosima.'

'I haven't felt special in a very long time.'

'Since Riccardo?'

'Yes, since Riccardo.'

He looked at her earnest face. 'I'm falling in love with you.'

'You barely know me.'

'That's irrelevant. It's about feeling you. I trust my instinct. You're as special as I think you are.'

'Tell me about you,' she said, as he buried his face in her neck.

'Do we have to talk?'

'I feel you too, Luca, but I also want to know the facts.'

'Then you'll kiss me back?'

She ran a finger down his bristly face. 'Then I'll kiss you until lunch.'

At midday Dennis Mendoros and his daughter, Stephanie, rolled up in his shiny Maserati *Quattro Porte*. Greek by nationality, Dennis was born in Sudan and raised in Yorkshire, though he had never lost the strong accent that English women found irresistible. He was blessed with dark, Mediterranean skin and intelligent brown eyes, but it was his smile, dazzling white against his tan, that could light up a small continent. Romina, who had always found Dennis attractive, enveloped him in her arms like a white linen butterfly.

'Stephanie,' she beamed, reluctantly pulling away from the girl's father. 'So lucky to have you too!' She ran her eyes over the leggy young woman who stood before her and momentarily entertained the idea of bringing her and Luca together. With long, glossy hair the colour of a chestnut pony's and her father's brown skin and eyes, she was a beauty. 'How old are you now, Stephanie?'

'Twenty-one.'

Romina struggled to hide her disappointment. 'So young,' she sighed. *Too young*, she thought. '*Che peccato!*'

She led them through the *palazzo* to the terrace, showing off the inner courtyard with its trickling fountain and lemon trees on the way. Stephanie admired the pretty pastel colours and elegant decoration. 'I'd love to live in a place like this, it's so serene.'

'You have to find your prince first, Stephanoula,' replied her father.

'There are plenty of handsome Italian boys in Incantellaria,' volunteered Romina.

'And if they so much as look at my daughter I will grind their bones to powder!'

Caradoc and Nanni were on the terrace, waiting for lunch and discussing the merits of the ancient philosophers; Ma was drinking lemonade in the shade, eavesdropping; Bill was in the garden working out where he wanted to create a grotto: while Sammy and the children were in their rooms changing out of their swimsuits.

Bill hurried up the garden to greet Dennis. 'My dear fellow, how good it is to see you!' he said, shaking him firmly by the hand.

'You have a beautiful home,' said Dennis admiringly. 'You're a very talented man, Bill.'

'I couldn't have done it without my wife.'

'It was a labour of love,' said Romina. 'Now, who do you know?' She proceeded to make the introductions, taking pleasure in assembling such an eclectic group of people.

'Dennis is an old friend,' she explained to her brother and the professor. 'He makes his own aeroplanes.'

'That is a little exaggeration, my love,' Dennis corrected. 'I'm an aeronautical engineer.'

'But he has flown helicopters and aeroplanes since he was a little boy. You're too modest, darling!'

'You're Greek,' observed the professor, narrowing his eyes like an iguana. 'With a little something else.'

'Born in Sudan.'

'From Kelbrook, Yorkshire' added Stephanie.

'A delicious mixture,' Romina gushed.

'Don't look too closely.' Dennis grinned mischievously. 'It's not good to look at a donkey when it's giving you a present.'

'Or as we'd say,' said Stephanie, 'don't look a gift-horse in the mouth.'

Nanni roared with laughter. 'I like you, Dennis.'

'Come, Stephanie.' The professor took her by the arm. 'Come and tell me a little bit about yourself. You're a very beautiful girl. I'm too old to enter the arena, but I'm not too old to admire from afar. You, my dear, have my total admiration.'

Luca arrived late for lunch, grinning at his good fortune. 'It's a beautiful day!' he exclaimed as he walked out on the terrace. Coco and Juno sprang down from the table like monkeys and threw their arms around his waist.

'Where have you been?' his mother asked.

'Up to no good, I suspect,' said Ma. 'He looks much too pleased with himself this morning.'

'I've been reading the papers in town,' Luca replied coolly.

'Why do you have to go into town all the time, when the best coffee is served here with the newspapers your father buys especially?'

'There's little to be had here in the way of adventure. Let the boy enjoy himself,' said Nanni, wriggling his toes as Porci took the liberty of lying across them.

'You know Dennis and Stephanie,' said Bill.

Dennis extended his hand. 'We haven't seen each other for a long time.'

'Just don't tell me I've grown,' laughed Luca.

'Nor me,' Stephanie added.

'But you have!' he retorted, walking around the table to kiss the young woman he had known as a teenager.

'Wait until she stands up,' Romina added. 'She has the longest legs I've ever seen.' *It's worth a try*, she thought.

After a while their conversation turned to the intruder and Bill took pleasure in telling Dennis how he had been accused by his wife of taking secret naps in the afternoons. 'I wish I had the time,' he lamented.

'Everyone has time if they want it,' Romina replied.

'Have you been down to the folly today?' Nanni asked his nephew.

'Not yet.'

'But you said you'd lie in wait and catch the intruder,' Romina cried. 'I'm almost too frightened to go in there now and it's my favourite place in the world!'

'Perhaps you ought to involve the police,' Stephanie suggested.

'What do you expect them to do? Guard the place?' said Romina. 'They're hopeless! No, Luca. You're going to catch her. You haven't got a job at the moment, so that will be your challenge. Whoever left that scarf, I want her out!'

After lunch, Luca took Dennis and Stephanie down to the folly while Coco and Juno drew pictures in the shade with their grandmother. He explained the history of the *palazzo* and the mystery intruder as they walked through the garden. 'I think I have an idea who it might be, but I'm keeping quiet until I'm sure.'

'So, what are you going to do?' asked Stephanie.

'I'm not sure but I think I need to set a trap.'

'A rat trap to catch the rat,' said Dennis. 'In which case you require a large piece of cheese.'

'Precisely.' Luca unlocked the door, disappointed to see that the bed was as smooth as his mother had left it the day before. 'No one's been sleeping in *my* bed,' he said in a deep, bear-like voice.

'Oh my goodness!' exclaimed Stephanie. 'This is the most exquisite place I have ever seen.' She wandered around marvelling at all the details. 'It's like a little love-nest. I can see why someone wants to come and sleep in here. It's enchanting!'

'The *Marchese* was a murderer,' said Dennis.

'But he murdered for love,' said Stephanie, running her hand over the smooth marble replica of Donatello's David. 'Imagine, the woman you love and believe to be an innocent, country girl is having an affair with a dangerous *mafia* boss. It's so romantic.'

'Why didn't he just kill the *mafia* boss?'

'*You always hurt the one you love,*' sang Luca. '*The one you shouldn't hurt at all.*' He sounded just like the professor.

'Well, I don't blame the woman who comes in here,' said Stephanie. 'Only it's a little sad to lie here on her own.'

'A little sad,' Luca repeated slowly, scratching his chin. 'You're right. The woman who lies here is desperately sad. She comes here to feel close to someone.' He was struck by an idea. 'Or because she's mourning someone.'

His heart began to race.

Alba.

Chapter 18

Romina was so alarmed at the thought of an intruder stealing into her folly that she eventually decided to report the
break-in to the police. She found the police station on the
square, a shabby building with three steps leading up to
doors made of sturdy wood. Inside, the air was stale with
tobacco and sweat. She crossed the room to the reception
desk, littered with papers and magazines, and waited for
someone to help her. The office itself was empty, but a
couple of *carabinieri* loitered around the entrance, discussing
mothers-in-law with loud guffaws, dropping ash on to the
floor.

Romina was not one to be kept waiting. She tapped her
fingers on the desk and exclaimed in a very loud voice: 'Is
anyone going to help me or do I have to cry murder?'

The two *carabinieri* stopped chatting and turned to the
woman. They swiftly looked her over, took in the expensive
jewellery and clothes, and deduced that this was a lady used
to getting what she wanted.

Eugenio murmured to his friend, 'I'll go.' The other man
pulled a face as if to say 'on your head be it', and made himself
scarce. '*Signora*, I'm so sorry to have kept you waiting,' he
said, trying to restore credibility.

Romina swept her eyes over his creased blue uniform and fancy epaulettes. 'There is obviously not a great deal of crime in Incantellaria,' she commented disdainfully.

'It's quiet today, thank God,' Eugenio replied. 'Would you like to sit down?'

'Yes, please,' she replied, following him to a worn leather sofa and sitting down. Eugenio sat opposite in an armchair.

'How can I help you?' he asked.

'My name is *Signora* Chancellor. I own the *palazzo*,' she began. Eugenio sat up straight. 'That's woken you up.'

'Palazzo Montelimone.'

'The very same.'

'I haven't been up there for years,' he muttered.

'Well, that rules you out of our inquiry then.'

'Inquiry?'

'We have an intruder, Inspector . . .?'

'Inspector Amato,' said Eugenio. The conversation was running away from him. 'What sort of intruder?'

'I think she's a woman because she left a scarf behind and it smelled of perfume. Not the sort of perfume I would choose, nor the scarf for that matter.'

'In the *palazzo*?'

'No, in the folly. How well do you know the *palazzo*, Inspector?'

'Well,' he replied. 'I had to go up there on many occasions in the past.'

'Really?'

'It was a ruin, but on clear nights you could see lights moving through the rooms.'

Romina tried to control her impatience. 'Are you superstitious, Inspector?'

'Not really, but there are enough people here who are.'

'I know. The staff talk of ghosts. It's quite ridiculous.'

He shrugged. 'A town like this never forgets a history tainted with blood.'

'How very melodramatic. So what did you make of those lights?'

'We found nothing.'

'Well, the light is back and I want you to look into it.'

He decided to humour her. She looked like the sort of woman who could create trouble if she felt she wasn't being taken seriously. 'Do you keep the folly locked?'

'Yes, at all times. I have the only key. So, someone is either picking the lock or has a key that I'm not aware of.'

'Have you thought about changing the lock?'

'Of course, but my son wants to catch the intruder.'

'I see.' So, Luca the hero had to save the *palazzo* as well as Cosima. 'Is there damage to the property?'

'Not really. I don't like to think of a stranger sleeping on the bed, though. It's very unhygienic.'

'No sign of a break-in?'

'No.'

'So your safety is not threatened?'

'No, not yet.' She narrowed her eyes. 'But, in a place like this, with the history you speak of, one can never be too sure.'

'You don't think it's someone who works at the *palazzo*? A housekeeper, for example, or a gardener? Someone who bears a grudge?'

'I'm a good judge of character, Inspector. I trust those who work for me. Besides, why would anyone bear a grudge? We've done nothing wrong. We simply bought a ruin and restored it to its former glory. What is the harm in that?'

'It still sounds like an inside job to me.'

'Well, it isn't. I know the people I live with. Anyway, they have far too much good taste to own a scarf like that one.'

'I'll come and have a look if you like, but I suspect there's not a great deal I can do. We don't have the resources to guard the door full-time.'

'So, I have to leave this to my son?'

'From what I have heard, he is more than capable.'

'I want you to come up all the same. Your presence will be very reassuring.' There was nothing remotely reassuring about Inspector Amato.

Luca spent the afternoon playing hide-and-seek with his daughters before taking them and Sammy to Fiorelli's for tea. Cosima was sitting at one of the round tables with Alba, deep in discussion. When she saw him, she smiled and waved.

'What will it be today?' she asked the children. 'Ice-cream again?' The girls nodded eagerly.

'And one for Greedy,' said Juno, wiggling her caterpillar into Cosima's face.

Luca watched Alba. Was it possible that she was the intruder? Sneaking into the folly to feel close to her dead mother? Like Rosa, Alba was eye-catching with her dark hair and light grey eyes, and her wide, infectious smile. But, unlike her daughter, she had a ripeness that gave her beauty depth. He took a seat and Cosima asked Fiero to make the coffee while she sat and chatted. He lit a cigarette and lowered his voice to make sure they couldn't be overheard.

'Can I see you tonight?'

'I'd like that.'

'It's impossible to look at you sitting there and not touch you.'

'I bet you say that to all the girls,' she teased.

'I used to say it to all the girls, but I never meant it. Now I mean it from the very bottom of my heart.'

She laughed incredulously. 'You're half Italian.'

'The other half is solid, reliable, trustworthy British.'

'Where shall we go?'

'Well, as you insist on keeping our friendship quiet, I suggest I pick you up at seven, we drive down the coast, find a little restaurant for dinner, then a pretty beach to walk along. Does that appeal to you?'

'It sounds lovely.'

'You won't have trouble getting away?'

She shook her head. 'They're used to me disappearing for hours. I like being on my own. They know that.'

Fiero brought his coffee. Luca blew smoke-rings and looked over to where the girls were playing with the local children, under Sammy's watchful eye. They were laughing and joining in as if they were old friends. After a while Juno began to jump off the bollard with Greedy, throwing him into the air and catching him as she jumped.

'Your children are enjoying themselves here,' said Alba. 'How long are they staying?'

'Until Friday,' Luca replied.

'By the end of the week they will have made friends with all the children in Incantellaria,' said Cosima. 'They won't want to leave.'

'Where is their mother?' Alba asked.

'Taking a holiday with her boyfriend.'

'Is he nice?'

'Nice enough.' Luca tried not to sound bitter.

'Do you think they'll marry?'

'I hope so. She deserves to be happy.'

'That's very gracious of you.'

'There's no point harbouring grudges.' He shrugged. 'We have our daughters to think about. Their happiness is worth more than ours.'

'I have a stepmother,' said Alba. 'I hated her while I was growing up. She wasn't my sort. Far too strident and hearty. But in the end I accepted her. She wasn't so bad. She gave me the best advice anyone had ever given me. On the strength of it I returned here. I've never regretted it.'

Luca remembered Fitzroy and his curiosity was aroused. 'Was there anything to keep you in England?' he asked carefully.

'Oh, yes. I was on the brink of marrying a darling man. He was adorable, but sadly not enough for me.' She took Cosima's hand. 'You see, I was in love with a little Italian girl who didn't have a mother. We had grown very close. When I left her I missed her so much she burned a hole in my heart. A hole that no one else could fill because it was her shape alone.' Cosima laughed at the familiar tale. Luca was beginning to see why Rosa was so jealous of her cousin. 'So, I left him for you, Cosima. And I've never looked back.'

The ice-creams arrived and the girls ran back to eat them. Rosa appeared with Alessandro, who had been to the doctor with a stomach complaint. His eyes lit up when he saw the girls and his stomach-ache miraculously disappeared at the prospect of a bowl of ice-cream. Rosa was not pleased to see Cosima sitting at the table with Luca as if she were part of his family, but she recovered a little when Luca gave her a smile and asked after her son.

'Children,' she shrugged. 'There's always something.'

Cosima got up. 'I'd better be going. Enjoy your ice-creams,' she said to the children. She didn't look at Luca for fear of provoking Rosa. He watched her walk off, admiring the gentle swing of her hips.

Francesco appeared from nowhere, skipping off after her, a bounce in his step that he hadn't had before. They were so close they were almost touching, separated only by a fine wall of vibration, but she was unaware that the child she mourned was right beside her. As if he read his thoughts, Francesco turned, grinned at Luca, then waved.

Rosa frowned as Luca laughed. 'What are you laughing at?'

'Nothing. Just a thought that popped into my head.'

'Aren't you going to share it?' She felt better now that her cousin had gone.

'I don't think you'd find it as funny as I do.'

'Try me?'

'Another time,' he said, looking at his watch. 'We'd better get going. It'll soon be time for the girls' bath.'

'That's okay,' said Sammy. 'It's holiday. They can stay up a little later if you like.'

'No. I need to get back too,' he said, not noticing Rosa's disappointment. All he could think about was Cosima and Francesco. Cosima went into the church. She needed time alone to think, somewhere to clear her head of the conflicting thoughts that filled it. The guilt didn't go away, but now she had something else to feel guilty about: her growing feelings for Luca.

She walked down the aisle, crossed herself in front of the altar, and took a seat. There were a few people walking around, looking at the glittering icons and frescoes, enjoying the serenity of the place. Cosima knelt and prayed for her son. She questioned Luca's credibility in seeing Francesco. Not that she thought he was making it up: she trusted him to be honest. But she worried that he might have imagined him, or mistaken someone else's child for hers. In spite of the evidence of the feather and the butterfly, and her own desire to believe, she feared some terrible disappointment would set her back to where she was before, alone and in despair.

She liked Luca. Love wasn't a word she felt comfortable using. Love was a word for Francesco. If she admitted she was falling in love with Luca, she felt she would somehow be subtracting love from her son. Luca had transformed her life in such a short time. One moment she was in the sea, wanting to end it all; the next she was wearing pretty dresses and blushing under his sympathetic gaze. It made her feel uneasy, as if she were a schoolgirl again, playing truant. If she didn't continue to mourn Francesco she was being a bad mother; she had taken her eye off him in life, and look what had happened. If she took her eye off him in death, then what? Did she deserve to be happy after her negligence? Would her guilt allow her to be happy?

These arguments jostled about in her head. If Francesco was dead, wasting her life in mourning wasn't going to bring him back. If he was in spirit, as Luca maintained, surely he would want her to be happy. He clearly didn't want her to die or he wouldn't have sought out Luca and begged him to rescue her. Then the voice of guilt argued that she should dress herself in black and return to her state of mourning, where she felt comfortable. Where she belonged.

When she opened her eyes it took a moment for them to adjust. She put her hand on the floor to push herself up and saw a feather on the floor by the cushion. Like the one she had found on the candle table, it was long and white. Surely, this was not a coincidence.

She looked around. There were no birds in the church and if someone had put it there while she prayed she would have noticed. It certainly hadn't been there when she sat down.

She walked unsteadily out of the church, the feather between her finger and thumb. She felt light-headed with joy. If this was a message from Francesco, then he must mean it was okay to see Luca. The feather was a blessing.

She sat on one of the benches in the square and watched the children playing. How she yearned to hold her son and feel his body against hers. How she longed to kiss his soft face and smell the familiar scent of his skin. She felt her eyes well with tears, then remembered Luca reassuring her that she was never alone. She stopped crying and twirled the feather around and around. If Luca was right, Francesco was beside her now, maybe sitting on this very bench. *If you're here, my love, show yourself to me so that I can know for sure.*

When Rosa and Alessandro returned home, Eugenio was waiting for them on the terrace.

'You're home early,' said Rosa, as Alessandro ran off to join his siblings in the garden.

'I had a very interesting visit today from the woman who owns the *palazzo*.'

'What did she want?'

'She says someone's been sleeping in the folly.'

'For goodness sake, she's mad.'

'She wants me to go and check it out.'

'What does she expect you to find?'

'A woman.'

'Why a woman?'

'Because they found a woman's scarf in there.'

'Why would anyone want to go and sleep in there? It's spooky.'

'I think she just wants reassurance.'

'Well, she's found the right man, then,' she said proudly.

'There's not a great deal I can do. She says her son wants to catch whoever it is, so she's not going to change the lock.'

'That's the first thing I'd do.'

Eugenio shot her a look. 'That place is a mystery if you ask me.'

'*Mamma* thinks it's haunted by the *Marchese*.'

'Perhaps,' Eugenio conceded. 'I'm going to go and take a look. Do you want to come?'

'No. I'm racked with curiosity, but I don't think it looks very professional to be accompanied by your wife. Just come back and tell me exactly what you find.'

Chapter 19

Luca picked up Cosima at the *trattoria* as arranged. She had changed into a black dress embroidered with small red flowers, and her hair was tied with a red ribbon. As he came closer he could smell the scent of lemons and felt the familiar ache of desire. He put his hand around her waist and pressed his lips to her neck.

She pulled away, looking around furtively. 'Not here,' she hissed. 'Someone might see.'

'Why should we hide? I want to shout my love from the rooftops!'

'Please don't.' She gave an embarrassed laugh. 'Come on, let's get out of here.'

They drove down the coast, along the winding road that hugged the hills. The sun began to slip down the sky, sprinkling the sea with glitter. With the windows open, the warm wind on their faces, they both felt exhilarated, as if they were young lovers stealing forbidden time alone together.

Cosima directed him up a narrow road to a little restaurant she knew hidden among the trees. They sat on the balcony, under a trellis of honeysuckle and lemons. Large urns were placed around the edge of the balcony full of pink

bougainvillea and white geraniums, and the smell of rosemary and olive oil wafted through the kitchen window. A
couple of black dogs slept on the red tiles in the fading
sunlight and birds came to peck at breadcrumbs on the
ground. A group of young children with grubby faces and
bare feet played on the hillside with a can of Fanta and some
sticks.

Luca took Cosima's hand across the table and stroked her
skin with his thumb. She turned and looked out over the sea.
'It's beautiful here,' she said softly, trying not to fuel her
doubts with thoughts of her son.

'*You're* beautiful,' he replied. 'You get more beautiful the
better I know you.'

She smiled. 'If I really am beautiful to you, I must cherish
you. It's not every day a man tells me I'm beautiful and means
it.'

'Oh, I mean it,' he said, looking deep into her eyes. 'I've
never meant anything so much in all my life.'

After a while a large, dark-skinned woman appeared with
the menu. She was as ripe as an autumn peach with pink
cheeks and big bulging eyes. Her grey hair was pulled back
into a loose bun, and long beaded earrings dangled from her
ears.

'Ah, this is the best view for young lovers like you,' she
said with a chuckle, handing them each a menu. '*Prosecco*?'

'Two *Bellinis*,' said Luca. 'To celebrate our first evening
together,' he added to Cosima in English.

The woman struck a match and lit the little hurricane lamp
in the centre of the table. 'There, that's better,' she said, standing back to admire it. 'Now you can enjoy a candle-lit dinner.
Take your time to look at the menu. I recommend the fish.
You can come around the back and choose from the tank.'

'This is a splendid place,' he said.

'It's famous. You don't think I'd bring you anywhere but the best?'

'So, you're not worried you're going to bump into someone you know?'

'I'm not worried, I just don't want to antagonise anyone.'

'Rosa.'

She lowered her eyes. 'She's not easy.'

'The way Alba talks about you, I'm not surprised.'

'Alba's like a mother to me.'

'I can't imagine Rosa's too happy about that.'

'Of course not. But she's not happy in herself.'

'Her marriage?'

Cosima sighed. 'She thinks Eugenio is not good enough for her. She wishes she were like her grandmother with lovers in every corner of Italy.'

'Valentina?'

'She's obsessed with her. It wouldn't surprise me if she were found murdered on the road to Naples in a car with some millionaire, draped in diamonds and furs. I don't think she's faithful to Eugenio for one minute. All she thinks about is material things she doesn't possess.'

'Unhappiness comes from wanting what one can't have.' He looked at her intently. 'I'd be unhappy if I couldn't have you.' He knitted his fingers through hers across the table. 'I want to make love to you.' She blushed and turned away, her gaze lost somewhere out to sea. 'I know. I won't push you, my darling. I just want you to know I desire you. We've got all the time in the world.'

'You'd wait that long?'

He barely recognised himself. 'I'd wait for you for ever.'

★   ★   ★

Eugenio had picked up his old Fiat from Gianni's. Rosa had tried to persuade him to buy a new car, but they didn't have the money to indulge in needless extravagances. She had stomped off in a huff, accusing him of not treating her well. 'You once called me Princess,' she had complained. 'Shame you can't treat me like one.' So he had bought her a pretty crystal necklace instead. It wasn't a car, but she had been pleased. Rosa was like a magpie: if it shone it gave her pleasure.

He was curious to see what the *palazzo* looked like now. During the lengthy building work the entire place had been hidden behind scaffolding and no one had been allowed into the grounds. The odd builder had come into the *trattoria* for coffee and given away a few details, but not enough to satisfy the curiosity of the locals. Now Eugenio motored up the sweeping drive, impressed at the beauty of the trees that lined the elegant curve of the approach. The gardens were manicured, large topiary balls clipped into perfect spheres, the lawn mowed, the borders weeded. The *palazzo* itself took his breath away. It was magnificent, with imposing towers and a grand entrance. The old stone blended with the new and the pink roof-tiles shone like copper beneath the setting sun.

He rang the bell. Romina opened the door and greeted him warmly. At her feet was a little pink pig in a nappy. 'Don't be alarmed,' she said coolly. 'This is Porci. A gift from my brother. So typical of Nanni to give me a pig!'

'Unusual to say the least,' said Eugenio. He couldn't wait to get home and tell Rosa about the sparkling collar around the animal's neck.

'Come through. We'll go straight to the folly.'

Eugenio followed her through the courtyard, marvelling at the splendour. How was he going to begin to describe it to his wife? He didn't have the vocabulary. *These people must be as rich as kings*, he thought. Outside, the rest of the house party sat playing cards or chatting, drinking glasses of white wine. A maid hovered, waiting to take orders. They must have turned the *palazzo* into a hotel, for no one would entertain so lavishly.

Romina didn't bother to introduce him to her guests. As they walked down the steps to the garden, the professor raised his eyes over his cards. 'I see young Luca is now out of a job.'

'The police will do nothing,' said Nanni.

'They should take fingerprints at least,' added Ma.

'Nothing has been stolen, has it?' said Dennis. 'No one hurt or threatened. For all they know, it could be one of us.'

'More likely one of *them*.' Ma nodded towards Ventura who was bustling about with a couple of young maids. 'In novels it's always disgruntled staff.'

'Or the hostess herself,' said Dennis with a laugh.

'My sister might be melodramatic,' said Nanni. 'But she's far too busy looking after all of us to bother creating a mystery for her own amusement.'

Down at the folly Romina unlocked the door and showed Eugenio inside. There was no evidence to suggest anyone had been lying on the bed. 'She doesn't come every night,' Romina explained.

Eugenio gave a low whistle. 'So this was the *Marchese's* love-nest.'

'How do you know it was his love-nest?'

'It's legendary. Valentina used to meet him here. It was their special place.'

'I haven't changed a thing. I kept it exactly as it was.'

'The *Marchese* was a notorious pervert,' he said with a chuckle. He leaned over to read the spines of the books neatly lined up in the bookcase. 'Erotica. That doesn't surprise me.'

'If he were alive I'd point the finger at him,' said Romina, folding her arms.

'He's dead and I still point the finger at him.'

'Don't be ridiculous! Dead people don't come back. When you're dead you're dead. That's it. Full stop.'

'Well, there's no sign of a break-in. Nothing stolen. No damage. Nothing.' He shrugged. 'As I said, there's nothing I can do until she turns up again. In that case, call me.'

'Maybe she won't come back. Maybe, she'll grow bored and go somewhere else,' said Romina hopefully.

'I'd take a good look at your staff, *signora*. And keep that key close to you at all times. I think you'll find it's nothing.'

After dinner, Luca and Cosima strolled along a small stony beach. It was twilight. The first stars were just visible, twinkling through an indigo sky, the waxing moon as shiny as a polished silver coin. He told her about his marriage, his divorce, his work and how it had all begun to suffocate him. He explained how coming to Incantellaria and meeting her had changed him.

'I feel alive, aware of all my senses. Aware of everything around me from the smallest flowers to the breeze on my face. I came here for some peace, so that I could work out where I wanted to go, what I wanted to do. I never expected to metamorphose into someone different.' He squeezed her hand. 'I never expected to fall in love.' They walked on in silence until he pressed her for an answer. 'And you? Are you falling in love with me too?'

She took a deep breath. 'Yes, Luca. I'm falling in love with you. But I'm afraid.'

'Of what? Rosa?'

'No, not my cousin. I'm afraid of allowing myself happiness. Whenever I feel happy something squeezes my heart to remind me of Francesco.'

'You don't feel you deserve happiness after what happened to your son?'

'Yes.'

He stopped and drew her into his arms. 'Francesco wants you to be happy. He doesn't blame you. If it wasn't for him you'd have drowned.'

'I want to believe.'

'Look, I saw him earlier today on the quay. When you left, he ran after you. He had a spring in his step. Then he grinned at me and waved.'

The longing glittered in her eyes. 'I want to believe with all my heart.'

'Trust me, Cosima. I wouldn't lie to you. This is all very new to me. I'm bewildered by it too.'

'Why didn't you tell me?'

'I didn't want to make you sad.'

'Don't you see? That is the one thing that will make me happy.'

They continued to walk, their arms wrapped around each other. Instead of Francesco's name hanging over them like an oppressive shadow, they talked about him openly. Cosima's anguish was lifted and she talked about her son with pleasure, recounting his antics and the funny things he had said. Luca was intrigued by the child who was only visible to him, but he longed for undeniable proof of his spiritual existence to give to Cosima. He had no idea how to talk to a spirit.

They sat on the pebbles and Cosima pushed her doubts to the very back of her mind. She let her desire take over and became aware only of the rough sensation of Luca's bristles against her skin, the warmth of his lips on hers, the strength of his body as he enveloped her. With Luca she felt safe. She felt herself again. The last three years she had been nothing more than a mother without a child to love. Now she felt like a woman again, loved by a man.

Eugenio came home from the *palazzo* to find Alba and Rosa preparing dinner. His wife fell on him with excitement. 'So, what's it like up there? Tell me everything.'

Alba went back into the kitchen to check on the pasta. She didn't want to hear about the *palazzo*.

'It's astonishing,' he said, taking off his cap and scratching his scalp. 'I saw the *Marchese*'s love-nest.'

'Did you find the intruder?'

'Just as I thought. Nothing.'

'How very dull. Not even a little ghostie?' Rosa ran a scarlet fingernail down his chest.

'Not even a little ghostie.'

'I'd like to make love to you in that little folly.'

'I don't think that will be possible, now the case is being handed over to Inspector Luca.' He didn't bother to hide the resentment in his voice.

'So, he's really going to guard the door?'

'I think so. How else is he going to find the intruder?'

'I love a mystery!'

'I don't think there is a mystery. But you know what? I think she's turned the place into a hotel.'

'You're not serious!'

'I am. There were so many people up there.'

'Don't tell *Mamma*. She'll be furious!'

'Don't tell me what?' said Alba, appearing in the doorway with a large bowl. Eugenio and Rosa exchanged glances.

'It looks like that woman has turned the *palazzo* into a hotel.'

Alba almost dropped the bowl. 'What? Are you sure?'

'She had so many guests. There must have been at least fifteen people on the terrace,' he exaggerated. 'Drinking wine, playing cards.'

'Won't it be good for business?' Rosa asked.

'Incantellaria can't take all these people.'

'I don't think fifteen are going to make a big difference.' Eugenio enjoyed teasing his mother-in-law.

'You don't know how many that place can hold. She might have fifty by August . . .' Alba sank into a chair. 'I don't like the thought of that place being turned into a palace of amusement. They're probably dining out on the history, taking tours around the rooms. It's not right.'

'She seems nice to me,' said Rosa. 'A little eccentric, but fun.'

'I won't have you going up there, do you hear!'

'You can't stop me, *Mamma*. I'm twenty-six. And anyway, what harm will it do? Romina's invited me with the children. They have a swimming pool.'

'I bet they do,' Alba interjected angrily. 'For all their guests.'

Rosa narrowed her eyes. 'Is it the guests you're worried about, or the fact that she's rebuilt the ruin?'

'I don't know.' Alba didn't want to discuss it any further. 'You can go up there if you must, but I'll never set foot in that evil place again.'

Chapter 20

The day after his dinner date with Cosima, Luca spent the morning in the pool with the children. Coco now threw herself into the water without inhibition, diving off her father's shoulders with a cry of delight. Little by little she gave way to the child in her. Her happiness was infectious as she settled back into the size of her skin.

At eleven, inspired by the desire to give Cosima something special, Luca set out to find the woman with the lemon farm. He remembered her name: Manfreda. So, he asked at the hotel in the square and was given directions. The farm was called La Marmella.

He drove along the same winding road he had travelled the evening before with Cosima, smiling as he envisaged handing her a basket of lemons and watching the surprise on her face. He didn't worry about Rosa finding out. When she saw how in love they were, she'd understand. He had only flirted with her mildly and, anyway, she was married.

After a few miles he reached the lemon grove on the hillside. The slope was planted with row upon row of trees, their rich green leaves shimmering beneath the midday sun. He turned into a drive lined with ancient plane trees, and drove across the shadows to the house at the end.

La Marmella was a charming Italian farmhouse made of sand-coloured stone with a weathered, pink-tiled roof and peeling yellow shutters. The façade was adorned with rampaging bougainvillea among whose little red flowers swarmed butterflies and bees. He parked in front of the house and pulled on a long iron pole to ring the bell inside. After a while he heard the scuffle of feet, the unbolting of locks and finally a small, scruffy little woman appeared. She was as delicate as a bird; her watery blue eyes alert.

'Hello, my name is Luca Chancellor, I'm a friend of Cosima . . .'

At the mention of Cosima's name the old lady's face softened. 'Cosima is a dear friend of mine, too,' she said. 'Come in.'

'I'm looking for a lady called Manfreda.'

'That is me. I'm not too old to answer my own front door.'

She led him into a colonnaded courtyard of cobbled stones. In the centre was an old well, now used as a flowerpot, over-flowing with orange bougainvillea. The place was in dire need of repair and repainting but its shabbiness had charm. The sun tumbled in through the open roof and a couple of doves flew out into the bright blue sky, their coos echoing against the ancient walls of the *palazzo*.

'You have a beautiful home,' said Luca.

'It's very old, like me. We could both do with a face-lift.' She held the door-frame for support. 'Let's go outside, it's a lovely day.'

They sat out on the terrace, overlooking the sea below. The garden was wild with voracious weeds and overgrown shrubs. Inky-green cypress trees swayed in the breeze and roses grew in abundance up a crumbling wall.

'I'm too old for a house of this size,' she explained dismissively. 'My sons live in Venice and Milan, my daughter in Geneva, and I'm rattling around here like a dice. Gelasio and Vicenzo run the lemon grove. It doesn't bring in much, but it gives me such pleasure and those young men have worked here for thirty years. Do you like lemons, Luca?'

'I adore lemons, *signora*.'

'Like Cosima,' she nodded knowingly. 'You're in love with her, aren't you?' Her question disarmed him. 'You're wondering how I know.'

'How *do* you know?'

'You have love written all over your face. There was a time when young men spoke about me with the same look of devotion. I haven't forgotten!' She turned serious. 'She's a very special woman.'

'That's why I wanted to come and meet you. I want to buy her lemons as a present. She says yours are the best in Italy.'

'How very sweet. I don't have much to do with them these days. I'm nearly a hundred!'

'You can't be!' he said gallantly.

'That's because I have the eyes of a young girl looking out of a decrepit old casing.'

'Cosima claims she can recognise your lemons from any others in the world!' Manfreda pulled a face at the absurdity of this idea. Luca shrugged. 'I believe her.'

'Then I'm flattered. It would be rude not to be! You can have as many lemons as you like. But first, tell me a little about you. I haven't seen anyone all day and I'm bored. I can still appreciate the company of a handsome young man. Give an old lady a treat. You're from London, aren't you?'

'Yes. Is my Italian so bad?'

'Not at all. In fact, it's very good for someone whose father is English.' Luca began to feel uneasy. 'I'm not a witch,' she reassured him. 'I don't have a broomstick and I'm afraid of heights. Cosima has told me about you.'

'I should have known,' he said. 'She's enormously fond of *you*. I'm sure she tells you everything.'

'I like to consider myself a grandmother to her. She lost her mother as a little girl and, although Alba has been as good as a mother can be, she will always carry the burden of rejection.' Her face crumpled. 'Then to lose her son as well. Cosima has suffered more than most. She's a bird with a broken wing. I'd do anything for her. Anything at all.'

At that moment a young girl appeared in the doorway. 'Ah, Violetta, you're back. Would you please bring us some lemonade? That's my maid, Violetta. She's Gelasio's daughter. A delight and very helpful.'

'You must have known Cosima all her life,' said Luca.

'Of course. She was an enchanting child, as she is an enchanting adult. You can imagine how I felt when she gave her heart to a married man. Such a precious human being throwing her life away for a man who would never treasure her as she deserved to be. She made a bad choice. But nothing in life is wasted. I know that through experience. Even the bad times are laden with important lessons to be learned. I'm ninety-six and I'm still learning, every day.' She leaned forward, her eyes as sharp as an eagle's. 'If she hadn't lost her heart to Riccardo she wouldn't have conceived Francesco. If she hadn't had Francesco she wouldn't have known unconditional love. Fate delivers with one hand and takes with the other. Now she has lost Francesco, who knows what Fate will deliver?' She smiled at him. 'You are going to be good for her, I can tell.'

'I want to protect her too. But she has to let me.'

'Give her time. She hasn't let another man into her heart since Riccardo.' Violetta emerged with a tray of glasses and a jug of lemonade. 'But lemons? That's a good start. I don't believe anyone has ever had the idea to give her lemons.'

Luca drove back to Incantellaria with a boot full of lemons to find Caradoc on the terrace reading Pushkin. 'Where have you been, young man? I haven't seen much of you in the last few days. It's a girl, isn't it? Not *my* girl?'

'Not your girl,' Luca reassured him. 'Yours is married.'

'Why haven't you told me? Aren't we partners in crime?' He stood up stiffly and shook out his legs.

'We are. I just wanted to see how it went before I told anyone.'

'Is she as juicy as a ripe fruit?'

'She puts all the fruit to shame.'

Caradoc nodded his approval and gave him a firm pat on the back. 'Not a word, I promise,' he said, limping over to the card table. 'Anyone fancy a rubber of bridge before dinner?'

There was no time for bridge because Coco and Juno were putting on a show. They performed a ballet on the terrace in the new tutus Ventura had made for them. Everyone was charged one euro to watch, and found a beautifully illustrated programme on their seat, made by the girls under the supervision of their grandmother. To great applause and a wolf-whistle from Caradoc, they pirouetted and twirled to the music of *Peter and the Wolf*.

As soon as he could get away after dinner, Luca met Cosima at the *trattoria*. 'Are you free to come with me?'

'It's not busy tonight. I'll tell my father I'm going out.' She disappeared into the restaurant, emerging a few minutes later with a cardigan over her shoulders.

'I have something for you,' he said. 'A little present. It's in the car boot.' He led her up the street to where he had parked the car in the square.

'What is it, a dog?'

'Better.' The boot swung open to reveal a basket full of lemons.

'Oh, Luca! They're beautiful!' She picked one up and pressed it to her nose. 'They're from La Marmella!'

'So you really can tell?'

'They're the best in the world. Thank you!' She flung her arms around his neck.

'If that's the reaction I get, I'll buy you lemons every day.'

'Then I will kiss you like this every day.' She pressed her lips to his. 'That's the best present you could ever give me.'

He closed the boot. 'Where do you want to go?'

'You choose.'

'Okay, let's go to the folly at the *palazzo*. I want to show it to you.'

She blushed. 'The *Marchese*'s love-nest.'

'The very same.'

'I went up there once with Eugenio when the *palazzo* was still a ruin. The folly was perfectly preserved.'

'My mother hasn't changed anything.'

'Do take me. I'd love to see it again.' He went to open the passenger door but she took his hand. 'No. I know a better way, a secret walk up the cliffs. I don't want to spend such a beautiful night in the car.'

She led him along the sea front to a secluded pebble beach. At the far end was a little grassy path that snaked its way up the hill. It was already dark, but the moon was sufficiently bright to illuminate their way. Crickets rattled in the bushes and the odd salamander scurried across the path before freezing in the grass until they had passed. They walked slowly, talking about nothing, enjoying the romance of the night and their secret excursion up the cliffs.

Finally they came to the folly. Luca was amazed how easy it was to get into the grounds of the *palazzo*, and wondered whether this was the way the mystery intruder entered.

Luca turned the key in the lock and slowly opened the door, half expecting to find someone inside. But, to his relief, the room was empty. He delved into his pocket for his lighter and lit the lamp on the dressing-table. The little room was warm and smelled pleasantly woody. He locked the door and watched Cosima wander around the room, taking in every detail, her excitement mounting. 'It's an erotic paradise,' she murmured. 'The books, the paintings, this statue here of Donatello's David.' She traced her fingers over the marble, lingering a moment on the wanton curve of his hip. 'The *Marchese* might have been a murderer but he was a great sensualist.'

'With exceedingly good taste.'

She pulled a book from the shelf. '*Casanova*,' she read the spine with a grin. She opened it at random and read out loud: '"*With that, she pulled off her cap, let her hair fall, took off her corset, and, drawing her arms out of her shift, displayed herself to my amorous eyes even as we see the sirens in Correggio's most beautiful canvas. But when I saw her move over to make room for me, I understood that it was time to reason no more and that love demanded I should seize the moment.*"'

'Love demands that I should seize the moment, too,' said Luca, moving closer.

She put the book down and walked deliberately over to the bed, avoiding him in a sensual dance, making him wait, enflaming his ardour. 'I imagine Valentina must have spent many happy hours in here,' she mused, running her fingers down the curtains that hung from the four posts. 'I wonder if he built this for her.'

'I know of a man who fell in love with an actress and built her a theatre.'

'How lovely. What would you build me?'

'A lemon grove.'

She turned to face him. 'Not much to ask for, is it?'

'Cheaper than diamonds and furs.'

'What would I build you?' She put her arms around his neck and stared into his eyes so that he could see her desire in all its nakedness.

'That's a good question.'

'A restaurant called Luca's.'

He laughed and brought his face closer so that his nose was almost touching hers. 'What would you cook for me there?'

'Cake,' she replied.

'You smell of lemon cake.'

'Then eat me, Luca.'

Luca needed no encouragement. He concentrated each one of his senses, savouring her as if committing every detail to memory. He kissed her neck, tracing his lips softly over her skin, sensing the rippling of her flesh as his touch made her shiver. He kissed her jaw and her cheek, her temple and her forehead and then he kissed her lips, opening his mouth to explore her more deeply. She unbuttoned his shirt and slid her hands to his chest and the firm muscles of his stomach. She let the cardigan slip off her shoulders with the straps of her dress and he traced his fingers over the smooth skin on her *décolletage*. The dress fell down her voluptuous figure, landing in a pool of silk at her feet. She stood before him in nothing but her black satin and lace panties, smiling shyly. He caught his breath at her curvaceous body in the golden candlelight. Her skin was brown and sleek, her stomach gently rounded, her thighs firm and shapely. Unable to control himself a moment longer he led her to the bed and laid her down on the quilt. She sank into the mattress, stretch-ing sensuously like a beautiful cat.

He struggled out of his shirt, then lay beside her, enjoying the warmth of her skin against his chest. He kissed the valley between her breasts then lower, to her stomach that trembled as his lips swept softly over it. With a laugh she pulled him up to kiss her again on the mouth while she undid the button on his jeans and pulled down the zip.

In the flickering light of the candle, on the *Marchese's* own bed, Luca slipped off Cosima's panties, then took a moment to savour the sight of her, naked and abandoned beside him. She lay without shame, her limbs carelessly draped across the bed, ready for him to feast upon. He took his time, tasting every inch of her with his tongue, devouring every delicious sight of her with his eyes.

Chapter 21

Claire usually telephoned the girls every evening before bed. Luca made himself scarce so he didn't have to speak to her. But the following morning Ventura handed him the telephone as he crossed the hall on his way out. He didn't expect it to be his ex-wife.

'Hello, Claire.'

'Luca, hi,' she replied, equally surprised. 'How are things?'

'We're having a great time.'

'Are the girls happy?'

Luca would normally have taken offence at her tone, which suggested they couldn't be anything but miserable with him. But his contentment made him resistant to her bitterness. 'They're having a blissful time. In the swimming pool most of the time. Even Coco's letting her hair down.'

'What do you mean, letting her hair down?'

'Being a child. Doing what every other little girl does.'

'Rather than what?'

Luca laughed at her defensiveness. 'Are *you* having a good time?'

'Yes.' Her voice was brittle. 'It was fabulous. John knows so many people, it was rather exhausting. Everyone was somebody, I felt rather inadequate.'

'You don't need to feel inadequate, Claire. You're probably more attractive than the lot of them put together.'

His unexpected compliment caught her off guard. 'I don't think so,' she mumbled, unsure how to deal with his flattery.

'Sure you are. Trust me. I notice every woman who passes me in the street. You're a hell of a lot more attractive than most. I wouldn't have married anything less than lovely.'

There was a pause. This new, easy-going Luca made her apprehensive. Even his voice sounded different. 'So no big-bottomed Italian has swept you off your feet, then?'

'I've got two small-bottomed English girls who keep me firmly on my feet most of the time!' She laughed and Luca sensed her relaxing.

'We left Barbados early. We got back this morning. I'm longing to see the girls. I've really missed them.'

'They've missed you too. But don't worry about them. It's important for you and John to spend time together. They're not his children and I'm sure he wants you to himself.'

'He adores them,' she snapped, suddenly suspicious.

'I'm sure he does. I'm only saying you need time for you. I'm really keen to have them back as soon as they break up. I've really enjoyed them. I'll miss them when they go.' He thought of leaving them at the airport and realised that he meant it. 'I think I hear them. Hold on.' Sure enough, they were coming in from an early swim with Sammy, their hair falling in long wet tendrils down their backs. 'Hi, girls. Guess who's on the telephone?'

'Mummy!' Juno shouted, breaking away from Sammy and Coco.

'I'll pass you over, Claire.'

★　　★　　★

Cosima walked up to the old lookout point and gazed out across the familiar stretch of ocean. It never looked the same. The light was always changing, subtly transforming the water with a spectrum of different shades. This morning the sky was cerulean, the sun a dazzling gold. The bright rays of light caught the waves as they rippled and rose, adorning their tips with diamonds. She was finally able to look at the sea without her stomach twisting with grief. She'd never get over losing Francesco – that kind of loss cuts a deep and lasting wound – but she'd find a way of living with it.

She thought of her night of love with Luca. Once hadn't been enough. They had enjoyed each other until their bodies ached with exhaustion and they lay like sated lions, bathed in the warm afterglow of love. The only thing barring her total happiness was guilt: guilt about Francesco; guilt about Rosa who watched her suspiciously, as if her pretty dresses and smile were an affront; guilt about being cheerful in the wake of such tragedy. In the dark hours of night she felt she didn't deserve to be loved. In the fresh light of day, she was flooded with fortitude. Life was for living. Francesco would want her to be happy. As Alba had told her, it took more courage to live.

Back at the *palazzo*, Romina was in a state of excitement at the arrival from London of the journalist from the *Sunday Times* magazine. After having spent half an hour deliberating what sort of image she wanted to project, she emerged on the terrace in a long green and purple Pucci kaftan over white trousers and gold sandals. She had scraped her hair off her face, holding it fast with a long white scarf that accentuated her bright eyes and the lively lines on her skin. She stepped through the French doors in a cloud of tuberose.

Ma, Caradoc, Dennis and Nanni were enjoying a late breakfast on the terrace. Juno and Coco were busy drawing with the artists' paper and crayons their grandmother had bought them, while Porci lay beside them grunting with pleasure. Much to Nanni's relief, Sammy was covered up in a white T-shirt over pink shorts, although the sight of her young brown thighs was enough to make him twitch with anxiety.

'Good morning, all.' Romina floated up to them like a giant butterfly. 'Where's my son?'

'Gone to have breakfast in town,' said Ma. 'He's been very elusive lately. Must be a local stray he's picked up.'

'*Pas devant* . . .' said Romina, glancing at the children. 'I hope he hasn't forgotten about the folly. Dennis, be a darling and go and check it later, will you? The journalist from the *Sunday Times* magazine is coming today and I don't want any nasty surprises. I hope he left the key with Ventura as I asked. Really, ever since Luca arrived he's been very distracted.'

'He's a young man, Romina,' said Caradoc in Luca's defence. 'Let him pick the juicy peach from the tree. He deserves to have some fun.'

'Of course he does. But he's promised to find the intruder.'

'For us to string up and roast on a spit,' Ma added.

'If she's a pretty girl . . .' interjected the professor.

'Then we'll sacrifice her to Luca,' said Nanni with a chuckle.

'That'll be far too good for her,' said Ma. 'We don't want to reward her for her intrusion.'

'And all the stress she's given me,' Romina added with a sniff.

'Haven't the police done anything to help?' said Caradoc.

'Of course not! They prance around with gold epaulettes and suntans looking very dashing, but they're as useful as shop dummies.'

Nanni finished his coffee and sat back in his chair, his belly as round and heavy as a wineskin. 'I think the intruder is settling in for a long and luxurious summer,' he said languidly. 'And I'm going to roll onto a sun-lounger, close my eyes, and reflect on the great philosophers of antiquity.'

'Don't work too hard!' said Ma. 'You might pull a muscle.'

'*Bella donna!*' Nanni sighed. 'I would agree with you if it weren't for the very obvious fact that I have none to pull.'

'Oh, I'm sure there are one or two little ones hidden away in that skull of yours!'

'Well, if you find them, do tell me. You'll make my day.'

Romina shook her head in fond disapproval. 'If you drank and smoked less, exercised a little and consumed half the quantity of food, you'd find a great deal more than two!'

Nanni sloped off across the terrace. 'And people wonder why I never married!'

Luca had breakfast at the *trattoria* but Rosa wasn't due in until later and Cosima wasn't expected at all. He wanted to telephone her, but was wary of getting her cousin on the line. He resolved to buy her a mobile telephone when he took the girls to the airport. He wanted to be able to contact her at all times. As charming as Incantellaria was, it was stuck in the past in spite of the attempts to drag it into the modern world with satellite dishes and internet access.

Alone with his *croissant* and coffee, Luca sat back and relived the previous night, remembering the scent of her, the taste of her, the feel of her, the sound of her sighs and the huskiness of her laugh. He had expected her to be virginal, somehow. She had looked so modest in her black mourning dress. But she had made love with the wantonness of a woman who lives for sensual pleasure and her lack of inhibition had held him captive. He didn't remember ever having enjoyed a woman so much. She was a creature of many layers, and he could barely restrain his impatience to peel away the next.

His erotic thoughts were interrupted by Stephanie, who had come into town to do some shopping. 'Do you mind if I join you?' she said, taking off her sunglasses.

'Please do. What will you have?'

'*Espresso* would be nice. Isn't it a beautiful morning?'

'Glorious,' Luca agreed, raising his hand to attract Fiero's attention. 'What have you done with your father?'

'He's up at the *palazzo*.'

'While the cat's away . . .'

'The mouse will shop.' She laughed, tossing her hair. 'But I'm doing some culture as well. The church is adorable. I can't imagine that statue ever weeping blood, though. Looks as solid as every other marble statue I've ever seen.'

'Miracles can't be explained.'

'Like magic.'

Luca shook his head. 'There's a world of difference between miracles and magic. So, Stephanie Kate, how many hopeful young men have you left behind in Yorkshire?'

Rosa walked down the hill into town. She felt particularly grumpy. The more Cosima laughed and smiled, the more disgruntled Rosa became. How was it possible to change so suddenly, from a woman in mourning to a woman in love? Surely such a dramatic metamorphosis was only possible if her previous state of misery had been a pretence, a passive-aggressive way of getting attention. Alba had come down heavily on her when she had suggested it, defending her niece with the ferocity of a tiger. In her opinion, Cosima had needed a catalyst to propel her out of her grief. Her failed suicide had shown her how much she wanted to live. Luca had demonstrated that it was possible for her to feel attractive again, and attracted. There was no doubt that Cosima was excited by him, but Rosa couldn't believe, didn't *want* to believe, that he could feel the same way about her.

When she reached the *trattoria*, there he was with his dark glasses, sky-blue shirt and the charisma that surrounded him like a dazzling mist. He was chatting and laughing with a very beautiful young woman she hadn't seen before. Rosa's fury dissipated. If he were in love with Cosima he wouldn't be flirting like that with another woman.

As she came on to the terrace, Luca waved her over. Rosa's heart flipped. She noticed him run his eyes appreciatively over her clingy red top and tight blue jeans, right down to her pretty scarlet toes peeping out of high-heeled sandals.

'How do you walk in those?' he asked.

'Practice,' she replied, putting her hands on her hips, striking a provocative pose. 'My feet aren't made for flat shoes.' She turned to his companion, clearly expecting to be introduced.

'Meet my old friend, Stephanie. She's from England.'

Rosa smiled warmly and shook her hand. 'It's good to meet an old friend of Luca's. Luca is now an old friend of mine!' She sat down without waiting for an invitation. 'So, how are you?'

'Good,' said Luca. 'Mother's in overdrive waiting for the *Sunday Times* journalist to show up.'

'Tell him to come down and see me. If he wants to know the truth about Incantellaria and all its murders and scandals, I know all there is to know. I have kept all the press cuttings that relate to my grandmother's murder.'

'Won't your mother murder *you* for divulging the gossip?'

'Not gossip, Luca, fact. It's not a secret. Everyone who was around at the time knows the story. My family tried to keep it secret, but how could they? People talked and journalists wrote it all up. Valentina was my grandmother and I have a right to do whatever I want with what I know. Besides, it was such a long time ago and it's a great story. My mother should relax about it, like my father, and give everyone a good read!'

'The famous Panfilo,' said Stephanie. 'I hope I'm around to meet him.'

'You're not staying long?' Rosa asked, trying to look sorry. 'Shame. My father's a wonderful character. Everyone loves him. I'll come up for the shoot,' she said, turning to Luca. 'I'd like to see the *palazzo*. It's been a long time since I've been up there.'

'The folly's the only thing you'll recognise.'

'The folly.' Rosa's eyes lit up. 'The *Marchese's* secret love-nest. There's something magical about that place.'

Luca thought of Cosima. 'And there, Rosa, I have to agree with you.'

Luca was disappointed that Cosima didn't come to the *trattoria*, but he wasn't surprised. He had promised to be tactful in front of Rosa and meeting at the family restaurant was awkward. They had arranged, instead, to have dinner again that evening. He planned to take her to the folly afterwards. As the days passed and no further evidence of disturbance was to be found, he was certain that the mystery Goldilocks had either decided to sleep somewhere else or been frightened off by their sudden determination to find her.

After lunch at the *palazzo*, Coco and Juno said goodbye to their grandparents who embraced them fondly.

'You'll come again soon, my darlings?' said Romina, her eyes filling with tears. 'I've grown used to your voices ringing out from the swimming pool. I shall miss you both terribly.'

Bill patted their heads as if they were dogs, but his gaze was full of affection. 'When you come back I will have completed my grotto,' he said proudly.

Coco tried to look excited although she didn't know what a grotto was.

'I shall miss Greedy,' said Caradoc, stroking the caterpillar.

'You can't have him!' Juno cried, snatching him away and nuzzling him.

'Divorce is a great sadness,' said Romina, as the girls walked away.

'It's better than the alternative,' said Caradoc. 'Unhappiness, rows, uncertainty. At least this way they are cherished by both parents without having to watch the two people they love most at each other's throats.'

'But I hardly ever see them.'

'You will see more of them, mark my words. Look at your son. When they arrived he didn't know what to do with them. Now he's a doting father. They'll be back.'

Luca climbed into the car with Sammy and waved as he motored down the drive. They chatted for a while, then fell silent. He could tell from their faces that all three were sad to leave. He tried to cheer them up, but soon he too withdrew into his thoughts, surprised how close they had grown in just a week. Sammy turned on the radio and listened to Italian pop songs. He glanced at the girls in the mirror. Italy had done them good. They looked radiant and healthy, their eyes shining, their cheeks rosy. Coco caught him watching her.

'Remember to telephone me every evening before bed, won't you, Coco?' She nodded, her eyes reassuringly responsive.

He turned his attention back to the road again but felt his heart swell with triumph. Their strengthened relationship had opened her up like a spring bud. Even though her eyes still betrayed too much knowledge of the adult world, she smiled with the innocence of a little girl. At the airport, the two girls stepped reluctantly out of the car. Juno took her father's hand, clutching Greedy against her chest. Coco walked beside him, carrying her pink bag with great importance.

'What have you got in there, darling?'

'Lots of things.'

'Like what?'

'Oh, sandwiches that Ventura made us. Biscuits. Pencils and paper. I'm going to draw you a picture on the plane.'

'I'd like that,' he said.

'I'm going to draw you one too!' Juno added, not to be outdone.

'I'm going to draw the *palazzo* with Granny and Grandpa waving goodbye.'

'I'm going to draw you as the naughty crocodile!' Juno giggled. 'With big white teeth and a long scaly tail.'

'Get Mummy to send them out. I'll put them up in my bedroom.'

'Can we come back soon?' Coco asked.

'As soon as you break up for the holidays.'

'You promise?'

'I promise.' He drew her into his arms. 'I'll be waiting for you.'

Chapter 22

Luca waved until the children were out of sight then walked slowly back to the car, a heaviness descending on him like cloud. He had grown accustomed to the sound of their voices, the feel of their small hands in his, their arms winding around his legs, their expectant faces smiling up at him. He fought off a wave of homesickness with thoughts of Cosima. He parked in the city and set about buying her a mobile telephone. This was a suitable distraction and soon his spirits lifted as her gentle expression broke through the cloud like sunshine. On his way back to the car he passed a jewellery shop and went inside.

At the sound of the taxi scrunching to a halt on the gravel outside, Romina swept through the grand entrance of the *palazzo* to greet the journalist. Porci, ignorant of the significance of this monumental event, trotted past her to sniff the tyres. If he were a dog he would have cocked his leg to show supremacy but, as he was only a little pig, he simply grunted and trotted on to roll down the grassy slope beyond.

The journalist did a double take at the sight of him, clad in his white nappy, and leaned closer to the window to get a better look. Romina couldn't contain her impatience. 'Don't be alarmed by Porci. He doesn't bite,' she said, smiling into the car.

'Extraordinary,' said the woman, gathering her enormous black leather handbag and shuffling across the seat. She had a chiselled, pale face with a deep red bob, square-cut like a spade. 'Wow, this is quite a palace!' As she stepped out of the car, Romina's eyes fell on her red fishnet tights, short denim skirt and black leather boots, and she recoiled.

'My dear, you're going to get very hot in those!'

'It was cold in London. I've got lighter clothes in my case.'

'I'm very glad to hear it. I'm Romina, your hostess.' She extended her hand formally.

'Fiyona Pritchett,' Fiyona replied, her scarlet lips curling into a smile. 'Fiyona with a "y".'

'Hello Fiyona with a "y". At last! Well, let's not stand out here dying of thirst.' Fiyona lifted her suitcase. 'No, no! Let the men do some work. I'll tell Ventura to get one of the boys to take it to your room.'

'Is it okay out here?'

'Well, I don't think Porci's going to run off with it!'

Fiyona followed her through the house to the terrace, gazing around her in fascination. 'This really is a stunning place,' she said.

'I know. Aren't we the luckiest people in the whole world? It was nothing but a ruin when we found it. Grass growing in the rooms, ivy climbing up the walls, animals making their homes in the pieces of furniture left behind. It was a terrible mess.'

'Has it been photographed yet?'

'No. Monday.'

'Good. I gather it has a bloody history.'

'A very dark history.'

'I'd like to talk to some of the locals.'

'Do you speak Italian?'

'Yes, that's why they sent me. I read French and Italian at university. Long time ago now, but I practise whenever I can.'

'My son will take you into town. He is the one mingling with the locals.' She raised her eyebrows suggestively. 'Recently divorced, I think he's making up for lost time.'

'He's just quit the City too, hasn't he?'

Romina was surprised. 'You know about Luca?'

'I've done my research.'

Outside, Caradoc, Nanni, Dennis and Ma were engrossed in a game of bridge. Romina introduced them before taking Fiyona to the table to offer her refreshment.

'I have Earl Grey or coffee,' she said.

'Coffee please, strong.'

Romina watched her with a growing sense of disappointment. Fiyona wasn't at all what she had expected. She was tough – clearly from a lower social stratum – and she wasn't pretty, though she was undoubtedly striking; her skin was translucent and her eyes an unlikely shade of green. Romina suspected she wore tinted contact lenses.

'Do you burn easily in the sun?'

'Yes. Can't go into it. I languish in the shade like an orchid.'

'You are very pale.'

'At least I don't have to worry about tanning. There's no point. Anyway, I think Nicole Kidman and Madonna have made it fashionable to be white.'

'You will certainly look younger for longer,' said Romina, determined to be kind.

'Not with my lifestyle. It's an uphill battle. I drink and I smoke and I like to stay up late. I'll always look older than I am.'

'So, how long have you written for the *Sunday Times*?'

'I've been a freelance journalist for twenty years.'

'Gracious, you must have started young!'

'I suppose I did. I get turned on by facts.' She narrowed her eyes. 'I like mysteries.'

'You'll find plenty of those here.'

'Oh, I already know about the *Marchese*, the girl he murdered, Valentina, and her long-suffering *fiancé* Thomas Arbuckle. Sadly, he won't talk. He's in his eighties now, bless! There's only so much you can pester people and I draw the line at harassment.'

'And you know that Valentina's brother murdered the *Marchese*?'

'No, that I didn't know. An act of revenge. That's logical.'

'People don't like to talk about the past. My son and the professor discovered that piece of information by talking to an old man in town.'

'None of this has ever been written anywhere?'

'Folklore.'

'And the people who really know aren't talking?'

'They don't want to dig up the past.'

'But I do. Digging up pasts is what I do best!'

Romina felt her disappointment melt away. After all, she didn't have to *like* the woman. The object was to write an article on the magnificence of the *palazzo* and its incredible transformation at the hands of two brilliantly talented people. The chances were that after she left, they'd never cross paths again.

'The truth is, I'd rather focus my attention on the present. Who lives here now? What happened to the previous owners? How does one build on such grim foundations? Can one ever really escape the past?'

'Please don't tell me that you believe in ghosts?'

Fiyona revealed two long eye-teeth, like a wolf. 'No, but hey, if there are any lurking around, I'd be only too delighted to meet them!'

Luca returned as the bridge game drew to a close with the four players going over the game in a heated post–mortem. Luca went over to introduce himself to the journalist.

'So, you're the famous Luca Chancellor. You're not at all what I expected.'

'Neither are you!'

'You look like a man who's been relaxing in the Italian sun for months.'

'I assume that's a good thing?'

'For someone who isn't intending to go back to the office.'

'I have no intention of doing anything for the moment.'

'Lucky you!'

He sat down and tapped a cigarette out of its packet. 'Have you shown Fiyona around, yet?' he asked his mother.

'She's only just arrived. How were the children?'

'Sad to leave, I think. They adored their stay.'

Romina beamed. 'I'm so pleased. I hope they'll come back soon.' She turned to Fiyona. 'My granddaughters. Delightful little girls. As pretty as my son is handsome.'

Fiyona watched him light up. 'I'm glad I'm not the only smoker.'

'Everyone smokes in Europe. It's only England and America where political correctness has gone crazy,' said Romina. 'Let's all have one, then we can be politically incorrect together.'

When Ventura appeared with a tray of cakes and fresh tea, the bridge players were drawn to the table like hungry dogs.

Nanni pulled out the chair beside Fiyona, catching a glimpse of her red fishnet tights. She glanced up at his beetroot face and grinned.

'Fun, aren't they? Not really appropriate for the Italian countryside, but I was in the city this morning.'

'They're very colourful,' he said, the sweat gathering on his forehead as he recalled the racy paintings of Toulouse-Lautrec. 'It is very hot today, don't you think?'

'I love the heat. As long as I'm not in direct sunlight.'

He noticed her pearly skin and ruby lips. 'You're born into the wrong century. Now brown is considered beautiful.'

She fixed him with her emerald eyes and blew a smoke-ring. 'Beauty's in the eyes of the beholder.'

'*Brava!* You're absolutely right.'

After tea Romina showed Fiyona around the *palazzo*, explaining all the rooms and what she and Bill had done to them. Fiyona was suitably impressed, but seemed more interested in the human story. 'Do you know in which room the murder took place?'

'No, I'm hoping you're going to find out and tell me!'

'I'll do my best. Someone, somewhere knows and I'll find him. I'm good at that. I did a piece recently on Eva Peron. You wouldn't believe the people who crawled out of the woodwork for that story. It was sensational.'

'How do you extract the information?'

'There are many ways. Some just want to tell their story, others are flattered I'm interested. There are those who need to offload and those who have just never been asked. Half the battle is finding the right people, the ones that history has swallowed with no trace, those who were right there during world historic events, of whom there are no records. Men without trace. Those are the ones I'm interested in.'

After the house they went to the folly. 'If you're interested in the history, this will enchant you,' Romina said proudly. 'Though I cannot boast any artistic input at all. I left it as I found it.' She turned the key and pushed open the door. Dennis had reported no evidence of ghosts or ghouls but she swept her eyes swiftly over the bed all the same. It was a great relief to find it as smooth as if she had made it herself.

Fiyona took in every detail with her acute powers of observation. 'This was built for Valentina?' she asked, lightly touching the silver brush and crystal pot of face cream in front of the Queen Anne mirror on the dressing-table. 'She was playing a dangerous game. As she sat here brushing her hair, I can't imagine she ever thought she'd be murdered by her lover. It's a room dedicated to sensual pleasure. Can you feel it?'

Romina looked uncomfortable. 'I'm not sure,' she said, running her hand down the silk curtains of the four-poster bed.

'That's what it is. The magic one feels in here is sex.' Fiyona grew more animated. 'I love it!'

'I should probably have changed it. What am I going to do with a house dedicated to the perverse desires of an old marquis?'

'No, you must leave it as it is. It's a museum. Don't touch a thing.'

Romina thought of telling her about the intruder, but the folly had remained untouched for some days now. There was every chance the trespasser had gone.

That night Luca took the key to the folly and met Cosima outside the church as arranged. She still felt superstitious about their relationship; that it would only survive if she lit daily candles to Francesco to reassure him that her love would never diminish. Her happiness was an uneasy condition, anchored so firmly in grief. Only when she was in Luca's arms could she let herself go. When they made love she stole her pleasure like a thief unworthy of such riches. When they were apart she nurtured her joy like a precious diamond, afraid of letting it show, as if it might shine through the darkness to give her away. Even though the darkness was comfortable, and it was what she felt she deserved, she was so tempted by the light.

It was a relief to see Luca standing in the shade of a plane tree, hands in pockets, patiently waiting for her. She ran up and threw her arms around his neck, allowing his strength to envelop her.

'Are you okay?'

'I'm fine. I'm just pleased to see you.'

'Where are we going?'

'Up the coast?'

'Wherever you want.'

'Somewhere we can be private.' Remembering where she was and the danger of being seen, she moved away and folded her arms. 'Where's your car?'

They drove up the coast, holding hands over the gear stick, the warm wind blowing in through the open windows and across their faces. They found a little restaurant in a small medieval town Cosima had never been to. It was picturesque with whitewashed houses with pink-tiled roofs and a small church with a pretty bell tower rising into the magenta sky. They sat under the awning on straw chairs, a candle lamp flickering in the centre of the table surrounded by a ring of scarlet flowers. They drank crisp white wine and held hands across the table. After they had eaten, Luca pulled a velvet pouch from his jacket pocket and handed it to her. 'I couldn't resist,' he explained. 'I was in Naples today and saw these in the window. I know we've only known each other a short time, but I want you to know how serious I am about you. I've played with the hearts of many women, but you're different. You're breaking through to a part of my heart I never knew was there. So, this is for you. Because you're different.'

She blinked back tears. 'I don't deserve you. I feel guilty for being so happy.'

'Don't feel guilty, my darling. Go on, open it.'

Tentatively, she loosened the little rope and peered inside. The present glittered through the darkness. He had bought her *real* jewellery. She opened her hand and poured the contents into her palm. When she saw the size of the diamonds she let out a gasp. She stared at the drop earrings as if they were stolen goods. 'You bought these for me? They're stunning.'

'They're antique. Put them on.'

With trembling fingers she took off her usual gold studs and replaced them with the new diamond earrings. The stones shone out against her milk chocolate skin, accentuating her white teeth and the clear whites of her eyes. The pear-shaped drops dangled as she moved her head.

'Put your hair up,' he said, longing to run his lips over the soft skin of her neck. She pulled a band off her wrist and swiftly tied her hair into a high pony-tail. 'Now they look spectacular.' Unable to contain her excitement she rushed around the table to embrace him.

'I have to see them on. I'll go and look in the bathroom mirror. Back in a second!'

Luca lit a cigarette and smiled with satisfaction. Giving had never afforded him such pleasure.

When she came back she walked slowly, the curve of her waist and hips emphasised by her clingy cotton dress. She leaned across the table, her eyes full of lust. 'Let's go to the folly and make love,' she breathed, her voice low and husky.

Luca needed no encouragement. He paid the bill and they left, running to the car like a pair of teenagers. Before he let her inside, he pressed her against the door and kissed her, running his lips over her neck and behind her ear where her new diamonds sparkled. He could feel the heat of her body and the rise and fall of her breasts. The smell of lemons, warm on her damp skin, was invitingly tangy. The drive to the *palazzo* only increased their ardour. Luca parked the car a little distance away from the front door and they crept through the trees. The moon lit up the sky like a Chinese lantern, illuminating their way through the damp undergrowth until they reached the folly. Luca was too hot with desire to care about the intruder. He lit a candle while Cosima pulled back the silk bedspread, unzipped her dress and dropped her panties to the floor. She was naked but for her diamond earrings and the lust that glinted in her eyes. He took off his jacket but before he had time to undress further, she moved towards him and unbuttoned his shirt, slipping it over his shoulders. Then she buried her face in his chest, kissing every inch of skin. The tension grew thick in the air with the scent of candle wax and lemons as they took their pleasure in that small folly designed for love.

Suddenly they were alerted to the sound of movement outside. Then, the rattling noise of a key in the lock, unsuccessfully attempting to turn against Luca's key. Then the shuffling of footsteps. Luca and Cosima froze. They lay entwined on the bed, barely daring to breathe. They sensed the person circling the folly, spying perhaps through the windows.

'Can he see us?' Cosima whispered.

'I hope not.' Were he dressed, Luca would have flung open the door to confront the intruder, man or woman. His nakedness rendered that idea farcical. By the time he struggled into his clothes the *voyeur* would be gone.

'What do we do?' she hissed.

'Nothing. We remain very still.' She made to speak again but he silenced her with a finger across her lips. 'Shhh, my darling. Nothing's going to ruin our night.'

Chapter 23

The following morning, as Luca had not come downstairs, Romina took Fiyona to the *trattoria* in the hope of finding Rosa. If anyone could help with her research it was sweet, garrulous Rosa.

It was a cloudy day. A grey front was approaching from the east, threatening rain. Fiyona had changed out of her red fishnet tights and skirt into a pair of jeans, pink flipflops and a denim jacket over a white T-shirt, her large handbag hanging over her shoulder like a penance. Romina's nostrils flared at the musky spice of her perfume. She looked like she could benefit from a thorough scrub. *Molto Inglese*, Romina thought. What was it about that type of English girl? She always looked grubby.

They found Rosa sitting outside chatting to Fiero. When she saw Romina, Rosa smiled and waved. '*Buon giorno*,' she said.

'*Buon giorno*, Rosa. I have someone to see you.' Romina ushered Fiyona forward.

'My name is Fiyona Pritchett, I'm a journalist for the *Sunday Times* magazine,' she said in fluent Italian.

Rosa was impressed. 'You speak very well!'

'I do my best,' Fiyona replied modestly. 'I like to practise. The only opportunity I get in London is with waiters.' She looked at Fiero and the young man's eyes lit up, responding enthusiastically to an unspoken message.

'Coffee, *signorina*?' he asked, grinning back at her.

'Black, please.'

'I'll have one too, Fiero,' said Rosa. Fiero turned on his heels and disappeared inside.

'So, you're writing the article about the *palazzo*?' said Rosa. 'Shall we sit down? Breakfast is on the house,' she added grandly. 'I know all there is to know about that place. My mother is Alba, Valentina's daughter. Just ask away. It's my favourite subject.'

'I'll leave you to it,' said Romina, looking at her watch. 'I have things to do at home. So many people, you know . . .'

'Give us an hour, if that's okay with Rosa,' Fiyona suggested.

'You can have all morning,' Rosa replied. 'It'll be quiet today and Fiero is here to help.' For a moment her face turned moody. 'I can't imagine Cosima will show up. She got home at four this morning and she's still in bed! Such a sudden transformation. She deserves an Oscar for that sort of performance!'

Romina narrowed her eyes. She had heard the car and her son's merry whistling some time after that. So that's who was keeping her son up to that ungodly hour of the morning.

'So, will your mother talk to me?' Fiyona put the tape recorder on the table and switched it on.

'No, she won't even go up to the *palazzo*. She's furious that it's been developed. I think she feels it should have been left to rot. She'll hate me talking to you but she forgets that Valentina was my grandmother. I'm very like her, you know.'

'There are no photographs of her . . .' Fiyona began.

'But there is a portrait. Wait, I'll get it for you.'

As Rosa rushed off to get the picture, Fiero returned with Fiyona's coffee. 'Would you like anything else?' he asked.

'I'd like you to talk to me. It's important that I practise my Italian,' she replied with a flirtatious smile. She placed a cigarette between her red lips. Fiero was quick to snap open his lighter. She leaned forward, steadying his hand with her own. 'You're very young, Fiero.'

'Twenty-five,' he replied, disarmed by her predatory expression. She looked him up and down.

'Italian men are more sophisticated than their British counterparts. Are you a good lover?'

Fiero ran his tongue over his bottom lip. 'You know how we Italians are. We live for making love. We live for women.'

'Shame I'm only here for such a short time, otherwise we could strike a deal. I'd teach you English if you'd teach me Italian. Get my drift?' He nodded, his nostrils flaring. 'Another time, perhaps.' Rosa returned with the picture of the reclining nude that hung inside, oblivious of the lascivious gleam in Fiero's eyes. She handed it to Fiyona. 'No one notices it now. But that is Valentina, painted by my grandfather.'

Fiyona read the handwriting beneath it: '*Valentina, reclining nude, Thomas Arbuckle, 1945.*'

'Isn't she beautiful?'

'Beguiling,' said Fiyona. 'Naughty smile. I can see the resemblance,' she added, grinning at Rosa.

Rosa was pleased. 'I'm not that naughty. Sadly, I don't have the opportunity.'

'You're married?'

'Yes. Three children. Very conventional!'

'Valentina might not have been so naughty had it not been wartime. She took lovers to survive.'

'I don't think she took up with Lupo Bianco to survive. For her he was a ticket to the high life in Naples. With him she could be someone different.'

'Simple village girl found in diamonds and furs,' said Fiyona, recalling the newspaper coverage of the murder. 'Terrible shock for your poor grandfather.'

'They were due to marry that day. So romantic, to be swept off your feet by a handsome foreigner! You know, they say that the statue of Christ didn't weep for the first time in years, predicting the tragedy.'

'You believe that?'

'Not really. They say it'll only weep again when all the ghosts are at peace.'

'They still think the old *Marchese* haunts the *palazzo?*'

Rosa turned serious. 'There *was* something strange going on. My husband is a policeman. Before Romina bought it there were dozens of sightings. Lights moving through rooms, strange noises. No one dared go up but him. He is extremely brave.'

'Did he find anything?'

She shrugged. 'Nothing. I have been up many times. It doesn't scare me. There was something beautiful about the ruin. It's not the same now.'

'I don't suppose you've come face to face with the ghost?' said Fiyona, exhaling a ribbon of smoke.

'I don't believe in ghosts,' Rosa laughed dismissively. 'But I wouldn't rule out a living ghost sneaking about trying to scare people. Romina complains of someone haunting the folly. She told my husband that someone sleeps in there and dragged him up to take a look.'

'She's eccentric but she doesn't strike me as superstitious,' said Fiyona.

'She's *northern* Italian. There's a big difference. People down here are very primitive.'

'So you don't believe the *Marchese*'s hanging around, repenting killing the woman he loved?'

'*Of course not*! Someone's just having some fun. Or the people of Incantellaria made it all up to stop anyone buying the *palazzo* and turning it into a hotel. They like their peace and they're rather proud of their history. They wanted to keep the place as it was, as a kind of morbid shrine. But they failed miserably.'

'Can I quote you on that?'

'You can quote me on anything you like. You can include a photograph too. After all, I'm the image of Valentina.'

'I can't use the drawing?'

'Absolutely not!' Rosa gasped, snatching it back. 'Only if you want another murder in Incantellaria!'

'Is it true that your great-uncle killed the *Marchese* for revenge?'

'Right there in the *palazzo*.'

'Do you know where?'

'In a leather chair in his sitting-room.' She drew a line slowly across her neck. 'They killed him like a pig.'

'They?'

Rosa flinched as if stung. 'I mean *him*,' she corrected, blushing. 'Falco.'

Fiyona chewed thoughtfully on her cheek. 'I see.'

'The police never properly investigated Valentina's murder. They assumed she was in the wrong place at the wrong time, caught in the middle of *mafia* crossfire. They never imagined that it was Lupo in the wrong place at the wrong time, that the *Marchese* killed Valentina and he just got in the way.' She leaned forward conspiratorially. 'In fact, he killed her because he didn't want my grandfather to take her away to England. If he couldn't have her he didn't want anyone else to have her. I think the *Marchese* was a shrewd old thing. I bet he knew she took other lovers and I don't imagine he minded. I remember my mother telling me that he collected beautiful things. He was an aesthete. Valentina was simply another one of his beautiful possessions. But when she fell in love with my grandfather, I mean, *really* in love, he couldn't take it. So he cut off his nose to spite his face and murdered the thing he loved so that no one else could have her. I'm surprised no one's made the film.'

'Maybe they will when they read my article. We have a two million circulation.'

Rosa's eyes widened. 'You mean two million people will read about me?'

Fiyona pandered to her vanity. 'Two million people will read about you and your family.'

'*Madonna!* Imagine that. I can act, you know. I'm a very good actress.'

'I don't doubt it,' Fiyona said truthfully.

Rosa looked wistful. 'I wish some handsome foreigner would drape me in diamonds and sweep me off somewhere else.'

'You don't like it here?'

'Nothing happens. I can see why Valentina walked on the dark side. War or no war, she had to make her own excitement.'

At twenty minutes past eleven Romina arrived to pick up Fiyona. They were still talking. Fiero hovered close, like a moth at Fiyona's flame.

'Haven't you two finished yet?' she asked.

'We're done,' said Fiyona, switching off her tape recorder. 'Thank you, Rosa, you've been very interesting.' She waved at Fiero. 'I'll see you later.'

Rosa looked affronted. 'You want to interview Fiero?'

'I want to talk to everyone. I don't like to leave any stone unturned.'

'He doesn't know anything.'

Fiyona shook her head shrewdly. 'Everyone knows something.' She winked at Fiero. 'I'll see you this evening.'

Back in the car, Romina asked if she had got what she needed. 'And some,' she replied happily. 'Valentina's star still shines brightly.'

'The naivety of youth. Rosa doesn't see the sordidness of the story, just the glamour.'

'It'll make great copy.'

'You should talk to her mother.'

'Apparently Alba won't speak.'

'Shame. I'm sure she knows a whole other dimension.'

'Rosa implied that more than one person killed the *Marchese.*'

'I thought it was just Falco.'

'Could have been a slip of the tongue.'

Romina shrugged. 'I'll ask my son. I think he's closer to that family than I previously thought.'

'It's important for the article. I like to get my facts right.'

'Leave it to me.'

That afternoon, when Rosa returned home, Cosima was still in her bedroom. She had been waiting all morning to talk to her, and couldn't wait another minute. As she reached the top of the stairs she could hear her cousin humming. She didn't bother to knock, but turned the handle and walked inside.

Cosima was sitting at her dressing-table, gazing at her reflection in the mirror. Dangling from her ears were the most magnificent diamonds. Rosa gasped, envy and fury rising in an uncontrollable swell.

'You should have knocked!' Cosima exclaimed, placing her hands over her ears in an attempt to hide the diamonds.

'I've already seen them, you fool! Don't think I don't know about you and Luca. I saw you together. So, he's given you diamonds!'

'Yes.' Cosima braced herself.

'I'm happy for you,' said Rosa briskly.

'You are?'

'Why wouldn't I be? I don't fancy Luca. Sure, I enjoy flirting with him, but I'm married.'

'I'm sorry now that I didn't tell you.'

'Why should you? I don't feel obliged to tell you everything.'

Cosima couldn't fail to notice the strain in her cousin's voice. Rosa's deliberate calm was more than a little disconcerting. Any moment she expected an object to come flying at her head.

'He gave them to me last night,' she confessed.

'Can I see?' Rosa sat on the bed. Cosima hesitated a moment before taking the earrings off and handing them to her. She stood up to let her cousin take her place in front of the mirror. Rosa was quick to push the little sticks through her ear lobes and stared at her reflection with childish pleasure. 'I've never seen anything more beautiful,' she whispered. 'They must have cost a fortune. As much as a house. He's obviously a millionaire. Trust you to find a rich man.'

'I never set out to find a man at all,' said Cosima uneasily.

'I should have been a little more cunning, but I was young and innocent when I married Eugenio. I had no understanding of life. Not like you, with all the wisdom of middle age.' She sighed. 'Lovely, but where are you going to wear them? Is he going to take you off to Naples?'

'No! I'll wear them just for him.'

'Maybe he'll sweep you off to London.'

Cosima was horrified. 'I'll never leave Incantellaria.'

'Why not? I'd give anything to leave this sleepy little place.'

'I can't!' Cosima's voice cracked.

'Why ever not?'

'Because I'll never leave Francesco.'

Luca spent the morning in bed. Outside the sky was grey; it looked like rain but there was sunshine in his heart. He couldn't believe his luck, how suddenly his life had turned around, how one woman in a magical little town could transform him. He had left London feeling lost and empty, having walked away from his life of twenty years. He didn't know what he was going to do; he was floating aimlessly like a piece of driftwood on the sea. Now his life was gaining purpose: loving Cosima and loving his children. That's what had been missing all along: love. Not the selfish love he had initially felt for Claire and the distant idea of love he had felt for his daughters, but the love that puts itself above one's own desires: loving another more than oneself. The realisation filled him with energy. Too excited to lie in bed he took a towel down to the little bay for a swim.

'He's in love,' said Ma, enjoying a pre-lunch Bloody Mary.

'And it's not with my girl,' added Caradoc happily. 'My money's on the widow.'

'The one who lost her little boy?'

'Yes. I never thought he'd crack her,' said Ma.

'Luca's very handsome and sweet,' said Stephanie. 'I'm not at all surprised. The waitress at the *trattoria*'s mad for him.'

Caradoc's eyes lit up. 'That's my girl! She's mad for me too!'

'Pipe dreams,' Ma scoffed. 'You're a silly old man!'

'One is never too old to dream,' protested Nanni, wondering where that naughty little journalist had got to.

'I hope he marries her and gives her another child,' said Stephanie wistfully.

Her father patted her knee. 'Ever the romantic, Stephanoula!'

'Bad blood,' said Ma darkly. 'I wouldn't go near that family if I were him. Imagine, Cosima's grandfather committed murder right here in this *palazzo*. The *Marchese* was slaughtered like an animal! Her great-aunt was murdered on the road to Naples having taken lovers and betrayed all of them. I'd think very carefully before dipping my snout into that trough!'

Caradoc shook his head. 'We all have family we're not proud of. But an individual shouldn't be judged on the errors of his ancestors.'

'Mark my words, Professor. You heard it here first. Nothing good will come out of that relationship.'

When Luca came up from the beach, his face red with exertion, his hair standing up in wet tufts, Ma put down her glass, determined to be the first to interrogate him. 'Now, Luca. We've been laying bets on you,' she shouted across the terrace.

He shot her a quizzical look. 'Laying bets on what exactly?'

'Who's luring you into town all the time? It's not just the coffee,' said Ma. He grinned at them all, a schoolboy on the point of announcing he'd won a prize.

'Ah, that smile says it all,' commented Caradoc. 'The cat that's got the cream!'

'You're in love. The question is, with whom?' said Ma.

'Don't tell her,' laughed Nanni, smoking languidly. 'A gentleman has no memory.'

'It's the widow,' said Caradoc. 'I'm right, am I not?'

Luca sat down. 'Am I that transparent?'

'Happiness is infectious. Your happiness is tickling us too,' said Caradoc.

'Or making us very envious,' Ma added dryly.

He looked helplessly at Stephanie. 'What do I do?'

'Are you appealing to me for help?'

'You're a young woman. Would you want your love life discussed by this group of eccentrics?'

'If they said positive things, I don't see why not.'

'Very well,' he replied. 'I am in love. I want to shout it to the skies, but she wants to keep it quiet.'

Ma narrowed her eyes. 'Then I should be very worried if I were you.'

'Worried? Why?'

'What does she have to hide? Is she already married?'

'She's definitely not married,' said Luca.

'The widow!' Caradoc clapped his arthritic old hands gleefully. 'I knew it.'

At that moment Romina and Fiyona arrived back from town. Nanni straightened at the sight of the redhead. He was sorry to see that she wasn't wearing fishnet stockings, but jeans. He felt himself grow hot, but the heat was strangely pleasurable. He took a gulp of Martini and leered at her.

Fiyona was as alert as a fox. She settled her long green eyes on him and licked her lips provocatively. 'So, Nanni, do you fancy a little promenade before lunch? I'd love to dip my toes in the sea.'

As Fiyona disappeared inside to change, Ventura emerged with the telephone. '*Signor* Luca.'

He took the handset, expecting it to be Claire. To his surprise it was Freya. 'Hi sweetheart, this is a nice surprise!'

'How are you?' She sounded tense.

'Well. Heaven here. When are you coming?'

'Perhaps sooner than you think.'

'Oh?'

'Do you remember last time we met, you thanked me for being there when you needed me?'

'Of course. That's what friends are for. You're not in trouble, are you?'

'Yes. Now it's I who need you.'

He felt his head spin. 'You do? What's going on?'

'Miles is having an affair.'

Luca wanted to laugh at the preposterous idea, but she sounded so upset, he maintained his composure. 'Are you sure?'

'I'm certain, Luca. What do I do?'

Now wasn't the time to tell Freya he was in love with Cosima. 'You come out here, now.'

'But what about the children?'

'They'll be fine with the nanny for a few days. Tell Miles you're giving him time to end it. He'll deny it, of course. But if you're sure, then you leave him once and once only. The second time, you don't go back.'

Chapter 24

Fiyona took off her flip-flops and dipped a foot into the water. Nanni noticed her toenails were painted black and he felt a frisson of excitement stir his sluggish loins. He was wheezing after their walk to the secluded beach, but concentrated on appearing as if it had cost him as little effort as it did her. 'I have a weakness for foreign men,' she said bluntly, lifting her sarong up her thighs as she walked a little further out to sea. 'I don't know whether it's the language, or just the fact that foreign men are different. Italian men make good lovers. There's poetry in the way they move, even if they're overweight and lazy, and they take pleasure from giving pleasure. I like that. Men on the whole are very selfish. It's all about getting their cocks in as quickly as possible.' Nanni wiped his brow with a hanky. She looked at him sweating on the pebbles. 'Why don't you come in?'

'I'm very much a land animal,' he replied, gazing longingly at the cool water but not wishing to take off his clothes in front of her.

'Can you swim?'

'Of course. But I'm a large man. I'd sink like the *Titanic*.'

'Then take off your shoes and come in. You look like you're about to explode!'

Affronted by her remark, he slipped off his shoes and socks, rolled up his trousers to reveal white calves, and stepped into the sea. He gave a nervous cry as he felt the cold water.

'There, bet that feels better!' she encouraged.

'It's accelerated my heartbeat. If I suffer a heart attack, I'll blame you.'

'If you suffer a heart attack, you won't be around to cast blame.' She walked over to him, then held her hands in the water until they were cool and placed them on his burning cheeks. He recoiled. 'Come now, doesn't that feel nice?'

'Just a little unexpected.'

'The best things in life are unexpected. I once died, you know. Yes, sounds odd, but I did. I died and came back. They said I should have been brain-damaged from having not breathed for so long, but I wasn't. A miracle perhaps. The point is, I now take life by the groin.' She placed her hand on his flies. 'If I fancy someone, I bed him. I'm not saving myself for Mr Right. There's much too much fun in looking for him. Don't pretend you don't fancy me. It's all in the eyes. I'm only here for the weekend and I intend to make the most of it. You're an intelligent man, and I adore clever men.'

Nanni was reminded of a red-haired girl he had fallen in love with at school. She had been just as precocious, taking him by the collar of his shirt and kissing him behind the fountain after mass so she could add another tick to her chart of conquests.

Fiyona widened her hypnotic green eyes. 'Do we have time for a little play before lunch?'

Luca sat with his mother in the drawing-room. 'I need to talk to you,' he said. 'It's Freya. She suspects Miles of having an affair and I think she should come out here right away, don't you?'

'Of course. Right away!'

'Miles needs a kick up the backside. He doesn't know how lucky he is to have Freya.'

'You always had a soft spot for her.'

'I still do, that's why I want to help.'

'Why doesn't she come out with her mother? A girl always needs her mother when the shit hits the fan.' Romina was already three steps ahead, calculating the chances of her son settling down with Freya. 'Yes, that's what I'll do. I'll telephone Rosemary right away and invite them.'

'That might be setting the cat among the pigeons,' said Luca, thinking of Fitz and Alba finding each other again after thirty years.

Romina frowned. 'I don't understand.'

'Don't worry, sometimes a few ruffled feathers is a good thing. I'll certainly derive a great deal of pleasure from it.'

Romina looked baffled.

Before she had the chance to enquire further, Bill strode through the French doors.

'Ah, there you are, darling.' He held out a little gold stud earring. 'I found this in the folly. A vital piece of evidence, I think.'

Luca recognised it at once as Cosima's and caught his breath.

'Well, we know now that the intruder is most certainly a woman,' Romina said, studying it closely.

'Unless it's a nose-ring,' Luca added, making light of it. 'Let's see?'

'Pity, we can't run a DNA test.'

'It's so small, it might have been there for years,' said Luca.

Bill shook his head. 'I doubt it. It was on the rug beside the bed. Definitely dropped there recently.'

'Then we have to find someone wearing only one earring,' said Romina. 'I'll leave you to it, Sherlock!'

'Seriously, Luca, you have to find her. Why aren't you camping in the folly yourself?'

'I thought you didn't want anyone sleeping in there.'

'Well, I've changed my mind. Where were you last night?'

'Out with a friend.'

'A girlfriend?'

'Yes.'

'Cosima?'

'How did you guess?'

'Rosa said her cousin got home at four in the morning. You came home shortly after that. It doesn't take a great mind to make the connection.'

'So Rosa's put two and two together as well?'

'Undoubtedly.'

'I'd better call Cosima.'

'Before you go, darling. Can you do something for me?'

'Sure.'

'It's about the *Sunday Times* piece. Rosa suggested to Fiyona that *two* men killed the *Marchese*. As far as anyone knows, it was just Valentina's brother, Falco. Wouldn't it be fun to discover that he had an accomplice? That would really give the article some spice!'

'Rosa will say anything! She's so melodramatic.'

'Cosima will know. Now you're intimate with her, you can find out. And darling, hurry up and catch the intruder. You're as frustrating as the police! I'm getting sick with impatience and worry. It's my folly. My pride and joy, and I don't dare go near it!'

Luca didn't say anything. He had no intention of doing either.

As Luca picked up his telephone, it rang. 'Cosima, I was just about to call you!' he said. 'How are you this morning?'

'Rosa knows. She knows about you and she knows about the diamonds.'

'Slow down, Cosi. There's nothing to worry about. You sound like she's caught you robbing a bank!'

'I though she was going to explode!'

'Look, my love, she's married, you're not. We're two single people who have found each other. There's nothing wrong with that. If Rosa's a little jealous, it's her problem.'

'I think she was up at the folly last night.'

'You do?'

'She said she already knew we were together because she saw us.'

'So, now we've found the intruder,' he said cheerfully.

'Intruder?'

'Long story. I'll tell you over dinner.'

'I can't imagine what she does up there in the middle of the night.'

'She's obsessed with Valentina. She thinks she *is* Valentina,' Luca replied. 'Maybe she lies there and dreams of the adventures she'll never live.'

'She's jealous because she sees the parallels between me and Valentina. Falling in love with an Englishman, being given beautiful diamonds.'

'Let's hope we enjoy a happier ending,' said Luca wryly. 'By the way, my father found your earring on the carpet.'

'Ah, I wondered where it went.'

'Well, don't wear the other one or my mother will notice and string you up. I'll come to the *trattoria* for lunch. Now our relationship is in the open I can shout about it. I want to show you off, Cosi!' She made to interrupt him with protests.

'I'm coming whether you like it or not. I'm glad we're no longer a secret. We're both too old to play these childish games.'

'Perhaps,' Cosima interrupted. 'But Rosa is not.'

Nanni and Fiyona came back from their walk looking flushed. Romina took one look at her brother and saw that his inertia had been whipped away to reveal a more confident man. She dropped her gaze to Fiyona. There was nothing new about the slouchy way she held herself or about her general grubbiness, but she seemed quite pleased with herself.

'*Madonna!*' Romina muttered under her breath. 'The girl's a tart!'

'That was lovely,' said Fiyona, flopping into a chair. 'Nothing beats the sea.'

'How was it for you?' Romina asked her brother.

He glanced at her guiltily. 'Good. I'm going to change for lunch. It is too hot for a man of my size.'

'Didn't the sea cool you down?' she enquired sarcastically.

'One would have thought so. But no, the climb up has made me hot again.'

He disappeared before she could interrogate him further. Once in his bedroom he permitted himself a broad, uninhibited smile. The last time he had had sex, over twenty years ago, had been a humiliating disaster. He still cringed. He wished the girl concerned dead so that the knowledge of his embarrassment had died with her. Since then he had avoided sex at all costs. But Fiyona had stirred something buried, and Lazarus had risen. He couldn't put his finger on what it was about her that attracted him. Her casual regard for sex, perhaps, and her no-fuss approach. She had wanted him and taken him without asking; and he had satisfied her. He barely recognised the man staring back at him from the mirror. As he undressed, he dared to wonder whether she'd be willing to do it again.

Luca drove into town and parked the car in the square. As he got out he spotted Francesco playing around a group of old widows sitting on a bench beneath a palm tree. He was blowing in their faces and laughing when they looked around in confusion. Luca shook his head at the boy's mischievous antics. His mother's happiness had clearly made him happy too, for his smile was broad and carefree. The boy sensed his presence and stopped blowing to look at him, then pointed to the church.

Luca walked through the big doors. The air was thick with incense, the candles twinkling through the gloom like small stars. When he couldn't see Cosima he wandered around, looking in the little chapels built out to the sides of the main church where tea lights flickered on glittering altars of their own. It was only when he reached the nave that he saw her, at the back of the church adjacent to the altar, deep in discussion with the priest. They were sitting whispering, their heads together. Luca watched them for a while, not wanting to interrupt. He thought he caught the words London and England.

When she saw him, Cosima looked startled, said something to the priest then stood up. 'Luca, can I introduce you to Father Felippo?' She beckoned him over.

Father Felippo got to his feet and sandwiched Luca's hand between his. 'It is a pleasure to meet you, Luca,' he said kindly. 'Cosima has told me a lot about you.'

Luca didn't know how to talk to a priest. 'You have a beautiful church.' It was a lame remark.

'Thank you. We like it, don't we, Cosima?'

'It's a place of great comfort and tranquillity,' she replied, smiling at Luca.

'I didn't want to interrupt,' he explained.

'That's all right, we've finished.' Father Felippo turned to Cosima. 'You'll be okay?'

She nodded. 'Thank you. Come, Luca, let's go and have lunch.'

'How did you know I was here?' she asked as they walked back down the aisle.

'Francesco showed me.'

'Francesco?'

'Yes, he was scaring a trio of old ladies by blowing in their faces. He pointed in here.' Luca shrugged. 'He's proving quite useful.'

Cosima wanted to believe more than anything in the world but, while she couldn't see Francesco herself, there remained a grain of doubt. 'I wish I could hold him,' she said softly.

'He's a spirit, Cosi. Not until you join him will you be able to hold him.'

They walked across the square in silence. Francesco had gone. The old ladies continued to gossip as if nothing had happened.

'I want to believe you, I really do. But are you telling me what I want to hear to make me happy? Is this all a trick to make me fall in love with you?'

He was shocked that she could doubt him. 'What have you and Father Felippo been talking about?'

'Nothing!' Tears welled in her eyes. 'But why is it only you who can see him? Why can't I?'

Luca held her upper arms. 'I don't know, Cosi. Please don't doubt me like this. I wish I could prove it to you, but I can't.'

'Maybe Francesco could tell you something that only he and I know?'

'He doesn't tell me anything at all. He's a little boy. He's probably as confused as we are. Most likely it hasn't even occurred to him. All he wants is to be close to you.'

'And I want to be close to him.' She looked around. 'Where is he now?'

'I can't see him.'

'You can't see him? Why not? Why do you only see him when I'm not with you? If you really can see him, then get him here now and talk to him!'

Luca looked pained. 'I can't,' he admitted. 'This is all new to me, you know. I don't know how it works either.'

Then he had a crazy idea. 'Come!' he instructed, taking her by the hand and dragging her across the square towards the old women. 'We'll ask them.'

'They'll think you're mad.'

'They can think what they like.'

The three women stopped talking and stared at them. Cosima winced with embarrassment while Luca introduced himself confidently. 'Good afternoon, ladies,' he said, bowing slightly. 'My name is Luca Chancellor. I'm sorry to interrupt such a tranquil scene, and my question is more than a little strange.' The three widows gazed up at him as if he were an alien. 'Tell me, a little while ago did you all feel as if someone was blowing into your faces? I know it sounds odd, but it's really important.' The smallest began to chew on her gums while the fat one muttered something inaudible.

The third grinned, revealing a set of small yellow teeth. 'So it was you!' she chuckled. 'If you weren't so handsome I'd knock you down with my handbag!'

The smallest leaned forward to take a better look. 'Was it you blowing on our faces? It's very rude, you know.'

'Promise you, it wasn't me,' he said, backing away. 'It was a spirit, but my friend here doesn't believe me.'

'A spirit?' they cried in unison, turning to each other in a flurry of excitement.

'So, believe me now?' said Luca.

'I have to,' she conceded.

He gazed steadily into her eyes. 'I wouldn't lie to you, Cosi. I promise I'll never lie to you.' They continued down to the quay in silence. As they neared the *trattoria*, he felt her stiffen at the sight of Rosa on the terrace. She was leaning over a table of young men in her red dress, her cleavage in full view.

They reached the terrace and Luca didn't let go of her hand. Rosa looked up and registered their hands held tightly and the closeness of their bodies as they walked. But she forced a smile and tried to make light of her feelings. 'Look at you two!' she exclaimed. 'If I wasn't married I'd be jealous.'

'Why don't you join us for lunch?'

She pulled a face. 'As if! Can't you see I'm working? No, you have lunch together. After all, you have to get to know each other!' She pointed to a table in the corner. 'It's quiet there. No one can eavesdrop.'

'Thank you, Rosa,' said Cosima sincerely.

'Look, I'm taking all the credit for getting you two together. If it wasn't for me you would still be moping around like an old lady.' She pointed a red nail at Luca. 'And you would still be mulling over your divorce. I'm happy for you and for me, because this good deed of mine might have erased some of the bad I've done in my past and gain me access to Heaven.

Now sit down and eat. Alfonso has made the most exquisite lobster.'

She went into the kitchen and sat down at the little wooden table. 'Romano, bring me a glass of wine, will you?'

'Are you all right, Rosa?' Alfonso asked. She had suddenly gone pale.

'I'm fine.' Romano brought her a glass and poured the wine. She swallowed a big gulp. 'That's better.' She shook her head in despair. 'Some people have all the luck!'

After dinner Fiyona took a taxi into town, reminding Romina of her appointment with Fiero.

'Now I know why she speaks such good Italian,' said Romina to Ma. 'She sleeps with all the waiters.'

'Your brother will be disappointed,' said Ma. 'She's thrown him into a lather of excitement.'

'Something needed to wake him up. Shame it's a tart.'

'She's an animal.' Ma gave a disapproving snort. 'She'll take anything that moves.'

'Particularly if it doesn't move very fast, like Nanni!'

'Sacrifice him ruthlessly if it guarantees a good article.'

Romina glanced at her brother, alone on the terrace with a glass of whisky. 'I hope he hasn't let us down.'

'Oh, I don't think she's very discerning.'

'I can't see that there's anything sexy about Nanni.'

Ma squinted thoughtfully. 'Oh, I don't know. There's someone for everyone.'

'Even you, Ma?'

Ma grinned ironically. 'I'm far too spiritual to indulge in earthly pleasures.'

'Earthly pleasure is all there is, Ma. Make hay while the sun shines.'

Chapter 25

It was dark. A salty wind swept in off the sea and raked cool fingers through Rosa's hair. She walked up the pebble beach, her eyes stinging with tears. She could hear the distant rumble of a party, the sudden uproar of laughter, the sound of merriment that only served to emphasise most cruelly her own discontent. She sat down, pulled her cardigan around her and gazed out to sea. Stars twinkled like fireflies, the moon shone brightly, lighting up the sea below, dragging her gaze out to the horizon. '*I was meant for better things than this,*' she thought. '*I was not meant for a small town, to live and die in obscurity. Now Cosima's stealing the life I should be leading. She'll go off to London and travel the world. Wear expensive clothes and diamonds.*' In frustration, she picked up a pebble and threw it into the water. It landed with a satisfactory plop.

She became aware of a shadowy figure at the other end of the beach. She stopped throwing stones and strained her eyes to get a better look. A man, she thought. He looked agitated, though she couldn't make out his features. For a moment she wondered whether he was going to wade out into the sea like Cosima. She wasn't about to go in after him and shrank back so he couldn't see her. He paced a small area, back and forth, his feet in the water. Finally, he walked off towards the little path that wound its way up the cliffs to the *palazzo* by way of the folly.

Rosa scrambled to her feet and hurried off in curious pursuit. She knew that path like the back of her hand, every twist and turn, every rise and fall. Taking care not to be seen or heard, she ran stealthily over the stones with the grace of a cat. It seemed that he, too, knew the path well. He didn't hesitate or stumble, but moved smoothly through the darkness.

Rosa followed at a safe distance. Her nerves were alert, ready to leap into the undergrowth should he turn around, but he walked on as if in a trance. It seemed that nothing could distract him from his purpose.

At last he disappeared into the trees. Rosa crept behind a large bush and waited. She heard the scuffle of footsteps around the folly, as if he were looking through the windows to check no one was in there. There was the sound of a key in the lock. She caught her breath, the excitement expanding in her chest. This was her chance to inject her life with a little adventure. After all, Valentina had made her own excitement.

She could see the warm glow of candlelight around the edges of the shutters, slipping into the darkness to expose the trespasser. So, there *was* an intruder after all, and he wasn't a ghost. But who was he and why was he there? Her pulse throbbing in her temples, she put her fingers on the handle and opened the door.

Cosima slept fitfully, her grief as constant a companion as the memory of her dead son. By day, Luca gave her courage and hope, but by night she was flooded with despair – the sense of falling into an abyss. Luca had tossed her a lifeline, but where would he take her? She couldn't leave Francesco. Nothing could take her away from Incantellaria, where all her memories lay imbedded in the soil. She would live there until the day she died, with or without Luca.

As she slipped into a deep sleep, a profound calm released her from the random ramblings of her mind. She was surrounded by whiteness and in that heavenly light she felt the presence of her son. He appeared before her as he had been in life – his eyes wide and smiling, his skin glossy brown, his cheeks the colour of the most perfect sunrise. He burrowed into her body and she wrapped her arms around him. She smelt the milky vanilla of his hair, felt his smooth skin against her lips, the warmth of his body against hers, and for the first time in three years she felt complete.

Finally, Francesco drew away. He looked at her with the loving eyes of a wise old man. 'You have to go back.'

'Don't make me go!'

'You must. It's not your time.'

'But I want to stay with you,' she pleaded.

He smiled as if the idea of them being apart was absurd. 'You know I'm always with you.'

'But I can't see you!'

'Trust, *Mamma*.' He slowly began to fade. 'Trust.'

She reached out to him through the whiteness. 'I love you, Francesco. Don't leave me. I can't live without you. Don't leave me! Please, come back!'

'It's all right, darling. You're having a nightmare.' Alba was leaning over her in her white nightdress. She looked around in panic. Francesco had gone. Alba stroked her head. 'It's okay. You're awake now.'

'I don't want to wake up.' She closed her eyes, willing herself to return to that strange white Heaven.

'It was a dream,' Alba reassured her.

'No. It was real. He was here. I could feel him, smell him. He was real!' She began to cry. Alba turned on the light and Cosima winced. 'Turn it off!' Alba ignored her and sat on the bed.

'It was Francesco in spirit.' Cosima gripped Alba's shoulders and opened her eyes wide. 'Luca said there was nothing in the world that would enable me to hold him. But he underestimated my son. Francesco found a way.'

Alba turned off the light and left Cosima to sleep. The older she got the more convinced she became that the spirit world was ever-present. She remembered the strong sense of Valentina's ghost in that very house when she had arrived all those years ago, and how she had moved on when Immacolata had finally let her go.

She climbed back into bed beside Panfilo, who had slept through his niece's plaintive cries, and lay down. Her mind jumped from thought to thought, willing herself to drift off again. Suddenly she heard the sound of humming outside. It could have been the whistle of the wind, or an owl, but it grew louder as the sound approached the house. Intrigued, she got out of bed and moved over to the window. There, walking with a bounce in her step, was Rosa. Alba was shocked. Her first thought was for Eugenio. If he found his wife weaving her way back home in the early hours of the morning, there'd be the most monumental row. She slipped on her dressing-gown and hurried downstairs, catching Rosa as she crept in through the side door like a burglar. 'Where in God's name have you been?' Alba demanded, hands on hips, her face pale in the moonlight that shone through the kitchen windows.

'For a walk.'

'At this hour of the night?'

'It's my favourite hour.'

'You're drunk.'

'I haven't drunk a drop. I'm just happy!' She smiled secretively.

'What have you to be so happy about when your husband lies alone in bed and your children . . .?'

'They never wake up in the night.'

'There's always a chance they will, and then what? Eugenio will wonder where you are.'

'I walk at night all the time.' She leaned against the side-board and folded her arms. 'I love to walk in the dark, along the cliffs, down on the beach by the sea. It makes me happy, *Mamma*. It gets me out of this claustrophobic house. Allows me to breathe. Tonight was special though. I'm happier than I have ever been. In fact, I never thought I could be so happy.'

Alba's face darkened. 'Who have you been with?'

'No one. Spirits.'

'What are you talking about?'

'I've been with spirits. Ghosts.' She shook her head as if her mother was too stupid to understand. 'Don't worry. I'm being silly. I'm tired now. If you don't mind I'll go to bed.'

'Don't let Eugenio catch you creeping out in the middle of the night.'

'He sleeps like a log.'

'Well, one of these days the log might just wake up and then you'll be in trouble.'

'I know how to deal with my husband. Men are all the same.'

Alba watched her daughter's insouciance with concern. 'The trouble with you, Rosa, is that you don't appreciate what you have.'

'How would you know? You never ask. It's always Cosima, Cosima, Cosima. I can't remember the last time you actually asked me how *I* was. But it doesn't matter.' She walked towards the stairs. 'By the way, Cosima and Luca are lovers.'

'I know.'

'Of course you do. You two are as thick as thieves.' She began to climb the stairs, leaving Alba smouldering with fury.

'Whatever you may think, I'm your mother and this is my house. Try looking past your own nose, Rosa. You always have been selfish!'

Rosa wanted to slam the bathroom door behind her, but she didn't want to wake Eugenio. She put her hands on the basin and inhaled, flaring her nostrils with anger. How dare her mother talk to her like that? She wasn't selfish. She just wanted to be the centre of her mother's world. Surely, as a daughter, that was her right? But Cosima occupied that place and had done ever since Francesco drowned. She stared at her face in the mirror and saw Valentina staring right back at her.

Now the likelihood was that Cosima would move to England with Luca. Well, she was welcome to him. Rosa no longer needed Luca to take her away; tonight, she had discovered that everything she needed was right here in Incantellaria and always had been.

Once again she climbed into bed believing her husband lay sleeping, trusting that he could not have heard her conversation with her mother. Once again Eugenio's heart spilled a little more blood.

The following morning was Sunday. Rosa hummed the entire way through breakfast, a secretive smile on her face, while Cosima ate in silence, clinging on to Francesco with all her senses. Panfilo went to Mass with Toto, Beata, Rosa,

Eugenio, the children and their cousins, leaving Alba at home with Cosima, who had made plans to see Luca.

Panfilo had kissed his wife tenderly, advising her to ignore the row with Rosa.

'Can't imagine where she gets it from,' he had laughed, the lines deepening into his handsome face.

'I've mellowed over the years,' Alba had said, reluctantly smiling back.

'And so will Rosa. She's young and spirited. We'll talk about it later, but perhaps she needs her own home.'

'On a policeman's salary?'

'No, on mine!'

The truth was Alba didn't want Rosa and Eugenio to move out. Whenever it had been mentioned she had thought of every possible excuse to prevent it. She had told them to wait until they had enough money to buy a nice big place. When Panfilo had suggested helping them financially, she had told him his offer would damage Eugenio's pride. Anyway, wasn't it convenient to have a babysitter on tap? Three children was a handful, but with their grandmother around the load became a great deal lighter. It was part of Italian culture for families to live together. That's the way Immacolata had lived and they had followed her example. Secretly, Alba feared the place would be lonely without them, especially with Panfilo away so much of the time. They were part of the fabric of the place and she cherished their company. She adored the children, took pleasure from reading them stories every night, tucking them into bed. She loved watching them playing in the olive grove.

But more than any of that they helped her deal with the loss of Francesco. If it hadn't been for Rosa and her family, Alba would have been dragged into the abyss with her niece.

As it was, she couldn't speak of her own heartbreak; if she went down that road she might never return.

Cosima was at the sink washing up, her mind still in a dream, when Luca's face appeared at the window. He came in, embraced her and kissed her cheek. Alba turned away, finding their intimacy overwhelming. 'I want to take you away for the day, if your family can spare you.'

'Of course, go.' Alba's spirits lifted as Cosima's face flushed with pleasure. 'You deserve some fun.'

Luca released her and leaned against the sideboard. 'My mother's unbearable this morning. I had to get out.'

'What's the matter with her?'

'The prospect of Panfilo coming to photograph the *palazzo* is more than her nerves can take. She's sitting in the lotus position on the terace, trying to calm down. Not easy with my father and the professor enjoying a heated political debate at the table next door!' He sighed. 'A whole troop of florists, stylists, make-up artists and assistants will descend on the place tomorrow so I'll need to escape then too.'

'You can help us at the *trattoria*,' Cosima suggested with a smile. 'Rosa's volunteered to help Panfilo.'

'I bet she has.'

Alba recalled her daughter's midnight escapade and wondered whether they knew something she didn't. 'I can't imagine he needs her,' she said, fishing for information.

'She has a fascination with that place,' said Cosima. 'I think she's sneaking up to the folly in the middle of the night.'

'What on earth for?'

'A little adventure?'

'In that dead old place?'

'It lives for her.'

Alba shook her head. 'I'm sure you're mistaken.'

'Well,' Luca said. 'Someone's been in there and my mother's given me the job of finding out who it is.'

'Rosa knows how I feel about the *palazzo*.' Alba was pale. She didn't want to talk about the *palazzo*, let alone imagine her daughter luxuriating in the tragedy of the past. Rosa knew how sacred it was to her.

'Mother's invited another couple to stay,' said Luca, changing the subject.

'It's like a hotel up there,' said Alba. Her voice sounded sharper than she intended.

'Getting more like a hotel by the minute,' Luca agreed. 'The professor and Ma Hemple are permanent fixtures I think; they'll be staying all summer for sure. I don't know how my parents put up with people hanging around all the time.'

'So, who have they invited now?' Cosima asked, putting away the plates she had dried.

'A charming old boy called Fitzroy Davenport.' Luca spoke slowly and deliberately, suddenly guilty about pretending not to know Alba's history. He watched her mouth fall open in surprise.

'Fitzroy Davenport?'

'The very same,' Luca replied. 'Do you know him?'

'Yes, we were lovers.'

Cosima stared at her aunt. Her candour was disarming. 'Lovers? When?'

Alba laughed. 'Long before I met Panfilo. When you were a little girl. I made a very wise choice back then, and I have never regretted it for a moment. It was either you, Cosima, or Fitz – I couldn't have both.'

'Poor Fitz,' said Luca.

'Well, he eventually married someone else. Who is she?'

'Rosemary,' Luca replied. 'Very . . . efficient.'

'You mean pushy. Oh really, Fitz, of all the women to choose. He was always going to be vulnerable to a woman like that! When are they coming?'

'Next weekend.'

'I can hardly wait. After all these years. Won't he be surprised?'

Luca recalled the wistful look on his face and the tender way he had spoken of her. '*Pleasantly* surprised,' he added with emphasis. For a moment he felt sorry for Rosemary, Alba being so much more beautiful, but he didn't mention that. Instead, he led Cosima out into the sunshine. He'd warned Alba that Fitzroy was coming. He'd meddled enough.

They lay together on the grass beneath the old lookout point. Cosima had an air of distraction, as if her mind were elsewhere. He ran his hand through her hair, scrunching it between his fingers, and swept his lips across her skin. 'What are you thinking about?'

'I had a dream last night,' she replied, smiling tentatively. 'I don't know what to make of it.'

'What was it about?'

'Francesco.'

Chapter 26

Nanni and Fiyona followed Caradoc's instructions and sat on a bench in the square outside the church. The sun shone, birds twittered in the trees or hopped on to the grass to peck at crumbs left for them by small children, and the church bell summoned people to Mass. Elderly men and women dressed in black surfaced in the square like crabs crawling out of crevices in rock, their heads covered with black hats or veils, their rosary beads rattling in their pockets. Young couples walked briskly across the square with their children, little girls in their best dresses, little boys scrubbed clean. It seemed the whole town emptied into the church. Everything was closed but for the hotel, outside which a couple of American tourists waited for a taxi with cameras slung over their shoulders, peering at a guidebook of Southern Italy.

Fiyona and Nanni waited like a pair of hyenas. With Fiyona, Nanni was transformed. He felt virile and sexy. He displayed his large belly and smoked a cigar. Fiyona seemed rather more interested in the young men, so dark and handsome with their Latin air of insouciance that so excited her. She couldn't help but smile at them and they smiled back, instantly recognising the availability in her eyes, like an 'open' sign hanging in a shop window.

She put a cigarette between her lips and lit it, letting the smoke dribble out through the side of her mouth. 'This town is full of old people,' she said. 'They must all know something.'

'We have to find the right person,' Nanni replied. 'Few will want to talk. People from the south are cagey.'

'Nothing cagey about the young,' she said, thinking of Fiero and their shameless flirting the night before.

'The young didn't live through the war.'

'Did your sister know about its history when she bought the place?'

'They fell in love with the *palazzo*. The history didn't interest them.'

'It does now.'

'It interests everyone now.' He flicked ash on to the ground.

'So she doesn't mind that an old man was murdered in her home?'

'Why should she? It happened long ago.'

'I wonder what Alba and her family think of your sister renovating it?'

'If Alba minded that much she wouldn't have chosen to live here. Besides, she never knew her mother. Valentina died when she was a baby.'

'But her uncle was a murderer.'

'He took revenge on his sister's death.'

'Still a murderer. I'm sure she'd rather the whole episode was forgotten.'

'Don't forget, Falco was never charged with the murder. The police believed it was the *mafia*. The case is closed.'

'Just Falco on his own, or did he have an accomplice?' She remembered Rosa's slip of the tongue.

'How many people does it take to kill a marquis?' Nanni chuckled. 'Perhaps there were three, who knows?'

'But I *want* to know,' she said with emphasis. 'I like to get the facts right. That's what makes me a good journalist.'

'I suppose that is an advantage. Most journalists I know make it up!'

After Mass the town filed out and dispersed. Fiyona scanned the herd of faces, even attempted to speak to one or two, but they looked at her in horror and shuffled away, muttering under their breath.

'This isn't going to be easy.'

'I told you, no one wants to talk to a stranger.'

'Then how did your nephew manage it?' She made another unsuccessful attempt, then saw a face she recognised. 'Rosa!' She caught the young woman's eye and waved.

Rosa broke away from her family. 'Hello, Fiyona. What are you doing here?'

'Mass,' Fiyona replied. Rosa raised her eyebrows. 'This is Nanni, Romina's brother.' Rosa shook his hand. 'Are those your children?' Fiyona asked as Rosa's family caught up with her.

'Yes, and my husband Eugenio. My father, Panfilo and my uncle Toto, his wife, Paola and his mother, Beata.'

'You have a big family,' said Fiyona, smiling her warmest smile.

'You haven't met the half of it!' laughed Rosa. 'We take up most of the church.'

'Do you live here in town?' Fiyona asked.

'Just outside. In the very house that Valentina lived in,' she hissed so that Beata wouldn't overhear.

'Dressed up like that you look even more like her.' Fiyona flattered her.

'Would you like to come for a drink?'

'I would love to,' Fiyona replied. 'Could I bring Nanni?'

'Of course.' Rosa turned to her father. 'I've asked them home for a drink.' Panfilo's face clouded. 'Don't look at me like that, *Papa*! My mother's shy of the *palazzo*,' she explained.

Fiyona was quick to turn up the charm. 'Don't worry, we wouldn't want to intrude. It's been so nice to meet you all. What a friendly, beautiful family you have, Panfilo. You must be very proud.'

Panfilo felt embarrassed. It wasn't in his nature to be rude. 'No, please. I welcome you into our home,' he said. Fiyona caught Nanni's eye, linked her arm through Rosa's and walked off towards Panfilo's car.

Alba busied herself in the house, tidying up the children's toys, folding their clothes, putting away their pencils and books. Then she decided to walk out to the old lookout point where her mother lay buried under the olive tree.

She was reminded of walking that path as a young girl, dreaming of Fitz, struggling with the choice she had to make – to remain in Italy with Cosima or return to England with Fitz. A bird of prey circled silently overhead, scouring the earth for mice and rabbits. She inhaled the scent of wild thyme and rosemary, swept her eyes over the hill where little yellow flowers flourished in the long grass, and felt her spirits soar. She would never tire of this landscape. Its beauty would always hold her captive.

She felt a frisson of excitement at the prospect of seeing Fitz again. Would he have changed? Would she feel anything for him? Or would her love be no more than a memory corroded by time, or a mirage in her past? She thought of him married to Rosemary and laughed out loud that he had fallen into the arms of a pushy woman. Fitz had always been affable, charming and gentle – vulnerable to a strong and determined woman. Alba had left him broken-hearted, but she had promised him she would wait. She had, at first, but he had not returned. Italy had filled the void Fitz had left, and Cosima had taught her that there were many different ways to love. Ultimately, Cosima's need had been greater than Fitz's. The little girl's welling eyes and disbelieving smile had shown her that she had done the right thing in returning. Then Panfilo turned up and she had fallen in love. 'In love' had faded with time, replaced by a love that was solid, deep and lasting. She wondered how things might have turned out had she not come back but married Fitz and lived in London. Would Fitz have had the strength of character to hold her? Would she have tired of him and gone back to her promiscuous ways? Would Italy have eventually been displaced by the shallow materialism and greed of the world she had returned to? What sort of woman would she have been?

She reached the olive tree and sat down on the grass. She remembered Fitz arriving in Incantellaria to ask her to marry him, her initial joy, and later her fear of leaving the family she had only just discovered. She recalled their escapade to the *palazzo*; climbing over the gate warped by time, rusted by many rainfalls; sneaking up the drive overgrown with shrubs and littered with branches, thorns and twigs. How the gardens had taken over and invaded the house, creeping in through the crumbling walls like snakes; the sinister cold that had pervaded the place, as if it were situated at the top of a mountain with its very own climate; the smell of rotting vegetation and neglect. But Fitz had accompanied her inside and she had felt more courageous with him beside her.

Finally they had reached a room that had a very different feel from the rest of the *palazzo*. Unlike the others, that one had vibrated with the warmth of the living. The remains of a fire were still hot in the grate and the air quivered with life. A leather chair was placed in front of the fire. They had had the strange feeling that they weren't alone. They had been right.

Alba recalled the albino, Nero. The man the *Marchese* had adopted as a little Neapolitan boy. He had been frail, with no front teeth, slowly drinking himself to death out of remorse and regret, pining for the man he had loved and lost. Because of him the *palazzo* had been given over to the ravages of nature. It had crumbled around him until all that remained was the room he lived in. The room in which the *Marchese* was murdered. He had wept when she had told him that she was Valentina's daughter and she, in turn, had wept when she learned that the *Marchese* had killed her mother. Fitz had helped put together the pieces of that tragic jigsaw; unveiling a final picture of love, jealousy and revenge.

After that, Alba vowed she'd never go up there again. While her father had believed Valentina loved him she had been lying in the folly with the *Marchese*. She had even given him the naked portrait Thomas had drawn of her and hung it by the bed which *she* had found with Fitz and returned to her father. He had been shocked to see it after all those years, having been so tormented by its disappearance at the time. But he hadn't wanted to be reminded of the woman who had so cruelly betrayed him and had given it back to her. She'd never forget the ruthless glint in his eyes when she had relayed how she and Fitz had turned detective and solved the *Marchese*'s murder. Falco had admitted responsibility, but it was only then that she had realised her own father's part in the plot. Rosa saw only the romance of her grandmother's seemingly glamorous life, but Alba knew the truth: that it was tawdry and dishonest. Valentina had hurt those who loved her the most. Thomas had never got over the deception. He had plunged the knife into the *Marchese*'s neck but the *Marchese*'s gleeful smile had never left him. '*You can kill me, but don't forget that I killed you first*,' he had said.

Knowing the truth about her father had brought Alba and Thomas very close. Now nothing could come between them. No secrets, no lies, only the truth that she had eventually shared with her family. It wasn't right to keep secrets from each other. She had learned that through experience.

Now she thought of Panfilo and his involvement with the *palazzo*. She feared the interest Romina had generated in renovating it. Now there would be an article in an international magazine, digging up the secrets they had no right to expose. People would come to Incantellaria out of curiosity to visit the scene. The story would no longer be hers but belong to the world. Her father had trusted her, now she had to trust her own family. She wasn't sure she could trust *all* of them. Rosa had inherited Valentina's genes and that frightened her.

Eventually, she got up and walked back through the olive grove. She imagined her family would be back from Mass. She heard laughter before she reached the house. Panfilo's voice rose above the others. She smiled as she thought of him. She was truly blessed. As she got nearer she saw that other members of the family had arrived – Toto's wife, Paola, and her children and grandchildren. The little ones played in the garden with Garibaldi, while the grown-ups drank *prosecco* and nibbled on *crostini* at the table beneath the vine. Alba greeted them warmly, then settled her pale eyes on the two strangers in their midst. 'This is Fiyona, and Nanni is Romina's brother,' said Rosa.

Alba made an effort not to show her displeasure. 'Welcome,' she said, sitting down beside Panfilo. 'So, you're staying up at the *palazzo*?'

'It's really beautiful,' volunteered Fiyona, watching Alba as if she were there to be studied, like an insect beneath a microscope.

Alba noticed her accent immediately. 'You're English.'

'So are you.'

'Whereabouts?'

'London.'

'I grew up in London, too. I lived on a houseboat on the Thames.'

'Aren't they rather damp in the winter?'

Alba could almost smell the paraffin and smiled with nostalgia. 'I loved it.'

'Is it still there?'

'No. It fell apart.' She didn't want to explain why they had scuttled the *Valentina*.

'What a shame. Some of them are very old.'

'And sturdier than mine.'

'Well, I live in Bloomsbury, in a house that's equally damp in winter,' said Fiyona with an affable chuckle. 'Lucky you living here!'

'The sun always shines in Italy,' said Panfilo, patting his wife's knee under the table.

'And if it doesn't, there's pasta,' Nanni added, rubbing his big tummy.

'I don't think you want for anything here,' said Fiyona, gazing around appreciatively. 'Incantellaria is paradise on earth. Have you seen what Romina and Bill have done to the *palazzo*? I gather it was a total ruin when they bought it.'

'No,' Alba replied shortly, not wanting to explain why.

'*Papa*'s going to photograph it tomorrow for the *Sunday Times* magazine,' said Rosa.

'You won't be disappointed,' said Nanni to Panfilo. 'My sister has immaculate taste. She has returned it to its former glory.'

Alba bristled. 'And what makes you think it was ever glorious?'

'It was clearly a masterpiece in terms of architecture,' Nanni argued, on the point of giving them a short lecture on the neo-classical period.

'And the decoration is incredible,' Fiyona added. 'You must go and see it. Surely, you knew that *palazzo* before it fell down?'

'I have no desire to go up there,' said Alba tightly.

'Do you know who lived there before?' The table fell silent. No one wanted to speak about that place and they were all aware of Alba. Fiyona, however, was undeterred. The *prosecco* had dulled her usually sharp senses. 'I know the famous Marchese Ovidio di Montelimone lived there once. But who lived there after he died? And why was it allowed to go to ruin?'

'We don't like to talk about the past,' said Panfilo, sensing his wife's simmering anger at such intrusive questioning by a stranger.

'But the past is so fascinating,' said Fiyona, stumbling on drunkenly. 'History should be made to live again. Sometimes it's only with hindsight that mysteries can be solved.'

'Why are you so interested in the history of the *palazzo*?' Alba asked.

'Because she's a journalist, Mother.'

Alba blanched, stunned that her own daughter could betray her. 'A journalist?'

Fiyona hadn't expected Rosa to blow her cover. 'I write for the *Sunday Times* magazine,' she admitted. 'I'm sorry, I thought you knew.'

Alba stared at Fiyona with such vitriol that the younger woman shrank. When Alba spoke she did so in English in order to make herself absolutely clear. 'You inveigle your way into my home, take my hospitality, drink my *prosecco* and eat my *crostini*, knowing all along that my mother was Valentina Fiorelli, murdered by the *Marchese* who lived in that *palazzo* you call glorious, with the intention of finding out as much as you can so that you can lift the lid on secrets kept for over fifty years?' She turned on her daughter. 'Oh, Rosa, you are naïve if you think this woman courted you for your friendship. Well, don't let me stop you all enjoying yourselves. Stay, have another drink why don't you? But if you'll excuse me, I'd rather not socialise with someone who's going to hurt the members of my family who were there when my mother was murdered and who, for the last fifty-six years, have tried to forget.'

She stalked into the house. Panfilo shook his head regretfully. 'I'm sorry,' he said politely, 'but I think you should leave.'

'Of course,' said Fiyona, rising unsteadily to her feet. 'Come on, Nanni.'

Nanni shook his head. 'My sister will be mortified that we have offended you.'

'Don't forget that Valentina was Alba's mother,' said Panfilo to Fiyona. 'And her father is still alive. If you have to write an article about the *palazzo*, write it with sensitivity for those still living.'

Fiyona swallowed hard. 'Of course.'

'I'll drive you back,' Eugenio volunteered.

'Don't worry, we'll walk,' said Nanni. 'I know the way.'

'Are you sure?' Rosa was furious that her mother had humiliated her in front of everyone.

Fiyona took Rosa's hand. Her lipstick had leaked into the lines around her mouth and bled on to her teeth. She had clearly drunk too much. 'I'm sorry, Rosa. But don't worry, two million people will read about *you*.'

Nanni led Fiyona up the hill. 'What a disaster!' he exclaimed, mortified.

'My fault. I pushed too hard.'

'What did you want to find out?'

'I like to have all the facts.'

'Don't you already have them?'

'I'm sure Falco wasn't alone when he murdered the *Marchese*.'

'So what?'

'I bet it was Thomas, Alba's father, who was with him.'

'And you thought Alba would tell you that?'

'I don't know what I thought. I forgot where I was.'

'You shamed us all!'

'I'm sorry. I feel dreadful. They're nice people.'

'Then drop it, Fiyona. Let it go.'

'But it would make such a good story.'

'Not if you hurt people.'

'I'm used to that.'

They walked through the woods. The trees towered above them, leaves shimmering in the breeze, parting to allow a luminous kaleidoscope of light to scatter on the path before them. Fiyona felt drunk and dizzy. It was very hot. 'I have to lie down a moment.'

Nanni was irritated, but he had no choice. He certainly couldn't carry her home.

She lay on her back and threw an arm across her eyes. 'That's better.' Then she began to laugh.

'What's so funny?' he asked, lying down beside her.

'I don't know. Us, this, now. There's something very funny about it.'

'I see nothing funny at all. It's okay for you. You will go home but we have to live in this place. My sister will kill you if Panfilo refuses to take the photographs tomorrow.'

'Bugger. What can I do?'

'I don't know,' he sighed, closing his eyes.

'I suppose a fuck's out of the question?'

Chapter 27

Panfilo found Alba fuming in their bedroom. 'Don't even try to persuade me that you photographing the *palazzo* is a good thing! What was that woman doing here anyway?'

'Rosa invited her,' Panfilo replied calmly.

'Rosa's a liability!'

'She's young and naïve.'

'Those people up there are nothing but trouble.'

Panfilo sat on the bed. 'You're irresistible when you're angry.'

'Don't try to appease me that way, I'm immune.'

'Look, they're going to photograph the place whether you like it or not. If it's not me, it'll be someone else.'

'I can't bear that bloody woman sniffing around the past like a detective. We're talking about my mother . . . and Daddy. What if she finds out that Daddy killed the *Marchese*?'

'She won't,' said Panfilo reassuringly. 'Who's going to tell her? No one knows but us.'

'And Rosa.'

'She's naïve but she's not stupid.'

'She's angry with me. You know how hot-blooded she is. She might not be stupid but she's a bloody fool. I should never have told her. What if Cosima tells Luca and he tells his mother? That woman's staying up at the *palazzo*, ears flapping like an elephant! I hate to think what they're all saying!'

'Calm down, Alba.' He pulled her down beside him.

'As you know, thirty years ago I discovered that Daddy murdered the *Marchese* with Falco. It was an act of revenge. "A matter of honour," he said. We never discussed it, but we had a silent understanding. If he finds out that I've told people – if it comes out in a British magazine – he'll be so disappointed in me. I can't bear to hurt him. I can't bear him to think less of me.'

'Why don't we just ask Rosa to keep quiet?'

'No, leave it. I'll talk to Cosima. She can find out from Luca. Unlike our daughter, Cosima can be trusted.'

'Alba, that's not fair,' said Panfilo gruffly. 'You've got to be more sensitive to Rosa. She's your daughter. You know, you were once as hot to handle as she is.'

'Rosa's way beyond what I ever was. She worries me. You know she sneaks off in the middle of the night? God knows what she's up to. I just hope she's sensible enough not to have an affair.'

Panfilo laughed. 'I don't think there's a great deal of temptation in Incantellaria!'

'If she wants something badly enough, she'll find it. She's longing for adventure. She's champing at the bit. She just doesn't know how lucky she is to have Eugenio.'

'Maybe she needs her own home . . .' he suggested carefully.

'That's not the answer.' She stood up. 'So, you're still determined to photograph the *palazzo*?'

'Yes,' he replied firmly. 'I have a commitment.'

'I don't want to see what they've done to it.'

'Very well.'

'So, don't even show me the photographs.'

'I won't.'

'I don't want to see the article when it comes out, either.'

'Fine.'

'Let's not speak of it again.'

Panfilo smiled at her melodramatic exit. The trouble was that Alba felt she owned Valentina's story and the *palazzo*. She couldn't bear to acknowledge that Valentina belonged to Incantellaria and the *palazzo* belonged to Romina and Bill Chancellor. He knew his wife better than she knew herself. He wouldn't be at all surprised if her curiosity eventually got the better of her.

That night Rosa could barely wait for Eugenio to fall asleep. She lay in bed, staring up at the ceiling, waiting for his breathing to grow deep and regular. She thought of her mother, watching from her bedroom window, suspecting that she was having an affair. Well, an affair of the mind, perhaps.

At last Eugenio slept. She crept out of bed, dressed in the bathroom and sneaked out of the house. She ran all the way up the path to the folly. The moon was bright, but she could have found her way there blindfolded, using an internal map and her senses. The feeling of excitement was intoxicating, as it must have been for Valentina. She must have trodden the same path to where the *Marchese* would have been waiting for her in the folly. She had believed Incantellaria devoid of excitement and adventure but it had been there all along, right under her pretty nose.

Finally, she reached the folly. All was quiet. She was alone. Luca was busy with her cousin. They were welcome to each other. She had better fish to fry. Inside, the folly glowed with the soft, dancing light of the candles he had lit.

'Ah, there you are, my dear. I was hoping you'd come.'

She closed the door behind her. 'I wouldn't miss this for the world,' she replied, sinking on to the bed. 'I've been looking forward to seeing you all day.'

When Romina laid eyes on the great Panfilo Pallavicini she was uncharacteristically speechless. He was simply the handsomest man she had ever seen, and that included Bill, as dear as he was. Instead of trying to talk, she threw her arms around him, enveloping him in Pucci and perfume, and planted loud kisses on his bristly cheeks.

'*Madonna!*' he exclaimed, laughing. 'I expected you to be very English.'

'I'm Italian,' she replied, finding her voice. 'One hundred per cent!'

He ran his eyes over the façade of the *palazzo*, muttering compliments in the superlative. 'You must have had a devil of an architect!'

'My husband,' said Romina proudly.

'*Complimenti!*'

'Thank you. Come on in. I'll show you around.'

They waded through vast black pots of cut flowers, and bags and boxes belonging to the crew, into the hall. Panfilo took in everything, sweeping his eyes over the walls, ceilings and furnishings. Years of experience had taught him to home in on the important features; little details that most people would overlook. He observed the light, different in every room, and the colours Romina had chosen for the walls. He admired her taste; it was flamboyant but faultless, and wished Alba would bury her pride and come and take a look. There was a time when she had always joined him on shoots and taken pleasure from snooping around beautiful houses.

Out on the terrace Romina introduced Panfilo to her friends. Dennis, Stephanie, Ma and Caradoc were playing cards. Nanni had taken Fiyona into town on the excuse of enjoying one final coffee before she left that afternoon. They were both too ashamed to face Panfilo. Porci trotted up to sniff the new arrival. 'My friends, this is the famous Panfilo Pallavicini!' Romina announced, opening her arms theatrically.

'The great Panfilo!' The professor exclaimed. 'We've been awaiting your arrival with anticipation.'

'What a peaceful sight!' Panfilo ran a hand through his long hair. 'Life up at the *palazzo* is good.'

'Up to a point,' grumbled Ma. 'It would be better if I was winning.'

'I'm going to show Panfilo the folly,' said Romina.

'I hope you don't find any ghosts,' Dennis called after her.

'I'm sure Luca has frightened them away,' Ma muttered sarcastically.

'Luca has been much too busy with the living to worry about the dead,' said Caradoc.

Panfilo followed Romina down the garden. 'My husband is constantly building things,' Romina explained. 'Now he's building a grotto out of tree stumps. What on earth will he think of next?'

'It's beautiful,' said Panfilo. 'You have done an incredible amount of work. It's hard to imagine that it was a ruin only two years ago.'

'There was something rather wonderful about the ruin, actually. I wish I had taken photographs. I'd like to make a book of before and after shots. A place as historic as this should be documented for posterity. All I have left of the past is the folly. Do you know it?'

'I've heard a lot about it from my daughter, but I've never been up here. It will be a pleasure to photograph. The only trouble is I don't know how I'm going to choose a few pictures out of so many. It requires a book, not just an article.'

'You are so right. That's what I think. Maybe you and I can write the book.'

'I think my wife would divorce me.'

Romina smiled. 'I shouldn't worry. You'd be snapped up before you wondered where you were going to lay your head at night!'

When they reached the folly, Romina was surprised to see Porci lying against the door. 'And what are you doing here, little pig?' She had an awful feeling that someone was inside.

'A pet?'

'My baby Porci,' she breathed, as the animal stood up to be let inside. Romina tried to look nonchalant, not wanting to give anything away, smiled confidently at Panfilo and opened the door. Porci trotted in. To her intense relief, the place was empty.

Panfilo gazed around the exquisite little building. The symmetry was perfect, the harmony as sensual as a beautiful piece of music. Romina threw open the shutters and let the sunlight tumble in, illuminating the books, the four-poster bed and the pretty dressing-table and desk. Then something made her look down to the ground outside the window; there, among the ferns, was a heap of cigarette butts.

Romina felt her fury mount. The intruder *had* to be found. This *had* to stop. Luca *had* to get a grip and catch her before she set fire to the place. But, not wanting to ruin the day she had been looking forward to for weeks, she gritted her teeth and shoved it out of her mind.

'Isn't it divine?' she said, smiling at Panfilo.

'It is more than divine,' he replied seriously. 'It's special.' He rubbed his fingers and thumb together. 'There's something in the air. I can't put it into words. It's a feeling, as if the air is charged with sorrow.'

'I call it love,' said Romina.

'Perhaps. Lost love. It's a sad feeling. Perhaps I can capture it.' He looked out of the window, working out where the sun rose and set. 'We'll do this last. When the sun is going down and the light is mellow.'

They heard the scuffle of feet as someone approached from the path. For a moment Romina thought it was the intruder and thanked God she was with Panfilo. Porci stared at the door expectantly. But it was Rosa's face that appeared in the doorway, flushed from having climbed the hill.

'Hi!' she said. 'I've come to help.'

Panfilo grinned at his daughter. 'Good. We can always do with an extra pair of hands.'

'Hello, Rosa, my dear,' Romina gushed with relief. 'I'm so pleased it is you.'

'Hi Romina, and hello little pig!' she exclaimed, scooping him up. Porci didn't resist. She sat on the bed and stroked him. 'This is the most comfortable bed ever!' she exclaimed, a wistful smile on her face as she recalled the night before.

'Don't get too comfortable. We've got work to do,' said Panfilo.

'When are you going to photograph it?'

'This evening,' he replied.

'Good,' said Rosa, putting Porci down and following her father out into the sunlight. 'This should be the main photograph.'

'You haven't seen the rest of the *palazzo* yet,' protested Romina, locking the door behind her.

'I can't imagine anything can be as perfect as this little folly. The very bed upon which my grandmother lay with the *Marchese.*'

'The very bed that catapulted her to her death,' Panfilo added dryly.

'Don't spoil it! Let me enjoy the romance.'

'There was no romance, Rosa. It was tawdry and decadent. There was nothing romantic about Valentina.'

Nanni and Fiyona deliberately stayed away from Fiorelli's in case Alba was there. Fiyona noticed a young *carabiniere* chatting up a pretty local woman, his gilded epaulettes shining in the morning sunshine and his eyes hidden behind a dashing pair of dark glasses.

'Back to London today, what a pity,' she said, dragging on a cigarette. 'I could get used to this life.'

'I can't imagine returning to Venice,' said Nanni.

'What's waiting for you in Venice?'

'Nothing.'

'Then stay.'

'I can't sponge off my sister indefinitely.'

'Why not? The others do.'

'They'll all leave in the end.'

'Only when they die.'

'Incantellaria does have a certain magic.'

'Palazzo Montelimone has a certain magic,' she corrected. 'The folly is something I'll never forget.'

'So, what are you going to write?' Nanni asked, waving at a waiter to order another double espresso.

'I will tell it as it is.'

'Which is?'

'That Romina and Bill, one of the most eccentric couples I have ever met, have built on foundations stained with blood to create a glorious home where peace and harmony co-exist with the resonance of mystery and murder. I will tell the story of Valentina and the *Marchese* and I will write that it is rumoured that Valentina's brother Falco sought revenge on the *Marchese* and killed him, but it has never been proven and the case is closed. I will mention the possibility that he had an accomplice who has never been named.'

'If you hadn't offended Alba, would you name her father?'

She thought a moment. 'No. I have a nose for sniffing out the truth and I sense Thomas Arbuckle was in on it. But while there's doubt, there's a chance I might make a mistake. And I don't make mistakes.'

'*Sei brava davvero*,' he marvelled.

'I'm not a good person. I've always been more intent on getting my articles right than sparing the feelings of those I write about. One forgets they're real people. And they *are* real people. The least I can do is consider them when I put pen to paper. Besides, I have a soft spot for Rosa and I'm falling in love with Incantellaria. If I offend everyone I'll never be able to come back. And you do want me to come back, don't you, Nanni?'

Nanni recalled their encounter on the beach and felt an ache in his loins. 'I'm going to miss you.'

'You're very sweet, Nanni,' she laughed.

'You don't leave until this afternoon. What are we going to do until then?'

Her crimson lips curled into a smile. There wasn't time to seduce the *carabiniere* and there was something rather endearing about Nanni. 'Well,' she said, leaning across the table. 'There's a little hotel right here in the square. We can't possibly go back to the *palazzo*. We're fugitives. Say we hide out for the morning and order room service for lunch?'

'That, my dear Fiyona, is the best idea you've had all day.'

Panfilo spent the day taking photographs, assisted by an enthusiastic youth called Mario. Rosa wandered from room to room, imagining what they were like in their glory days and being no help at all. Romina shadowed the stylist and florist who arranged the rooms to their best advantage, enhancing the shots with large vases of white lilies and dusty pink roses. For the family picture, the make-up artist spent an hour painting her face and styling her hair while she insisted on brushing Porci for his part in the portrait. Bill was reluctant to be photographed, but his wife insisted. After all, she explained, it was only right that the public should see how handsome he was too!

Panfilo settled them on the terrace with the ocean behind them. Romina cradled Porci like a baby and scratched his fat tummy, while he grunted with pleasure and paddled with one hind leg. At least Romina had removed his nappy. Panfilo looked over the Polaroids with satisfaction.

At the end of the day they moved down to the folly. The light was softer now as the sun turned the heavens pink. Romina insisted on leaving the folly as it was. No flowers, no bowls of fruit, no enhancement of any kind. The magic was already there. She was right; it was perfect just the way it was.

Panfilo was on the point of taking the shots with film when, all of a sudden, the lights flickered and went out.

'*Madonna!*' Romina exclaimed. 'There really is a ghost in this place!'

'It's the *Marchese!*' Rosa announced excitedly. Porci gave an anxious grunt and trotted off into the bushes. Mario ran about checking extension leads and the plugs that connected to the generator. There was no electricity in the folly itself.

'Is it possible to take shots without lights?' Romina asked.

Panfilo shook his head. 'I don't think there's enough natural light.' He turned to his assistant. 'What's wrong? Is it the generator?'

'No, everything works perfectly. Try again.'

Panfilo switched the lights on. They worked. Without wasting time he set about focusing the cameras. Just as he was about to take the first shot the lights flickered for a few seconds before going out again. One bulb exploded, spraying the floor with broken glass.

'This is spooky!' squealed Rosa.

'What is it?' Romina asked anxiously.

'Someone doesn't want us to photograph the folly,' said Panfilo darkly.

'Or he doesn't want us to take it with artificial light,' Rosa suggested. 'Try without. Go on!'

'Very well,' Panfilo sighed, certain it was too dark. 'I'll take a Polaroid.'

They waited a moment while the Polaroid developed. Romina recalled the cigarette stubs on the ground outside the window and wondered whether these strange goings-on had something to do with the person responsible for those. Finally, Panfilo pulled back the black film to reveal the picture. 'Right, it's perfect,' he said, astonished. 'Let's not waste another minute.' And he set about taking the photographs as quickly as he could, before the light changed.

'Must be the *Marchese*, don't you think?' said Rosa. 'Wouldn't he want his folly to be pictured at its best? He knew it would look better in natural light.'

'I don't believe in ghosts,' Romina muttered.

'I'm not so sure any more,' Rosa said. 'I think there's a lot out there that we can't see.'

'You sound like my mother,' Romina said scathingly. 'She was delusional to the point of insanity!'

Rosa was left staring at the photograph. The light that illuminated the folly was not only natural, but supernatural.

When Panfilo returned home, he was careful not to mention his day up at the *palazzo*. Rosa, too, had agreed to keep quiet. She didn't want to antagonise her mother and she was still smarting from the consequences of having invited that journalist up for a drink after Mass. Alba didn't ask. They sat at the dinner table, skirting around the subject like skaters around a hole in the ice. Cosima had enjoyed a shopping trip to Naples with Luca and was wearing one of the new dresses he had bought her. Rosa eyed it enviously, but then she remembered her new friend and the anticipation of seeing him that night erased her envy like sun burning off mist.

Panfilo left the Polaroids where Alba was sure to find them. Just as he had predicted, she was unable to contain her curiosity. When the household went to bed, she crept downstairs to look at them.

Chapter 28

'So, Luca,' said Caradoc, swilling the ice around in his glass of whisky. 'How's the widow?'

They sat outside on the terrace. It was late. Dusty moths and little midges hovered around the hurricane lamps and crickets chirruped in the undergrowth. Ventura had cleared away dinner. Romina and Bill had retired to bed, exhausted by a day spent photographing the *palazzo*. Ma had retreated inside to listen to Nanni playing the piano. To her surprise he played like a concert pianist, his long fingers dancing effortlessly over the keys. Dennis and Stephanie had reluctantly motored off in his shiny Maserati just after tea, promising to return the following summer. Romina had watched them drive away with regret. Stephanie would have been good for Luca, despite her youth. Still, there was always Freya.

'She's not a widow,' Luca explained. 'She's never been married.'

'Ah, she's a dark horse. Defying convention and having a child out of wedlock.'

'She fascinates me.'

'Fascination is a good thing. Myrtle fascinated me. The trouble is no one has since.'

'Not even Rosa?'

'My girl? She's lovely, Rosa.' He took a sip of whisky. 'A man's never too old to appreciate a beautiful woman. But my heart is sealed with Myrtle's kisses. I've had my fill in this life. I look forward to meeting my Myrtle in the next.'

'You believe you will?'

'I know it.' He put his hand on his heart. 'I feel it in here.'

Luca leaned forwards, arms on knees, keen to confide in the professor. 'Do you remember the little boy I saw in the church?'

'At the *festa*? Yes, I remember. I thought it better not to mention it.'

'You're a true friend, Caradoc.'

'So, have you seen him again?'

'Lots of times. He's Cosima's dead son. I believe he's stuck here because of her grief. Do you think we can ground spirits by the very force of our will?'

'I don't see why not. We're all energy, aren't we? We're all connected. But perhaps he's stuck here of his own volition?'

'Tied to his mother by love?'

'He's all she has. Maybe he doesn't want to leave her alone in her grief.'

'But she doesn't have to be alone. You told me that love comes when you think you don't need it. And that once you've discovered true love you can't imagine how you ever lived without it. Well, I know what you mean. I've fallen in love. Really in love. You were right.'

'The only good thing about being old is being wise.'

'Some people grow old without acquiring wisdom along the way.'

'I pity those poor fellows. Does she love you back?'

'I think she's beginning to. The trouble is her guilt.'

'That's only natural. You have to give her time. Judging by your lack of plans, time is something you have rather a lot of.'

'I've told her about Francesco. That I have seen him in spirit.'

'Does she believe you?'

'She wants to. But she's suspicious. I wish he'd give me something concrete so I can prove to her that he exists.'

'It's hard to believe what one cannot see or touch.'

'I don't want her to think I'm a fraud, using her son to get to her.'

'I'm sure she knows you better than that.'

'She's The One, Caradoc. I know she's The One.'

The professor smiled indulgently. 'Then tell her, my boy.'

'Until she lets Francesco go, I don't think she'll give herself to me.'

'Do you want to marry her?'

'Yes, I think I do.'

'And take her back to London?'

'I can't imagine her in London. Taking Cosima away from Incantellaria is like taking a beautiful panther out of the jungle and putting her in a zoo.'

'Have you asked her how she feels about the zoo?'

Luca recalled her whispered conversation with the priest. 'I think I already know the answer.'

'Then why don't you stay here?'

'And do what?'

'Necessity is the mother of invention.'

'Join the family business?' Luca laughed. 'I don't think it's my thing, brewing coffee all day.'

'You'll think of something. If you love her, you'll work it out.'

'I do love her, therefore I *will* work it out.'

Caradoc looked at him with fatherly concern. 'There's one thing you have to do first,' he said gravely.

'And what's that, Professor?'

'You have to work out who *you* are. What *you* want out of your life. You have to find out what gives you the most joy, then you will know your life's purpose. I think the answer will surprise you.'

'Do you already know?' Luca was surprised.

'If I did, I'd be a great deal more helpful. But *you* do. Look deep inside you and wait for the answer to materialise.'

Alba sat down at Panfilo's desk and studied the Polaroids. There were fifteen of them. Fifteen windows into the past. She took her time with each picture, scrutinising every detail, straining her memory to remember what the place had looked like when she had been there with Fitz. She couldn't help but admire Romina for having recreated it with such flair and good taste. It really was beautiful, in every respect, transformed with light and love. She laughed aloud at her self-delusion. The eerie picture she had nurtured in her mind for nearly three decades, fed with her fears and foolish fantasies, no longer existed. Romina had banished the ghosts by opening the shutters and letting in the sunshine. What had been an evil den of iniquity was now a perfectly pleasant family home. She wished she had the courage to ask if she could see it, but her pride prevented her. She couldn't bear to admit she had been wrong.

Finally, she came to the picture of the folly. It was exactly as it had been thirty years ago. Not one item had been moved or changed. The bed was the same, with the faded curtains and silk bedspread. The little dressing-table complete with pots of creams and glass phials of perfume. The Queen Anne mirror into which her mother must have so often gazed, was still at an angle, as was the chair upon which she must have sat while the *Marchese* lay waiting for her on the bed. The pretty little desk. The strangest thing of all, however, was the light. There was something other-worldly about it, as if it was illuminated not from the outside, but from within.

Alba returned to her bedroom to find Panfilo sitting up in bed engrossed in a book. He looked at her over his reading glasses and guessed that she had looked at the Polaroids. Alba had no intention of admitting she had been snooping; she undressed and climbed into bed without a word. After a while, Panfilo switched off the light and snuggled up behind her, winding his arm around her waist and pulling her against him. She could sense him staring at her through the darkness, feel the unformed words balancing on his lips.

'Don't say it,' she warned.

'Don't say what?'

'That you know.'

'That I know what?'

'I've seen them, okay.'

'Have you?' He played ignorant.

'I still have no desire to go up there though.'

'Of course you don't.' He kissed her neck.

'I couldn't help looking at them. They were there on your desk. You put them there on purpose.'

'It's my desk!'

'They were in plain view.'

'On *my* desk.'

'I didn't want to see them, but I couldn't help it.'

'You're a prisoner of your own convictions, Alba. I couldn't care less whether you looked at them or not.'

She rolled over and let him wrap his arms around her. 'Here's the one place in the world I feel totally safe,' she whispered. 'Here, pressed up against you.'

'As irrational as you can be, we belong together.'

'You think I'm irrational?'

'You rather enjoy a melodrama.'

'I do not!'

'Just a little bit.'

'You're absolutely wrong about that,' she insisted.

'But you're irresistible.'

'I'm glad I have at least one redeeming feature.'

'You have many. Now stop talking and let me kiss you.'

He placed his lips on hers and felt her smile beneath them.

Feeling reckless, Luca drove to Naples to buy Cosima a ring. Caradoc was right: love had hit him when he had least expected it and now he couldn't imagine ever living without it. Cosima filled his soul with something warm and sweet, right to the very farthest corners. He liked who he was when he was with her. She had no idea how wealthy he was, but loved him for himself. He would buy her the world if she let him. If only he could buy her back her son.

It didn't take long to find a ring he felt would suit her. It had to be a diamond and it had to be simple. The ring stood out from all the others in the same way that Cosima stood out from all the other women he had ever met. A large solitaire. As big as a candy.

He recalled buying an engagement ring for Claire. He hadn't chosen it himself but had sent her off to design it with a jeweller she was fond of. He had simply paid the bill, which was less than he had expected. Back then she hadn't been spoiled. During the ten years of their marriage she had acquired a knack for homing in on the most expensive items in the shop – and shopping had been her greatest pleasure. From Rodeo Drive to via della Spiga to Bond Street, Claire had a vast capacity to acquire and she never wore a party dress twice. Cosima was from a simple family and she had simple tastes. Unlike her cousin, Cosima seemed content with what she had. Perhaps the death of her son had taught her the unimportance of material wealth. The only things of any value to her were the people she loved. He recalled her face when he had given her the earrings and her pleasure filled his heart with bubbles. He wanted to buy her every jewel in the shop.

As he drove back down the coast he decided it was time he brought his own car out to Italy. If he was going to settle here he needed to put down some roots, make a home, think of something constructive to do. He imagined making love to her. He imagined spending the rest of his life with her. He couldn't wait to propose in the good old-fashioned way. But Freya was arriving that weekend with her mother and stepfather so he'd have to wait until they had gone. Then he would take Cosima to the beach at sunset and go down on bended knee. At his age there was no point wasting time.

Back at the *palazzo*, Romina confronted him about the intruder. 'I was showing Panfilo the folly yesterday when I threw open the shutters to see, to my horror, a pile of cigarette butts outside the window. Imagine! This woman could set fire to the place. You have to find her, Luca, and make it soon. Enough of your romancing. Really, you should be taking stock after having put your children through such a terrible divorce, not throwing yourself into the arms of unsuitable girls.'

Luca deliberated which thoughtless statement he should address first. Then he felt the bulk of the engagement ring in his pocket and his intolerance evaporated. 'Look, Mother,' he said calmly. 'I know who she is.'

'You do?' She threw up her arms. 'How long have you known?'

'A while.'

'Who is she?'

'That I can't divulge. I need to speak to her first. But rest assured, she poses no threat to your safety.'

'What a relief!'

He looked at his mother sternly. 'On another note, my romancing, as you put it, has nothing to do with you. I'm old enough to choose my own girlfriend without you writing her off as unsuitable.'

'But darling, you don't have a very good track record.'

'I think I've learned from my mistake.'

'So you go from one extreme to the other. Cosima is a simple girl from a simple little town. She is not sophisticated enough for you. You need a woman who's seen the world, not a provincial.'

'I don't think you know what I need,' he replied, controlling his irritation.

'I'm your mother. Of course I know what you need.'

He could only laugh at her delusion. 'You never change!'

'You'll move on from Cosima, then find someone in the middle. Like Freya. Don't pretend you aren't a little in love with her. You were green with jealousy when she married Miles. She, too, has made a mistake. Now you can both leave your mistakes behind and start afresh together. The *palazzo* is big enough for six children.'

'You're dreaming.'

'It's only natural that I should want more grandchildren. If Bill had let me I would have had a dozen children of my own.'

'Freya's not for me, Mother.'

'She's always been for you. Sometimes the one you love is . . .'

'Right beneath my nose,' he said, finishing the cliché for her.

'Exactly. Now her husband is straying it's a good excuse for her to bail out.'

'She loves Miles. Don't you think she should try to win him back, for the sake of her children?'

'That depends how far the rot has set in. Perhaps it is irreparable.' She smiled mischievously. 'When she sees you, she won't want to win Miles back!'

'I love Cosima,' he stated firmly.

'You *think* you love Cosima.'

'No, Mother. I *know* I love Cosima.' She opened her mouth but he silenced her. 'Don't even think about telling me how I should feel.'

She rolled her eyes. 'Just don't do anything rash. Take her to London first and see how she fits in. I think you'll find she's a fish out of water.'

But Luca didn't have the will to argue his case. He didn't need to. He had already made up his mind.

Chapter 29

Freya, Rosemary and Fitz arrived in Incantellaria on a perfect sunny day. Romina had arranged for them to come in by boat in order to enjoy the sight of the medieval town from the sea, the way it was built to be seen. Fitz's stomach churned with nerves. He hadn't been back in thirty years. He didn't even know whether Alba still lived there. Perhaps they had sold the family *trattoria* and moved away. Thirty years was a long time. He shrank at the thought of finding another restaurant in the place of Fiorelli's. In his heart he wanted everything to be just as it was; even her.

He couldn't confide in Rosemary. She had always been disdainful of Incantellaria, ever since he had told her about Alba and that she had tried to get him to follow her there. It had been Rosemary who had finally dissuaded him, and over the months that followed they had grown close. The only reason she had come now was because she didn't want him to encounter his old love on his own. So, he didn't communicate his longing. He could only hold on to the railing at the back of the boat and wait. Preparing himself for the worst, he envisaged nightclubs and smart boutiques, expensive hotels and a beach crowded with under-dressed, over-bejewelled Euro-trash.

Freya hadn't told her mother about Miles's affair. She didn't want to worry her. But she had done as Luca had advised and confronted Miles. Of course he had denied it, accusing her of being paranoid, of not trusting him. But she was certain. The evidence weighed too heavily against him. The telephone calls, the texts she'd read on the sly, the evenings away playing bridge. She knew the woman's name: Felicity Cranley. One of his regular bridge four. She wasn't even very pretty. With the plane ticket to Naples in her handbag, she had given him an ultimatum. He had one chance. The next time she'd take the children with her and she wouldn't come back. Miles had been stunned into silence.

There was something wonderfully liberating about sitting in that boat without her husband and children. Alone with the wind in her hair, the scent of salt and thyme in the air, the anticipation of seeing her old flame, Luca, burning a hole in her stomach. She felt her excitement mount and looked over at her stepfather who had blanched the colour of a stick of celery. She assumed he was seasick, and smiled sympathetically. Rosemary noticed too and rubbed his back. How could he explain what was making him ill? Surely after thirty years . . .?

When the boat motored around the cliffs and into the bay of Incantellaria, the three passengers stared at the exquisite view without uttering a word. Fitz scanned the sea front for Fiorelli's but they were still too far away. He was encouraged, however, by the fact that little seemed to have changed. Blue boats were still dragged up on to the stony beach, the buildings were familiar, and above them rose the mosaic dome of the church of San Pasquale. Memories assaulted him like loose pages of a diary carried on the wind. Snippets of his visit, from the moment he saw Alba on the quay to their leaving together, in no particular order, tossed out by his subconscious. He tried to hold on to them, to savour them one by one, but they were already landing and it was Romina, not Alba, who was waving at them from the quay.

As they disembarked to Romina's enthusiastic welcome, Fitz raised his eyes to where Fiorelli's had once been. It was still there.

'You look better,' said Rosemary. 'Poor Fitz got so seasick,' she explained.

'Oh dear! Was it terribly bumpy out there?'

'A little,' said Rosemary. 'Better now, darling?'

'Much,' Fitz replied, feeling restored.

'Luca's waiting for you at the *palazzo*,' said Romina to Freya. 'He is so excited to see you.'

'I'm excited to see him,' said Freya. 'I've been longing to see your place.'

'You won't be disappointed. It's just been photographed for the *Sunday Times* magazine. Panfilo Pallavicini took the photographs himself.'

'How wonderful,' Rosemary gushed, not wanting to expose her ignorance. The name meant nothing to her.

'I booked two taxis. My car is too small to fit us all in and I wasn't sure how much luggage you had.' She dropped her eyes to the row of navy Globetrotters. Rosemary travelled heavy. 'Just as well,' she added.

'I hate not having the right thing to wear,' Rosemary explained. 'I almost brought the kitchen sink, but assumed you already had one.'

Romina laughed. 'A few actually.' Fitz's gaze lingered on the *trattoria*, imagining Alba as she had been thirty years before with her funny short hair and simple floral print dress, so different from the Londoner she had been in Mary Quant mini skirts and blue suede boots. Her defiance had gone: in its place a serenity, a contentment he had envied. He wondered what she was like now. Whether she had held on to that inner peace or whether she had moved back to a metropolis and her old redoubtable self. He half expected her to run out, arms outstretched, to greet him. But he saw only strangers on the terrace.

'That's Fiorelli's,' said Romina. 'Luca spends his entire time in there drinking coffee. We'll go there if you like, the food is very good. The lady who owns it is married to Panfilo the photographer.' Fitz wondered whether she was talking about Alba. He wanted to enquire, but Rosemary's ears were as sharp as a fox terrier's. He didn't want to upset her.

'Well, this is very beautiful,' Rosemary conceded as they climbed into the car. 'A quaint little place, but very charming.'

'It has a fascinating history.'

'Really? I can't imagine anything has ever happened here. It looks very sleepy.'

'I will tell you over lunch. It's a wonderful story and we, in the *palazzo*, are at the very heart of it.'

Fitz remembered the town surprisingly well. It was a lot busier than it had been thirty years ago, and the satellite dishes certainly hadn't been there then, but it was mostly unchanged. He felt a frisson as they drove up the hill. The last time he had seen the *palazzo* had been with Alba, when they had climbed over the gates and explored the ruin. Nothing had ever held her back from getting what she wanted.

They arrived at the gates, the same gates that he and Alba had scaled, and swept up beneath the cypress trees. There was nothing sinister about the place now. It had been rebuilt and repainted, the gardens brought to heel and tamed. He imagined it looked a lot like it had when it was originally built. Romina and Bill had restored it so cleverly it didn't look new.

Freya was enchanted by Incantellaria and the *palazzo*. She could see why Luca hadn't wanted to return to London. Surrounded by such harmony she would be the same. She wished she had been able to bring her children with her. How they would love the fairytale palace and the pretty town.

When Luca heard the cars on the gravel he went to the front to greet the new arrivals.

'Luca!' Freya climbed out of the car and rushed over, arms wide. Romina smiled. The boy didn't know what was good for him. 'You look so well!' Freya gushed. 'You're brown and relaxed! The rest has done you the world of good.'

'It will do you the power of good too. A little sunbathing by the pool, walks along the beach, time to think . . .' He didn't want to spoil her arrival by telling her about Cosima. He'd find the right moment. He was sure she'd be happy for him.

'I'm so pleased you encouraged me to come out,' she said, linking her arm through his. 'Miles couldn't believe it. I think he's still in shock.'

'He deserves more than shock.'

'A few days away is just what I need to get my head straight. I've had a ghastly time of it, I really have.'

'Let's go and have something to drink. I want to introduce you to two very dear friends of mine.'

'Oh?' She looked up at him, forgetting all about her children and her philandering husband in the warmth of his attention.

'Then I'll show you around.'

Outside, Ma, Nanni and Caradoc sat chatting on the terrace while Porci slept on the tiles in the sunshine, his belly round in spite of his apparent lack of appetite. The men stood up politely for Freya, but Ma remained in her seat, too sleepy and fat to move.

'This is the in-crowd of Incantellaria. Here's where it's all at,' said Luca, grinning broadly. 'My uncle Nanni, eccentric bringer of the pig: Professor Caradoc Macausland, the wisest man in Christendom; and Ma Hemple, possibly the grumpiest woman this side of Naples.'

Ma extended her hand. 'He's so wrong about me. I'm by far the most good-natured person here. He just doesn't understand my sense of humour. Too many years working in a bank with Sloanosauruses'

Freya giggled. 'I can tell he's wrong about you, Ma.'

'It's a pleasure to meet another pretty girl,' said Caradoc.

'The professor has a keen eye for the ladies,' Luca explained.

'I have a lovely girl down at the *trattoria*. She's called Rosa and she's as lovely as a spring rose.'

'She's a tart,' Ma corrected. 'Caradoc can't tell the difference.'

'At our age we don't really care,' said Nanni, recalling Fiyona's white flesh and red pubic hair. 'We'll take what we're given.'

'Look who's here!' Romina called to her husband.

'What a stunning place you have, Bill,' said Rosemary, marching over to kiss him.

'We've done our best.'

'You've done better than your best,' Fitz corrected, remembering what it had been like as a ruin. Most of the balustrade had collapsed and the tiles had been so covered with moss and weeds as to be entirely hidden. A putrid stench had poisoned the air; now he felt the garden restore him. It smelt sweet, of cut grass, pine and gardenia. He inhaled, expanding his chest like a peacock, taking pleasure from stepping back into the past.

Ventura and a butler brought out wine and *crostini* and they sat chatting. Ma took an instant dislike to Rosemary, which wasn't a surprise; Ma disliked pretentiousness. Rosemary was out of her comfort zone and felt inadequate. She was better on home soil and among her own sort. Foreigners made her feel uneasy, as did people who felt happy around them. Although Fitz hadn't mentioned Incantellaria in thirty years, and had barely raised an eyebrow when Bill and Romina had invited them to stay, there was something about his silence, as if he were hiding in it. She wasn't jealous of Alba; after all Rosemary was his wife, but Incantellaria was a part of Fitz's past that she had no claim on, so she was automatically suspicious of the place. But Fitz had wanted to come, he was keen to see what Romina and Bill had done to their home, and she couldn't let him walk down memory lane on his own.

Ma took to Fitz on sight. It wasn't just that he was handsome; he was genuine. There was no pretence in Fitz. He pulled Porci on to his lap and nuzzled him. The little pig grunted with pleasure, exposing his tummy which Fitz duly scratched. He was enthusiastic about everything, even Ma's sense of humour, which was rare so soon after meeting her, and she didn't mind that he gently teased her. In fact, she rather liked it.

As for Freya, Ma watched her with Luca. Romina had told her they were very old friends and that Freya suspected her husband of having an affair. Ma couldn't understand why people got married in the first place; it wasn't in a man's nature to remain faithful. That Freya was enamoured of Luca was plain to see. Luca was clearly fond of her. But love? If Romina were a dog, she'd be barking up the wrong tree. The object of Luca's desire was in an entirely different forest. Ma sat back to watch events unfold. Love was the best spectator sport.

During lunch Romina enlightened her new guests with the bloody history of the *palazzo*. Fitz's face was a mask, giving nothing away. Rosemary and Freya were gripped, hanging on her every word. 'And guess what, Valentina's family still live here in Incantellaria,' she said when she had finished the story. Fitz's mask slipped a moment and he went pink. 'Valentina's daughter owns the *trattoria*. It's still the family business.'

Rosemary gritted her teeth and retained her composure. She had hoped Fitz's great love would have moved away, or died. 'Alba's married, presumably,' she said.

'Yes, to Panfilo!' Romina reminded them.

'The photographer,' Rosemary recalled. Freya remembered her stepfather going very quiet when they had mentioned Incantellaria.

'You've been here before, haven't you, Fitz?' said Romina.

'A long time ago.'

'Did you come here, to the *palazzo*?'

'It was a ruin.'

Romina rubbed her hands together gleefully. 'What was it like?'

Rosemary sat up straight as Fitz told the table of the eerie cold, the rotten smell, the overgrown garden and the crumbling palace. 'We were exploring,' he explained.

'We?' said Ma.

'An old friend.'

His evasiveness aroused Ma's interest. 'An old friend. How very mysterious.'

'Not at all,' said Fitz, coolly. 'It was Alba. I haven't seen her in thirty years.'

The table fell silent. Rosemary was appalled that he had mentioned Alba by name; he had somehow insulted her by bringing up his old love. Freya was astonished that the woman Fitz had nearly married was so closely tied to the story Romina had told them of the murder in the *palazzo*. The men looked at Fitz with admiration – Alba was a beauty.

'Well, aren't you a dark horse!' said Bill, passing around the wine. 'What will Alba think when you turn up at the *trattoria*?'

'I shouldn't think she will even remember me. It was thirty years ago.'

'You don't have to go to the *trattoria*,' said Rosemary with a strained smile. 'We can stay here. I can't think of anywhere nicer.'

'Of course you should go.' Ma saw through Rosemary's silly ploy. 'You can't come all the way out here and not see her.'

'I'd be very curious to see an old flame!' agreed Romina.

'Don't get too excited.' Fitz tried to make light of it. He could sense Rosemary's discomfort as if she had suddenly grown a skin of prickles.

'I won't miss this,' said Ma. 'It reminds me of a Shakespeare play.'

'Which one?' asked Caradoc.

'Ah, that depends how things pan out!'

Rosemary felt as though she were drowning. 'It'll be fun,' she said, wanting to add '*at my expense*'. She checked herself. She was being unreasonable. After all, it was thirty years ago.

While the oldies slept off their lunch, Luca gave Freya a guided tour of the property. He knew he should tell her about Cosima, but he didn't want to put her in an awkward position. She had come to seek refuge from her troubled marriage. The last thing she needed to hear was that he was on the point of asking Cosima to marry him. It wasn't fair that his joy should detract from the purpose of her visit.

He felt bad at having flirted with her, and wanted to take back everything he had said that had been inappropriate. She had been right; while he had felt insecure, she had been a calm, familiar harbour. But he was a man for the high seas and, now he had regained his strength, he no longer wanted that safety. He hoped she wasn't thinking of leaving Miles.

He took her around the gardens and down to the folly, which she found as enchanting as he knew she would. They sat on the bed where he had made love to Cosima and finally, after discussing the beauty of the little building and the tragedy of its history, they talked about Miles.

'I never thought Miles would be the type to stray,' she said, curling a lock of hair behind her ear. 'He's not exactly a ladies' man.'

'Who is she?'

'One of his regular bridge four. She's not even attractive. She's got lanky brown hair and a round face.' They both laughed.

'What's got into the man?'

'I don't know. Maybe I'm too wholesome for him.'

'Wholesome is a good thing,' said Luca kindly.

'Maybe he wants dirty sex, someone who'll do all the kinky things I don't want to do.'

'What kinky things don't you want to do?' Luca couldn't help himself.

She blushed. 'I don't know. Miles hasn't exactly asked me to do anything. He's very conventional. I'm just trying to find an explanation.'

'So, you gave him an ultimatum?'

'I told him to finish it or I'll take the children and leave him.'

'I imagine you put the fear of God in him?'

'I think I did.'

'I'm sure he'll do what's right.'

'But can I trust him now? I'm not sure I can.'

'You have four children who need you to trust him, or at least to make the marriage work.'

'Yours have adjusted, haven't they?'

'Yes, I think so. But I wouldn't wish it on anyone. Coco and Juno came for a week and it was great, but naturally they'd be better off if Claire and I had stayed together.'

'But now they have the best of both worlds. Time with Mummy in England and time here with Daddy.'

'It hasn't been easy for them. Every child wants their parents to love each other.' He looked at her steadily. 'Do you still love Miles?'

She didn't hesitate. 'Of course. But he's hurt me.'

'If you didn't love him he wouldn't have the power to hurt you.'

'We've been married for ten years. I can't imagine life without him. I was arrogant enough to think I was the centre of his world. I never imagined he'd fall in love with someone else. I feel as if he's knocked the wind out of me.' She smiled sheepishly. 'I'm not so arrogant any more.'

Luca touched her shoulder. 'You'll go back in a few days and he'll have ditched the dog. You're going to have to make a real effort not to let it destroy you.'

'I know. If he gives her up, I've got to let it go. It won't be easy.'

'But you've shown him you mean business.'

'I don't think he ever imagined I'd just run off like this.' She grinned. 'I think you've put the wind up him, Luca.'

'Me?'

'Yes. I told him I was coming out here to see you. If anyone can provoke his jealousy, it's you.'

'I'm glad I'm helpful.'

'You're more than helpful,' she replied, squeezing his hand. 'You're a real friend.'

Chapter 30

Fitz was nervous about seeing Alba again in spite of the fact that they had both married and found happiness with other people. Thirty years could be reduced to almost nothing when it came to the emotions. Alba had broken his heart. Rosemary had put a plaster over the wound, but beneath the superficial healing it still remained open. He didn't suffer the same acute pain as in those first few months after she had left, and time served to dull the discomfort, but the ache was always there. A niggling regret. A longing for something precious. He often wondered about her and fantasised about what might have been. Now, gazing at the beauty that was Incantellaria, he wondered whether he would have been happy here. He wished he could say with certainty that he would not.

Romina loved nothing more than what she described as a 'situation'. She would have never imagined Fitzroy Davenport and Alba Pallavicini together. He was so incredibly English – a cigar and slippers sort of man – while Alba was so Italian. Her father might have been English, but Incantellaria had brought out the Italian in her. She and Fitz were as different as a Great Dane and a sleek black panther. She didn't see the parallels with her own marriage – Romina wasn't a woman who was self-aware. If things had been different, Fitz might have ended up running the *trattoria* instead of being married to the well-meaning but bossy Rosemary. She could barely restrain her impatience to thrust the former lovers together and wished she could whisk Rosemary off to give them time to talk about the past without her hanging over them like a fearsome judge. Rosemary wouldn't allow them a moment alone. Women like her were fragile beneath their brittle exteriors and seething with jealousy. She had done well to ensnare Fitz and Fitz was a fool to have got caught!

After a guided tour around Palazzo Montelimone, Romina gathered up the house party and squeezed them into Nanni's car and her little yellow Fiat. Freya stayed with Luca in the folly. She had no desire to watch Fitz and his old girlfriend humiliate her mother.

Alba had made an effort with her appearance. Not that she didn't normally, but today she knew the chances of Fitz walking into the *trattoria* were very high and she wanted to look her best. She had washed her hair, leaving it to fall down her back in shiny waves, and chosen a black dress imprinted with red and green flowers that hugged her curvaceous body, emphasising the swell of her breasts and the rounded lines of her hips and bottom. She wasn't as slim as she had been when Fitz had known her, but she knew she looked good for a grandmother. There came a time in a woman's life when she had to choose between her face and her figure. Alba had reached that point and chosen her face. The extra pounds made her skin look plump and youthful but her waist was thicker than she would have liked. She painted her eyelashes and applied a little blusher, hoping no one would notice and draw attention to it. She hadn't told Panfilo that Fitz was coming. The chances were they wouldn't meet. Panfilo had gone to Milan for a few days and, even if he were to come home, a man as self-assured as Panfilo wouldn't be concerned about the sudden arrival of an old flame of hers. She didn't even think he'd be curious. As she left the house she hoped Fitz would pay her a visit after all the trouble she had gone to.

It seemed everyone was at the *trattoria* that day. Rosa and Cosima were serving tables while Toto was chatting to the regulars. Lunchtime was busy. A big boat brought tourists from Sorrento and there was barely a spare seat in the whole town. Alba was so distracted that she didn't notice Rosa's smug smile or the way she bounced off the balls of her feet when she walked. The two barely spoke to one other. Only Cosima commented on Alba's appearance, telling her how good she looked. Alba grinned at her and replied '*Vecchio pollo fa buon brodo* – Old chicken makes good broth.'

By teatime, Alba's excitement had waned. She had sat at the table in the corner going through the accounts for long enough, barely daring to go out in case Fitz turned up and caught her off guard. She wasn't sure how to react. She didn't usually spend all day in the *trattoria*. 'I'm going home,' she said to Cosima at last. Her good mood had deflated. She was like a girl who'd been stood up on her first date. 'You can hold the fort with your father and Rosa. I'll see you later.' As Alba strode off across the terrace, something made her stop in her tracks.

There, walking up the quay, was Fitzroy Davenport. He hadn't changed at all, perhaps a little grey around the temples and a little more weathered, but he had those boyish good looks that didn't age very much. He saw her too and his face opened into a wide, infectious smile. He forgot about Rosemary, a few yards behind him. It was thirty years ago and he was striding towards the love of his life.

'My God, I can't believe it's you,' he said, kissing her cheek. 'I can't believe you're still here. You haven't changed a bit!' She smiled up at him and Fitz saw beyond the fifty-six-year-old woman to the girl he had fallen in love with.

'I said I'd wait for you,' she whispered. His face clouded. 'Well, I couldn't wait for ever, could I?' She was teasing, but beneath his laugh he was choked with regret.

'I should have known better.'

'So, how do you like your old friend?' said Romina, as if she were the mastermind of their reunion.

'Very much,' Fitz replied, reluctantly letting Alba go. He felt his wife at his side. She linked her arm through his possessively. 'This is Rosemary,' he said. 'My wife.'

Alba took in the perky woman Fitz had married instead of her. 'Welcome to Incantellaria.'

'Very nice to meet you,' replied Rosemary, who had already noted Alba's dark beauty and astonishingly pale eyes. 'I've heard so much about you.'

Fitz knew what Alba would think of Rosemary and the laughter in her eyes confirmed his suspicions. 'Come, let's find a table where we can all sit and catch up,' she said, leading the way across the terrace.

'I must sit in the shade,' said Ma, helping Caradoc as he walked stiffly, leaning on his stick.

'Where's the lovely Rosa?' he asked.

'She's gone home to her children.'

'Words cannot express my disappointment!'

'Well, isn't that a relief!' said Ma. 'You can keep quiet then.'

They all sat down. Alba wished she could be alone with Fitz, but it was impossible. That wife of his reminded her of her stepmother, the woman she had rudely referred to as the

Buffalo. Who'd have thought that Fitz would end up with a woman like her? She noticed the helpless look in his eyes. He wished he were alone with her, too. Instead, they had to catch up in front of a curious audience and a jealous wife. She raised her hand and summoned her niece. 'Cosima, why don't you bring everyone tea and coffee?'

Cosima pulled out a pad and pencil. 'So, Fitz,' said Alba, leaning into the table. 'Do you still have dogs and a smelly old Volvo?'

'Why didn't Luca and Freya join us?' Ma asked.

'They've got a lot of catching up to do,' Romina replied. She noticed Cosima's pencil pause over the paper as Nanni and Caradoc gave her their orders.

'Freya has always had a soft spot for Luca,' said Rosemary, trying not to listen to her husband's conversation with Alba.

'Bad timing,' said Romina, deliberately raising her voice. 'They would have been perfect together.'

'Luca's handsome but fickle. I can't say I'm surprised his marriage broke up. That man's not made for monogamy.'

'I think you'll find Luca's heart is well and truly full,' Caradoc interjected, catching Cosima's eye.

Cosima smiled at him gratefully, although she felt sick in her stomach. Luca hadn't mentioned Freya. Nor had he mentioned she was staying at the *palazzo*. Her anger began to simmer. It wasn't the fact that he was with another woman that set her off balance, but the fact that he hadn't told her.

Once everyone had given their order, Cosima retreated inside. She took the mobile phone out of her pocket and switched it off. If he was capable of lying about that, what else was he capable of lying about? If she couldn't trust him, what was the point in having a relationship?

Luca and Freya stayed in the folly until six. They talked about Miles in great detail. Luca listened patiently and tried to give good advice though the subject was beginning to bore him. As late afternoon turned the little folly amber, he suggested a walk down on the beach, then that they make their way around the bay to meet the others at the *trattoria*. He knew he had to tell her about Cosima. If she believed he was available for her, the idea of leaving her husband might seem more attractive. He didn't want to give her false hope. More importantly he didn't want to upset Cosima.

The sea stretched out before them, sparkling in the evening light. A few boats cut through the ocean, gleaming white in the sunshine, and sea birds wheeled on the air. Freya breathed in the scent of wild thyme that grew among the rocks and felt her spirits grow light despite her husband's infidelity. Incantellaria had entered her soul through all her senses. She watched Luca in front of her. He walked tall, his shoulders back, his skin tanned by the sun, his hair gleaming in the light. She felt as if she were the one indulging in the affair. She recalled Luca telling her that letting her go was the stupidest thing he had ever done. Then she blushed when she remembered how he had wanted to make love to her. She hadn't forgotten about 1979 either, the summer they had been lovers. She hadn't forgotten a single detail. He had been her very first. She smiled as she wondered what it would be like, now that she was no longer innocent. They could make love – after all they were unfinished business – and no one would be any the wiser. Then she could return home to Miles, and only she would know the sweetness of her revenge.

'You know, there's a story of red carnations being swept up the beach by a mystery tide,' said Luca, putting his hands in his pockets and feeling the bulk of Cosima's ring.

'Do you believe it really happened?'

'It certainly happened. But who put them there? The Mediterranean has no tide.'

'And Jesus weeping blood?'

'A clever priest.'

'Do you believe in anything you can't see?' she asked, remembering his clash with Hugo.

'Yes, I do.'

He thought of Francesco but couldn't begin to explain all the strange things that had happened to him over the past week. What a vastness he and Cosima shared, and what depth the bond that it had engendered. Fond as he was of Freya, he didn't have the will to share it with her. 'Listen, there's something I want to tell you.'

Rosa was walking down to the beach with Alessandro and Olivia when she saw Luca in the distance with a strange woman. She hissed at her children to be quiet, then stood watching them. They were deep in conversation, standing very close. Rosa saw him pull out a little box and give it to her. The mystery woman was pretty. Rosa could tell, even from that distance. Her long, fine hair blew about on the breeze and her pale skin seemed translucent against the backdrop of the sea. She was slim and willowy with long legs and arms, even though she was wearing an unflattering pair of shorts. The woman took the box. Rosa's anger mounted. Did Cosima know they were here? The woman hesitated before opening it, gesturing to him as if in protest. But he encouraged her by pushing her hand. When she saw what was inside, she shook her head, closed the box and threw her arms around him. They held each other close, as close as lovers, for what felt like an indecently long time. Dizzy with rage, Rosa took her children by the hand, turned around, and walked back up the path, her mind racing with possibilities. No wonder he had flirted with *her*. She had seen him flirting with Stephanie too. He was a playboy. She had had a narrow escape. Cosima wasn't so lucky; she was as vulnerable as a sitting duck to a huntsman. She should never have trusted him. Rosa knew she had to do what was right for her cousin. Blood was thicker than water; she had to be told.

Luca held Freya against him. 'I knew you'd understand.'

She pulled away and gave him back the box. Her eyes sparkled like the sea. 'It's beautiful. She'll love it. What woman wouldn't?'

'I've been longing to share it with you. I just didn't know whether it was right to tell you, considering the trouble you're having with Miles.'

'It's great news, Luca. I'm happy for you. It's given me something else to think about other than myself.'

'That's very generous of you.'

'Not at all. We're friends, right? I was there when you needed me. Now you're here when I need you. You see, I was right. You loved what I represented. Told you we'd laugh about that conversation one day.'

'I'm not laughing,' he replied bashfully. 'I'm too ashamed.'

'Don't be. I find it hilarious. Mind you, you became instantly more attractive to me the minute Miles played around. Bad timing, I guess. We're just not destined to be.' She linked her arm through his as they set off up the beach. 'At least I'm lucky enough to have you as my friend, even though I know we'll never finish what we started.'

'My loss,' he said diplomatically.

'Mine too! Now, why don't you introduce me to the lucky girl!'

Cosima was so incensed she went home early, leaving Alba on the terrace talking to Fitz and his stringy wife. At home she found Rosa waiting for her in the kitchen, her face apprehensive. The children were outside on the terrace with Beata who was listening to Alessandro reading from his school book.

'I need to talk to you,' said Rosa.

'Well, I'm not in the mood,' Cosima replied, stalking over to the fridge to grab some lemon juice.

'It's about Luca.'

'I don't want to talk about him.'

Rosa looked puzzled. 'You know?'

'About what?' She poured the juice into a glass and leaned back against the sideboard.

'His girlfriend.'

'*I'm* his girlfriend,' Cosima stated, giving her cousin a withering look. 'If you're talking about the girl who's staying up at the *palazzo*, I already know. I heard them talking about her at the *trattoria*.'

'You mean he didn't tell you himself?'

Cosima stared into her glass. 'No, but I'm sure he meant to.' She averted her eyes, not wanting to reveal the depth of his betrayal.

Rosa took a laboured breath and plunged in. 'Well, I saw them on the beach together.'

'When?'

'Just now. They were very close. He pulled out a little box and gave it to her. She opened it and fell into his arms.' The blood drained from Cosima's face. 'I wish I hadn't seen them,' Rosa continued. 'I wish I wasn't the one to have to tell you.'

'Are you sure?'

'I'm not lying. *He's* the liar!'

'I don't believe you! Give me one reason why I should?'

Cosima's reaction to the betrayal had surprised Rosa. Aside from all their daily bickering, when all was condensed down to the very last drop of blood, Cosima was family. She loved her. 'You're not just my cousin, Cosi, you're my sister.'

Cosima dissolved into tears. 'Oh God, Rosa. Do you think he's lied about everything?'

'I wouldn't trust a word he says.'

She thought of Francesco and felt her hope drain away like water down a plughole, leaving everything as black as it had been before. She shook her head, unable to voice her despair. When Luca and Freya reached the *trattoria*, Romina was still there with Alba, Rosemary and Fitz, Nanni, Ma and Caradoc.

'Come and join us, darling,' said Rosemary.

Alba looked her over, wondering whether Freya was Fitz's daughter. 'Freya's my stepdaughter,' said Fitz, reading her mind. 'My daughter in everything but blood.'

'She's beautiful,' said Alba.

'I'm very proud.'

'Where's Cosima?' Luca asked.

Alba had been so distracted by Fitz, she hadn't noticed her niece. 'She must have gone home.'

'Damn! I want to introduce her to Freya.'

'Maybe you should go and find her,' Caradoc suggested, communicating that all was not well.

'Is she all right?' Luca asked, bending over the professor.

'You hadn't told her about Freya, had you?'

Luca rolled his eyes at his stupidity. He had let his ego get in the way of common sense. 'Is she furious?'

'As only a truly passionate Latin woman can be.'

Luca left Freya with the group and ran up to the square to get a taxi. He dialled Cosima's number but it went straight through to voicemail. He felt his anxiety like an invisible weight on his chest. If she had switched off her telephone, she must be furious with him. He scanned beneath the trees lining the road around the *piazza*, but there were no taxis. He thrust his hands in his pockets, wondering what to do, when he spotted Eugenio smoking on the steps of the police station, talking to another *carabiniere*. When Eugenio saw him, he raised his eyebrows in recognition. '*Buon giorno.*'

'Hey, you wouldn't help me out, would you?'

'What can I do?'

'I need a lift up to your house. I have to see Cosima urgently.'

Eugenio tossed his cigarette butt on to the ground and squashed it beneath his boot. 'Come, I'll give you a lift. If it is a matter of urgency.' Luca followed him to the police car parked on the curb.

'Have you found the intruder yet?' Eugenio asked as they climbed in.

'Not yet,' Luca replied. He didn't want to mention he suspected Eugenio's wife.

Eugenio was secretly pleased. 'I thought you were going to guard the door?'

'I have had better things to do with my time.'

'Is Cosima okay?'

'I hope so. Just a misunderstanding.'

'She's very fragile,' Eugenio said, his tone laden with foreboding.

'Which is why I need to clear this up as quickly as possible.'

Chapter 31

When Luca arrived at Cosima's house, he leapt out of the car and ran down the hill. Beata was outside on the terrace with Rosa and the children, who were eating large bowls of pasta. When Rosa saw him, her face frosted over. He knew something was very wrong. '*Buona sera*,' he said politely to Beata, who smiled at him in ignorance. Rosa stood up and walked into the kitchen. Luca followed her.

'Rosa, what's happened?'

She swung around, hands on hips and began to shout at him. 'How dare you betray my cousin? We all fell under your spell. Well, aren't we a bunch of provincial fools?'

'What are you talking about?'

'You might as well turn around and leave because you're not welcome here any more. If Falco were alive he'd have *you* murdered in your *palazzo*!'

'I don't understand! I haven't betrayed anyone.'

Rosa laughed, though it was more of a wild cackle than a laugh. 'Don't lie to me! I saw you.'

'Saw me. Where?' Then it hit him. 'You saw me on the beach with Freya.'

'Is that her name? Nice!'

'It wasn't what it seemed.'

'It never is. You're all so bloody predictable. Why can't men come up with something original instead of the old clichés.'

Eugenio came in as they both fell silent. 'Am I interrupting anything?'

'Don't worry, Luca's just leaving.'

'You can't walk off without hearing my explanation.'

'If Rosa asks you to leave, you leave,' said Eugenio coldly.

'It's okay, Eugenio.' She sighed dramatically and turned around. 'It had better be good.' Luca pulled the little box out of his pocket. Rosa looked at it suspiciously. 'That's the box you gave Freya.'

'Yes, it is. If I had wanted her to have it I wouldn't be holding it in my hand now.'

Rosa opened the box. '*Madonna!*' She whistled, showing it to her husband.

'It's for Cosima. I'm going to ask her to marry me.'

'Then why did you give it to Freya?'

'I didn't. I was showing it to her.'

'Funny to show another woman an engagement ring!'

'Freya's an old friend,' he explained patiently. 'She's left her husband because he's having an affair. She had nowhere else to run to. I couldn't tell her about Cosima straight away. I didn't think it fair to tell her my good news when she was so unhappy. So I waited until I felt it was the right time. She was happy for me. We embraced as friends, Rosa.'

'Why didn't you tell Cosima she was coming?'

'Because I was afraid she wouldn't like it.'

Rosa pulled a face. 'Well, that's honest, at least – and you're right, she doesn't like it.'

'Look! I wouldn't betray Cosima. I *love* her.'

Rosa handed the ring back. 'You'd better love her with all your heart and all your soul because believe me, if you make her unhappy, you'll regret it. My family has a history of seeking revenge in the most violent way.'

'Now, will you tell me where she is?'

'I don't know.'

'You have no idea?'

'She just ran off.' He took his telephone out of his pocket. 'Don't bother. She doesn't want to speak to you.'

'I *have* to find her.'

'Rosa?' Eugenio felt sorry for Luca. He too knew what it was like to love too much.

'All right, I have an idea where she *might* have gone.'

'Where?'

'Come with me. I'll show you. Eugenio – you're driving.'

Fitz returned to the *palazzo* with Rosemary, Freya, Romina, Ma, Nanni and Caradoc. All the way back in the car he stared out of the window, chewing on his regret that he wasn't able to spend time alone with Alba. Rosemary wittered on about the scenery and how beautiful it was, anything rather than talk about Alba. Romina could read Fitz's thoughts that were as transparent as if he were made of glass.

'I'm going to have a rest before dinner,' said the professor, shaking out his legs as he walked unsteadily into the hall.

'I think I'll do the same,' said Ma. 'What a tiring afternoon. Being on a perpetual holiday is quite exhausting.'

'Fancy a game of cards?' Nanni asked Fitz.

Fitz turned dutifully to his wife. 'What would you like to do, darling?'

Romina was quick to intervene. 'Darling Rosemary, I have just the thing for you and Freya. A precious little shop full of exquisite Italian crafts that you would adore. Most of the things you have admired of mine come from there. It's called Casa Giovanna and it's a secret little place off the beaten track. It will be closed tomorrow, but if I telephone Imelda she will keep it open now just for us. What do you say?'

'Oh, I'd love to.' Rosemary thought a little retail therapy was just what she needed after having had to sit with Fitz's beautiful ex-girlfriend for a couple of hours.

'I don't suppose Luca's back?' Freya asked wistfully. 'I hope he's okay.'

'He'll be back in time for dinner,' said Romina, opening the door. 'Come, let's not waste another minute!' She caught Fitz's eye and winked.

'So, what do you say?' Nanni persisted.

'Later perhaps. For now, I'd like to take a walk down memory lane.'

'A rain check then,' said Nanni, bending down to pat Porci.

Fitz stood on the gravel, deliberating what to do, unable to get Alba out of his mind. He knew the way to her house. He remembered the old lookout point, the olive tree and Valentina's grave. Some memories never fade. He'd go by way of the folly, down the path. He hoped she'd be there.

Alba was downhearted. She cursed his possessive wife for not leaving them alone together. Trust Fitz to wind up with a woman like that. He must have married her by default; she was too brisk and brittle to love. A woman who liked to be in control of everything. Knowing Fitz as she did, he would have gone along with it. Oh, he was happy enough, but there were many degrees of happiness and she'd wager good money that his happiness only reached half its capacity.

Once home she sat talking to Beata, who told her that Rosa and Eugenio had disappeared with Luca in great haste.

She had heard Rosa shouting in the kitchen but she didn't know what it had been about. Alba rolled her eyes. Her first thoughts were for Cosima. She felt a constant nagging in the pit of her stomach that her niece might do something stupid. She was so used to the girl's fragility, she always expected the worst. But Beata didn't know where Cosima was.

'Perhaps she's gone for a walk,' said Alba, getting up. 'I'm going to have a shower. It's been a long day.'

'You've been at the *trattoria* all day?'

'You know who showed up? Fitz. Do you remember him?'

'Of course I remember him. What a nice surprise. What's he doing here?'

'He's staying up at the *palazzo*.'

'Oh? Are you going up there?'

'Absolutely not. Wild horses couldn't drag me there.'

'Is he married?'

'Yes, to a real busybody!' It was good to share her feelings with Beata. 'The silly woman wouldn't leave us alone. I really wanted to talk to him on my own. It's been thirty years, I can't imagine why his wife is so possessive.'

'Because you're a very beautiful woman, Alba.'

'Not any more.'

'Oh yes you are. The years have been kind, because they have been happy.'

'I'm hardly going to steal him, am I? She could have been generous and offered to leave us. But no, that was too much to bear. She had to hang around and listen. She didn't know what we were talking about.'

'Poor old Fitz. He always had the potential to marry a strong woman.'

'Well, he didn't want me enough to follow me out here. It's his fault. No one asked him to marry Rosemary.'

'But you have Panfilo. You got what you deserved, Alba: the best.'

Alba went upstairs and took a shower. Memories rained down with the water and she began humming, taking pleasure from mental pictures she hadn't looked at in so many years. She remembered her houseboat on Cheyne Walk and her favourite pair of blue suede clog boots she had bought from Biba. She remembered the goat she had tethered to the roof of Viv's boat, to eat the grass and flowers she had planted there, and imagined her old friend's horrified face when she discovered it. She wondered where Viv was now and whether anyone bothered reading her books any more. She had been a very different person then.

She finished showering and rubbed rose oil into her skin before dressing. It was hot in her bedroom. The window was wide open, the sounds of crickets floating in on the breeze. As she buttoned her dress she went over to look out across the garden and down to the sea beyond. It was then that she heard a low masculine voice. It was unmistakeable. He was speaking shockingly bad Italian to Beata, who was listening to him patiently. It belonged to Fitz.

She ran downstairs, then composed herself a moment in the kitchen before going out on to the terrace. 'Oh, it's you, Fitz!' she exclaimed, feigning surprise.

'I was just . . .' He was about to make up a story about passing by coincidence. But Alba would see through that. 'I wanted to see you,' he said simply.

'Where's your wife?'

'Shopping.'

'Do you fancy a walk? We could go down to the old look-out point.'

'I'd love that.'

'Will you stay until Rosa comes home, Beata?'

'I'll stay as long as you need me, my dear. You go off and have a nice time.' Beata smiled, she wasn't so old that she couldn't remember what it was like to be in the company of an attractive man.

Fitz put his hands in his pockets, bid goodnight to Beata, then followed Alba down the olive grove towards the cliffs. The sun was setting, turning the sky to crimson and gold just above the horizon.

'This place is just the same, isn't it?' he said, glancing at her. 'You haven't changed either, Alba.'

'We only really change on the outside. When I'm with you, I'm twenty-five again.'

'I should have come after you.'

'No, you did what you felt was right.'

'It wasn't right. *You* were right for me. It's like the last thirty years haven't happened. I don't know why I lacked courage.'

'How soon after I left did you meet Rosemary?'

'Weeks.'

'That soon? Weren't you a little sad?'

'I was devastated. I missed you terribly. At one point I nearly came back, but by then Rosemary was on the scene. She managed to convince me that I wouldn't be happy in Italy. She told me that if you'd really loved me you would have put me above Italy.'

'It wasn't just Italy, Fitz. It was Cosima too. She's like a daughter to me, you know. I have never once regretted coming back.'

'I've regretted not following you a million times.'

'But you're happy with Rosemary?'

'I was happy with you. I'm content with Rosemary. She's a good woman. She looks after me. It's not passionate like it was with you and we certainly don't laugh as much.' He gazed at her tenderly. 'You were the great love of my life, Alba. There'll never be another you.'

'I'm flattered. We did have fun, didn't we?' She began to walk with a bounce in her step. With Fitz she felt head-strong and mischievous, as if she were young and playful again and not a grandmother who had to conform to stereotype.

'I've thought about you often over the years. It's crazy to think of you being a grandmother. You're frozen in my mind as you were when you left.'

'I'm afraid I'm a lot older and fatter than I was.'

'No, you're more beautiful now because your face shows your wisdom. You've calmed down, too, I can tell.'

'How do you know?'

'You were incredibly selfish when I met you.'

'I was not!'

'You were promiscuous, wilful, obstinate and wild. You had everyone running around after you. That's why I fell in love with you because you were like a wild animal. So, Alba, who tamed you?'

'A photographer called Panfilo.'

'Great name,' he conceded.

'Great man.'

'Has he made you happy? Or will there only be one Fitz?' She pushed him playfully. 'I'm afraid I can't tell you what you want to hear. I'll tell it the way it is. He's the love of my life. Who knows what would have become of us had we danced off into the sunset, but Panfilo has made me very happy.'

Fitz struggled to hide his disappointment. 'I'd rather you told me you'd been miserable for the last thirty years!'

'And then what? You'd leave Rosemary, I'd leave Panfilo and we'd start a life together? You know that would be impossible.'

'I can't say I haven't thought about it.'

'You *are* funny.'

'I'm an old man now. I'm entitled to dream.'

'You're not old! There's no excuse for that sort of dream. You made your bed, now you must lie in it.'

They reached the olive tree and sat down. 'So, where's Viv these days?'

'She's dead, Alba.'

'Good God!' Alba blanched at the news of her old friend. 'Viv, dead?'

'She died about ten years ago.'

'She was my one true friend. She stuck with me through thick and thin, the only person I could talk to. It's sad we lost touch. But let's not dwell on sad things. Tell me about England. It's years since I've been back. Tell me about you.' She lay on her side, holding her head up with her hand. 'I'm listening. I want to hear everything. This is the only chance we'll get.'

'Oh, I don't know. If Rosemary finds us, we'll have the rest of my life!'

Eugenio drove the car through the gates of La Marmella. 'Why do you think she'll be here?' Luca asked Rosa.

'If she's not here I don't know where she'll be.'

'Oh, God!' he groaned. 'If she's not here I'll slit my throat!'

The car rattled up the drive. Lemon trees glimmered in the evening light. Flies hovered among the leaves and a spray of small birds took off to the skies. Luca felt sick with worry. He knew how fragile she was. Cosima must think he had betrayed her. That he was a liar. That he had used Francesco to get to her like some low-life fraud. He silently prayed that she was here with Manfreda, the one woman who could vouch for his integrity. The car stopped outside the front door and Luca climbed out and rang the bell. He shuffled from foot to foot with impatience. The few seconds it took for Manfreda to reach it felt like a lifetime. When she finally opened the door, Luca practically fell in with eagerness.

'Manfreda!' he exclaimed. 'Is she here?'

'Of course she's here,' she replied calmly. 'Come in.' She stood aside to let him pass. 'Hello Rosa, Eugenio.' She chuckled. 'You've brought everyone!'

'Is she okay?'

'She's fine,' said Manfreda gravely. 'But you, young man, have a lot of explaining to do.' She waggled a bony finger at him.

'I know. Where is she?'

'On the terrace.'

She turned to Rosa. 'Violetta has made the most delicious *limoncello*. Come, let's have some. It's in the kitchen.' She led them away. Rosa looked over her shoulder, wishing she could be present for their making-up. Eugenio couldn't have cared less. The prospect of a glass of *limoncello* was infinitely more enticing than watching a reunion between Cosima and Luca.

Luca walked on to the terrace. There at the table sat Cosima – and Francesco. Luca did a double-take. For a split second he thought the child was real, but then he recognised the luminous quality of his body, as if he were made of transparent colours, like a rainbow. He decided now wouldn't be the moment to mention his presence.

Cosima looked at him with a distant expression in her eyes. A barrier had grown up between them behind which she sat stiffly, like a stranger.

'I'm sorry, Cosi. I should have told you about Freya.'

'I'm listening.'

'She's an old friend. My oldest friend. I didn't behave very well when I last saw her. I've never liked her husband. He's an ass. So I flirted with her, knowing that she was married and unavailable. I told her she was the only woman I'd ever loved, that now I was divorced I could see that the woman I have always looked for had been right by my side all along. Then I came out here and met you.' He reached for her hand, but she withdrew it, placing it on her lap. He persevered. 'Now she's discovered her husband is having an affair. I invited her out to cheer her up. I didn't tell you because I didn't want to upset *you* and I needed to tell her about you in my own time so I wouldn't upset *her*. I guess I tried to please you both and ended up hurting the woman I love the most. Down on the beach I broke it to her that I'm no longer available. That my heart is with you.' He took a deep breath. 'I didn't imagine it would be like this,' he said, taking out the little jewellery box. 'I fantasised that we'd be in some romantic spot.' Her eyes fell on the box. 'I showed this to Freya. I wanted her to know how serious I am about you.' He pushed it towards her. 'I love you, Cosi. I've never lied to you. And I never will. I want to spend the rest of my life with you.'

Francesco watched his mother take the box. She bit her lip while she deliberated what to do, until curiosity got the better of her and she opened it. Without waiting for her permission, Luca took her left hand and slipped the ring on the fourth finger. 'Please forgive me, my darling.' A fat tear trickled down her cheek. 'Please say you'll marry me?'

She shook her head and pulled off the ring, replacing it carefully in its box. 'I cannot marry you.'

Luca felt the world fall away. 'You can't? Why?'

'Because I can't live anywhere else but here.'

'Why not?'

'I can never leave Francesco!' She swallowed.

Francesco stared at her sadly. Then he looked at Luca, his brown eyes large and pleading.

'Francesco is right beside you,' he said softly. 'He's right there in that chair.'

Cosima looked at the empty space beside her. 'Stop, Luca. Don't . . .'

'He's here, I swear it,' he insisted.

'Don't torment me!' Her face turned white with fury. 'Don't use my son to get to me!'

Luca closed his eyes and took a deep breath. He emptied his head of thoughts so that Francesco could transmit into the void.

'Talk to me, Francesco,' he said. 'Your mother needs you now, and so do I.'

He waited. Cosima remained totally still, staring at him incredulously. At first all he could hear was his heart thumping in his ears. If he failed she'd lose all trust. He had to communicate with Francesco. His life depended on it.

In the silence of his mind words formed sentences that were not of his making. Slowly Luca repeated what he heard. He didn't open his eyes for fear of breaking the moment and he didn't think of Cosima's reaction, but concentrated on holding on to the voice, a shiver of excitement washing over him for at last being able to communicate with her son.

'I left my toys around the house to get your attention, *Mamma*, but you always blamed my cousins. You never imagined it was me. I tried so hard for you to notice me. I'm always with you, every day and every night. I have never left your side, but you cannot see me which makes me sad. I'm sorry I ran after the feather. One minute I was in the water and the next I was on the beach, shouting at you, but you didn't see me and you didn't hear me. I wanted to make you better so I put my butterfly on your pillow but you got cross with Alessandro. You didn't know it was me, wanting to say sorry. Alessandro saw me but he was too afraid to tell you. I gave him a yellow rose to give you, but you didn't imagine it was me. Don't you remember? Yellow is my favourite colour. I put a white feather on the candle table in the church, then at your feet when you knelt in prayer. There was no other way to reach you. Only Luca can see me and he doesn't know why. Some children can see me too, which is fun for it is very lonely like this. I try to reach the light, but I'm so heavy with your sorrow that I can't jump high enough. One day you'll know that dying isn't an end but life going on in a different way. I know now that it was my time to return home. It was already decided before I was born. The one thing we take with us is love. I carry your love with me, *Mamma*, in my heart.'

Francesco stopped talking. Luca's eyes were wet with tears. He looked across at Cosima; her hand was over her mouth and her fingers were trembling. Neither spoke.

Francesco moved his hand and placed his fingers on the box. It was barely discernible at first, but then it gained a little speed as Francesco moved the box across the table. The little box moved right before their eyes, seemingly all by itself, until it stopped in front of Cosima.

Francesco looked up at his mother. 'I want you to be happy,' he said.

Luca tried to speak but all that came out was a croak. He cleared his throat, then repeated what Francesco had said.

'Ask him one thing,' Cosima whispered. 'What is the name of his favourite butterfly?'

Luca didn't need to ask. Francesco was already replying. 'My Morfino.'

Cosima began to cry. 'That was his special name for it. The Morfino. Tell him I hope Heaven is full of Morfini.'

'He says one day you'll come and see for yourself.'

Cosima opened the box and placed the ring on her finger. 'I want to be happy, too,' she said. 'But I don't want to leave Incantellaria.'

'So, you'll marry me?'

'Yes, if you'll stay here with me.'

He took her hand across the table. 'If you want to stay here, stay here you will. My happiness depends on yours, Cosi.' He laughed as Francesco placed his hand on top of theirs. 'We have your son's blessing. Now let's keep quiet until we've got my daughters' blessing too.'

Chapter 32

When Manfreda hobbled laboriously on to the terrace, followed by Rosa and Eugenio, she was pleased to see that peace had been restored. The large diamond on Cosima's finger shone almost as brightly as the light in her eyes.

Rosa put down the tray of drinks and embraced her cousin. She only felt a mild twinge of envy for the beautiful diamond and Cosima's good fortune. 'I'm happy Luca's not the liar I thought he was,' she said, then turned to Luca and added, 'I'm sorry I doubted you.'

'It's all resolved. Cosima's agreed to marry me. I'm dizzy with happiness.'

'We must tell *Mamma*,' said Rosa.

'We'll tell no one until I've told my daughters. Then I'll ask Toto for your hand in marriage and announce it for all of Incantellaria to hear!'

Manfreda sat back in her chair, content. 'Everything is as it should be,' she said, folding her hands in her lap.

'Well, almost,' interjected Luca. 'Rosa, there's something I've been wanting to ask you for some time.'

'What's that?'

'Are you the intruder at the folly?'

Eugenio was quick to reply for her. 'Don't be ridiculous!

What would Rosa want with the folly?' But as he spoke he knew he was wrong. 'Rosa?'

She poured a drink for herself and sat down. 'No, I'm not the intruder. At least, not the *original* intruder.'

Eugenio looked at her in surprise. 'So that is where you disappear off to at night?'

'You know?'

'Of course I know. I watch you leave and I watch you return, but I don't know where you go.'

She took his hand, horrified. 'You must think I . . .?'

'I trust you,' he interjected. 'At least, I *want* to trust you.'

'Please don't tell *Mamma*!'

'Just tell us the truth.'

'Who's the *original* intruder?' Luca asked, intrigued.

'You know the strange lights in the *palazzo* and the reports of noises in the middle of the night? The place is haunted and has been for years, but not by the dead. I like to walk up the beach in the middle of the night.' She smiled apologetically at Eugenio and squeezed his hand. 'Don't be angry with me, it's a way of clearing my head and having time alone. I love the darkness. I feel exhilarated when I'm walking that path in the dark. The sea looks beautiful beneath the moon and I can hear everything, even the rattling of my own thoughts. But then, one night, I felt compelled to walk up to the folly. I make no secret of my fascination with my grandmother, Cosima. Her life was tragic but I see the romance of it. It would make *Mamma* mad, but the folly attracted me like a magnet. I wanted to be near Valentina and I was curious to see whether Romina had changed it or whether she had seen what I saw in there and kept it just the way it was.' Rosa felt a frisson as she held everyone in her thrall. 'So I walked that path I know so well and reached that darling little house. But there was a light on inside. The flickering of a candle that shone through the gaps in the shutters. I could either turn around and go home, or open the door and see who was in there. Incantellaria is a sleepy little place, nothing much happens here. Now was my chance to live an adventure of my own. So I opened the door.'

'Who was it?' Luca asked.

Rosa grinned secretively. 'Let me make a telephone call. Then I'll show you.'

'You have to tell us!' Cosima exclaimed.

'No, I want you to see for yourselves.' She turned to her husband. 'I'm sorry.'

Eugenio's fears dissolved in the sweet light of her smile for only he knew how hard it was for Rosa to apologise.

Cosima gave Manfreda an affectionate hug. 'Thank you,' she whispered into the old woman's ear.

'Don't thank me. This is what you deserve. It is time to open your heart to happiness.'

Alba and Fitz watched the sun descend into the sea. The land was bathed in a dusky purple light.

'This is the best time of day,' Alba said contentedly.

'I don't want it to end. I don't want to return to my life. I want to stay here with you, pretending that it's thirty years ago. That we're young and in love.'

'We're not the same people we were.'

'Do people change that much?'

'Yes, life moulds us. Incantellaria has moulded me. I watched the arrogant girl in a mini skirt and clog boots sink with the *Valentina*.'

'No, she's still there inside you,' said Fitz, grinning raffishly. 'I can see her.'

'Well, thankfully no one else can.'

'Because they wouldn't recognise her if she slapped them across the face. I recognise her because I love her.'

'You're an incurable romantic.'

'You once told me that was my problem.'

'You remember?'

'Yes, you said that you didn't believe in love or marriage.'

'You see, people change.'

'And I told you that when I fall in love, I lose my heart completely. Once gone, I can never get it back.'

'Oh, Fitz.' She took his hand. 'Are you in love with a memory?'

'I let you go. The stupidest thing I ever did in my life.'

'Don't worry, you've got Rosemary,' she teased.

Alba felt a wave of exhilaration wash over her. Perhaps the girl in a mini skirt and clog boots really was still inside her. 'Hey, Fitz. Why don't we sneak up to the *palazzo* again, just the two of us?'

'Why would you want to do that?'

'Because I haven't been up there since we broke in thirty years ago. I haven't dared. But with you, I dare.'

He held out his hand to help her up. 'Let's go to the folly. No one will have to know. We can sneak in there together. Apparently, Romina hasn't changed a single thing.'

'She hasn't,' he replied. 'I've seen it, and it's exactly as it was when your mother combed her hair at the dressing-table.'

'Oh Fitz, I'm trembling with nerves.'

'Don't be scared. We're in this together. If it wasn't for my stiffening joints I'd believe I was a young man again.'

'You are a young man inside,' she said. 'I recognise him, because I loved him.'

'Tell me you still do.'

'If you remember, I also told you there are many ways of loving.'

'So you still love me.'

She set off up the hill. 'I still love you, Fitz,' she shouted back.

He hurried after her. 'And I love you for loving me still!'

Rosa parked the car a little way down the hill from the *palazzo*. They didn't want Romina to find them sneaking around. Cosima took Luca's hand and followed Rosa through the trees until they reached the folly. It was dark. A misty moon rose slowly into the navy sky and the sparkling eyes of a thousand stars began their nocturnal vigil. The breeze rustled through the leaves and invisible crickets sang their habitual song in the undergrowth.

Rosa opened the door. Inside, the warm glow of candle-light illuminated the room. Rosa walked in. Eugenio, Luca and Cosima followed, craning their necks to see who was inside. There at the back window, smoking into the night air, stood a man. He was so thin his trousers hung off him, cinched at the waist by a belt, leaving his ankles exposed. He wore a white shirt and the little hair that he had was as white as goose down. The hand that held the cigarette was bony, covered in skin as diaphanous as moths' wings, mottled pink and brown. The room was filled with the same sweet perfume that had clung to the mysterious scarf.

'Nero?' said Rosa softly. The old man turned. When he saw she wasn't alone he seemed to shiver with pleasure.

'So, we have company tonight,' he said languidly. '*Che bello!*'

'This is my husband, Eugenio, my cousin, Cosima, and her *fiancé*, Luca.'

'Ah, Eugenio, I have heard only good things about you.' Eugenio didn't know what to say: he could never have imagined this. 'And Luca, welcome.' He settled his pale eyes on Cosima, devouring her features. 'It's a pleasure to meet you, Cosima. I can see the resemblance,' he added, extending his hand. Cosima shook it. The skin was as cold and damp as a corpse. 'But you, Rosa, are the one who has inherited your grandmother's face.'

'You're the *Marchese*'s adopted son?' said Luca incredulously.

'The very same. This was my special place. Ovidio loved this more than anywhere else in the world. When he died I let the *palazzo* go.' He waved his hand, dismissive of his past. 'I fell apart and the *palazzo* fell apart around me. But this, this I looked after, for Ovidio. And he's still here. Can you feel him?' Cosima looked around warily. 'Well, sit down everyone. Let's not stand on ceremony.'

He pulled out the chair in front of the dressing-table and Rosa threw herself on to the bed as if she owned it, patting the place beside her for Eugenio to join her. Luca and Cosima, uncomfortably aware that Nero had probably watched them making love, sat together on the floor.

'You can imagine my delight when I first saw Rosa. I thought Valentina had risen from the dead. We're friends, aren't we, Rosa?'

'Nero was so sad when I found him. He was like a lost dog, lingering over the body of his dead master. A pitiful sight.'

'Where do you live?' Cosima asked.

'In a small house in the hills not far from here. I bought it with the last of Ovidio's fortune when the *palazzo* became uninhabitable. I struggled to hold on to it, truly I did, but it was rotting around me. In the end I was forced to go. But like a homing pigeon I came back every day and watched it slowly sink into the garden. I left this folly as it was because everything in it was chosen specifically for here by Ovidio. These books, the statue, paintings, furniture, rugs, none of it has any value anywhere else but here, in Ovidio's folly. So I left it like a shrine.'

'Isn't that romantic?'

'You couldn't count on my mother keeping it the way it was,' said Luca.

'No, I tried to frighten people away but I wasn't a very convincing ghost!'

'So, it was you who haunted the *palazzo*?' said Eugenio.

'I've wandered those corridors at night when everyone's asleep.' He clearly felt the *palazzo* still belonged to him. 'I know every corner, every crevice.'

'No wonder Ventura complains about ghosts,' said Luca.

'She need not be afraid. The only person this ghost has hurt is himself. So, it is your family who live here now?'

'Yes,' Luca replied.

'I was lucky it fell into such sensitive hands. It was a gamble I had to take. I needed the money, so I had to sell.'

'He likes what your mother's done to the *palazzo*,' said Rosa.

'She thinks she's captured the beauty of the original building,' said Luca.

'It's not the same,' Nero replied sharply. 'It's not at all like it was. I've got a book of old photographs to prove it. But,' he conceded graciously, 'she has good taste. Ovidio appreciated good taste.'

'Nero and I talk long into the night, don't we, Nero? You'd be amazed at the people he met with Ovidio. Grandees from all over Europe came and stayed here when he was a boy. The Aga Khan, the Duke and Duchess of Windsor . . . I could listen to Nero's stories for hours.' She glanced at her husband for his approval. He looked at her lovingly, relieved beyond words that Nero wasn't the young lover he had feared.

'And I could talk for hours. I don't like people on the whole, I'm happier with memories of those I loved who are dead. But Rosa and I are friends. I'm no longer alone. How ironic that the granddaughter of the woman who stole Ovidio's heart is now my consolation.'

At that moment the door opened and Alba's face peered in, shocked to see that the folly wasn't empty.

'*Mamma!*' Rosa sat up guiltily.

'What are *you* doing here? Oh my God! Nero?'

'Alba,' said Nero, pleased to see his audience was growing. 'Is that Fitz?' Fitz walked in behind Alba.

'Come in, don't be shy. Aren't the years just falling away!'

'Rosa, how do you know Nero?' Alba was baffled. She thought him dead long ago.

'I found him here.' She shrugged, as if it was the most natural thing in the world.

'Now we've found the intruder, the only thing left is to tell Mother.'

Fitz looked anxiously at Alba. He thought of Rosemary discovering them here together and barely dared contemplate the consequences. 'I should go,' he said.

'Don't go,' interjected Nero. 'We're having a *salon*. We must make it a nightly event. It'll be the most desirable *salon* in Italy.'

As Fitz turned to leave, he bumped straight into Romina who had appeared in the doorway with Rosemary like a pair of schoolmistresses walking in on an illicit midnight feast. 'What on earth is going on? Who is that?' She pointed at Nero.

'You must be Romina,' said Nero, standing up. 'Allow me to introduce myself. My name is Nero. Palazzo Montelimone was once mine.'

'Nero?' she repeated. '*Madonna!* The world could not get any stranger! So you are the intruder? *Che fascinante!* I've always wondered. Luca, run to the house and bring some wine, I need a drink. Move over, Rosa my darling, I must sit down. Nero, who'd have thought *you* would come back from the dead?'

'I've never felt more alive.' He grinned, revealing a gap where his two front teeth had been.

'My dear friend, tell me all about the *Marchese*. I'm longing to know.' At that moment Porci hurried past her, straight into the outstretched arms of Nero.

'Hello, little pig. I know what you want.' He withdrew a wedge of cake from his pocket which Porci ate greedily.

'Well, that's another mystery solved,' muttered Romina, sitting down.

Rosemary glared at her husband. 'What are *you* doing here?' she demanded. 'We've been looking all over for you!'

Everyone stared at Fitz and Alba. For a moment they floundered, not knowing what to say.

Rosa saw an opportunity to make peace with her mother. 'It's all *my* fault,' she said, climbing off the bed. 'Nero is *my* friend. I wanted to introduce him to Eugenio, my mother and Cosi, so we crept up here uninvited only to be discovered by Fitz and Luca, coming to trap the intruder.' She threw up her hands. 'We're guilty as charged.'

'But the *real* intruder is me,' said Nero. 'That's a warmer word than ghost. I like it!'

'If I had known you were the intruder, Nero, I would have invited you in for a drink,' said Romina.

'You would?'

'Of course. This is your folly. Thanks to you, it has been perfectly preserved. To be honest, I never really felt it belonged to me, which is why I didn't touch it. I must have known, somewhere deep inside my soul, that it was possessed by someone else, someone who had more right to it than me.'

'You are a woman of excellent taste. Ovidio would have held you in high esteem. I have a book of old photographs. Perhaps you would like to see what the *palazzo* looked like in its prime, before we let it succumb to the elements?'

'I would adore to see it! And I would adore for you to come here as often as you like, so long as you entertain me with wonderful stories of the *Marchese*.'

'Nothing would give me greater pleasure.' He kissed her hand. 'You are not only beautiful but blessed with a dazzling intelligence. I am humbled by the glare of it. My gratitude is overwhelming. Do you mind if I have a cigarette?'

Rosemary relaxed her shoulders. 'I'm sorry,' she muttered, slipping her hand around Fitz's arm. 'I've been so worried.'

'About what?'

She shook her head, not wanting to discuss her fears within earshot of Alba. 'Silly woman's worries. You're fine, that's all that matters.'

Alba smiled at her daughter. It was a small smile but Rosa felt her pride like the heat of the sun. She had won her mother's admiration and her gratitude. Things were going to be different now.

When Luca returned with glasses and wine, he brought the rest of the house party with him. They all crammed into the folly, opened the bottles, and listened enraptured while Nero brought the past alive with colourful tales of dukes and princes and the inimitable *Marchese*.

Luca took Cosima's hand. The ring sparkled on her finger like a bright star, but no one seemed to notice, until he caught the professor looking across at him with a father's affection. His gaze dropped to Cosima's ring and the professor gave Luca a wink and a discreet, but laudatory nod.

Chapter 33

Luca told his parents that he was returning to London to touch base, pay bills and catch up with his friends. He didn't tell them of his marriage plans, and he didn't tell Cosima of his plans for their future. He just took a plane back with the intention of kick-starting the rest of his life with the woman who had made it all possible.

He left the *palazzo* in a state of excitement. Romina had all but adopted Nero, renaming the folly after him and inviting him to stay there whenever he liked. She spent hours on the terrace, with the old photographs of the *palazzo* and all the elegant people the *Marchese* had entertained in decadent magnificence. She welcomed Nero's evening *salons* with Rosa, and Eugenio, so relieved that Nero was not the hand-some stranger he had imagined, allowed her to see him as often as she wanted. The decrepit old Nero was no competi-tion for Eugenio; Rosa's enthusiastic love-making, without the stimulus of a row, was testament of that.

Fitz, Rosemary and Freya returned to England. Miles was at the end of his tether, afraid to the point of making himself ill that his wife would leave him for Luca. If it hadn't been for Cosima, she might well have done. But she accepted his apol-ogy and believed him when he told her he had finished his affair and would never stray again. He could barely take his hands off her, following her around the house like an adoring puppy. Freya found this mildly irritating, but she was pleased to be back where she belonged. She didn't need to sleep with Luca to redress the balance; she was holding all the cards.

Fitz knew he would never see Alba again. He lodged her safely in the very furthest corner of his heart along with his regret and a little sadness. There was no point longing for the unattainable. Alba and he were a chapter closed long ago. Now he would return to his life and look forward. He would try not to think of what might have been, or lament his lack of courage; he was too old to sour the years he had left. But she held all his love and always would.

While Luca was away, Nero became part of the *palazzo* 'family' along with Nanni, Caradoc and Ma, who seemed likely to stay on well after the summer was over. Porci's infatuation with Nero grew more intense with each passing day, dozing off at his feet to the languid undulations of his beautiful Italian. Bill accepted his wife's eccentric posse in his easygoing way. Having a group of friends around her all the time was what made her happy. He concentrated on the garden and began formulating an idea to build another folly, one dedicated to beauty and learning, for Romina.

Back in London, the overwhelming noise of the city and the strange sense of being alone in the midst of millions of people unsettled Luca. He breathed in the polluted air, grimaced at the crowds jostling on the pavements and sat in traffic while the knot of frustration grew tighter in his stomach. He went back to his empty house and felt emptiness engulf him again.

He drove to Kensington to surprise the girls. He could hear their laughter before he rang the bell and felt his excitement mount. Normally he would have taken presents, but this time, in his hurry to see them, he had forgotten.

When Claire saw him she flushed with surprise. 'What are you doing here?' Before he could reply, Coco and Juno pushed past her into his arms. He hugged them both, kissing their warm faces and rubbing his nose in their hair.

'I've missed you!' he breathed, realising how true it was.

'Greedy wants to see you!' said Juno, skipping off to the playroom to retrieve her caterpillar.

'How are you, Coco?'

'Are we going out to Italy again soon?' she asked.

'If you'd like to.'

'I like the swimming pool.'

'So do I.'

She giggled. 'You're the Naughty Crocodile!'

He tickled her ribs. 'You know what Naughty Crocodiles do, don't you?'

'Eat children!' she laughed, running off down the corridor.

'You had better come in,' said Claire.

'Are you alone?'

'If you're referring to John, yes, I'm alone.'

'Good. I need to talk to you and the girls.'

'What about?' Her stomach lurched at the horrendous possibilities.

He patted her back. 'Nothing to be afraid of, Claire.' He watched her shoulders drop. 'I have some news I want to share.'

'Okay. Let's go into the kitchen. Would you like a cup of tea?'

'Cup of coffee, please. Do you have a biscuit?'

Claire summoned the girls and they all sat around the table. Luca suddenly felt apprehensive. He feared his news might be unwelcome to his daughters, that they might feel threatened by the presence of another woman laying claim to their father's heart. 'So, what's the news?' Claire placed a coffee cup in front of him.

He looked at his daughters' expectant faces. 'I'm moving to Italy.'

'You're going to live in Incantellaria?' Claire said, astonished. 'What on earth are you going to do there?'

He ignored her and waited for his daughters to respond. 'I hope you'll come and visit me every holiday and for half-terms. Mummy and I will share you.'

Juno's eyes lit up. 'When is the next holiday?'

'Soon,' said Luca. Claire remained silent while the coffee percolated, calculating what the consequences of his move would be for her.

'So, you're happy about me moving to Incantellaria?' he asked Coco.

'Yes,' she said importantly. 'Very happy.'

'You know Mummy has a friend called John?' Claire stared at him warily. The girls nodded. 'Mummy would be lonely without John. Well, Daddy is lonely on his own in Incantellaria. If Mummy and Daddy can't be together, the next best thing is Mummy and Daddy finding new friends. Mummy has found hers, and Daddy . . .'

'You're getting married,' said Coco nonchalantly.

Claire flushed again. 'Are you?'

'Yes,' he replied carefully. 'I have found the woman I would like to spend the rest of my life with.'

'Who is she?' Claire felt she had just been punched in the stomach.

'She's called Cosima,' Luca replied. 'You might remember her,' he said to the girls.

'She's very pretty,' said Coco, pleased to be in the know. 'She's got lovely thick hair and a nice smile. I could tell she liked you, Daddy.'

'Do I remember her?' Juno asked.

'Greedy remembers her,' said Coco.

'So, you give me your blessing?'

'Yes,' said Coco.

'Me too!' said Juno, making Greedy nod in agreement.

'Then that's settled.'

Coco was quick to spot an opportunity. 'Can we be bridesmaids?'

Luca felt his spirits soar. His daughters approved of his choice. There was only one more thing to do.

'Claire, I want to settle the money side without going to court,' he said.

'Okay. Girls, why don't you go off and play? Daddy and I have some talking to do. Boring stuff.' The girls ran off, chattering excitedly about their father's wedding. Luca handed her an envelope. 'Why have you put your sword away?'

'Because I'm happy, Claire, and I want you to be happy, too.'

'Really?'

'Yes, we have two beautiful little girls. We made them together. We might not have worked out, but we did something right.'

She opened the envelope and pulled out the neatly folded letter. He watched her read it. 'Are you joking?' she gasped.

'Why? Isn't it enough?'

She stared at him as if he had just handed her the world on a plate. 'It's more than enough. You'd be richer if you took me to court!'

'I don't want to take you to court and I don't want to be richer. You deserve it. We were married for ten years. I spoiled you rotten. I can't expect you to live with less than you had when we were married.'

She folded her arms. 'Then it's well and truly over,' she said, trying to mask her sadness. 'Were we ever happy?'

'When Coco and Juno were born, we were the happiest two people on earth.'

'She must be one hell of a woman to make you live over there.'

'She is.'

'What are you going to do?'

'Ah, that's the million dollar question.' But his smile implied that he already knew.

Luca spent a fortnight in London sorting out his affairs and seeing the few friends who really mattered. With the help of his old secretary he answered the towering pile of invitations and letters that had accumulated over the weeks he had been away and put his house on the market. He telephoned Cosima every morning and every evening and with each day that passed his longing for her grew. He wouldn't miss London and he wouldn't miss the City. Those days were gone. He was embarking on a new life and the thought of it filled him with excitement.

He drove out to Italy in his Aston Martin, the roof down, the wind in his hair, thoughts of Cosima dominating his mind. He sang loudly to Andrea Boccelli and felt his spirits soar. In the midst of such beauty, in the face of such a positive future, he now understood why a certain thought had inexplicably popped into his head that night in his mews house. *Darkness is only the absence of light.* It was up to him to find the light inside him, and he had.

There was one thing he had to do before seeing Cosima. One vital thing upon which all his plans depended. With a suspended heart, he motored through the gates of La Marmella.

Chapter 34

Cosima was taking an order on the terrace of the *trattoria* when Luca sauntered into view. When she registered his features, surprise caused her cheeks to flush a pretty shade of pink, her face softening with affection.

'Excuse me,' she said to the old lady. 'Fiero, would you take over!' Fiero nodded, wondering why Luca carried a large basket of lemons.

Cosima melted against him as if his embrace was the only place in the world where she felt secure and at peace. 'I've missed you.'

'I've missed you, too,' he replied, kissing her temple. 'You're more beautiful than I remember.'

She pulled away and laughed at the basket of lemons. 'You're funny,' she said. 'Can I guess where they're from!'

'They're from *your* farm.'

She frowned. '*My* farm?'

'Yes, *your* farm.'

'I never knew I had a farm.'

'I've just bought you the most beautiful farm overlooking the sea. We're going to cultivate lemons and grow old together.'

She picked up a lemon and put it to her nose. For a moment she looked bewildered. 'But I swear these are from La Marmella.'

'They are.'

She dropped the lemon back into the basket and made to speak but nothing came out. Her eyes widened and welled with happiness. 'You've bought La Marmella for me?'

'I've bought La Marmella for *us*. You're going to be my wife and the future will be what we make of it.'

'I don't believe it! What about Manfreda?'

'Of course Manfreda knew all along. She was just waiting for me to make her an offer so she could go and live with her son in Venice. She's been longing to sell the place. You said I should plant a seed and watch it grow. Well, so I shall.'

'I'm overwhelmed!'

'The professor told me to look deep inside myself and work out what is important. Well, I have. You're important, Cosima. You and my children and any future children we might have together. Nothing is more important than love. Francesco has taught me that. I can't take my worldly goods with me when I die, but I will take my love.'

When Cosima stepped into the aisle of the little church of San Pasquale, Luca noticed that besides Toto, on whose arm she walked, and Coco, Juno, Olivia and Domenica who were bridesmaids, and Alessandro who was her only page, another little boy walked with her that only he could see. It was right that Francesco should give her away, for he had brought them together; the little Italian matchmaker.

Cosima knew that her son was with her for he had told her himself in her dream. Now she believed, in spite of not being able to see him herself. She knew that if she sat quietly, closed her eyes and asked him, he would come close.

Now she walked on her father's arm and felt a wave of relief. She could begin a new chapter knowing that she had her son's blessing. Knowing that loving Luca did not detract from loving Francesco, that there was no limit to her heart's capacity. Her long ivory dress rustled as she stepped over the stone floor, her new shoes peeping out from beneath to remind her of her shopping day in Naples with Alba and Rosa, when the three of them had laughed with the simple joy of being together. The veil that covered her face was the one that Alba had worn on her wedding day.

Romina had organized the make-up artist from the *Sunday Times* magazine shoot to put Cosima's hair up and decorate it with the small yellow flowers she had insisted upon dominating all the displays. Her smooth skin shone and her deep brown eyes glittered at the good fortune that now smiled upon her. Luca stood handsome and tall, ready to take her from her father and lead her into the future. She knew he would never leave her, because Francesco had chosen him and he would never let her down. They held hands before Father Felippo to make their wedding vows. The altar candles flickered, the incense filled the air with its woody perfume, and Francesco watched his Brazilian Blue Morpho fly off his hand and flutter into the air. Father Felippo noticed the rare creature and commented that the butterfly was surely a good omen. The congregation gasped at the miracle of it. Never had they seen such a beautiful butterfly in Incantellaria. Luca and Cosima smiled at each other knowingly.

Romina dabbed her eyes with a silk handkerchief and Bill put his arm around her. She didn't like to admit when she was wrong, but she conceded quietly to herself that perhaps her son knew what he wanted after all. The professor grinned as Luca knelt before the altar on the cushions Beata had embroidered especially for them. He knew that the boy had finally worked out what he wanted from his life, what was important. It was very simple, but it eluded most people. He silently took credit for showing him the way. He couldn't take credit for love: Luca had found that all on his own. Ma was astonished to discover a tear trembling on the top of her lip. She brushed it off, appalled at the emotions that bubbled to the surface of her armour, breaking through to expose her soft heart. Nanni witnessed it and raised his eyebrows in mock surprise. Ma wasn't too moved to scowl back at him.

Rosa squeezed Eugenio's hand. 'Do you remember when it was us?' she whispered.

'Of course.'

'I was more beautiful.'

'Without doubt, my love. No bride has ever been, nor ever will be, more dazzling than you.'

Rosa nudged him playfully then turned her eyes back to the bride and groom who were about to make their way back up the aisle. She saw the anxious faces of her children as they were shuffled into position by Coco. The congregation stood. The music rang out as Cosima and Luca set off towards their future.

One person was missing in the procession that filed out into the sunshine. One person who had now been released with joy to step into a light of his own. The little Italian matchmaker felt his spirit grow bigger and brighter, filled with the infinite light of unconditional love. There, ahead of him, stood Immacolata, Falco and Valentina, together with others who had gone before whom he had never known, but now recognised from the eternal current of life. At last he was home.

Epilogue

Father Felippo returned to the church after the wedding party had gone on to Alba and Panfilo's house for the party. He had chuckled at the sight of Luca and Cosima departing in a horse-drawn cart full of lemons. She had been so anxious to remain in Incantellaria, among all her memories of her son, that she had contemplated a life alone. He had advised her that if Luca loved her enough he would stay. He congratulated himself that he had been right.

He was going up the aisle towards the altar to blow out the candles when something caught his attention at the back. He looked at the marble statue of Christ. There, against the shiny white stone, was a thin ribbon of red blood trickling from his right eye. Father Felippo gasped, his whole body trembling with awe. Hastily, he crossed himself, then dropped to his knees, humbled that it should be he and he alone who witnessed the miracle.

A few minutes later he checked that the blood was still there, then ran down the aisle as fast as he could, shouting '*Miracolo, miracolo, miracolo!*' at the top of his voice. Soon, the entire town was crowding into the small building. Old women wailed and old men wept while the young gazed in wonder that a miracle should happen in the modern world. The church bells continued to ring out and everyone anticipated a tremendous party, except Alba, her family and guests, who were enjoying a party of their own.

'The day Christ weeps tears of blood, all the ghosts shall be at peace,' said the priest, remembering the strange feathers and the butterfly. 'And so they are.'

Acknowledgements

For years I have wanted to write this book. Having seen spirits on and off all my life, I am certain our lives do not end in death, but that we all eventually return home from where we came. The people we love and lose are always around us, watching us and loving us. Life does not end in death; it just takes us to another shore.

I couldn't have written it without the help of a very special and dear friend, Susan Dabbs. She is an extraordinary woman with an astonishing gift who has opened my eyes to the fascinating world of Spirit. It is a lifelong adventure and I am enjoying every new discovery.

Since childhood my father and I have enjoyed long discussions about life and death. Over the years he has fanned my interest and answered my questions with wisdom and open-mindedness. We have exchanged books and ideas and our shared fascination has brought us closer together. Without his encouragement I wouldn't have begun to write this book.

I want to thank my mother, too, for reading my manuscripts with a keen eye for detail. She's a loyal supporter and her applause means a great deal to me. She has taught me many things in my life, but most importantly she has taught me about love.

I'm very grateful to my agent, Sheila Crowley. I feel she belongs exclusively to me as she has the amazing gift of making all her authors feel they are uniquely important. She's a dear friend and wise counsel who works tirelessly on my behalf and is never too busy to listen. Thank you.

I'd also like to thank my editor, Suzanne Baboneau, Clare Hey, and the brilliant team at Simon & Schuster UK who have made my books the successes they are. I am so grateful.

Our children, Lily and Sasha, are my greatest inspiration and joy. All my books are dedicated to them.

And my darling husband, Sebag, my most faithful supporter, and devoted *consigliere*, thank you.

Read on . . .
For an exclusive excerpt of *Songs of Love and War*, the
stunning new novel from Santa Montefiore,
out now

Hardback ISBN: 978-1-47113-584-2
Ebook ISBN: 978-1-47113-587-3

**SIMON &
SCHUSTER**

London · New York · Sydney · Toronto · New Delhi

A CBS COMPANY

Prologue

Co. Cork, Ireland, 1925

The two little boys with grubby faces and scuffed knees reached the rusted iron gate by way of a barely distinguishable track that branched off the main road and cut through the forest in a sleepy curve. On the other side of the gate, forgotten behind trees, were the charred remains of Castle Deverill, once home to one of the grandest Anglo-Irish families in the land before it was consumed in a fire three years before. The drystone wall that encircled the property had collapsed in places due to neglect, the voracious appetite of the forest and harsh winter winds. Moss spread undeterred, weeds seeded themselves indiscriminately, grass grew like tufts of hair along the top of the wall and ivy spread its leafy fingers over the stones, swallowing entire sections completely so that little of it remained to be seen. The boys were unfazed by the large sign that warned trespassers of prosecution or the dark driveway ahead that was littered with mouldy leaves, twigs and mud, swept onto it season after desolate season. The padlock clanked ineffectively against its chain as the boys pushed the gates apart and slipped through.

On the other side, the forest was silent and soggy, for the summer was ended and autumn had blown in with icy gales and cold rain. Once, the drive had been lined on either side with red rhododendron bushes but now they were partly obscured by dense nettles, ferns and overgrown laurel. The boys ran past them, oblivious of what the shrubs represented, unaware that that very drive had once witnessed carriages bearing the finest in the county to the magnificent castle overlooking the sea. Now the drive was little more than a dirt track and the castle lay in ruins. Only ravens and pigeons ventured there, and intrepid little boys intent on adventure, confident that no one would discover them in this forgotten place.

The children hurried excitedly through the wild grasses to play among the remnants of the once stately rooms. The sweeping staircase had long gone and the centre chimneys had fallen through the roof and formed a mountain of bricks below for the boys to scale. In the west wing the surviving part of the roof remained as sturdy beams that straddled two of the enduring walls, like the exposed ribcage of a giant animal left to decay in the open air.

The boys were too distracted to feel the sorrow that hung over the place or to hear the plaintive echo of the past. They were too young to have an awareness of nostalgia and the melancholic sense of mortality it induces. The ghosts who dwelt there, mourning the loss of their home and their brief lives, were as wind blowing in off the water. The boys heard the moaning of the empty windows and the whistling about the remaining chimney stacks and felt only a frisson of exhilaration, for the eeriness served to enhance their pleasure, not diminish it. The ghosts might as well have been alone for the attention the boys paid them.

Over the front door, one of the boys was able to make out some Latin letters, tarnished by soot, half-concealed in the blackened lintel. '*Castellum Deverillis regnum 1662,*' he read out.

'What does that mean?' asked the smaller boy.

'Everyone around here knows what that means. A Deverill's castle is his kingdom.'

The smaller child laughed. 'Not much of a kingdom now,' he said. They went from room to room in the fading light like a pair of urchins, excavating hopefully where the ground was soft. Their gentle chatter mingled with the croaking of ravens and the cooing of pigeons, and the ghosts were appeased as they remembered their own boyhoods and the games they had played in the sumptuous gardens of the castle. For once, the castle had been magnificent.

At the turn of the century there had been a walled garden, abundant with every sort of fruit and vegetable to feed the Deverill family and their servants. There had been a rose garden, an arboretum and a maze where the Deverill children had routinely lost themselves and each other among the yew hedges. There had been elaborate glass houses where tomatoes had grown among orchids and figs, and yellow cowslips had reflected the summer sun in the wild-flower garden where the ladies of the house had enjoyed picnics and afternoons full of laughter and gossip. Those gardens had once been a paradise but now they smelt of decay. A shadow lingered in spite of the sunshine and year after year bindweed slowly choked the gardens to death. Nothing remained of the castle's former beauty, except a savage splendour of sorts, made all the more arresting by its tragedy.

At the rattling sound of a motor car the boys stopped their digging. The noise grew louder as the car advanced up the drive. They looked at each other in bewilderment and crept hastily through the rooms to the front, where they peered out of a glassless window to see a shiny Ford Model T making its way past the castle before halting at the steps leading up to where the front door had once been.

Consumed with curiosity, they elbowed each other in their effort to get a closer look, while at the same time careful to keep their heads concealed behind the wall. The boys' jaws fell open at the sight of the car with its soft top and smoothly curved lines. The sun bounced off the sleek green bonnet and the silver headlights shone like frog's eyes. Then the driver's door opened and a man stepped out wearing a brown felt hat and smart camel coat. He swept his eyes over the castle, taking a moment to absorb the dramatic vision. He shook his head and pulled a face as if to acknowledge the sheer scale of the misfortune that had destroyed such a beautiful castle. Then he walked round to the passenger door and opened it.

He held out his hand and a small black glove reached out and took it. The boys were so still that, were it not for their pink faces and black hair, they might have been a pair of mischievous cherub statues. With mounting interest they watched the woman step out. She wore an elegant dress of a deep emerald green and a long black coat, with a black cloche hat pulled low over her face. Only her scarlet lips could be seen below it, somehow shocking against her white skin. Glittering beneath her right shoulder was a large diamond star brooch. The boys' eyes widened for she looked as if she came from another world; the sort of world that had once inhabited this fine castle before it was swept away.

The woman stood at the foot of the darkened walls and lifted her chin. She took the man's hand and turned to face him. 'As God is my witness,' she said, and the boys had to strain their ears to hear her. 'I will rebuild this castle.' She paused and the man made no move to hurry her. At length she returned her gaze to the castle and her jaw stiffened. 'After all, I have as much right as any of the others.'

Chapter 1

Kitty Deverill was nine years old. For other children, born on other days, turning nine was of no great significance. But for Kitty, born on the ninth day of the ninth month in the year 1900, turning nine had been very significant indeed. It wasn't her mother, the beautiful and narcissistic Maud, who had put those ideas into the young child's head; Maud was not interested in Kitty. She had two other daughters who were soon to come of age and a cherished son at Eton who was the light in his mother's eyes. In the five years between Harry and Kitty's births Maud had suffered three miscarriages induced by riding hard over the hills around Ballinakelly; Maud did not want her pleasure halted by an inconvenient pregnancy. However, no amount of reckless galloping managed to unburden her of her fourth child, who, contrary to expectation, was a weak and squeaking girl with red hair and transparent skin, more like a scrawny kitten than a human baby. Maud had turned her face away in disgust and refused to acknowledge her. In fact, she had quite rejected her child, declining to allow her friends to visit, donning her riding habit and setting off with the hunt as if the birth had never happened. For a woman so enraptured with her own beauty an ugly baby was an affront. No, Maud would never have put ideas into Kitty's head that she was in any way special or important.

It was her paternal grandmother, Adeline, Lady Deverill, who told her that the year 1900 was auspicious and that her date of birth was also remarkable, on account of it containing so many nines. Kitty was a child of Mars, Adeline would remind her when they sat together in Adeline's private sitting room on the first floor, one of the few rooms of the castle that was always warm. This meant that her life would be defined by conflict – a testing hand of cards dealt by a God who surely knew that Kitty would rise to the challenge with courage and wisdom. Adeline told her much else besides, and Kitty far preferred her stories of angels and demons to the dry tales her Scottish governess read her, and even to the kitchen maids' tittle-tattle, mostly local gossip Kitty was too young to understand. Adeline Deverill knew about *things*. Things at which Kitty's grandfather rolled his eyes and dismissed as 'blarney', things her father mocked with affection and things that caused Kitty's mother great concern. Maud Deverill was less amused by tales of spirits, stone circles and curses and instructed Miss Grieve, Kitty's Scottish governess, to punish the child if she ever indulged in what she considered to be 'ghastly peasant superstition'. Miss Grieve, with her tight lips and tight vowels, was only too happy to whack the palms of Kitty's hands with a riding crop. Therefore the child had learned to be secretive. She had grown as furtive as a fox, indulging her interest only with her grandmother, in the warmth of her little den that smelt of turf fire and lilac.

Kitty didn't live in the castle: that was where her

grandparents lived and what, one day, her father would inherit, along with the title of Lord Deverill, dating back to the seventeenth century. Kitty lived on the estate in the old Hunting Lodge, positioned by the river, within walking distance of the castle. Overlooked by her mother and too cunning for her governess, the child was able to run wild about the gardens and surrounding countryside and to play with the local Catholic children who took to the fields with their Tommy cans. Had her mother known she would have developed a fever and retired to her room for a week to get over the trauma. As it was, Maud was often so distracted that she seemed to forget entirely that she had a fourth child and was irritated when Miss Grieve reminded her.

Kitty's greatest friend and ally was Bridie, the raven-haired daughter of Lady Deverill's cook, Mrs Doyle. Born in the same year, only a month apart, Kitty believed them to be 'spiritual sisters' due to the proximity of their birth dates and the fact that they had been thrown together at Castle Deverill, where Bridie would help her mother in the kitchen, peeling potatoes and washing up, while Kitty loitered around the big wooden table stealing the odd carrot when Mrs Doyle wasn't looking. They might have different parents, Kitty told Bridie, but their souls were eternally connected. Beneath their material bodies they were creatures of light and there was very little difference between them. Grateful for Kitty's friendship, Bridie believed her.

Because of her unconventional view of the world, Adeline was happy to turn a blind eye to the girls playing together. She loved her strange little granddaughter who was so much like herself. In Kitty she found an ally in a family who scoffed at the idea of fairies and trembled at the mention of ghosts while claiming not to believe in them. She was certain that souls inhabited physical bodies in order to live on earth and learn important lessons for their spiritual evolution. Thus, a person's position and wealth was merely a costume required for the part they were playing and not a reflection of their worth as a soul. In Adeline's opinion a tramp was as valuable as a king and so she treated everyone with equal respect. What was the harm of Kitty and Bridie enjoying each other's company? she asked herself. Kitty's sisters were too old to play with her, and Celia, her English cousin, only came to visit in the summer, so the poor child was friendless and lonely. Were it not for Bridie, Kitty might be in danger of running off with the leprechauns and goblins and be lost to them forever.

One story in particular fascinated Kitty above all others: the Cursing of Barton Deverill. The whole family knew it, but no one besides Kitty's grandmother, and Kitty herself, believed it. They didn't just believe, they *knew* it to be true. It was that knowing that bonded grandmother and grand-daughter firmly and irreversibly, because Adeline had a gift she had never shared with anyone, not even her husband, and little Kitty had inherited it.

'Let me tell you about the Cursing of Barton Deverill,' said Kitty to Bridie one Saturday afternoon in winter, holding the candle steady in their dark lair beneath the back staircase, which was an old, disused cupboard in the servants' quarters of the castle. The light illuminated Kitty's white face so that her big grey eyes looked strangely old, like a witch's, and Bridie felt a shiver ripple across her skin, something close to fear. She had heard her mother speak of the Banshee and its shriek that pre-warned of death.

'Who was Barton Deverill?' Bridie asked, her musical Irish accent in sharp contrast to Kitty's clipped English vowels.

'He was the first Lord Deverill and he built this castle,' Kitty replied, keeping her voice low for dramatic effect. 'He was a right brute.'

'What did he do?'

'He took land that wasn't his and built on it.'

'Who did the land belong to?'

'The O'Learys.'

'The O'Learys?' Bridie's black eyes widened and her cheeks flushed. 'You don't mean *our* Jack O'Leary?'

'The very same. I can tell you there is no love lost between the Deverills and the O'Learys.'

'What happened?'

'Barton Deverill, my ancestor, was a supporter of King Charles I of England. When his armies were defeated by Cromwell, he ran off to France with the King. Later, when King Charles II was crowned, he rewarded Barton for his loyalty with a title and these lands where he built this castle. Hence the family motto: A Deverill's castle is his kingdom. The trouble was those lands didn't belong to the King, they belonged to the O'Learys. So, when they were made to leave, old Maggie O'Leary, who was a witch . . .'

Bridie laughed nervously. 'She wasn't really a witch!'

Kitty was very serious. 'She was so. She had a cauldron and a black cat that could turn a person to stone with one look of its big green eyes.'

'Just because she had a cauldron and a cat doesn't mean she was a witch,' Bridie argued.

'Maggie O'Leary was a witch and everyone knew it. She put a curse on Barton Deverill.'

Bridie's laughter caught in her throat. 'What was the curse?'

'That Barton Deverill and every male heir after him will never leave Castle Deverill but remain between worlds until an O'Leary returns to live on the land. It's very unfair because Grandpa and Father will have to hang around here as ghosts, possibly forever. Grandma says that it is very unlikely that a Deverill will ever marry an O'Leary!'

'You never know. They've come up in the world since then,' Bridie added helpfully, thinking of Jack O'Leary whose father was the local vet.

'No, they are all doomed, even my brother Harry.' Kitty sighed. 'None of them believes it, but I do. It makes me sad to know their fate.'

'So, are you telling me that Barton Deverill is still here?' Bridie asked.

Kitty's eyes widened. 'He's still here and he's not very happy about it.'

'You don't really believe that, do you?'

'I *know* it,' said Kitty emphatically. 'I can *see* him.' She bit her lip, aware that she might have given too much away.

Now Bridie was more interested. She knew her friend wasn't a liar. 'How can you see him if he's a ghost?'

Kitty leaned forward and whispered, 'Because I see dead people.' The candle flame flickered eerily as if to corroborate her claim and Bridie shivered.

'You can see dead people?'

'I can and I do. All the time.'

'You've never told me before.'

'That's because I didn't know if I could trust you.'

'What are they like, dead people?'

'Transparent. Some are light, some are dark. Some are loving and some aren't.' Kitty shrugged. 'Barton Deverill is quite dark. I don't think he was a very nice man when he was alive.'

'Doesn't it scare you?'

'It used to, until Grandma taught me not to be afraid. She sees them too. It's a gift, she says. But I'm not allowed to tell anyone.' She unconsciously rubbed the palm of her hand with her thumb.

'They'll lock you away,' Bridie said and her voice quivered. 'They do that, don't you know. They lock people away in the red-brick in Cork City for less and they never come out. Never.'

'Then you'd better not tell on me.'

'Oh, I wouldn't.'

Kitty brightened. 'Do you want to see one?'

'A ghost?'

'Barton Deverill.'

The blood drained from Bridie's cheeks. 'I don't know . . .'

'Come on, I'll introduce you.' Kitty blew out the candle and pushed open the door.

The two girls hurried along the passageway. Regardless of the disparity of their colouring, they could have been sisters as they skipped off together for they were similar in height and build. However, there was a marked difference in their clothes and countenance. While Kitty's dress was white, embellished with fine lace and silk, tied at the waist with a pale blue bow, Bridie's was brown and shapeless and made from a coarse, scratchy frieze. Kitty wore black lace-up boots that reached mid-calf, and thick black stockings, while Bridie's feet were bare and dirty. Kitty's governess brushed her hair and pinned it off her face with ribbons; Bridie received no such attention and her hair was tangled and unwashed, almost reaching as far as her waist. The difference was not only marked in their attire but in the way they looked out onto the world. Kitty had the steady, lofty gaze of a child born to privilege and entitlement, while Bridie had the feral stare of a waif who was always hungry, and yet there was an underlying need in Kitty that bridged the gap between them. Were it not for the loving company of her grandparents and the sporadic attention lavished on her by her father when he wasn't out hunting, shooting game or at the races, Kitty would have been starved of love. It was this longing that gave balance to their friendship, for Kitty needed Bridie just as much as Bridie needed her.

While Kitty was unaware of these differences, Bridie, who heard her parents and brothers complaining endlessly about their lot, was very conscious of them. However, she liked Kitty too much to give way to jealousy, and she was too flattered by her friendship to risk losing it. She accepted her position with the passive compliance of a sheep.

The two girls heard Mrs Doyle grumbling to one of the maids in the kitchen but they scurried on up the back staircase as quiet as kittens, aware that if they were caught their playtime would be over and Bridie summoned to wash up at the sink.

No one ever went up to the western tower. It was chilly and damp at the top of the castle and the spiral staircase was in need of repair. Two of the wooden steps had collapsed and Kitty and Bridie had to jump over the gaps. Bridie breathed easily now because no one would find them there. Kitty pushed open the heavy door at the top of the stairs and peered around it. Then she turned back to her friend. 'Come,' she whispered. 'Don't be frightened. He won't hurt you.'

Bridie's heart began to race. Was she really going to see a ghost? Kitty seemed so sure. Tentatively and with high expectations, Bridie followed Kitty into the room. She looked at Kitty. Kitty was smiling at a tatty old armchair as if someone was sitting in it. But Bridie saw nothing besides the faded burgundy silk. However, the room was colder than the rest of the castle and she shivered and hugged herself in a bid to keep warm.

'Well, can't you see him?' Kitty asked.

'I can't see anything,' said Bridie, wanting to very much.

'But he's *there*!' Kitty exclaimed, pointing to the chair. 'Look *harder*.'

Bridie looked as hard as she could until her eyes watered. 'I don't doubt you, Kitty, but I can see nothing but the chair.'

Kitty was visibly disappointed. She stared at the man scowling in the armchair, his feet propped up on a stool, his hands folded over his big belly, and wondered how it was possible for her to see someone so clearly when Bridie couldn't. 'But he's right in front of your nose. This is my friend, Bridie,' Kitty said to Barton Deverill. 'She can't see you.'

Barton shook his head and rolled his eyes. That didn't surprise him. He'd been stuck in this tower for nearly two hundred years and in all that time only the very few had seen him – most unintentionally. At first it had been quite amusing being a ghost but now he was bored of observing the many generations of Deverills who came and went, and even more disenchanted by the ones, like him, who remained stuck in the castle as spirits. He wasn't keen on company and there were now too many furious Lord Deverills floating about the corridors to be easily avoided. This tower was the only place he could be free of them, and their wrath at discovering suddenly, upon dying, that the Cursing of Barton Deverill was not simply a family legend but an immutable truth. With the benefit of hindsight, they would have gladly taken an O'Leary for a bride and subsequently ensured their eternal rest as a free soul in Paradise. As it was they were too late. They were stuck and there was nothing they could do about it except rant at *him* for having built the castle on O'Leary land in the first place.

Now Barton turned his jaded eyes onto the eerie little girl whose face had turned red with indignation, as if it were somehow *his* fault that her plain friend was unable to see him. He folded his arms and sighed. He wasn't in the mood for conversation. The fact that she sought him out from time to time did not make her his friend and did not give her permission to show him off like an exotic animal in a menagerie.

Kitty watched him stand up and walk through the wall. 'He's gone,' she said, dropping her shoulders in defeat.

'Where?'

'I don't know. He's quite bad-tempered, but so would *I* be if I were stuck between worlds.'

'Shall we leave now?' Bridie's teeth were chattering.

Kitty sighed. 'I suppose we must.' They made their way back down the spiral staircase. 'You won't tell anyone, will you?'

'I cross my heart and hope to die,' Bridie replied solemnly, wondering suddenly whether her friend wasn't a little over-imaginative.

In the bowels of the castle Mrs Doyle was expertly making butterballs between two ridged wooden paddles, while the scrawny kitchen maids were busy peeling potatoes, beating eggs and plucking fowl for that evening's dinner party, to which Lady Deverill had invited her two spinster sisters, Laurel and Hazel, known affectionately as the Shrubs, Kitty's parents, Bertie and Maud, and the Rector and his wife. Once a month Lady Deverill invited the Rector for dinner, which was an obligation and a great trial because he was greedy and pompous and prone to spouting unsolicited sermons from his seat at her table. Lady Deverill didn't think much of him, but it was her duty as Doyenne of Ballinakelly and a member of the Church of Ireland, so she instructed the cook, brought in flowers from the greenhouses and somewhat mischievously invited her sisters to divert him with their tedious and incessant chatter.

When Mrs Doyle saw Bridie she pursed her lips. 'Bridie, what are you doing loitering in the corridor when I have a banquet to cook? Come and make yourself useful and pluck this partridge.' She held up the bird by its neck. Bridie pulled a face at Kitty and went to join the kitchen maids at the long oak table in the middle of the room. Mrs Doyle glanced at Kitty, who was standing in the doorway with her long white face and secretive mouth that always curled at the corners, as if she had exclusive knowledge of something important, and wondered what she was thinking. There was something in that child's eyes that put the heart crossways in her. She couldn't explain what it was and she didn't resent the girls playing together, but Bridie's mother didn't think any good would come of their friendship when, as they grew older, their lives would inevitably take them down different paths and Bridie would be left feeling the coldness and anguish of Kitty's rejection. She went back to her butter. When she looked up again Kitty had gone.

Songs of Love and War

Santa Montefiore

Their lives were mapped out ahead of them. But love and war will change everything...

West Cork, Ireland, 1900. The year marks the start of a new century, and the birth of three very different women: Kitty Deverill, the flame-haired Anglo-Irish daughter of the castle, Bridie Doyle, the daughter of the Irish cook and Celia Deverill, Kitty's flamboyant English cousin.

Together they grow up in the dreamy grounds of the family's grand estate, Castle Deverill. Yet their peaceful way of life is threatened when Ireland's struggle for independence reaches their isolated part of the country.

A bastion of British supremacy, the castle itself is in danger of destruction as the war closes in around it, and Kitty, in love with the rebel Jack O'Leary and enflamed by her own sense of patriotism, is torn between loyalty to her Anglo-Irish family and her deep love of Ireland and Jack...

HB ISBN 978-1-47113-584-2

EBOOK ISBN 978-1-47113-587-3

FIND OUT MORE
ABOUT SANTA MONTEFIORE

Santa Montefiore is the author of fourteen sweeping novels. To find out more about her and her writing, visit her website at

www.santamontefiore.co.uk

Sign up for Santa's newsletter and keep up to date with all her news.

Or connect with her on Facebook at

http://www.facebook.com/santa.montefiore

Born in England in 1970, Santa Montefiore grew up in Hampshire. She is married to historian Simon Sebag-Montefiore. They live with their two children, Lily and Sasha, in London.

Visit her at www.santamontefiore.com
and sign up for her newsletter.

Praise for *The Italian Matchmaker*:

'A gripping romance. It is as believable as the writing is beautiful'
Sunday Telegraph

'Montefiore is adept at writing perceptive character analyses and her writing is funny, too . . . It is the kind of transfixing narrative that we have come to expect from Montefiore'
Sunday Express

Praise for Santa Montefiore:

'Santa Montefiore is the new Rosamunde Pilcher' *Daily Mail*

'Engaging and charming' Penny Vincenzi

'Sophisticated, irresistible backdrops and brilliantly drawn characters' Elin Hilderbrand, author of *The Matchmaker*

'One of our personal favourites and bestselling authors, sweeping stories of love and families spanning continents and decades' *The Times*

'Anyone who likes Joanne Harris or Mary Wesley will love Montefiore' *Mail on Sunday*